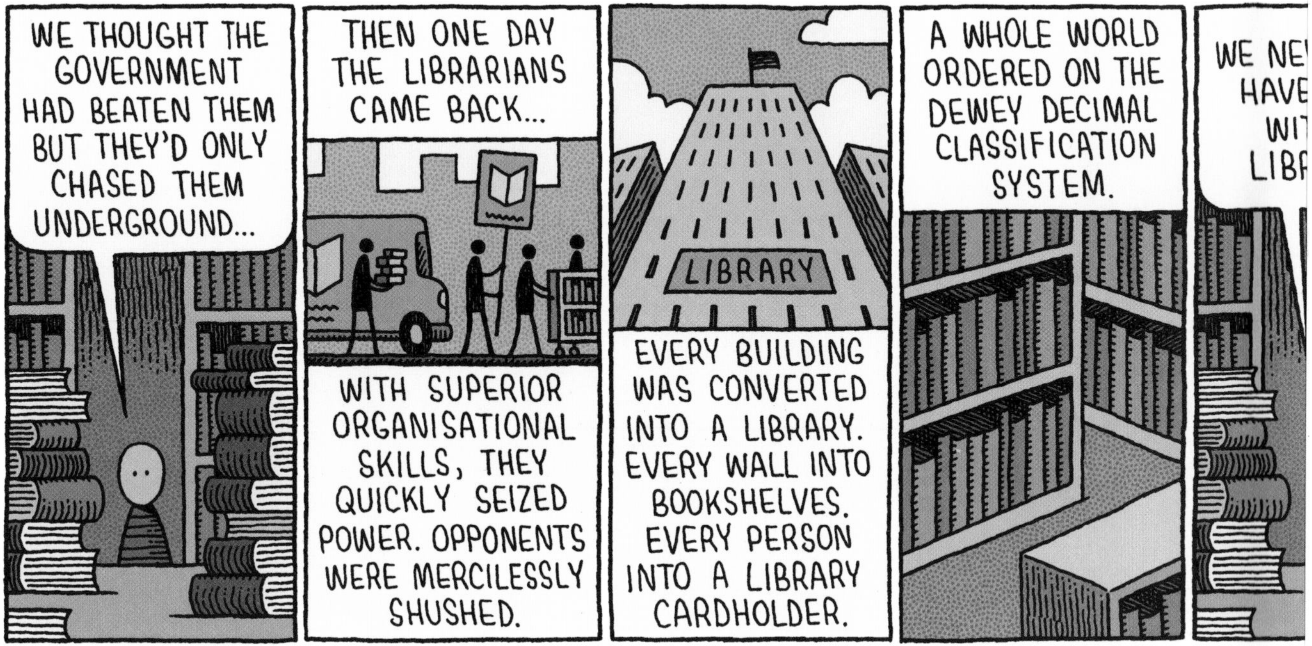
WE THOUGHT THE GOVERNMENT HAD BEATEN THEM BUT THEY'D ONLY CHASED THEM UNDERGROUND...
THEN ONE DAY THE LIBRARIANS CAME BACK...
WITH SUPERIOR ORGANISATIONAL SKILLS, THEY QUICKLY SEIZED POWER. OPPONENTS WERE MERCILESSLY SHUSHED.
LIBRARY
EVERY BUILDING WAS CONVERTED INTO A LIBRARY. EVERY WALL INTO BOOKSHELVES. EVERY PERSON INTO A LIBRARY CARDHOLDER.
A WHOLE WORLD ORDERED ON THE DEWEY DECIMAL CLASSIFICATION SYSTEM.

FOR FRED, BERT, GEORGE, LAILA & TEDDY

ENTIRE CONTENTS ©2022 TOM GAULD

THESE CARTOONS WERE ORIGINALLY
PUBLISHED IN THE GUARDIAN

DRAWNANDQUARTERLY.COM

ISBN 978-1-77046-616-6
FIRST EDITION: OCTOBER 2022
PRINTED IN CHINA
10 9 8 7 6 5 4 3 2 1

CATALOGUING DATA AVAILABLE FROM
LIBRARY AND ARCHIVES CANADA

PUBLISHED IN THE USA BY DRAWN
& QUARTERLY, A CLIENT PUBLISHER
OF FARRAR, STRAUS AND GIROUX

PUBLISHED IN CANADA BY DRAWN
& QUARTERLY, A CLIENT PUBLISHER
OF RAINCOAST BOOKS

FSC
www.fsc.org
MIX
Paper | Supporting
responsible forestry
FSC™ C005748

REVENGE OF THE LIBRARIANS

CARTOONS BY
TOM GAULD

DRAWN & QUARTERLY

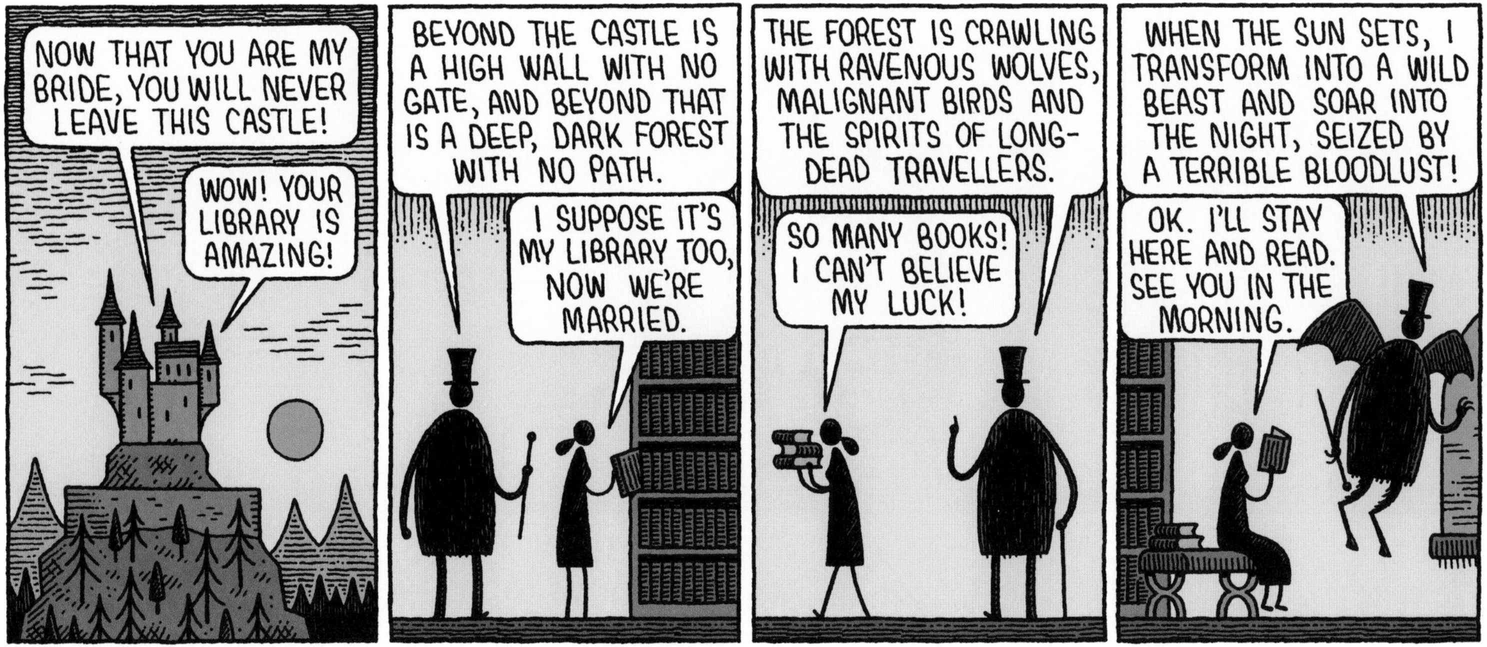
NOW THAT YOU ARE MY BRIDE, YOU WILL NEVER LEAVE THIS CASTLE!
WOW! YOUR LIBRARY IS AMAZING!
BEYOND THE CASTLE IS A HIGH WALL WITH NO GATE, AND BEYOND THAT IS A DEEP, DARK FOREST WITH NO PATH.
I SUPPOSE IT'S MY LIBRARY TOO, NOW WE'RE MARRIED.
THE FOREST IS CRAWLING WITH RAVENOUS WOLVES, MALIGNANT BIRDS AND THE SPIRITS OF LONG-DEAD TRAVELLERS.
SO MANY BOOKS! I CAN'T BELIEVE MY LUCK!
WHEN THE SUN SETS, I TRANSFORM INTO A WILD BEAST AND SOAR INTO THE NIGHT, SEIZED BY A TERRIBLE BLOODLUST!
OK. I'LL STAY HERE AND READ. SEE YOU IN THE MORNING.

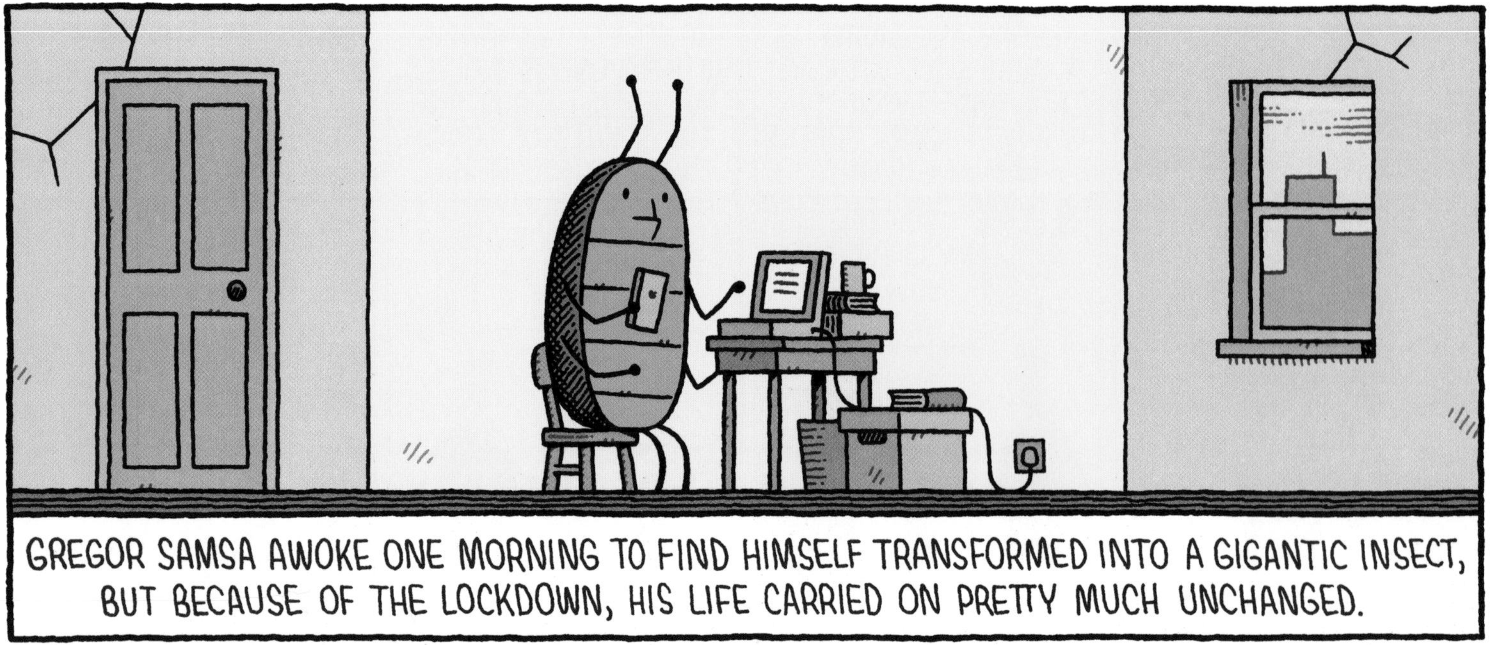

GREGOR SAMSA AWOKE ONE MORNING TO FIND HIMSELF TRANSFORMED INTO A GIGANTIC INSECT, BUT BECAUSE OF THE LOCKDOWN, HIS LIFE CARRIED ON PRETTY MUCH UNCHANGED.

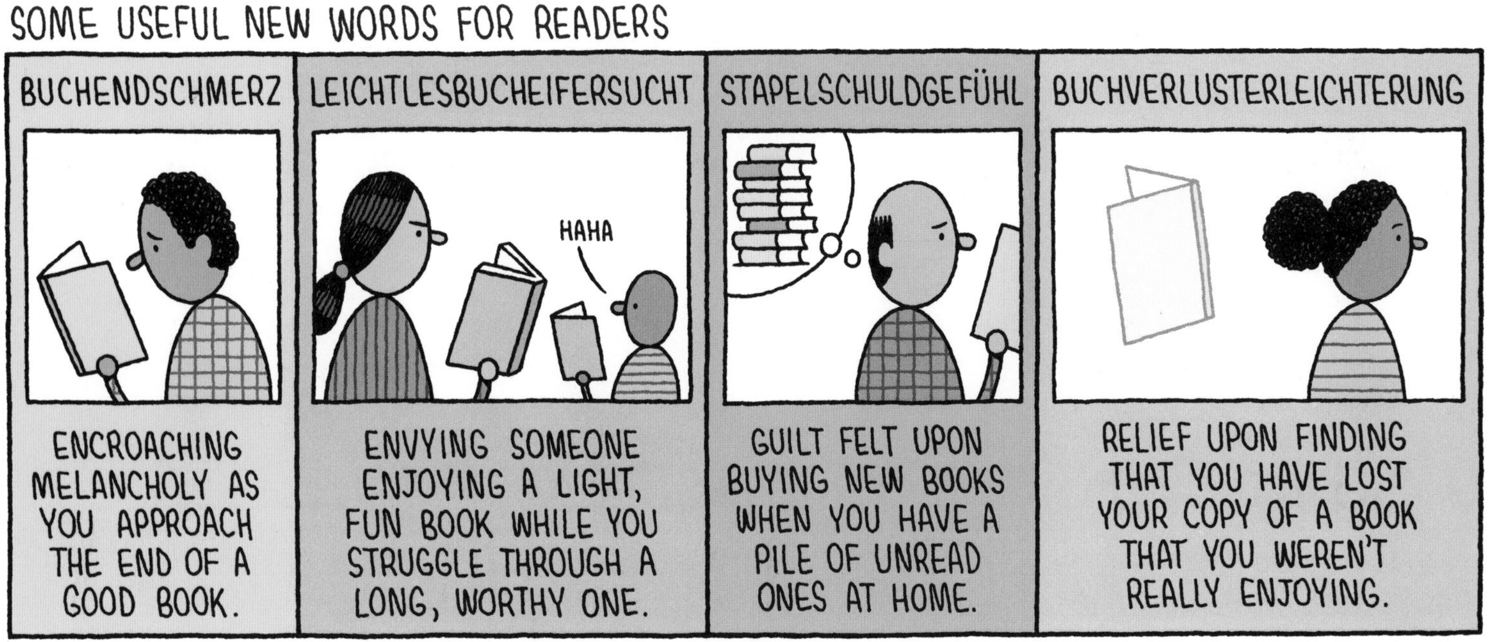
SOME USEFUL NEW WORDS FOR READERS
BUCHENDSCHMERZ
ENCROACHING MELANCHOLY AS YOU APPROACH THE END OF A GOOD BOOK.
LEICHTLESBUCHEIFERSUCHT
HAHA
ENVYING SOMEONE ENJOYING A LIGHT, FUN BOOK WHILE YOU STRUGGLE THROUGH A LONG, WORTHY ONE.
STAPELSCHULDGEFÜHL
GUILT FELT UPON BUYING NEW BOOKS WHEN YOU HAVE A PILE OF UNREAD ONES AT HOME.
BUCHVERLUSTERLEICHTERUNG
RELIEF UPON FINDING THAT YOU HAVE LOST YOUR COPY OF A BOOK THAT YOU WEREN'T REALLY ENJOYING.

MATHEMATICAL PROBLEMS FOR NOVELISTS

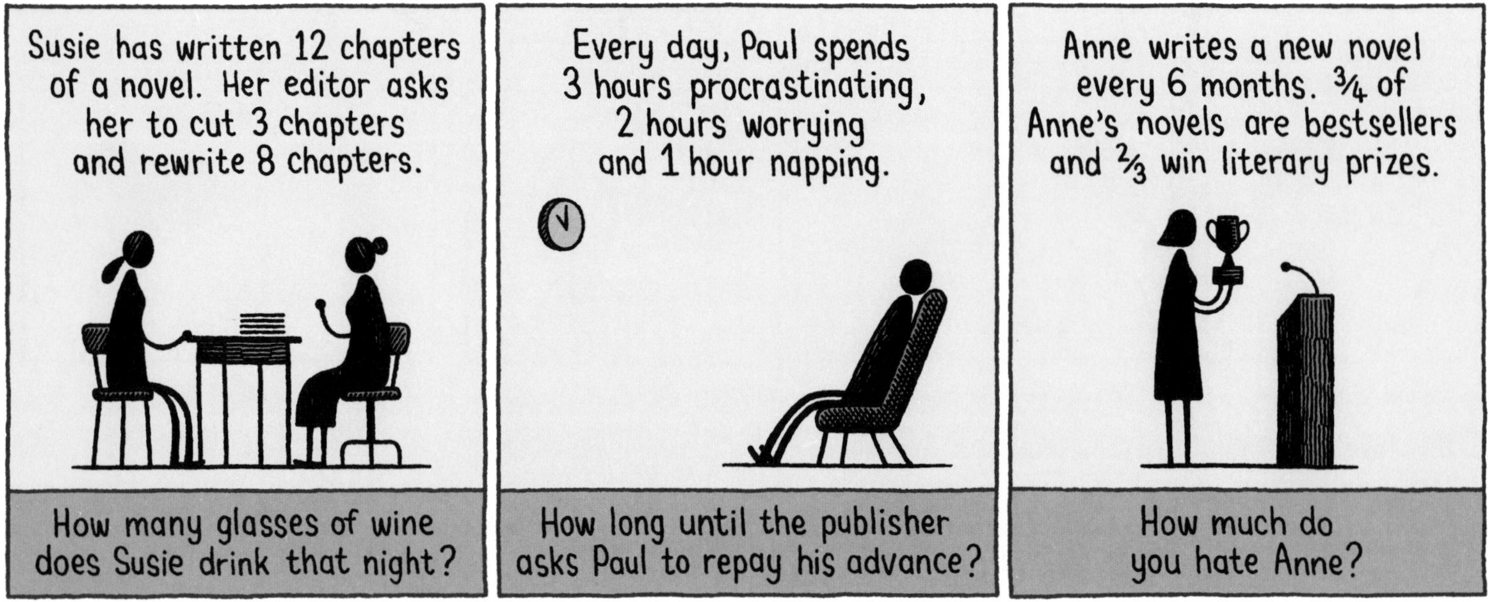
Susie has written 12 chapters of a novel. Her editor asks her to cut 3 chapters and rewrite 8 chapters.
How many glasses of wine does Susie drink that night?
Every day, Paul spends 3 hours procrastinating, 2 hours worrying and 1 hour napping.
How long until the publisher asks Paul to repay his advance?
Anne writes a new novel every 6 months. ¾ of Anne's novels are bestsellers and ⅔ win literary prizes.
How much do you hate Anne?

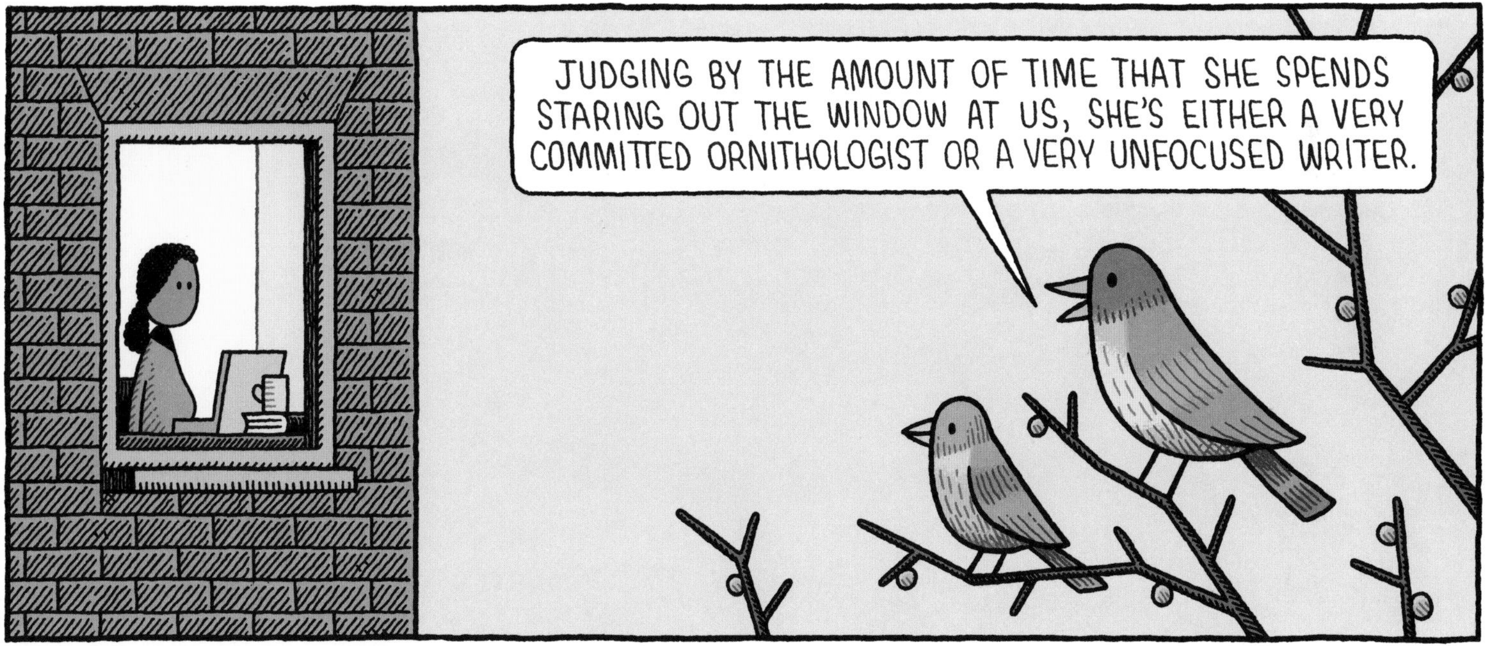
JUDGING BY THE AMOUNT OF TIME THAT SHE SPENDS STARING OUT THE WINDOW AT US, SHE'S EITHER A VERY COMMITTED ORNITHOLOGIST OR A VERY UNFOCUSED WRITER.

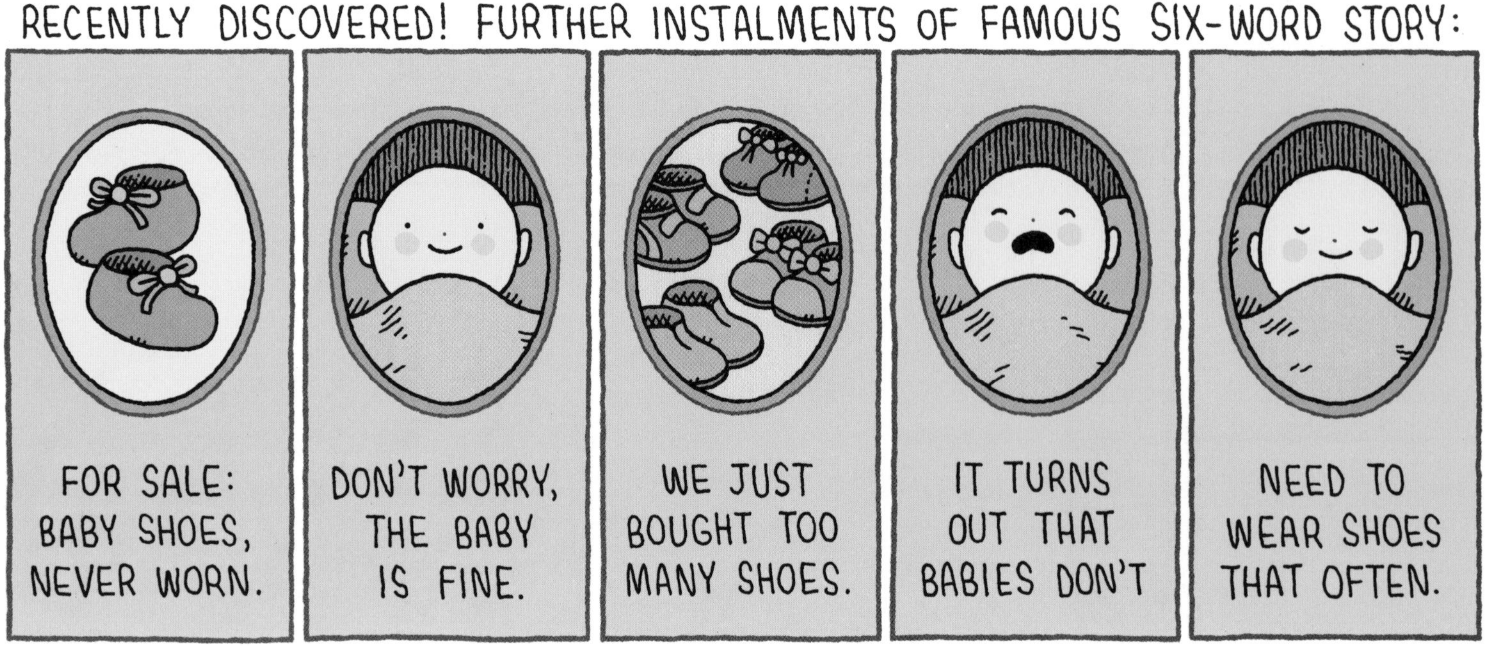
RECENTLY DISCOVERED! FURTHER INSTALMENTS OF FAMOUS SIX-WORD STORY:
FOR SALE: BABY SHOES, NEVER WORN.
DON'T WORRY, THE BABY IS FINE.
WE JUST BOUGHT TOO MANY SHOES.
IT TURNS OUT THAT BABIES DON'T
NEED TO WEAR SHOES THAT OFTEN.

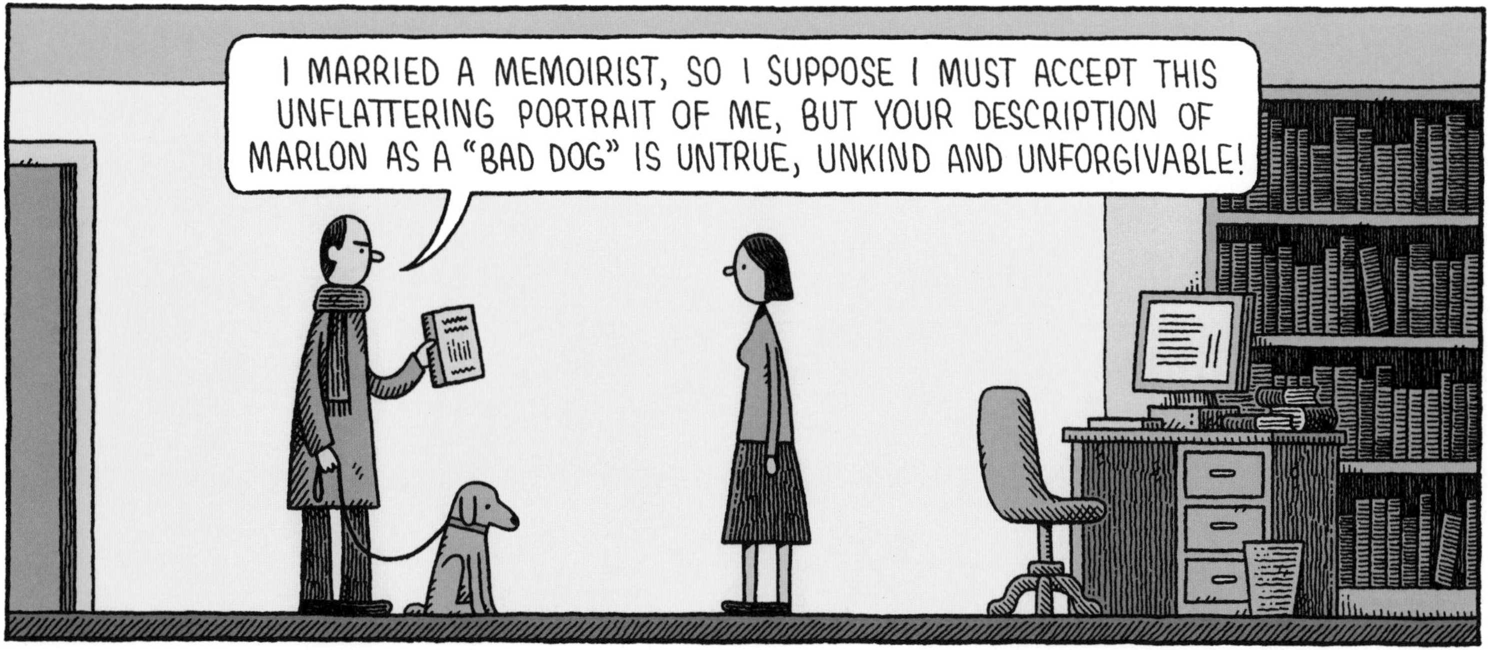
I MARRIED A MEMOIRIST, SO I SUPPOSE I MUST ACCEPT THIS UNFLATTERING PORTRAIT OF ME, BUT YOUR DESCRIPTION OF MARLON AS A "BAD DOG" IS UNTRUE, UNKIND AND UNFORGIVABLE!

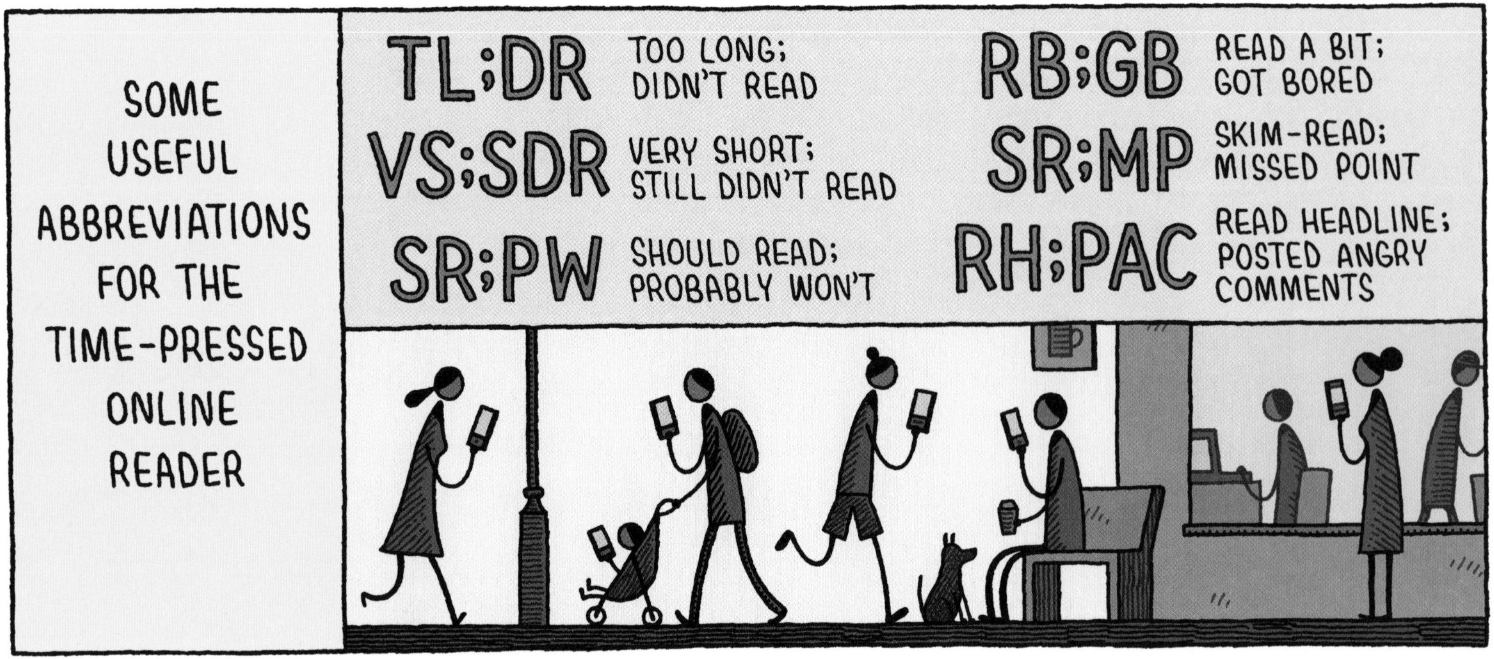
SOME USEFUL ABBREVIATIONS FOR THE TIME-PRESSED ONLINE READER
TL;DR
TOO LONG; DIDN'T READ
VS;SDR
VERY SHORT; STILL DIDN'T READ
SR;PW
SHOULD READ; PROBABLY WON'T
RB;GB
READ A BIT; GOT BORED
SR;MP
SKIM-READ; MISSED POINT
RH;PAC
READ HEADLINE; POSTED ANGRY COMMENTS

THE BOOKSHOP CAT AND THE PANDEMIC

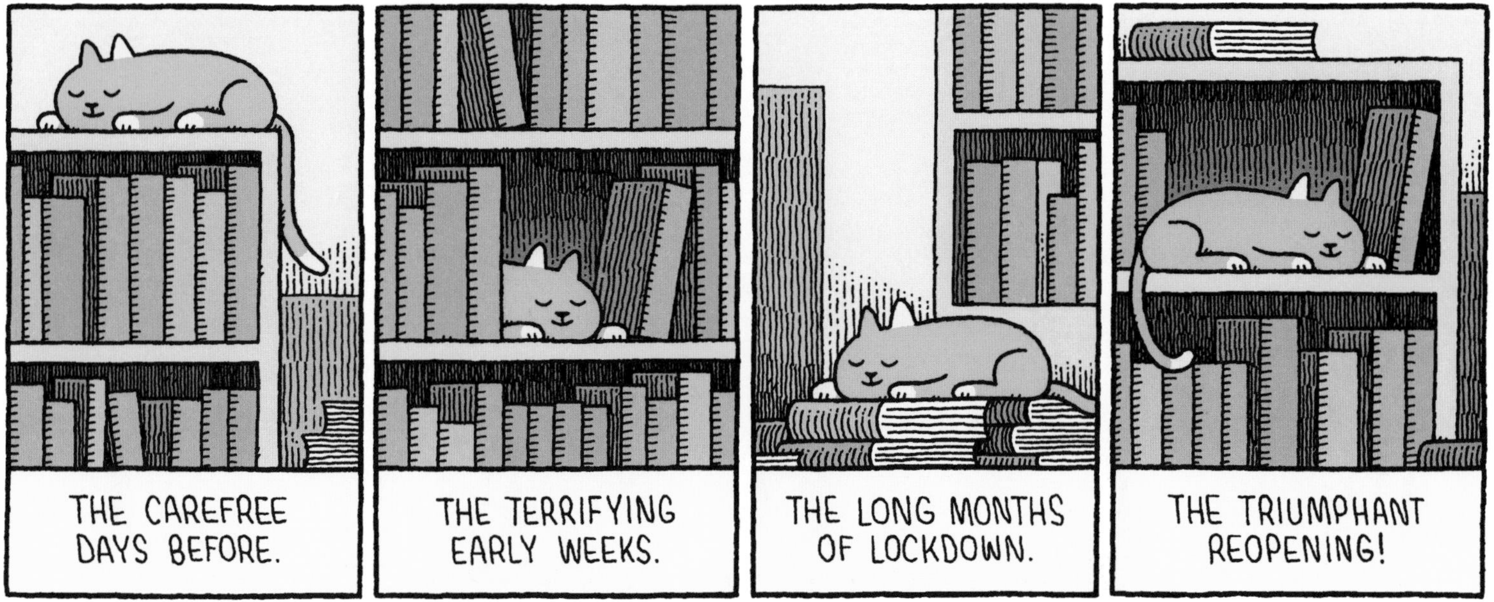
THE CAREFREE DAYS BEFORE.
THE TERRIFYING EARLY WEEKS.
THE LONG MONTHS OF LOCKDOWN.
THE TRIUMPHANT REOPENING!

THE WRITER AT WORK...

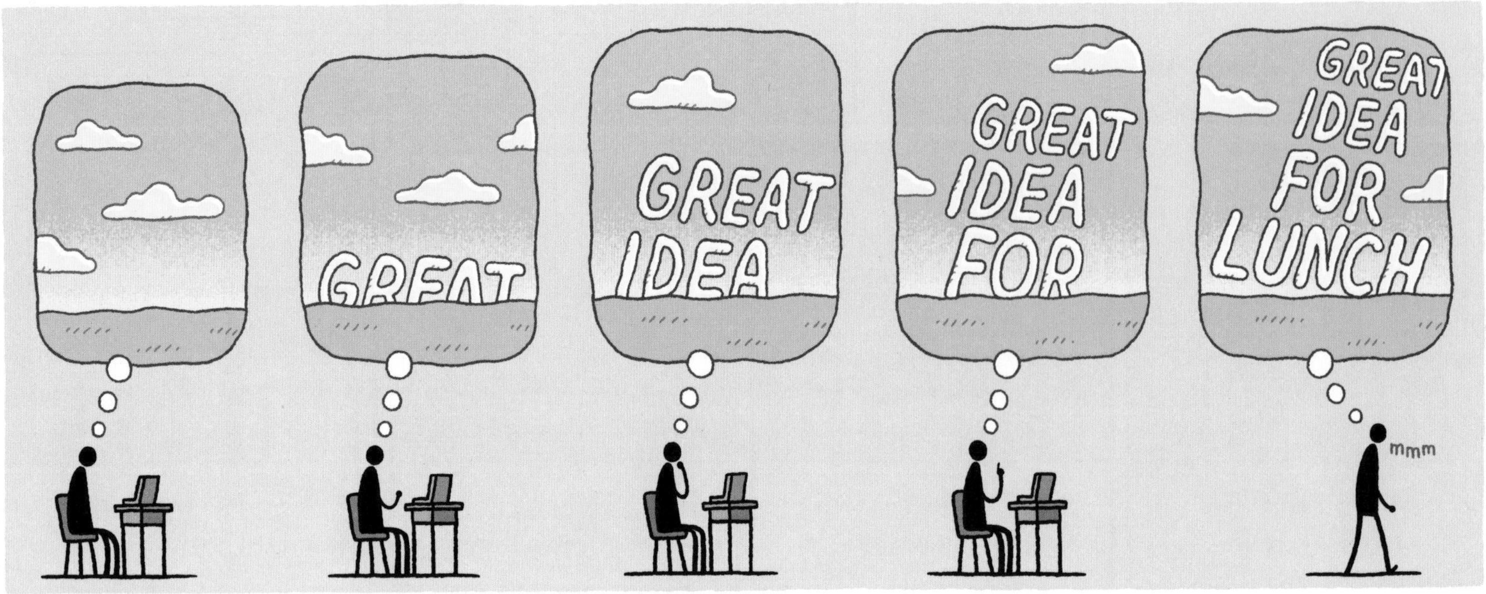
GREAT
GREAT IDEA
GREAT IDEA FOR
GREAT IDEA FOR LUNCH
mmm

THE SPERM WHALE AND THE COLOSSAL SQUID HAD NEVER BEEN CLOSE FRIENDS,
BUT WHEN THE LONDON REVIEW OF BOOKS PUBLISHED THE SQUID'S VITRIOLIC CRITIQUE
OF THE WHALE'S SECOND VOLUME OF POETRY, THE TWO BECAME MORTAL ENEMIES.

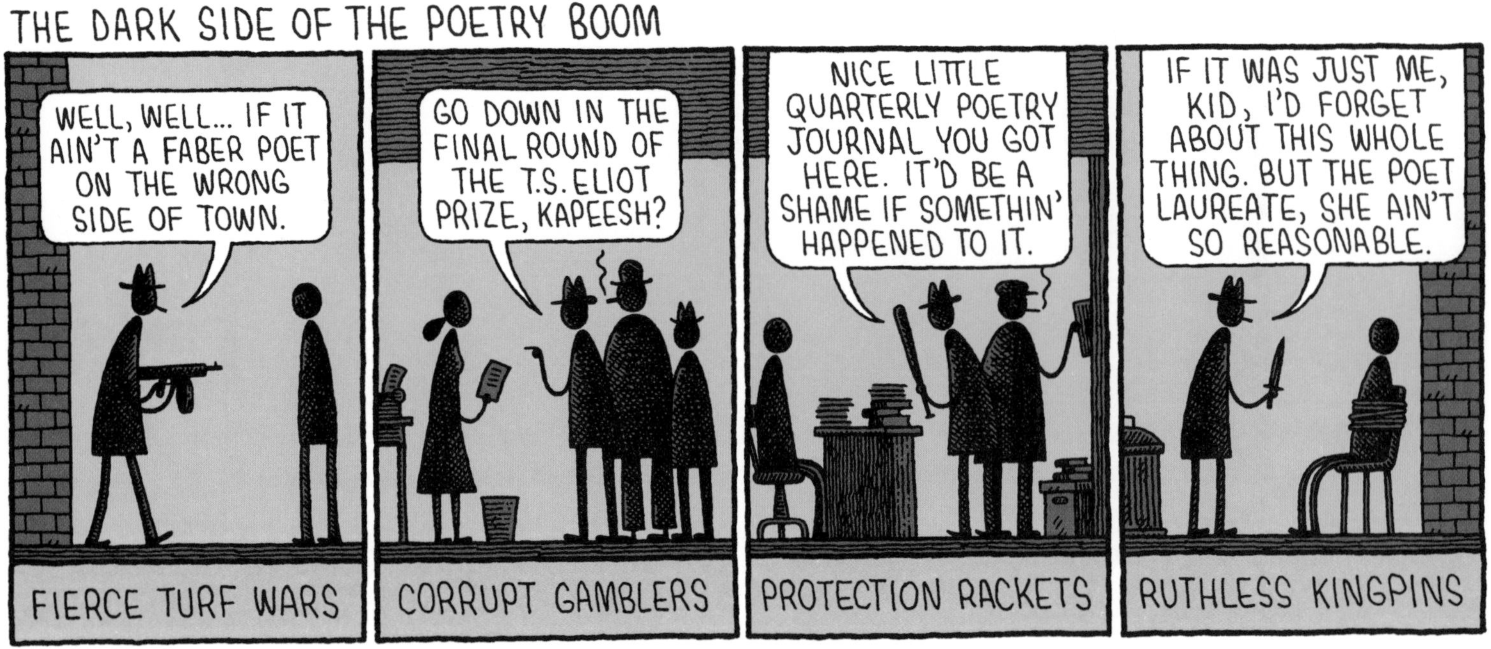
THE DARK SIDE OF THE POETRY BOOM
WELL, WELL... IF IT AIN'T A FABER POET ON THE WRONG SIDE OF TOWN.
FIERCE TURF WARS
GO DOWN IN THE FINAL ROUND OF THE T.S. ELIOT PRIZE, KAPEESH?
CORRUPT GAMBLERS
NICE LITTLE QUARTERLY POETRY JOURNAL YOU GOT HERE. IT'D BE A SHAME IF SOMETHIN' HAPPENED TO IT.
PROTECTION RACKETS
IF IT WAS JUST ME, KID, I'D FORGET ABOUT THIS WHOLE THING. BUT THE POET LAUREATE, SHE AIN'T SO REASONABLE.
RUTHLESS KINGPINS

SUMMER READING FOR CONSPIRACY THEORISTS

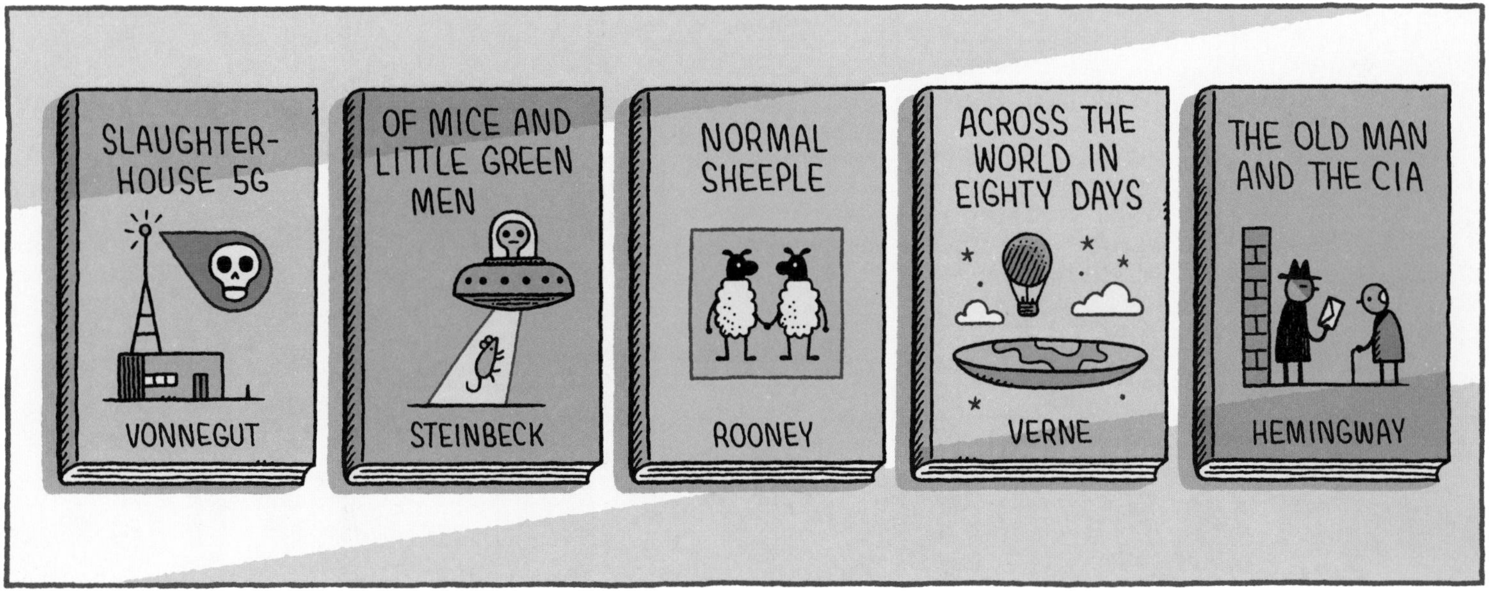
SLAUGHTER-HOUSE 5G
VONNEGUT
OF MICE AND LITTLE GREEN MEN
STEINBECK
NORMAL SHEEPLE
ROONEY
ACROSS THE WORLD IN EIGHTY DAYS
VERNE
THE OLD MAN AND THE CIA
HEMINGWAY

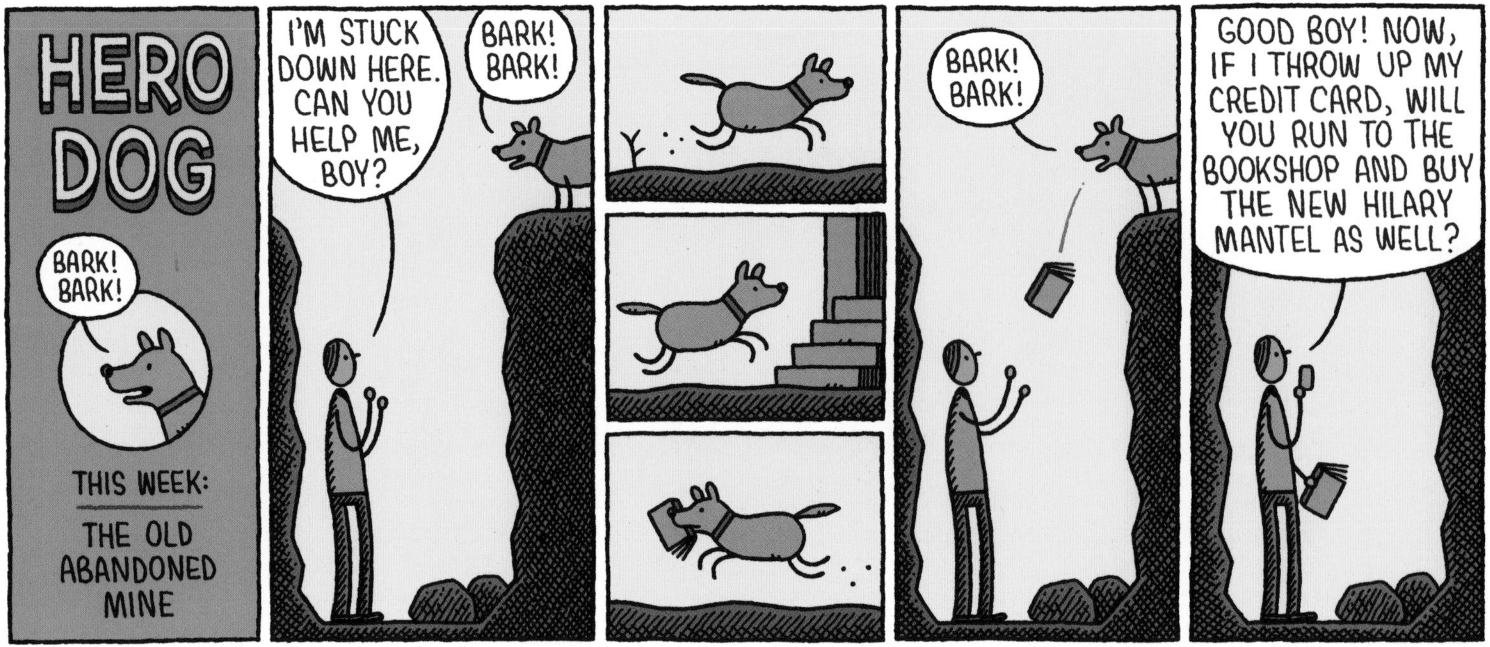
HERO DOG
BARK! BARK!
THIS WEEK:
THE OLD ABANDONED MINE
I'M STUCK DOWN HERE. CAN YOU HELP ME, BOY?
BARK! BARK!
BARK! BARK!
GOOD BOY! NOW, IF I THROW UP MY CREDIT CARD, WILL YOU RUN TO THE BOOKSHOP AND BUY THE NEW HILARY MANTEL AS WELL?

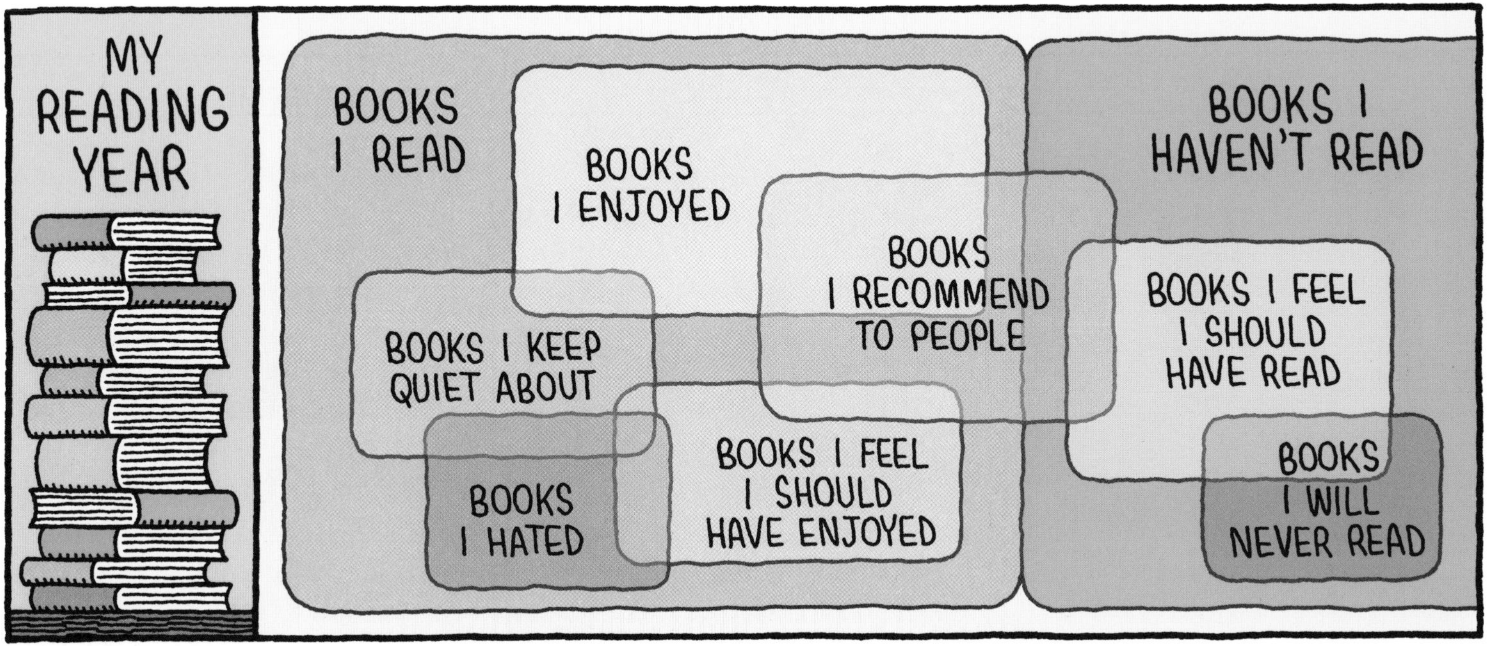

MY READING YEAR
BOOKS I READ
BOOKS I ENJOYED
BOOKS I RECOMMEND TO PEOPLE
BOOKS I KEEP QUIET ABOUT
BOOKS I HATED
BOOKS I FEEL I SHOULD HAVE ENJOYED
BOOKS I HAVEN'T READ
BOOKS I FEEL I SHOULD HAVE READ
BOOKS I WILL NEVER READ

GREAT LOST SENTENCES

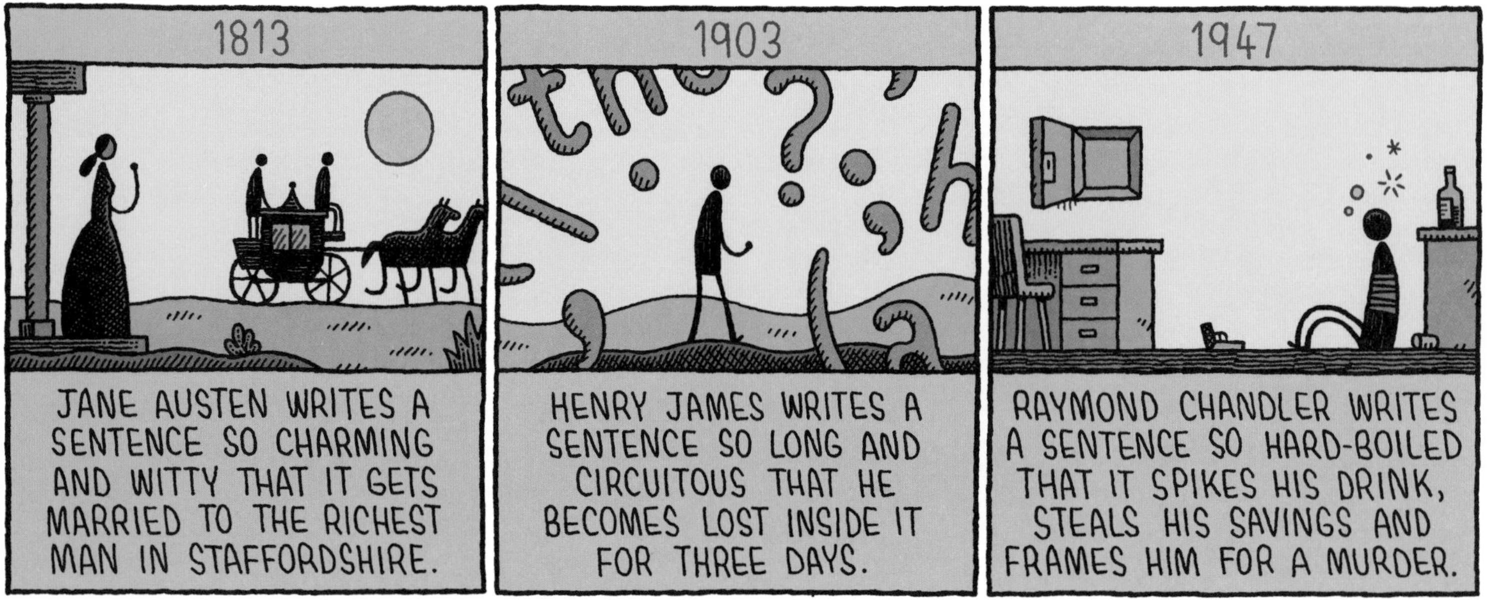
1813
JANE AUSTEN WRITES A SENTENCE SO CHARMING AND WITTY THAT IT GETS MARRIED TO THE RICHEST MAN IN STAFFORDSHIRE.
1903
HENRY JAMES WRITES A SENTENCE SO LONG AND CIRCUITOUS THAT HE BECOMES LOST INSIDE IT FOR THREE DAYS.
1947
RAYMOND CHANDLER WRITES A SENTENCE SO HARD-BOILED THAT IT SPIKES HIS DRINK, STEALS HIS SAVINGS AND FRAMES HIM FOR A MURDER.

WAITING FOR GODOT TO JOIN THE ZOOM MEETING

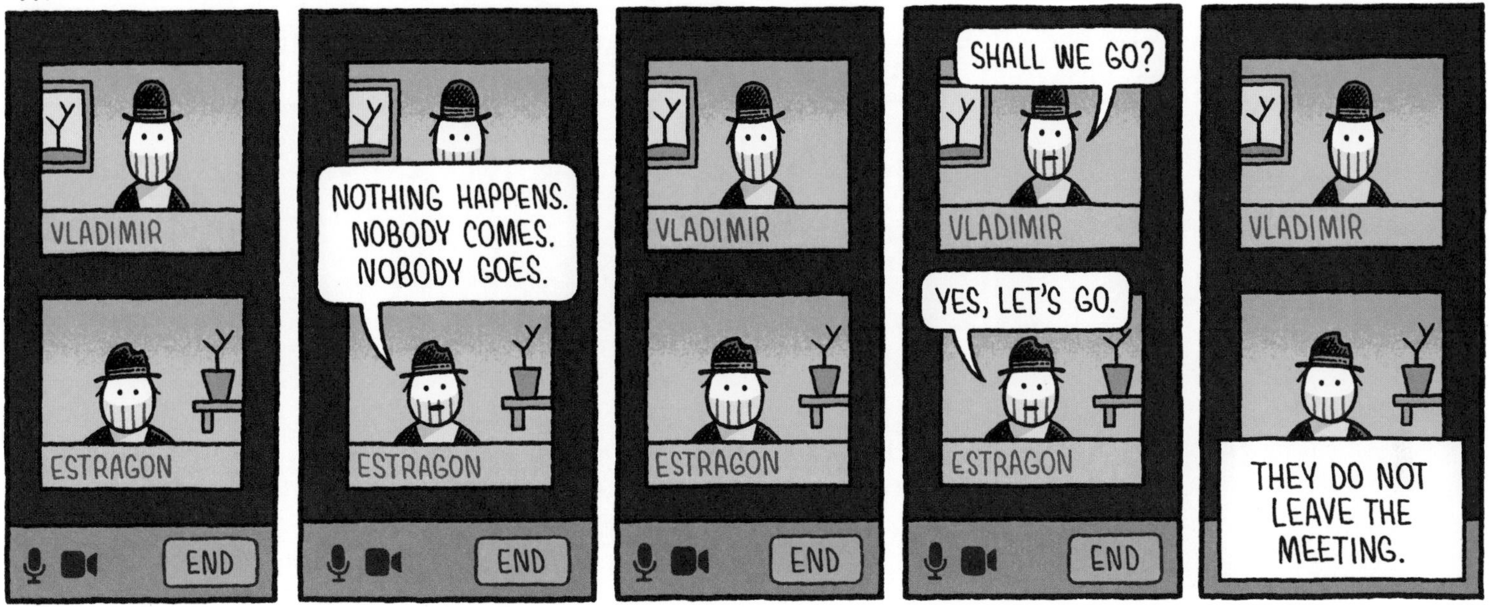
VLADIMIR
ESTRAGON
END
NOTHING HAPPENS. NOBODY COMES. NOBODY GOES.
VLADIMIR
ESTRAGON
END
SHALL WE GO?
VLADIMIR
YES, LET'S GO.
ESTRAGON
END
VLADIMIR
THEY DO NOT LEAVE THE MEETING.

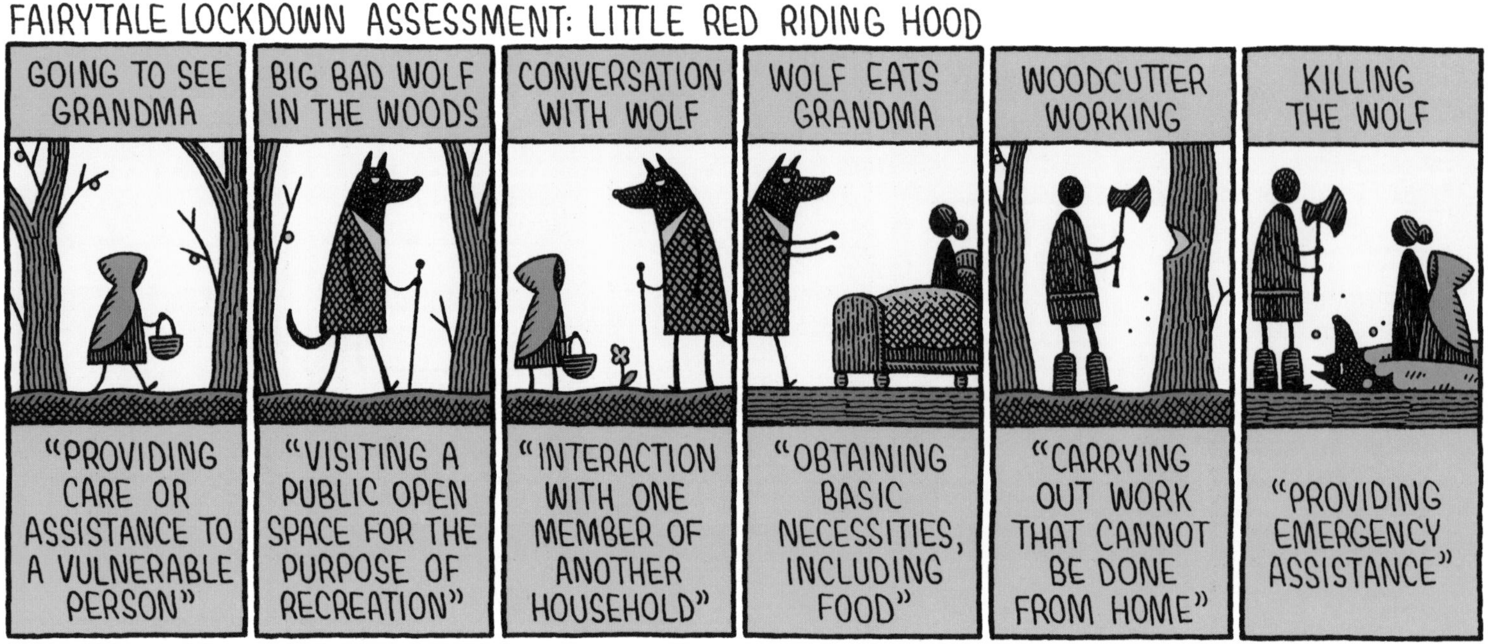

FAIRYTALE LOCKDOWN ASSESSMENT: LITTLE RED RIDING HOOD
GOING TO SEE GRANDMA
"PROVIDING CARE OR ASSISTANCE TO A VULNERABLE PERSON"
BIG BAD WOLF IN THE WOODS
"VISITING A PUBLIC OPEN SPACE FOR THE PURPOSE OF RECREATION"
CONVERSATION WITH WOLF
"INTERACTION WITH ONE MEMBER OF ANOTHER HOUSEHOLD"
WOLF EATS GRANDMA
"OBTAINING BASIC NECESSITIES, INCLUDING FOOD"
WOODCUTTER WORKING
"CARRYING OUT WORK THAT CANNOT BE DONE FROM HOME"
KILLING THE WOLF
"PROVIDING EMERGENCY ASSISTANCE"

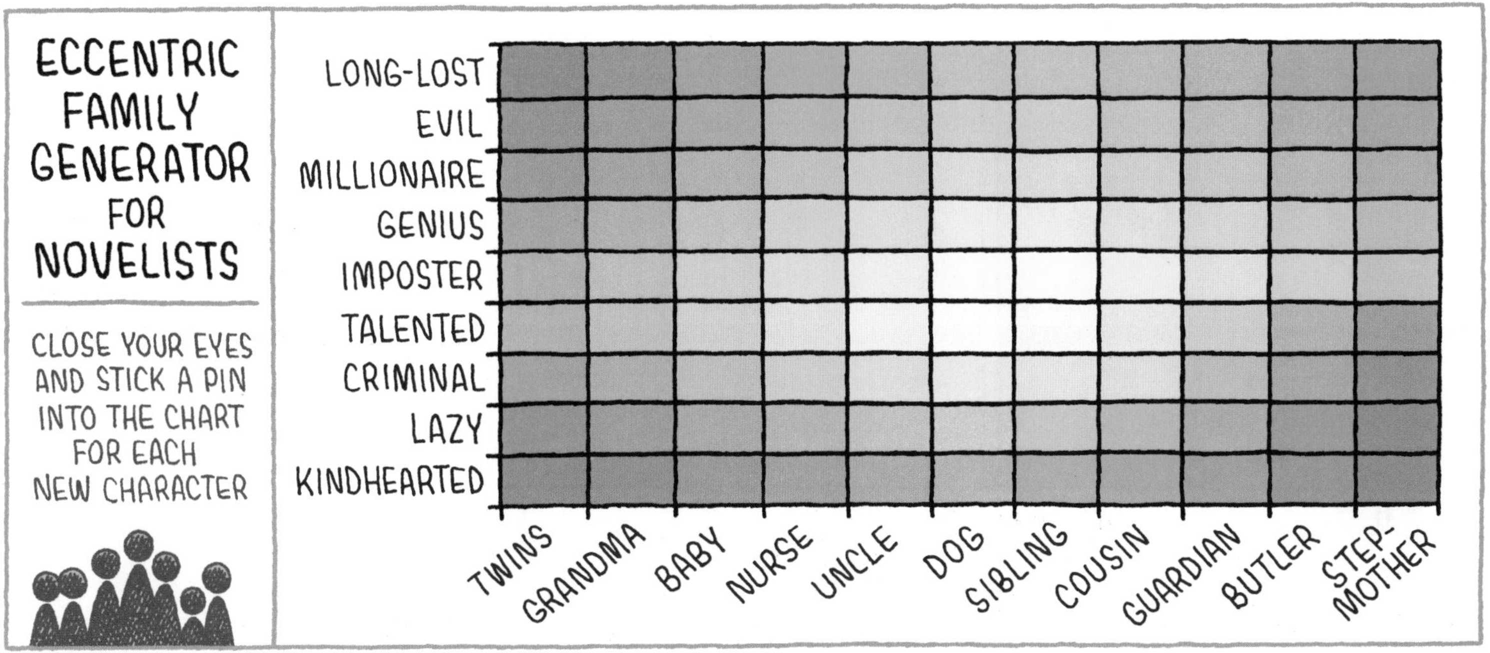
ECCENTRIC FAMILY GENERATOR FOR NOVELISTS
CLOSE YOUR EYES AND STICK A PIN INTO THE CHART FOR EACH NEW CHARACTER
LONG-LOST
EVIL
MILLIONAIRE
GENIUS
IMPOSTER
TALENTED
CRIMINAL
LAZY
KINDHEARTED
TWINS
GRANDMA
BABY
NURSE
UNCLE
DOG
SIBLING
COUSIN
GUARDIAN
BUTLER
STEP-MOTHER

THE LIBRARIES HAVE REOPENED SO THE LIBRARIANS MUST RESUME THEIR RIGOROUS TRAINING REGIME

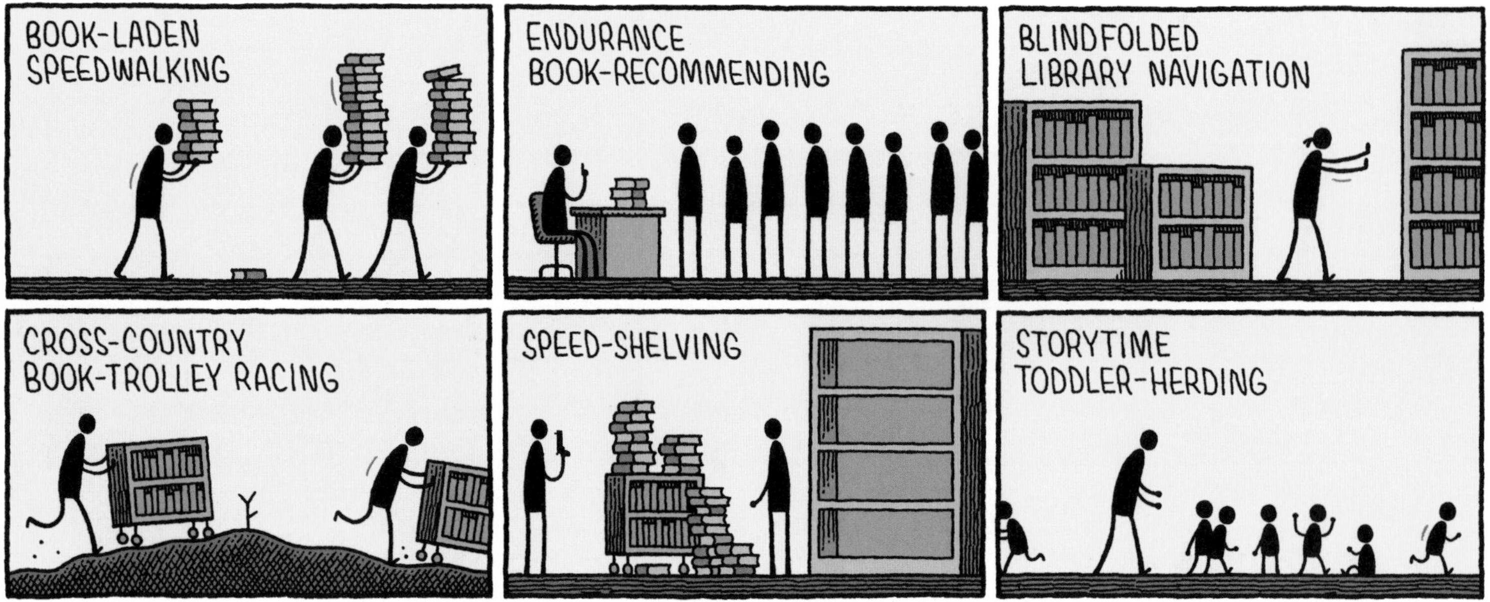

BOOK-LADEN SPEEDWALKING
ENDURANCE BOOK-RECOMMENDING
BLINDFOLDED LIBRARY NAVIGATION
CROSS-COUNTRY BOOK-TROLLEY RACING
SPEED-SHELVING
STORYTIME TODDLER-HERDING

DIFFICULT TIMES FOR WRITERS

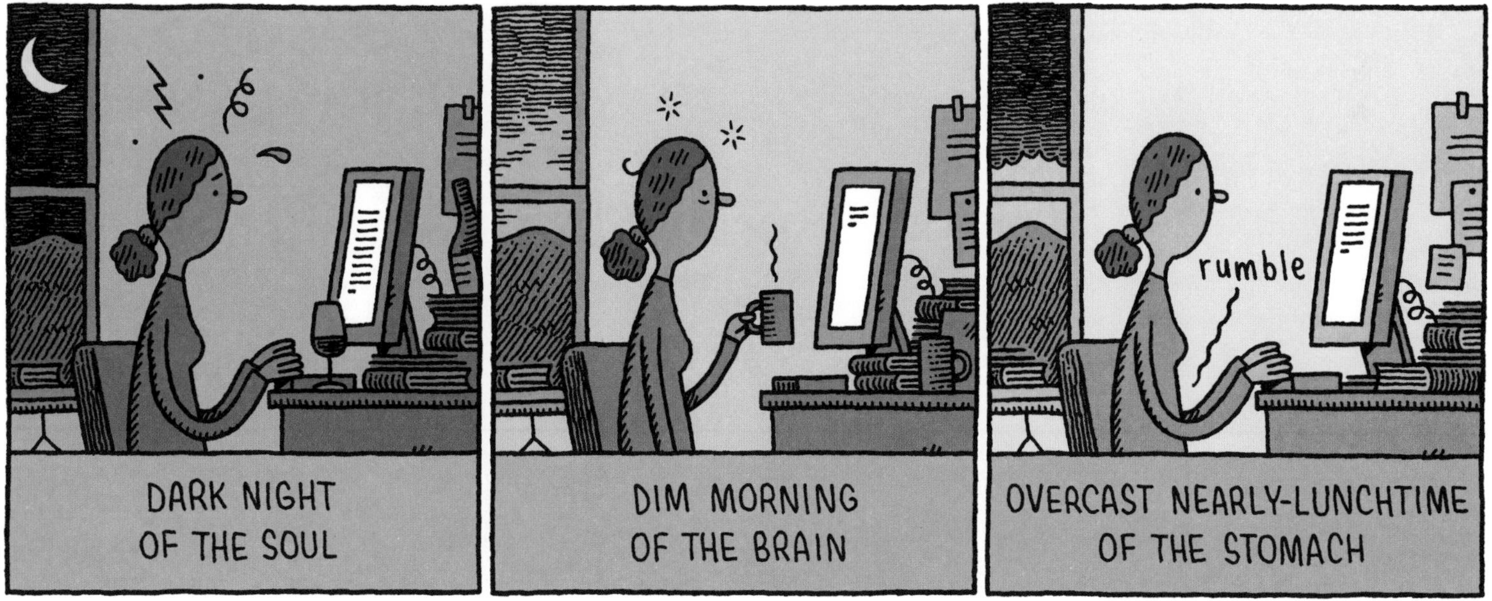
DARK NIGHT
OF THE SOUL
DIM MORNING
OF THE BRAIN
rumble
OVERCAST NEARLY-LUNCHTIME
OF THE STOMACH

HUNTING FOR EASTER EGGS WITH WERNER HERZOG

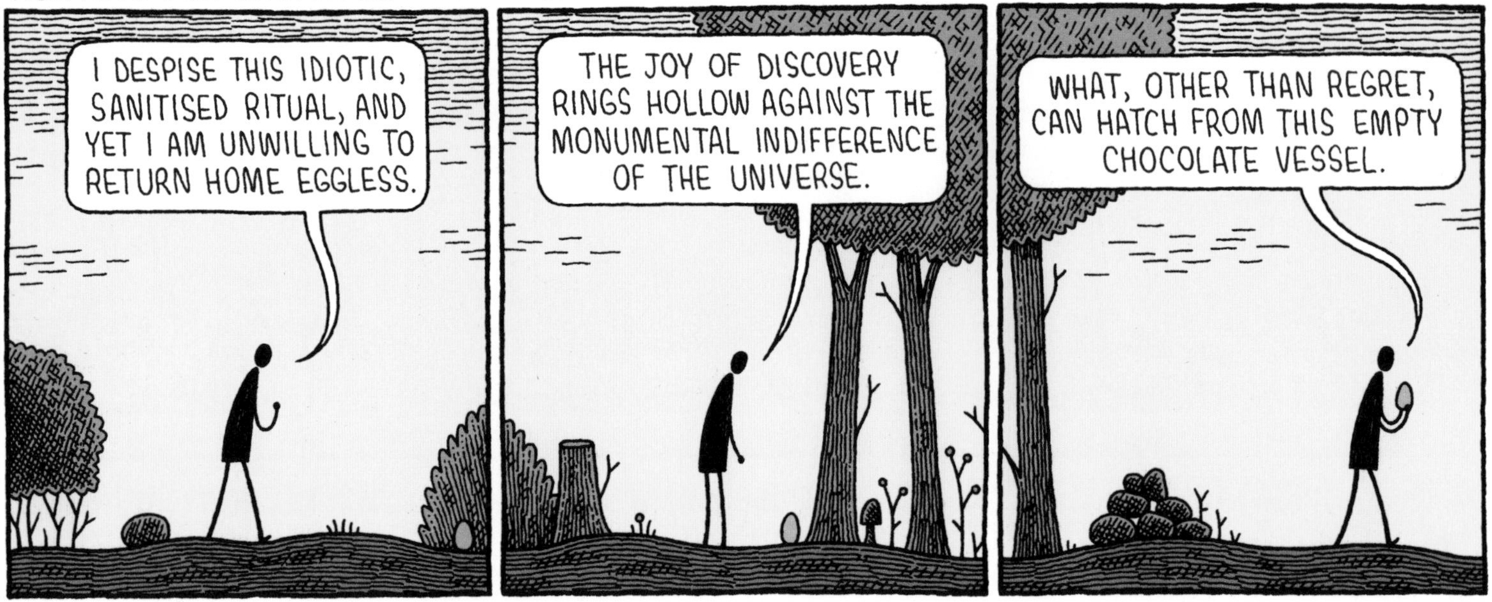
I DESPISE THIS IDIOTIC, SANITISED RITUAL, AND YET I AM UNWILLING TO RETURN HOME EGGLESS.
THE JOY OF DISCOVERY RINGS HOLLOW AGAINST THE MONUMENTAL INDIFFERENCE OF THE UNIVERSE.
WHAT, OTHER THAN REGRET, CAN HATCH FROM THIS EMPTY CHOCOLATE VESSEL.

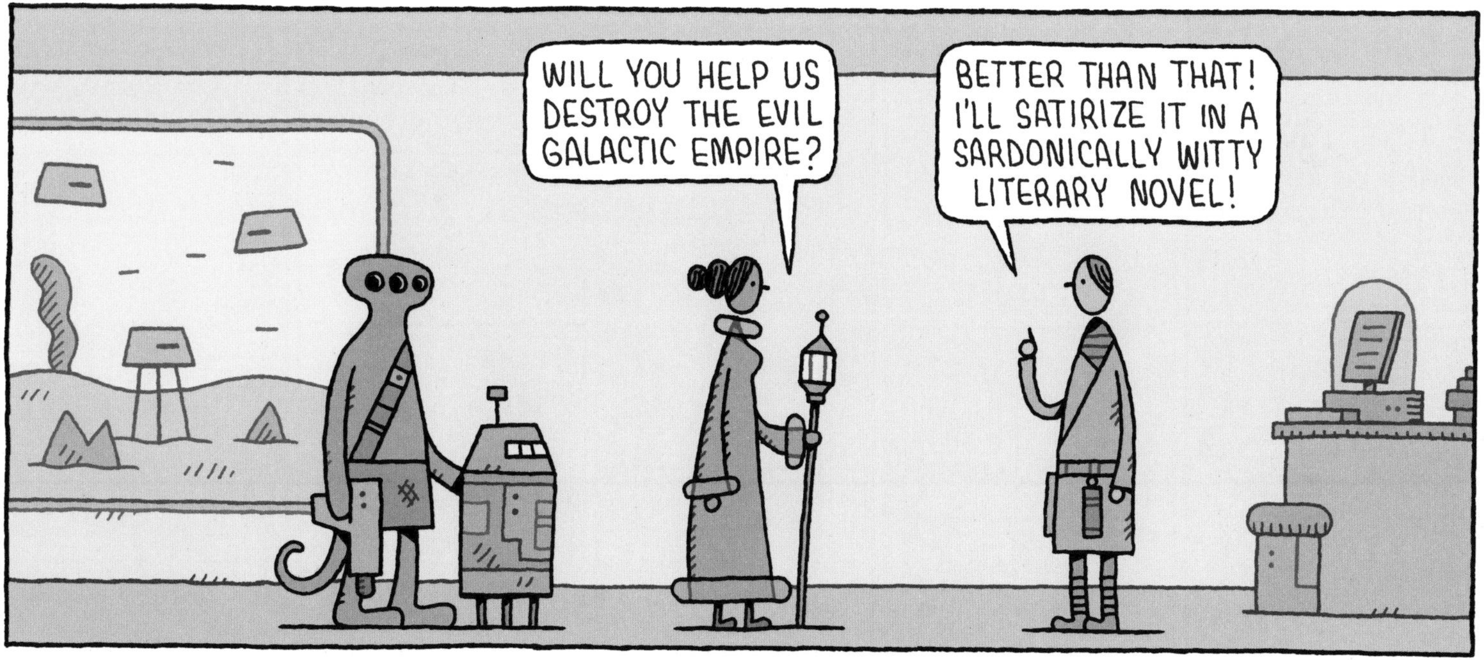
WILL YOU HELP US DESTROY THE EVIL GALACTIC EMPIRE?
BETTER THAN THAT! I'LL SATIRIZE IT IN A SARDONICALLY WITTY LITERARY NOVEL!

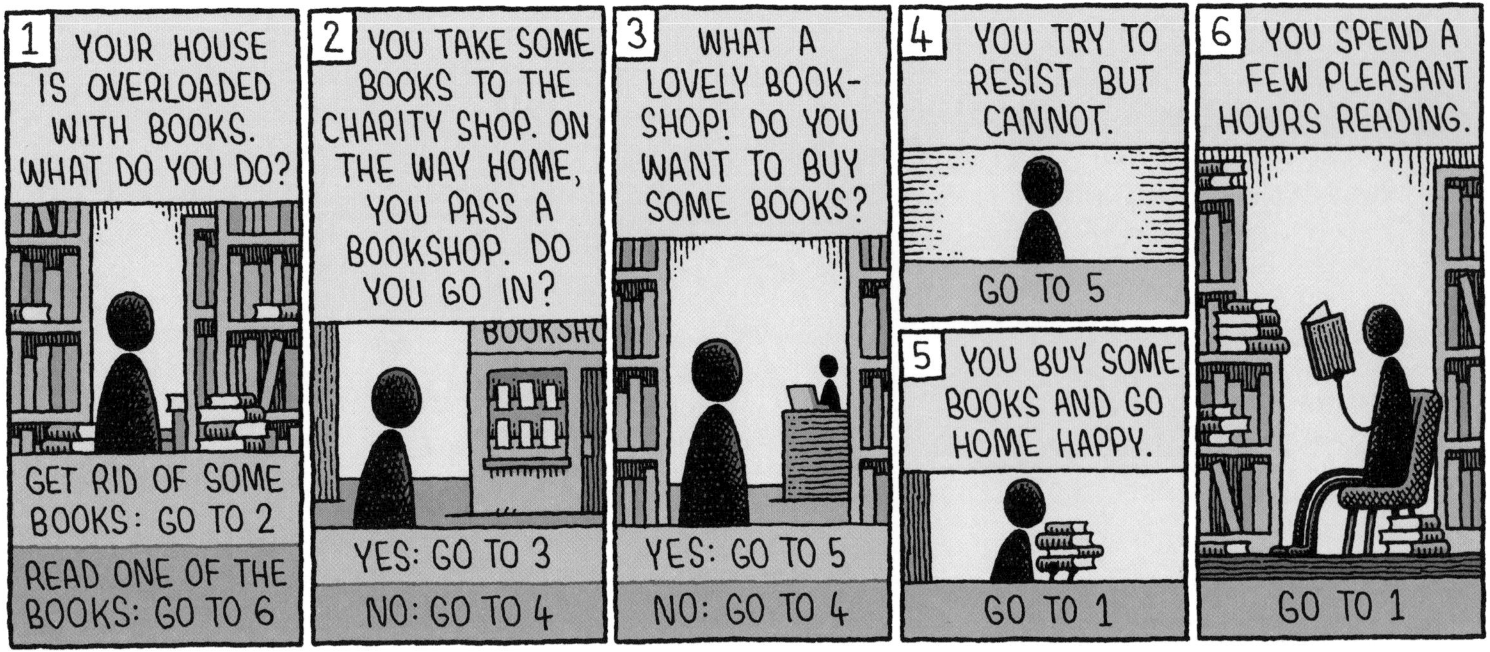
1
YOUR HOUSE IS OVERLOADED WITH BOOKS. WHAT DO YOU DO?
GET RID OF SOME BOOKS: GO TO 2
READ ONE OF THE BOOKS: GO TO 6
2
YOU TAKE SOME BOOKS TO THE CHARITY SHOP. ON THE WAY HOME, YOU PASS A BOOKSHOP. DO YOU GO IN?
YES: GO TO 3
NO: GO TO 4
3
WHAT A LOVELY BOOK-SHOP! DO YOU WANT TO BUY SOME BOOKS?
YES: GO TO 5
NO: GO TO 4
4
YOU TRY TO RESIST BUT CANNOT.
GO TO 5
5
YOU BUY SOME BOOKS AND GO HOME HAPPY.
GO TO 1
6
YOU SPEND A FEW PLEASANT HOURS READING.
GO TO 1

ROAD SIGNS FOR A GOTHIC NOVEL

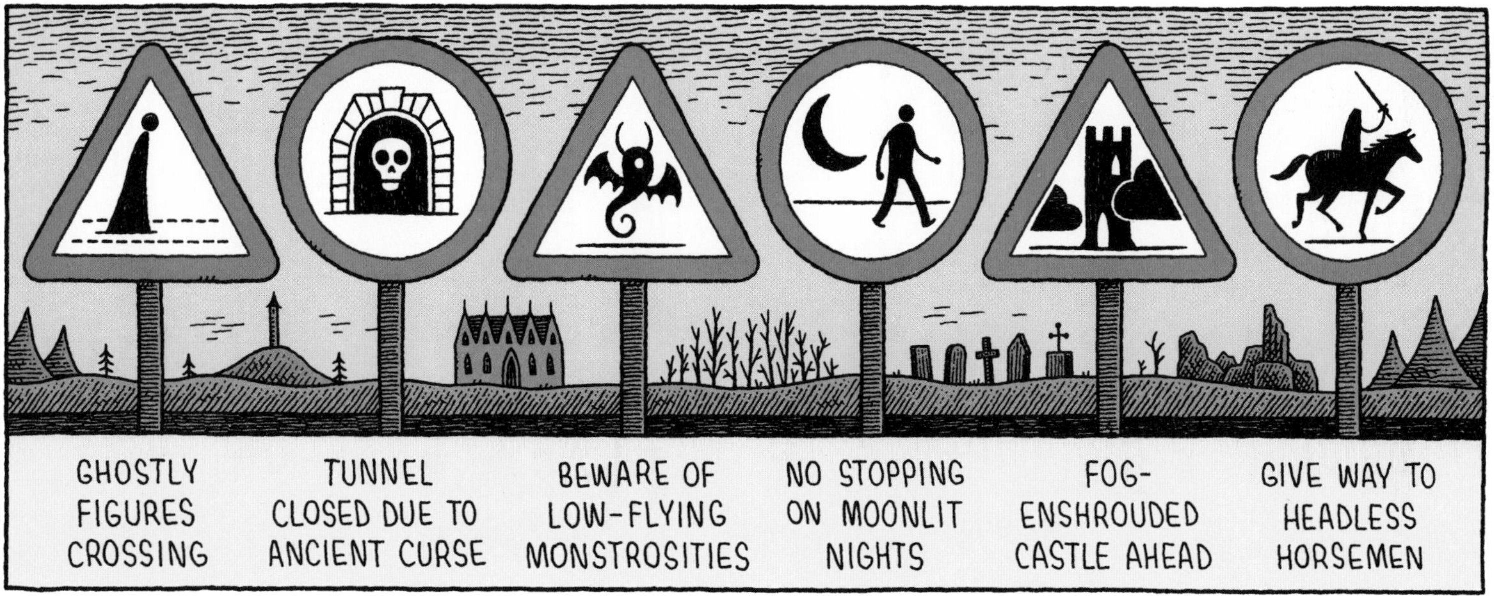
GHOSTLY FIGURES CROSSING
TUNNEL CLOSED DUE TO ANCIENT CURSE
BEWARE OF LOW-FLYING MONSTROSITIES
NO STOPPING ON MOONLIT NIGHTS
FOG-ENSHROUDED CASTLE AHEAD
GIVE WAY TO HEADLESS HORSEMEN

SOME LITERARY COLLECTIVE NOUNS

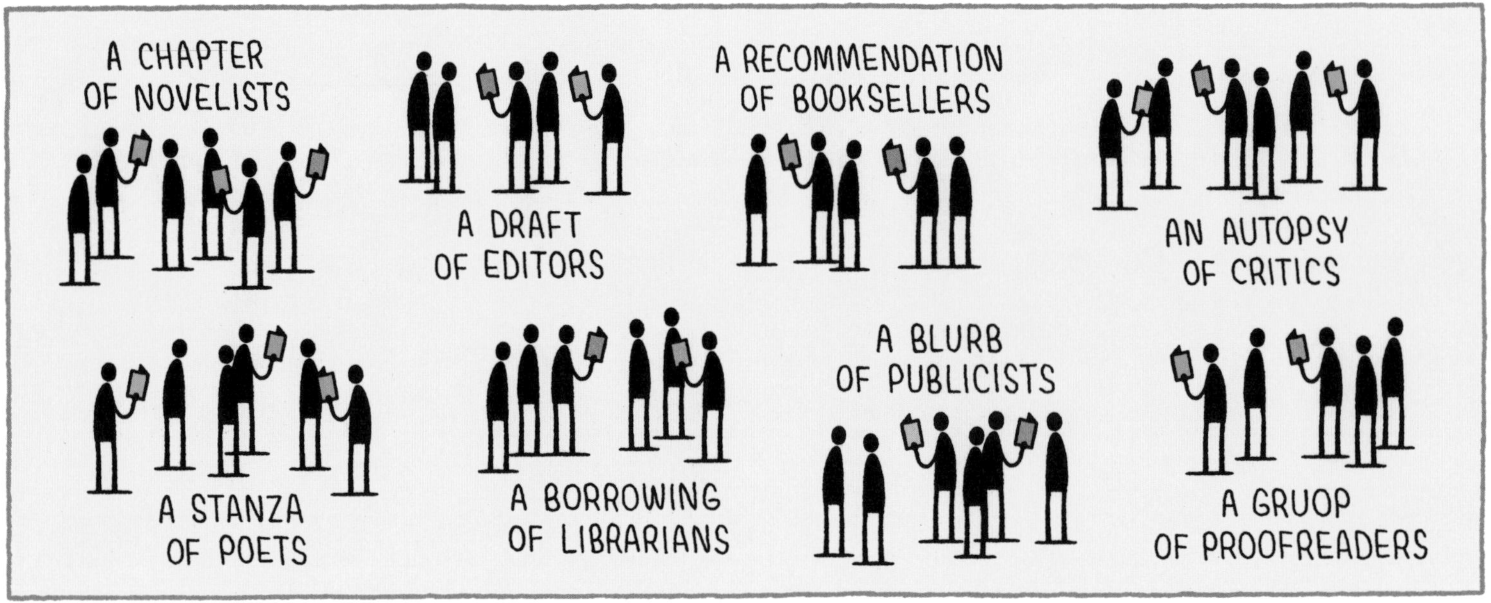
A CHAPTER OF NOVELISTS
A DRAFT OF EDITORS
A RECOMMENDATION OF BOOKSELLERS
AN AUTOPSY OF CRITICS
A STANZA OF POETS
A BORROWING OF LIBRARIANS
A BLURB OF PUBLICISTS
A GRUOP OF PROOFREADERS

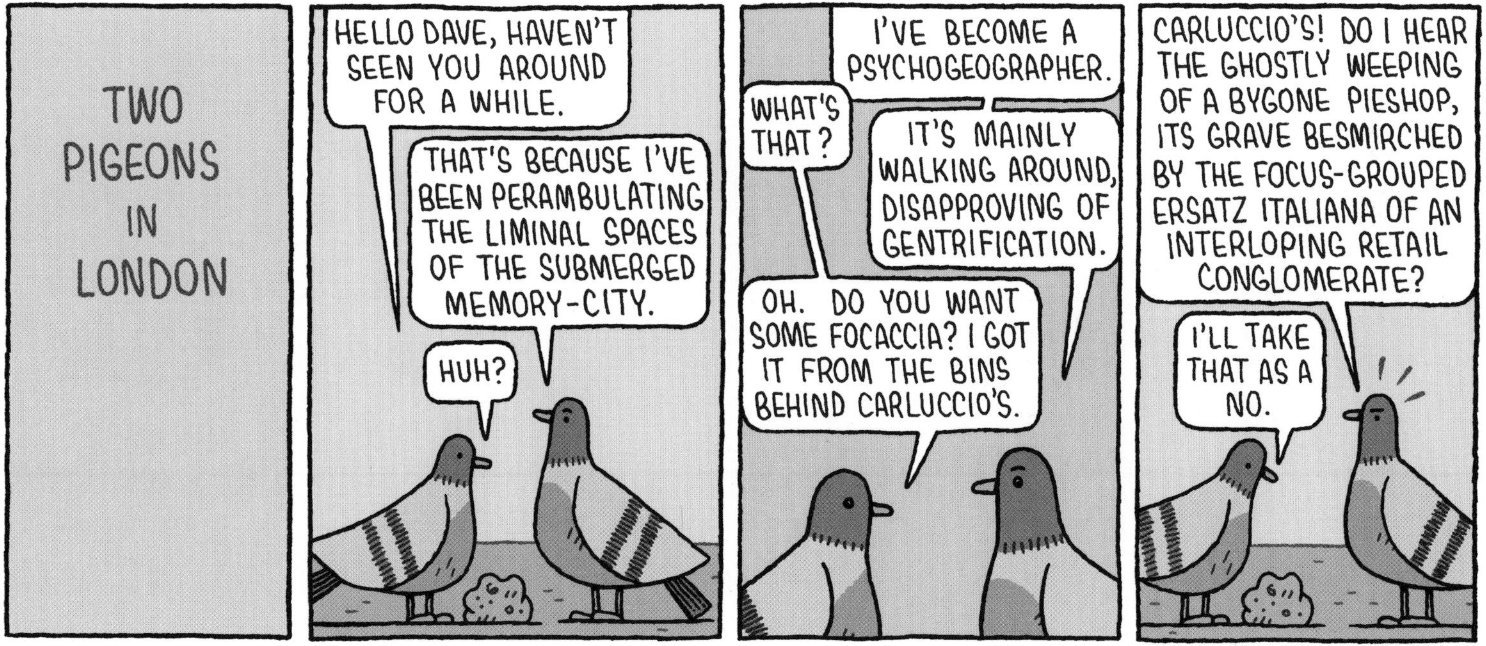

TWO PIGEONS IN LONDON
HELLO DAVE, HAVEN'T SEEN YOU AROUND FOR A WHILE.
THAT'S BECAUSE I'VE BEEN PERAMBULATING THE LIMINAL SPACES OF THE SUBMERGED MEMORY-CITY.
HUH?
I'VE BECOME A PSYCHOGEOGRAPHER.
WHAT'S THAT?
IT'S MAINLY WALKING AROUND, DISAPPROVING OF GENTRIFICATION.
OH. DO YOU WANT SOME FOCACCIA? I GOT IT FROM THE BINS BEHIND CARLUCCIO'S.
CARLUCCIO'S! DO I HEAR THE GHOSTLY WEEPING OF A BYGONE PIESHOP, ITS GRAVE BESMIRCHED BY THE FOCUS-GROUPED ERSATZ ITALIANA OF AN INTERLOPING RETAIL CONGLOMERATE?
I'LL TAKE THAT AS A NO.

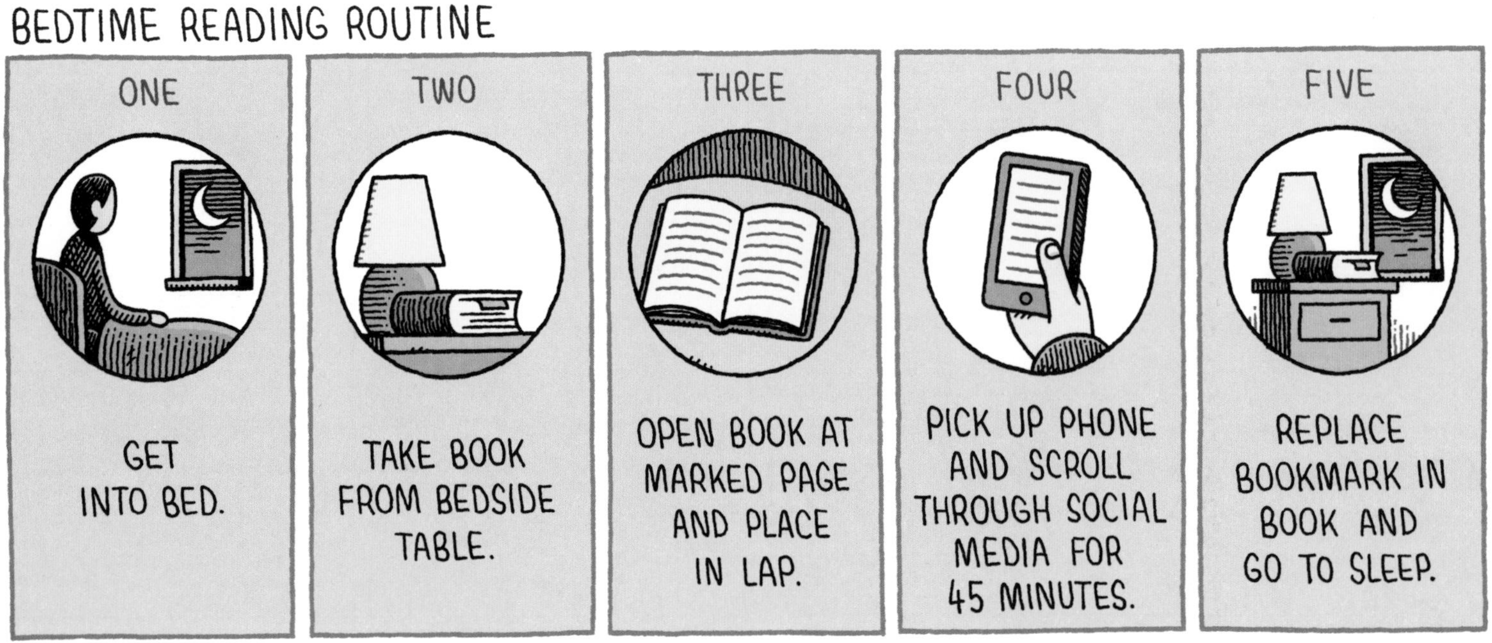
BEDTIME READING ROUTINE
ONE
GET INTO BED.
TWO
TAKE BOOK FROM BEDSIDE TABLE.
THREE
OPEN BOOK AT MARKED PAGE AND PLACE IN LAP.
FOUR
PICK UP PHONE AND SCROLL THROUGH SOCIAL MEDIA FOR 45 MINUTES.
FIVE
REPLACE BOOKMARK IN BOOK AND GO TO SLEEP.

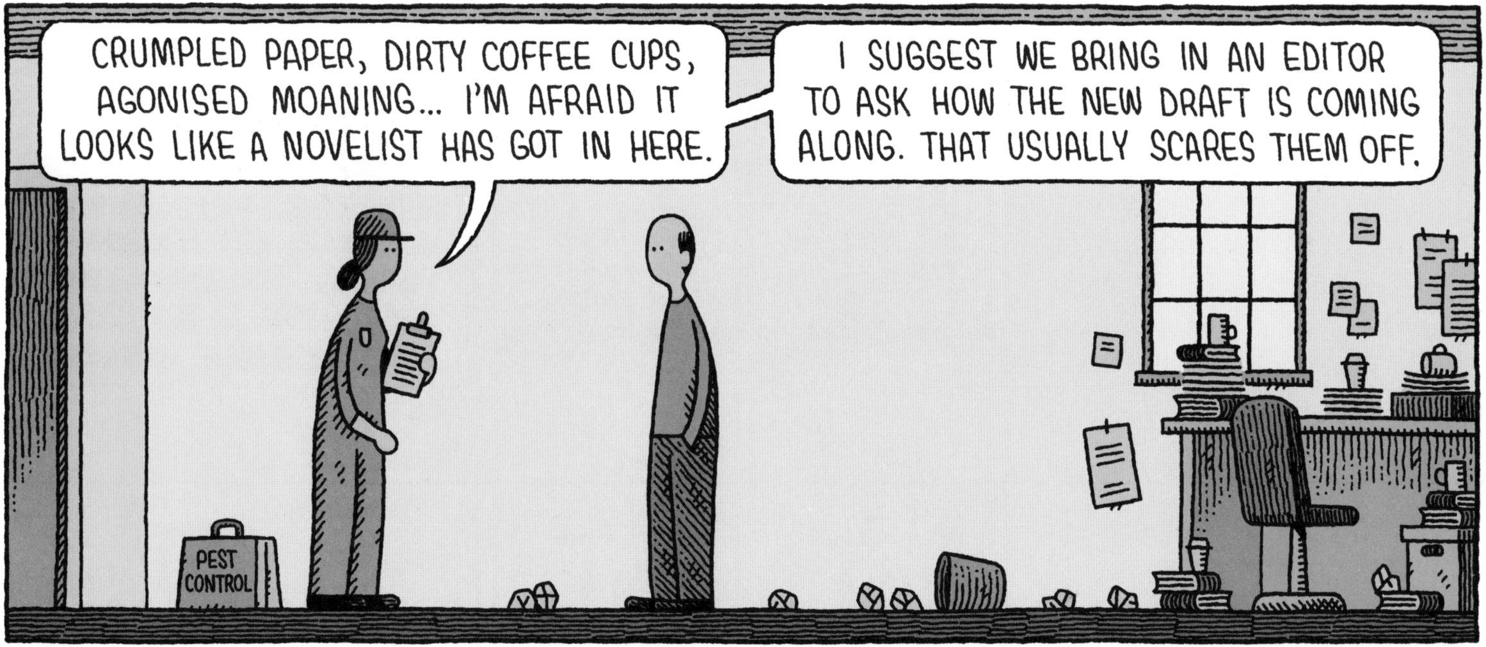
CRUMPLED PAPER, DIRTY COFFEE CUPS, AGONISED MOANING... I'M AFRAID IT LOOKS LIKE A NOVELIST HAS GOT IN HERE.
I SUGGEST WE BRING IN AN EDITOR TO ASK HOW THE NEW DRAFT IS COMING ALONG. THAT USUALLY SCARES THEM OFF.
PEST CONTROL

NEW YEAR'S RESOLUTION

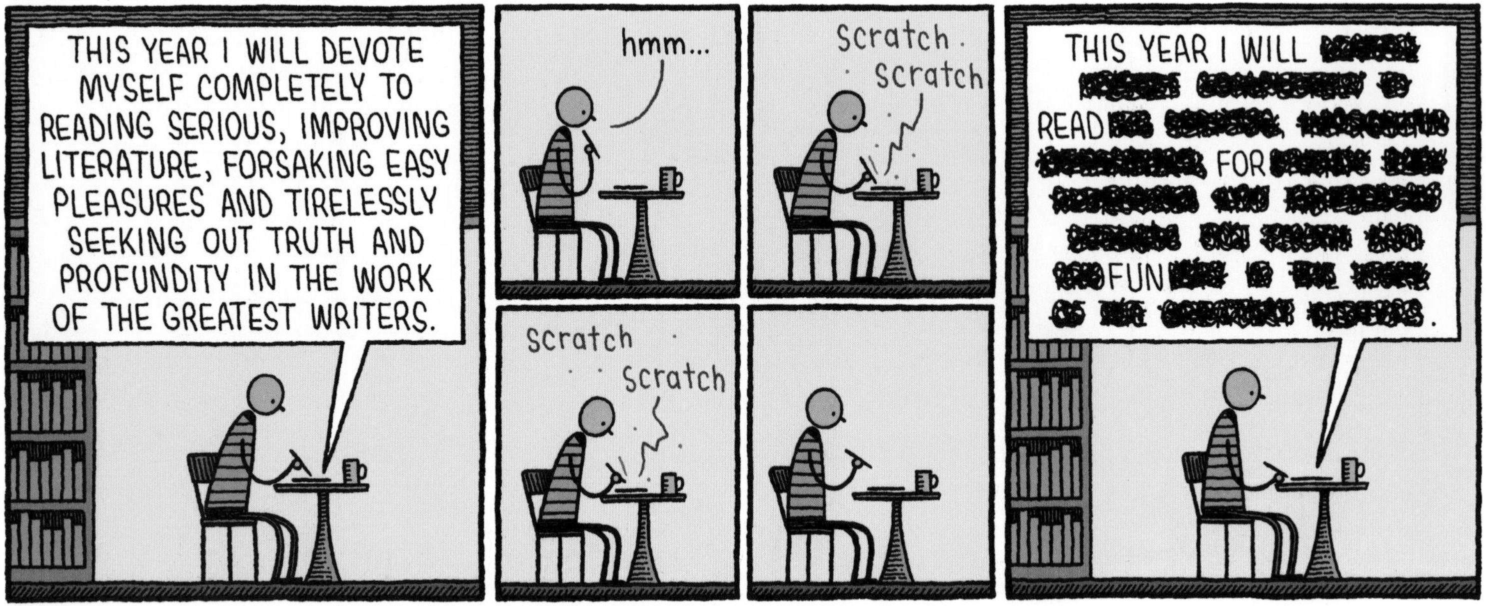

THIS YEAR I WILL DEVOTE MYSELF COMPLETELY TO READING SERIOUS, IMPROVING LITERATURE, FORSAKING EASY PLEASURES AND TIRELESSLY SEEKING OUT TRUTH AND PROFUNDITY IN THE WORK OF THE GREATEST WRITERS.
hmm...
Scratch . . Scratch
Scratch . . . Scratch
THIS YEAR I WILL [redacted] READ [redacted], [redacted], FOR [redacted] FUN [redacted].

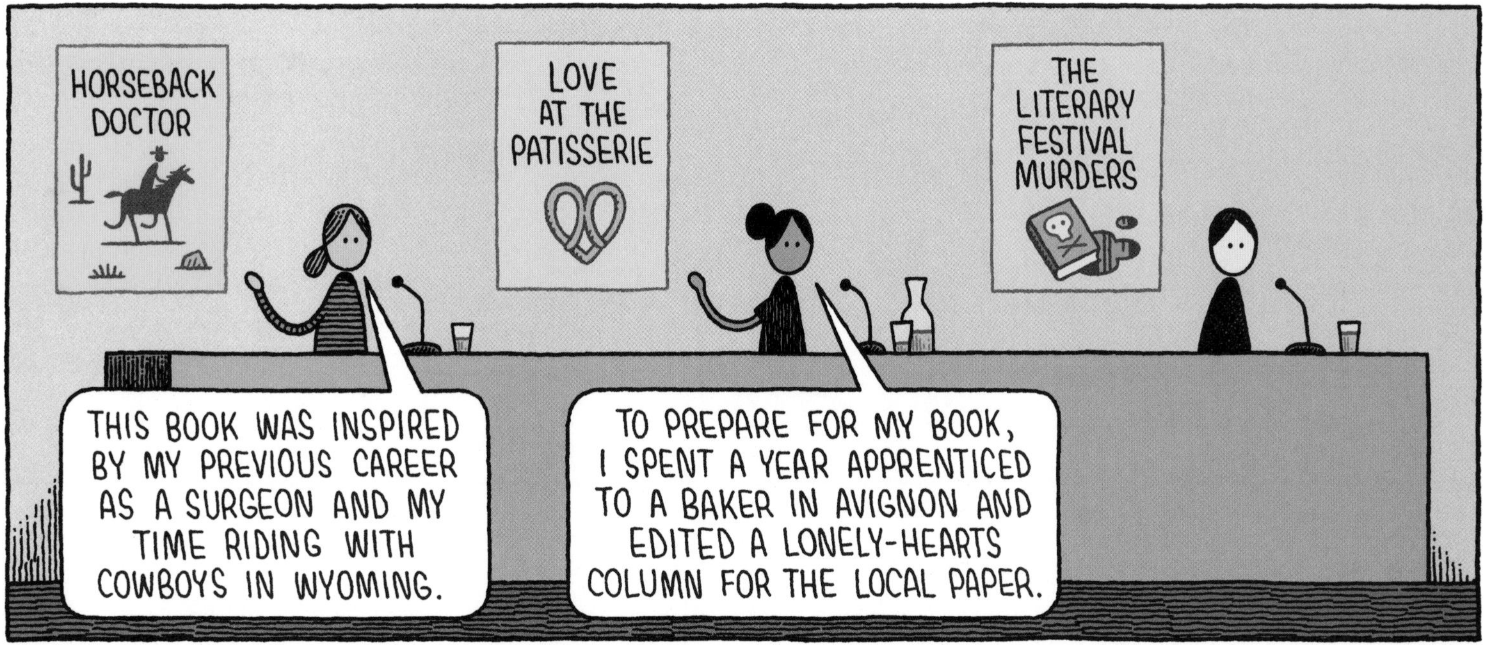
HORSEBACK DOCTOR
LOVE AT THE PATISSERIE
THE LITERARY FESTIVAL MURDERS
THIS BOOK WAS INSPIRED BY MY PREVIOUS CAREER AS A SURGEON AND MY TIME RIDING WITH COWBOYS IN WYOMING.
TO PREPARE FOR MY BOOK, I SPENT A YEAR APPRENTICED TO A BAKER IN AVIGNON AND EDITED A LONELY-HEARTS COLUMN FOR THE LOCAL PAPER.

SUPERNATURAL ENEMIES OF THE WRITER

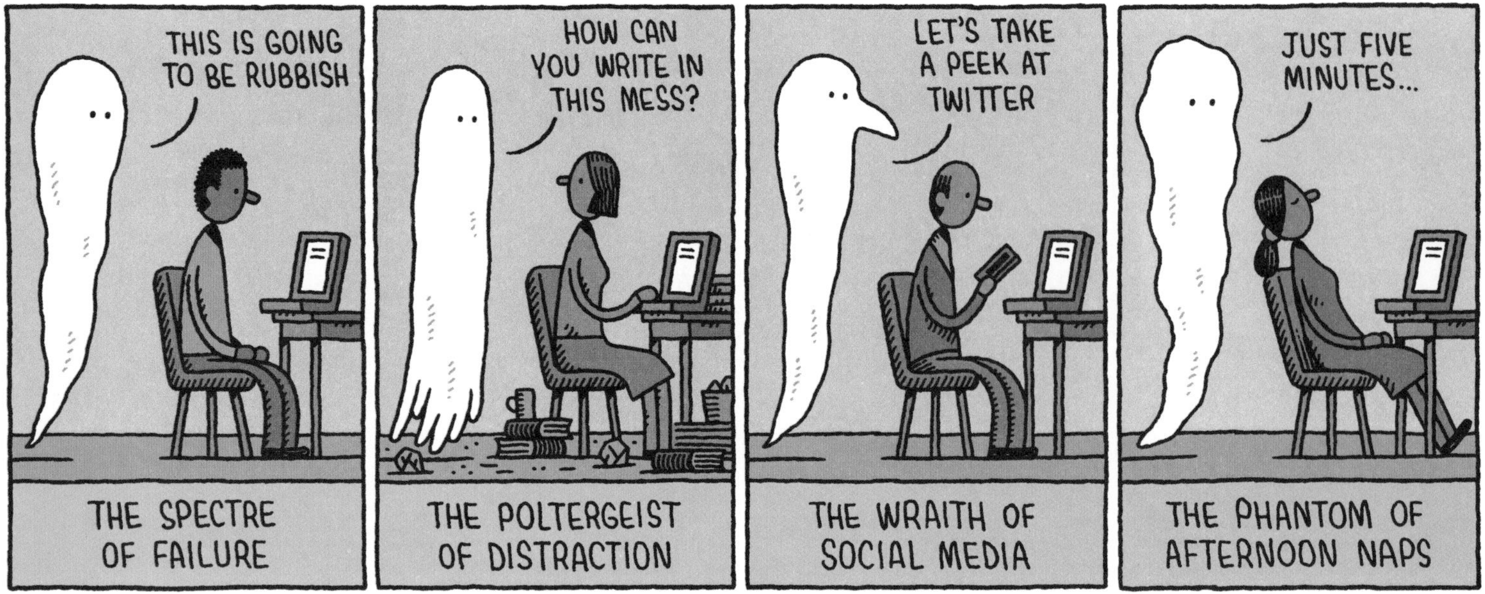
THIS IS GOING TO BE RUBBISH
THE SPECTRE OF FAILURE
HOW CAN YOU WRITE IN THIS MESS?
THE POLTERGEIST OF DISTRACTION
LET'S TAKE A PEEK AT TWITTER
THE WRAITH OF SOCIAL MEDIA
JUST FIVE MINUTES...
THE PHANTOM OF AFTERNOON NAPS

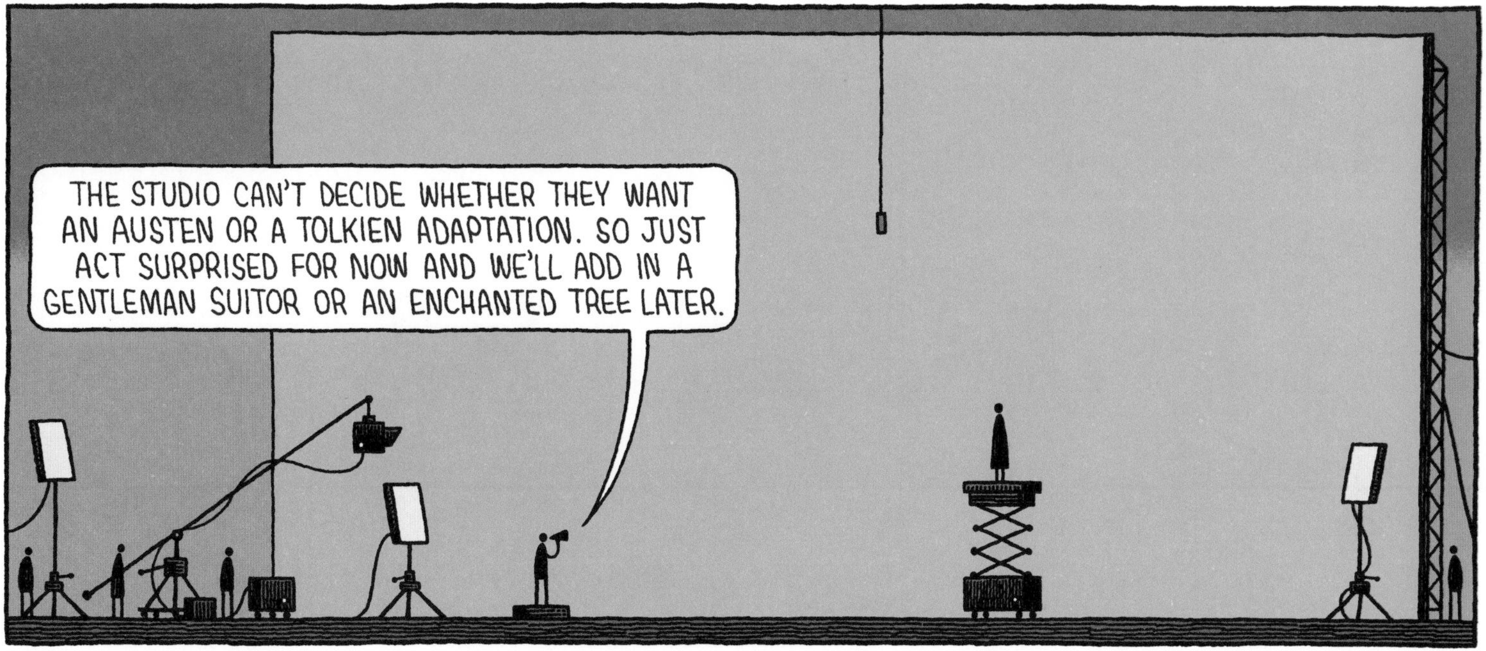
THE STUDIO CAN'T DECIDE WHETHER THEY WANT AN AUSTEN OR A TOLKIEN ADAPTATION. SO JUST ACT SURPRISED FOR NOW AND WE'LL ADD IN A GENTLEMAN SUITOR OR AN ENCHANTED TREE LATER.

HOW TO TELL IF YOUR CAT IS INTERESTED IN THE NOVEL YOU ARE WRITING

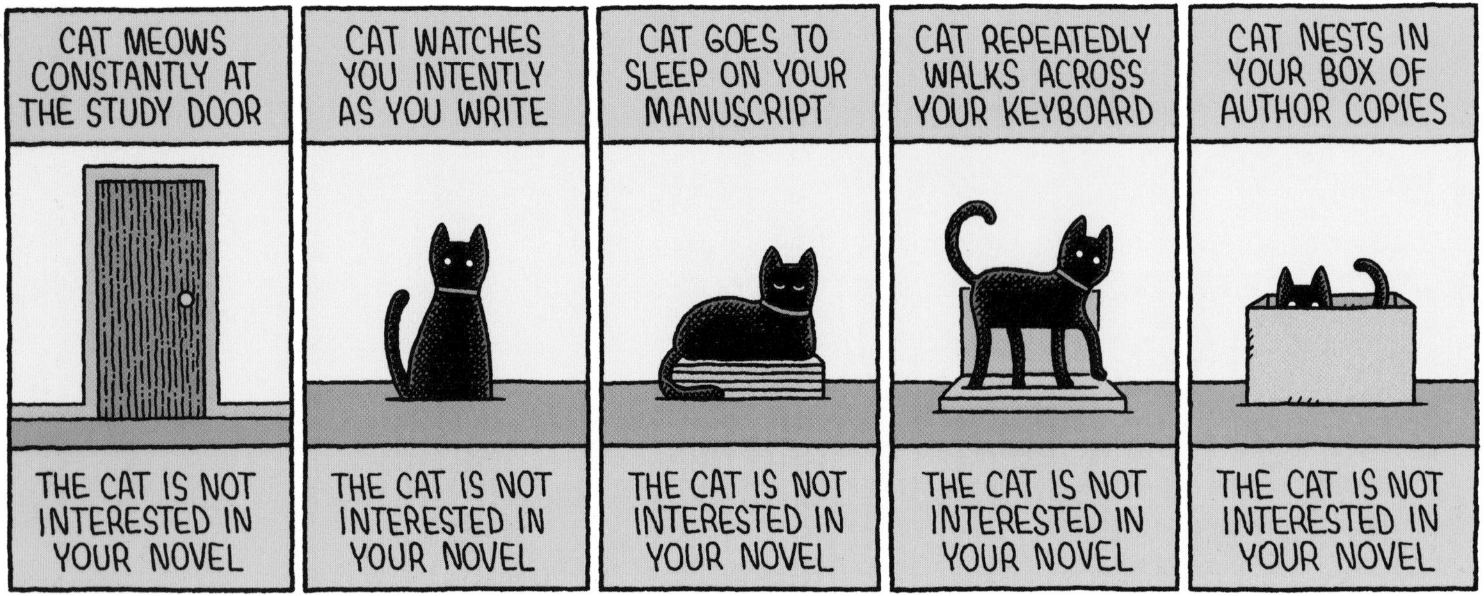
CAT MEOWS CONSTANTLY AT THE STUDY DOOR
THE CAT IS NOT INTERESTED IN YOUR NOVEL
CAT WATCHES YOU INTENTLY AS YOU WRITE
THE CAT IS NOT INTERESTED IN YOUR NOVEL
CAT GOES TO SLEEP ON YOUR MANUSCRIPT
THE CAT IS NOT INTERESTED IN YOUR NOVEL
CAT REPEATEDLY WALKS ACROSS YOUR KEYBOARD
THE CAT IS NOT INTERESTED IN YOUR NOVEL
CAT NESTS IN YOUR BOX OF AUTHOR COPIES
THE CAT IS NOT INTERESTED IN YOUR NOVEL

THE RECLUSIVE AUTHOR TELLS US ABOUT HIS WRITING DAY

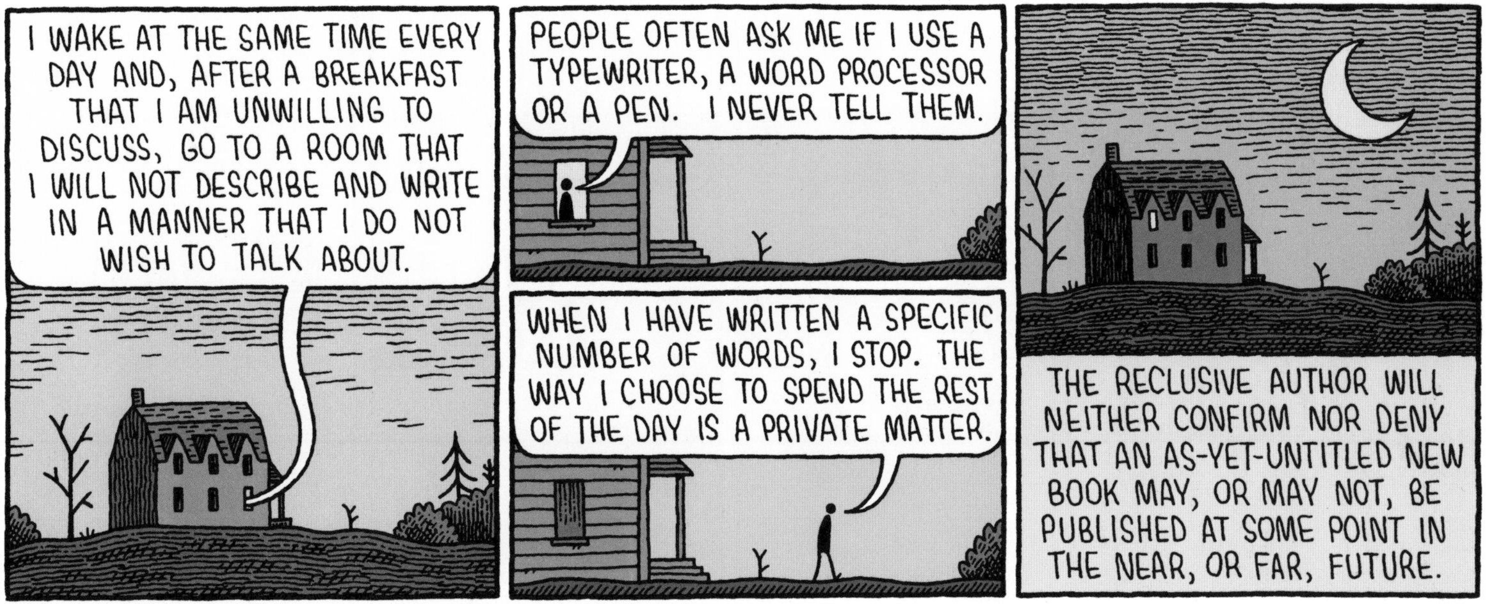
I WAKE AT THE SAME TIME EVERY DAY AND, AFTER A BREAKFAST THAT I AM UNWILLING TO DISCUSS, GO TO A ROOM THAT I WILL NOT DESCRIBE AND WRITE IN A MANNER THAT I DO NOT WISH TO TALK ABOUT.
PEOPLE OFTEN ASK ME IF I USE A TYPEWRITER, A WORD PROCESSOR OR A PEN. I NEVER TELL THEM.
WHEN I HAVE WRITTEN A SPECIFIC NUMBER OF WORDS, I STOP. THE WAY I CHOOSE TO SPEND THE REST OF THE DAY IS A PRIVATE MATTER.
THE RECLUSIVE AUTHOR WILL NEITHER CONFIRM NOR DENY THAT AN AS-YET-UNTITLED NEW BOOK MAY, OR MAY NOT, BE PUBLISHED AT SOME POINT IN THE NEAR, OR FAR, FUTURE.

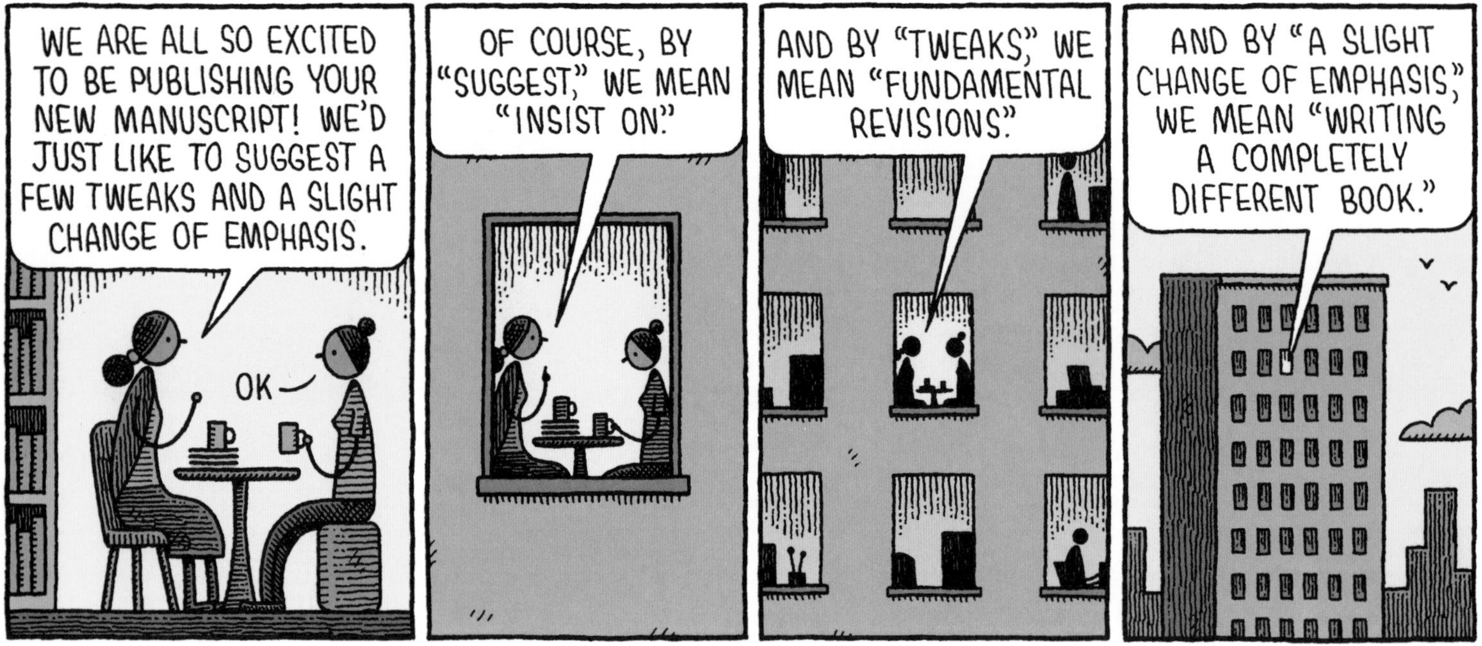
WE ARE ALL SO EXCITED TO BE PUBLISHING YOUR NEW MANUSCRIPT! WE'D JUST LIKE TO SUGGEST A FEW TWEAKS AND A SLIGHT CHANGE OF EMPHASIS.
OK
OF COURSE, BY "SUGGEST," WE MEAN "INSIST ON."
AND BY "TWEAKS," WE MEAN "FUNDAMENTAL REVISIONS."
AND BY "A SLIGHT CHANGE OF EMPHASIS," WE MEAN "WRITING A COMPLETELY DIFFERENT BOOK."

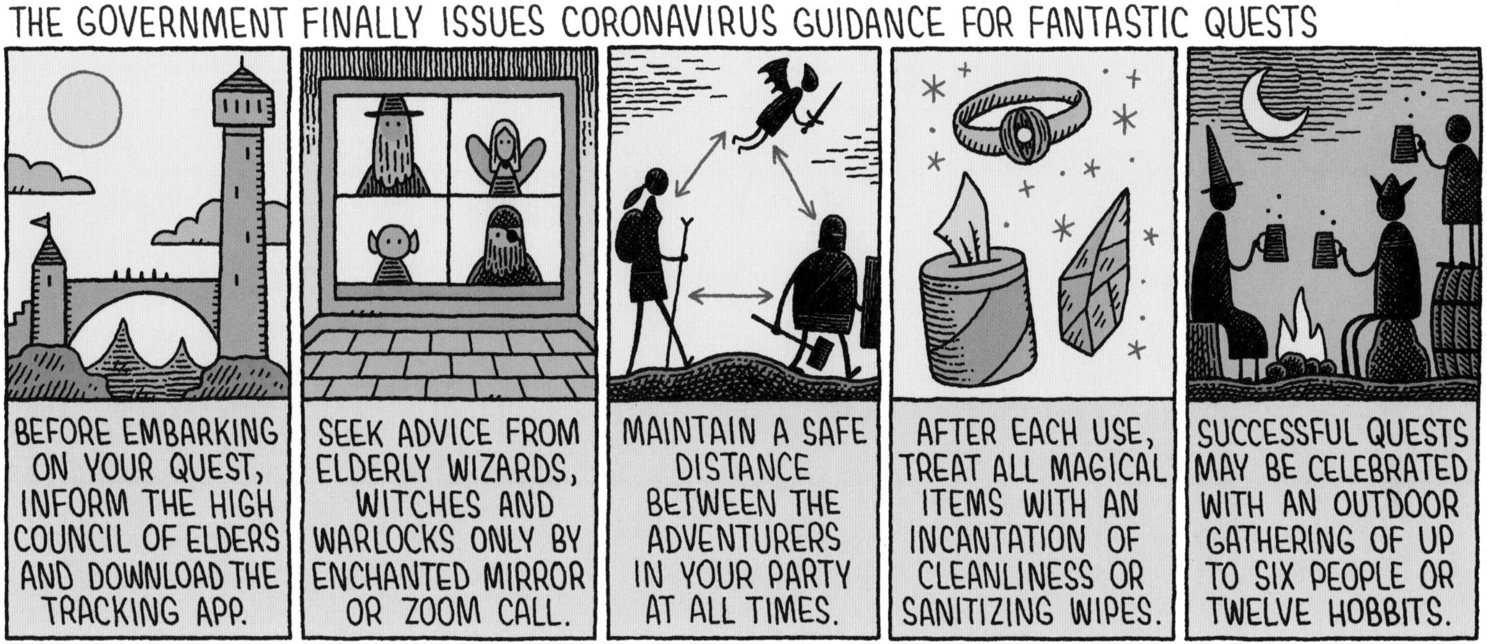
THE GOVERNMENT FINALLY ISSUES CORONAVIRUS GUIDANCE FOR FANTASTIC QUESTS
BEFORE EMBARKING ON YOUR QUEST, INFORM THE HIGH COUNCIL OF ELDERS AND DOWNLOAD THE TRACKING APP.
SEEK ADVICE FROM ELDERLY WIZARDS, WITCHES AND WARLOCKS ONLY BY ENCHANTED MIRROR OR ZOOM CALL.
MAINTAIN A SAFE DISTANCE BETWEEN THE ADVENTURERS IN YOUR PARTY AT ALL TIMES.
AFTER EACH USE, TREAT ALL MAGICAL ITEMS WITH AN INCANTATION OF CLEANLINESS OR SANITIZING WIPES.
SUCCESSFUL QUESTS MAY BE CELEBRATED WITH AN OUTDOOR GATHERING OF UP TO SIX PEOPLE OR TWELVE HOBBITS.

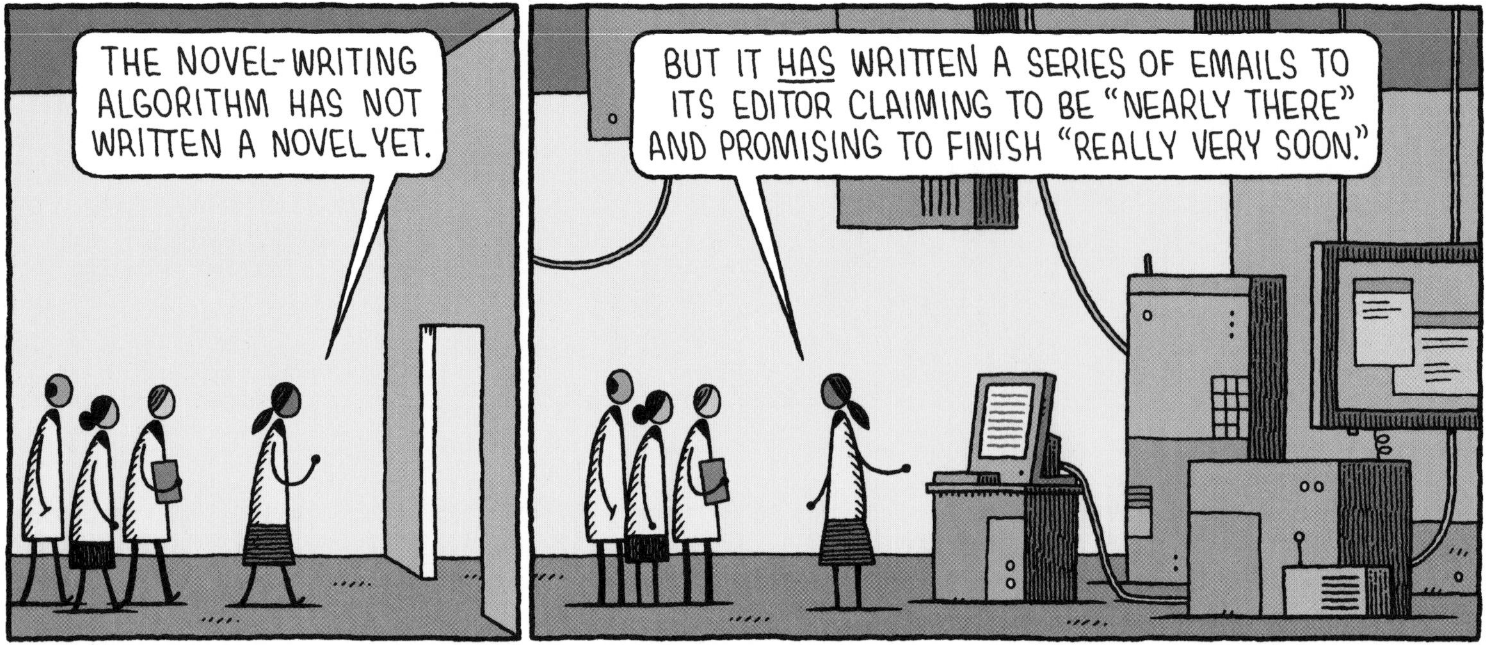
THE NOVEL-WRITING ALGORITHM HAS NOT WRITTEN A NOVEL YET.
BUT IT HAS WRITTEN A SERIES OF EMAILS TO ITS EDITOR CLAIMING TO BE "NEARLY THERE" AND PROMISING TO FINISH "REALLY VERY SOON."

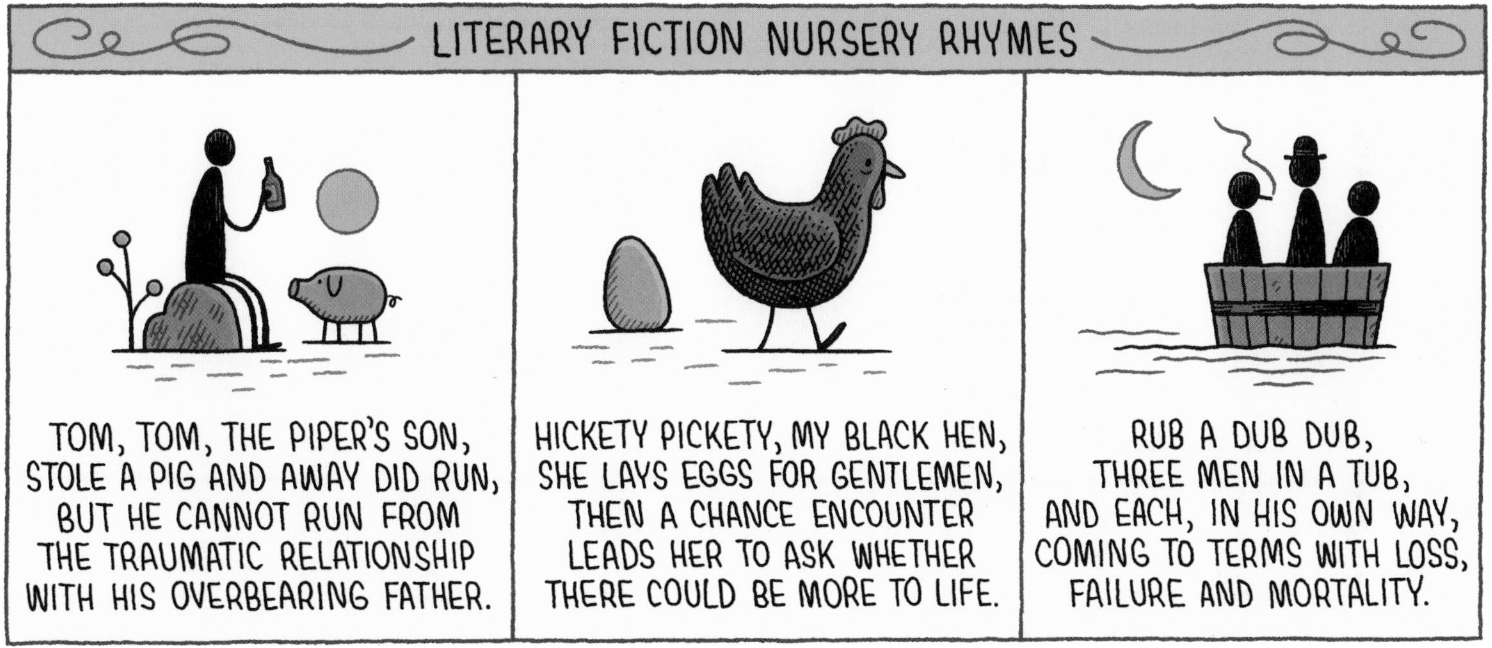
LITERARY FICTION NURSERY RHYMES
TOM, TOM, THE PIPER'S SON, STOLE A PIG AND AWAY DID RUN, BUT HE CANNOT RUN FROM THE TRAUMATIC RELATIONSHIP WITH HIS OVERBEARING FATHER.
HICKETY PICKETY, MY BLACK HEN, SHE LAYS EGGS FOR GENTLEMEN, THEN A CHANCE ENCOUNTER LEADS HER TO ASK WHETHER THERE COULD BE MORE TO LIFE.
RUB A DUB DUB, THREE MEN IN A TUB, AND EACH, IN HIS OWN WAY, COMING TO TERMS WITH LOSS, FAILURE AND MORTALITY.

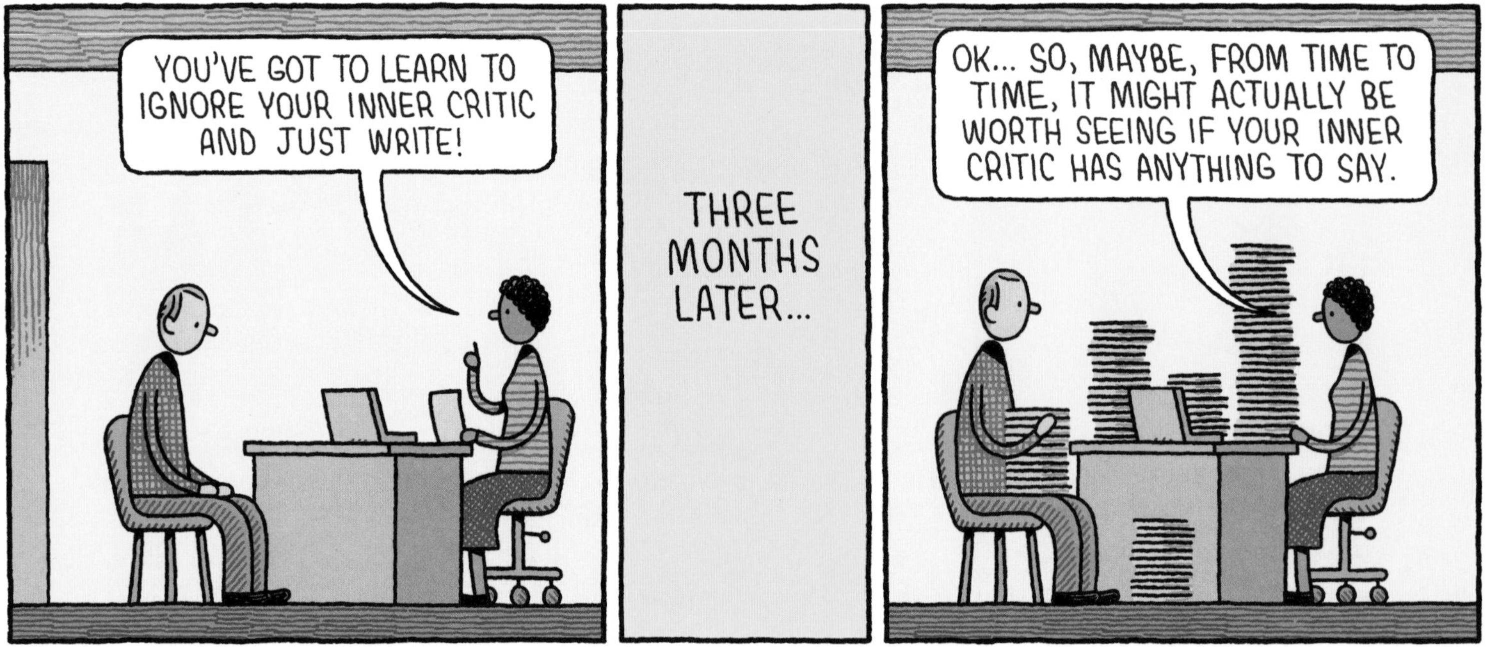
YOU'VE GOT TO LEARN TO IGNORE YOUR INNER CRITIC AND JUST WRITE!
THREE MONTHS LATER...
OK... SO, MAYBE, FROM TIME TO TIME, IT MIGHT ACTUALLY BE WORTH SEEING IF YOUR INNER CRITIC HAS ANYTHING TO SAY.

COMING SOON! PREQUELS TO CLASSIC NOVELS...

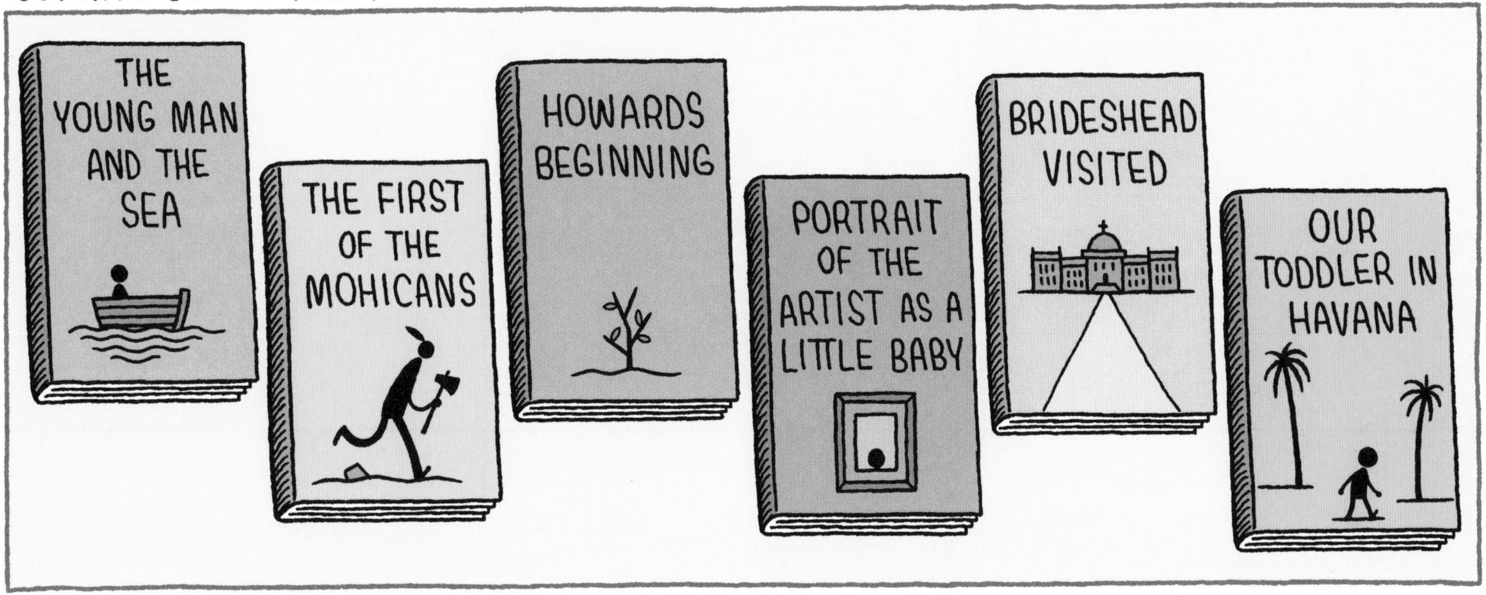
THE YOUNG MAN AND THE SEA
THE FIRST OF THE MOHICANS
HOWARDS BEGINNING
PORTRAIT OF THE ARTIST AS A LITTLE BABY
BRIDESHEAD VISITED
OUR TODDLER IN HAVANA

AN AUTUMN WALK INSPIRES THE NATURE POET AND THE DETECTIVE NOVELIST

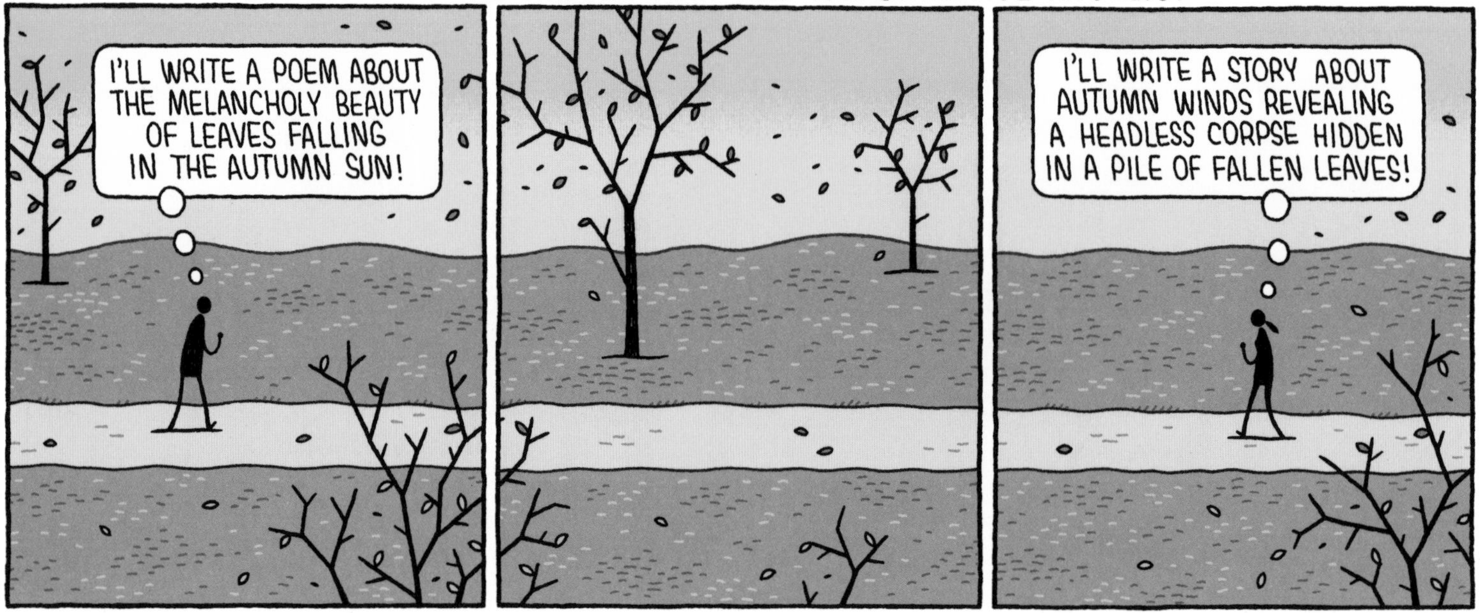
I'LL WRITE A POEM ABOUT THE MELANCHOLY BEAUTY OF LEAVES FALLING IN THE AUTUMN SUN!
I'LL WRITE A STORY ABOUT AUTUMN WINDS REVEALING A HEADLESS CORPSE HIDDEN IN A PILE OF FALLEN LEAVES!

THRILLER CONCEPT GENERATOR – Choose one option from each set

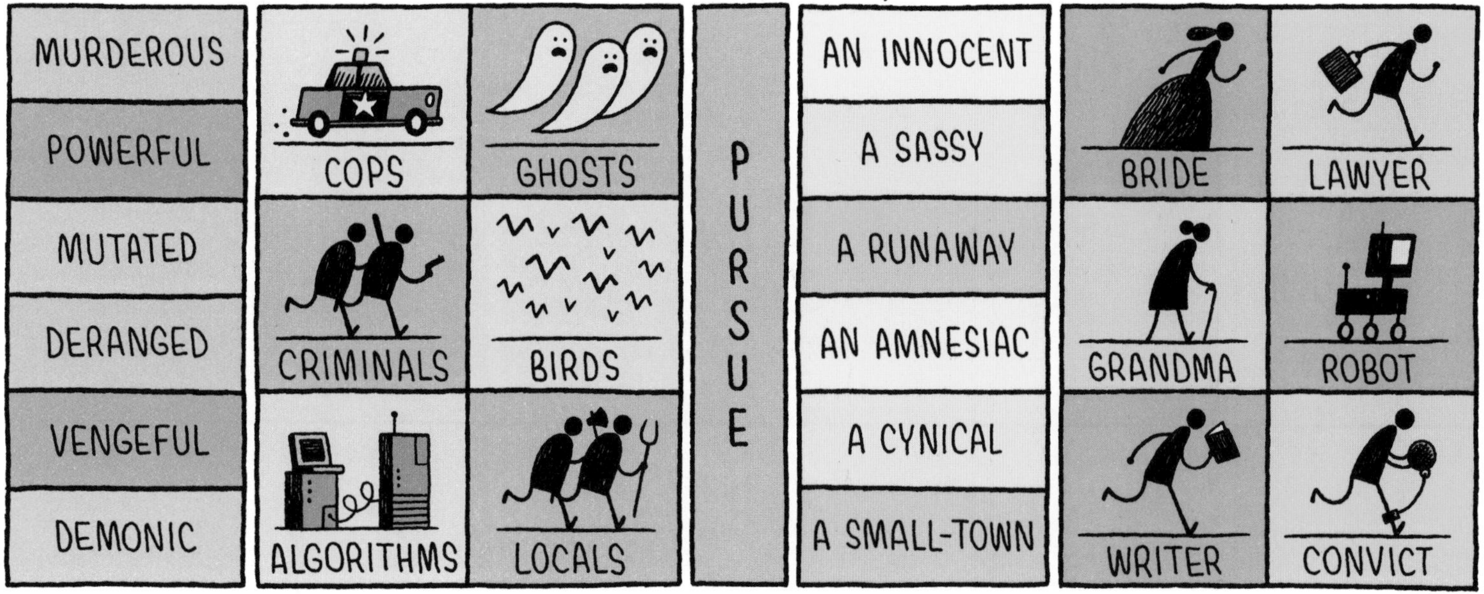
MURDEROUS
POWERFUL
MUTATED
DERANGED
VENGEFUL
DEMONIC
COPS
GHOSTS
CRIMINALS
BIRDS
ALGORITHMS
LOCALS
PURSUE
AN INNOCENT
A SASSY
A RUNAWAY
AN AMNESIAC
A CYNICAL
A SMALL-TOWN
BRIDE
LAWYER
GRANDMA
ROBOT
WRITER
CONVICT

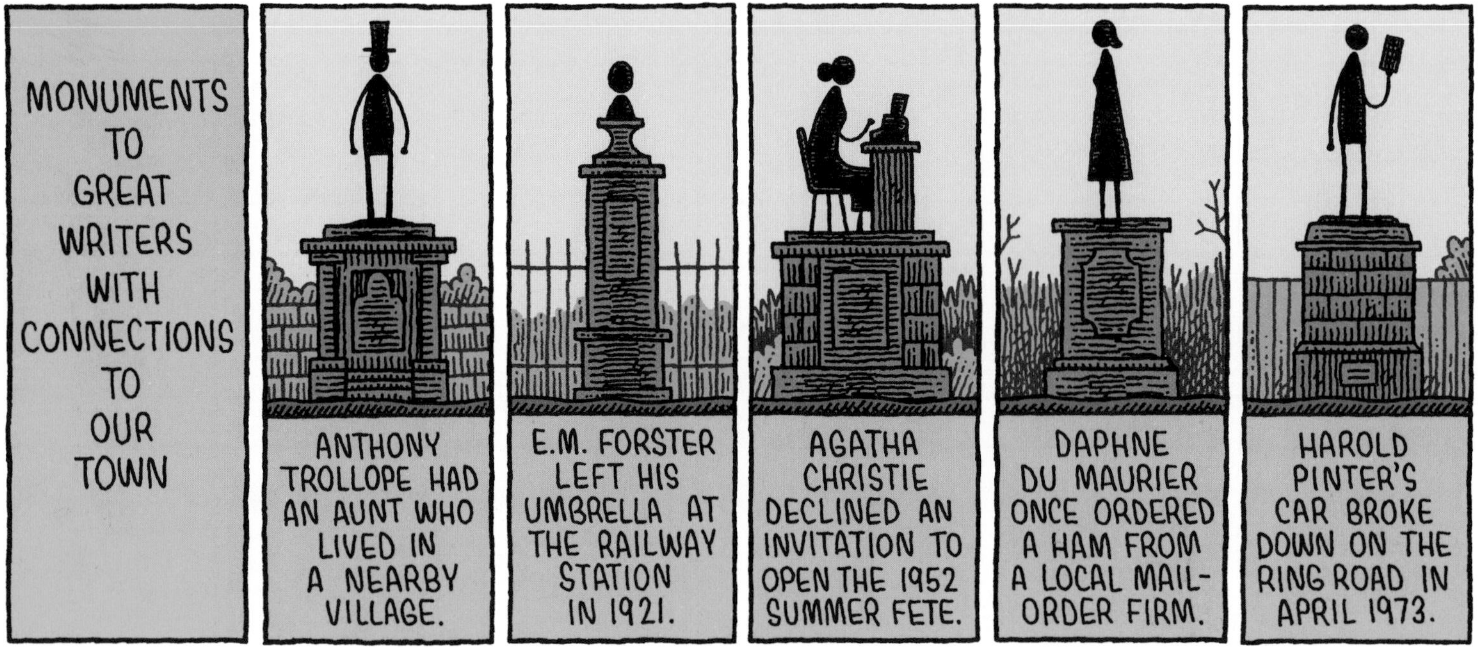
MONUMENTS TO GREAT WRITERS WITH CONNECTIONS TO OUR TOWN
ANTHONY TROLLOPE HAD AN AUNT WHO LIVED IN A NEARBY VILLAGE.
E.M. FORSTER LEFT HIS UMBRELLA AT THE RAILWAY STATION IN 1921.
AGATHA CHRISTIE DECLINED AN INVITATION TO OPEN THE 1952 SUMMER FETE.
DAPHNE DU MAURIER ONCE ORDERED A HAM FROM A LOCAL MAIL-ORDER FIRM.
HAROLD PINTER'S CAR BROKE DOWN ON THE RING ROAD IN APRIL 1973.

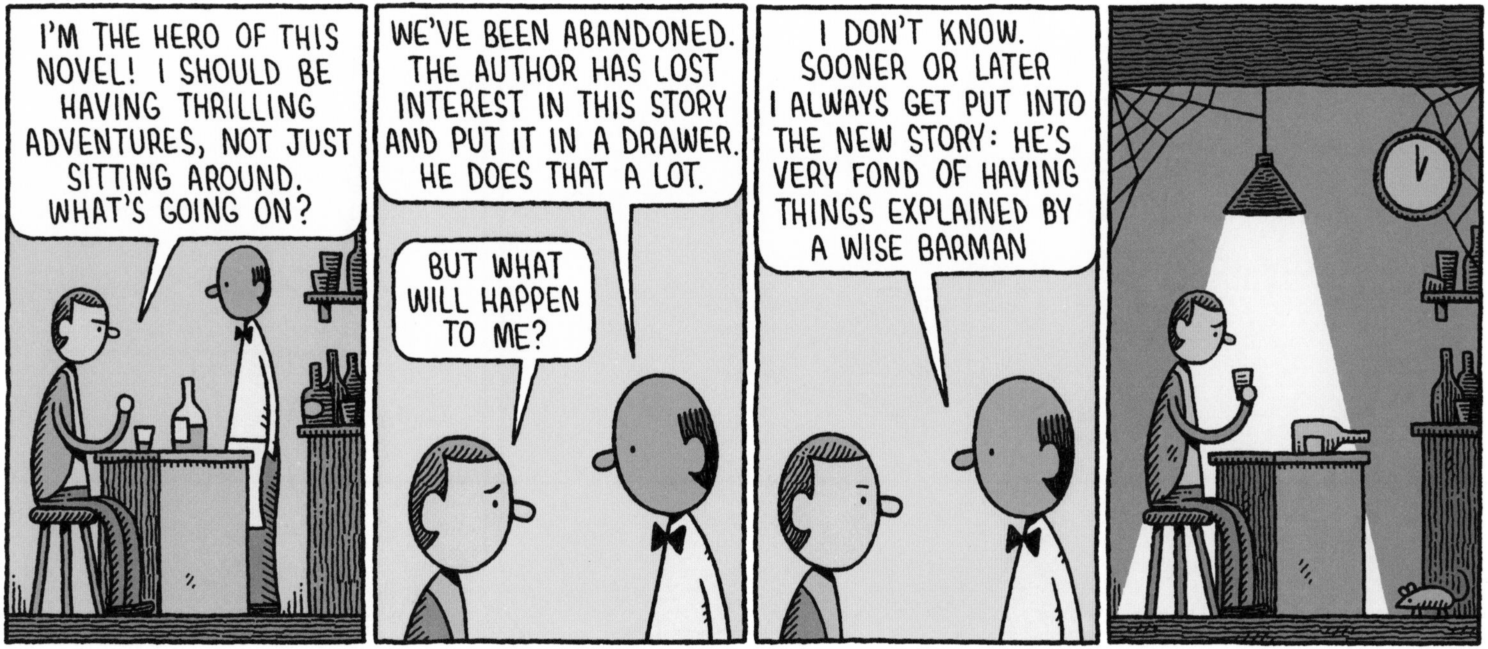

I'M THE HERO OF THIS NOVEL! I SHOULD BE HAVING THRILLING ADVENTURES, NOT JUST SITTING AROUND. WHAT'S GOING ON?
WE'VE BEEN ABANDONED. THE AUTHOR HAS LOST INTEREST IN THIS STORY AND PUT IT IN A DRAWER. HE DOES THAT A LOT.
BUT WHAT WILL HAPPEN TO ME?
I DON'T KNOW. SOONER OR LATER I ALWAYS GET PUT INTO THE NEW STORY: HE'S VERY FOND OF HAVING THINGS EXPLAINED BY A WISE BARMAN

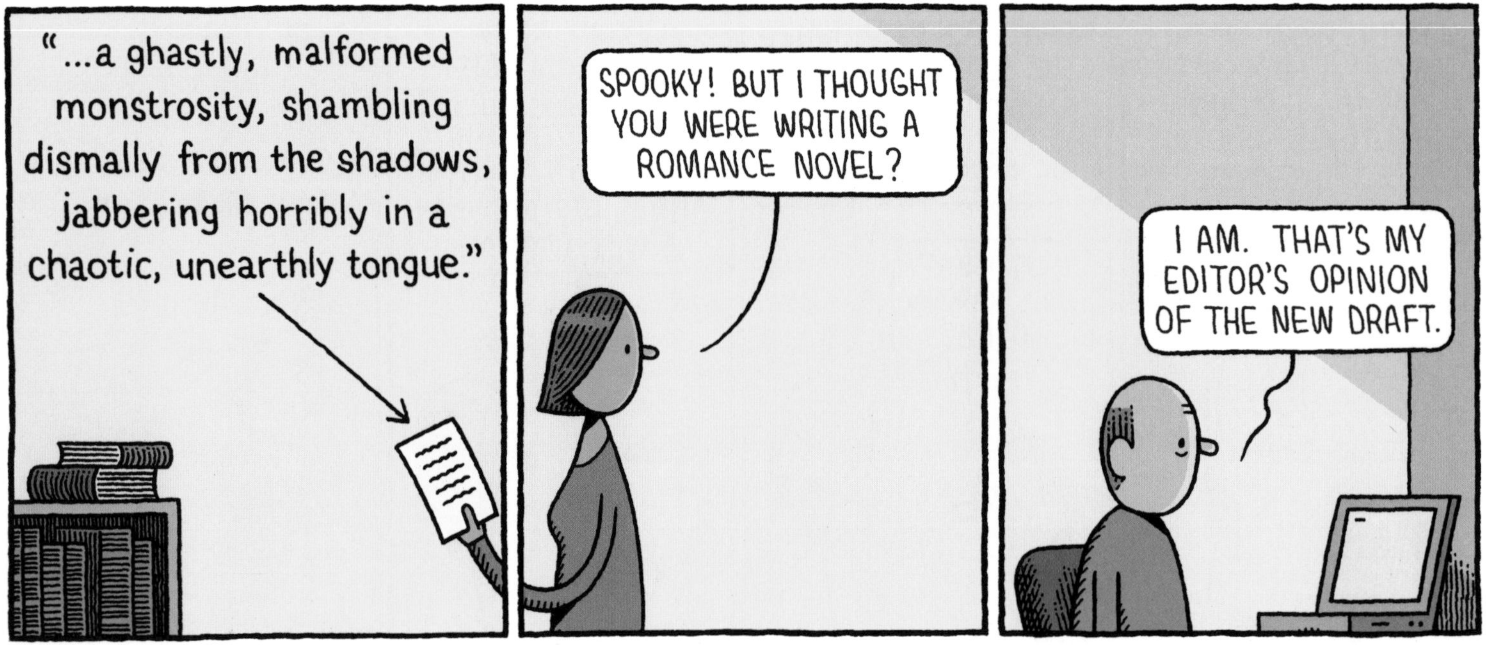
"...a ghastly, malformed monstrosity, shambling dismally from the shadows, jabbering horribly in a chaotic, unearthly tongue."
SPOOKY! BUT I THOUGHT YOU WERE WRITING A ROMANCE NOVEL?
I AM. THAT'S MY EDITOR'S OPINION OF THE NEW DRAFT.

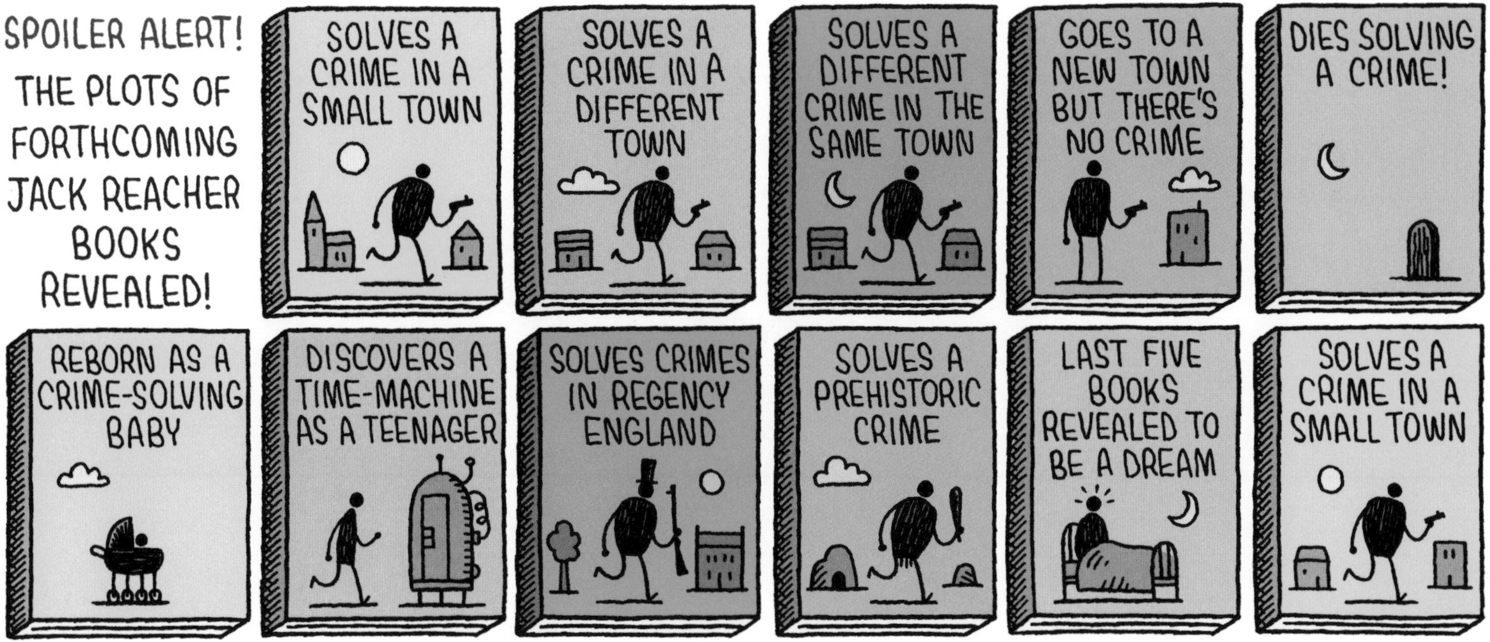
SPOILER ALERT! THE PLOTS OF FORTHCOMING JACK REACHER BOOKS REVEALED!
SOLVES A CRIME IN A SMALL TOWN
SOLVES A CRIME IN A DIFFERENT TOWN
SOLVES A DIFFERENT CRIME IN THE SAME TOWN
GOES TO A NEW TOWN BUT THERE'S NO CRIME
DIES SOLVING A CRIME!
REBORN AS A CRIME-SOLVING BABY
DISCOVERS A TIME-MACHINE AS A TEENAGER
SOLVES CRIMES IN REGENCY ENGLAND
SOLVES A PREHISTORIC CRIME
LAST FIVE BOOKS REVEALED TO BE A DREAM
SOLVES A CRIME IN A SMALL TOWN

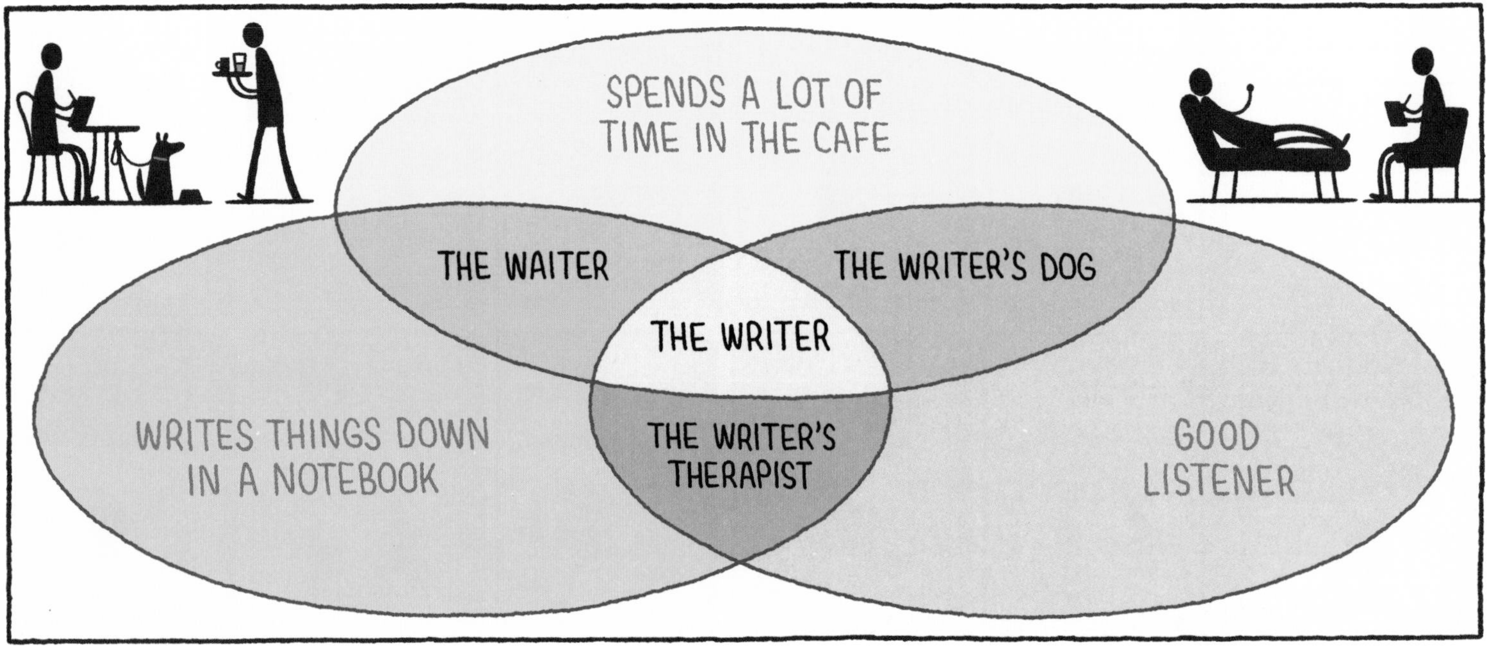
SPENDS A LOT OF
TIME IN THE CAFE
THE WAITER
THE WRITER'S DOG
THE WRITER
WRITES THINGS DOWN
IN A NOTEBOOK
THE WRITER'S
THERAPIST
GOOD
LISTENER

KARL MARX, 1851

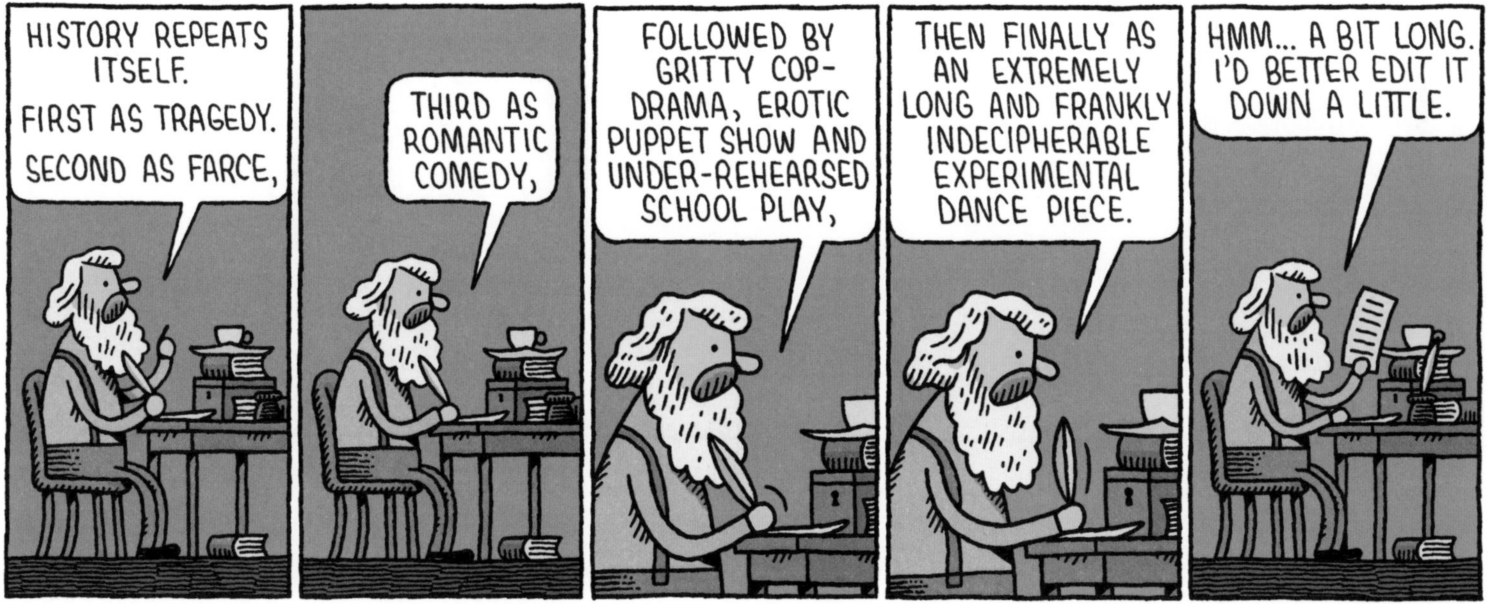
HISTORY REPEATS ITSELF. FIRST AS TRAGEDY. SECOND AS FARCE,
THIRD AS ROMANTIC COMEDY,
FOLLOWED BY GRITTY COP-DRAMA, EROTIC PUPPET SHOW AND UNDER-REHEARSED SCHOOL PLAY,
THEN FINALLY AS AN EXTREMELY LONG AND FRANKLY INDECIPHERABLE EXPERIMENTAL DANCE PIECE.
HMM... A BIT LONG. I'D BETTER EDIT IT DOWN A LITTLE.

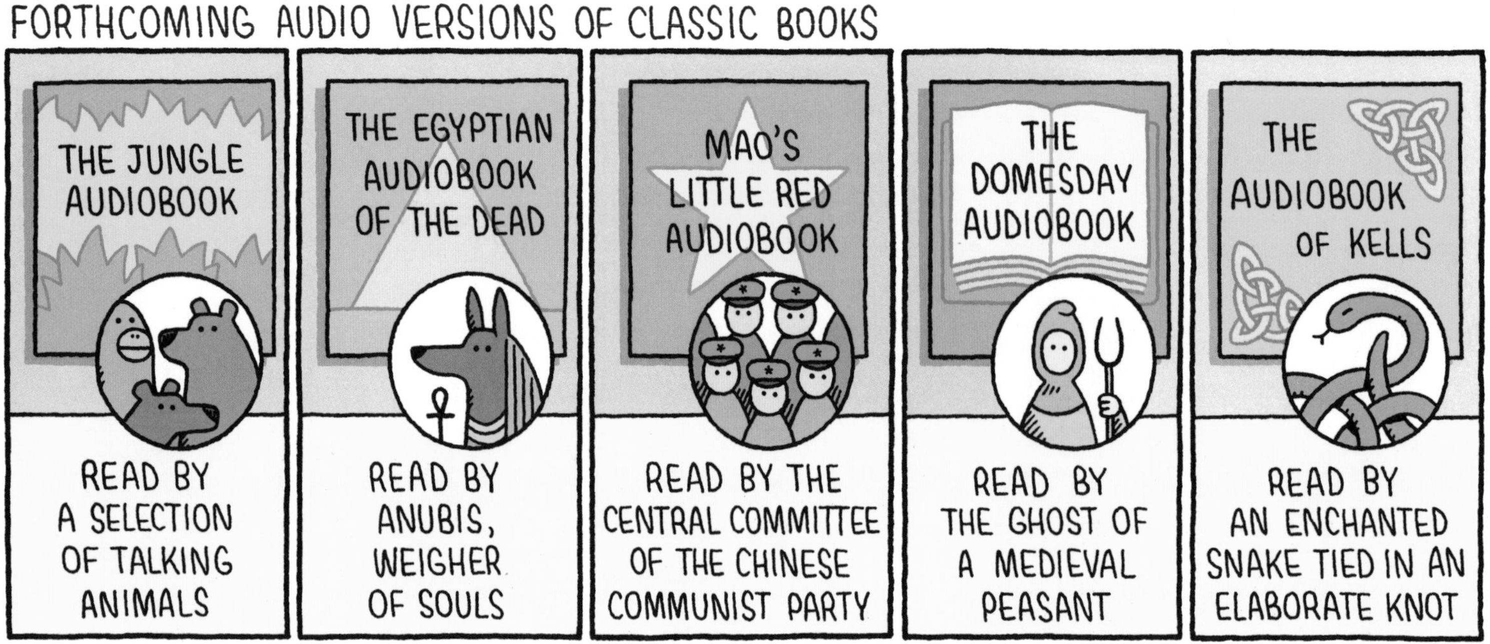
FORTHCOMING AUDIO VERSIONS OF CLASSIC BOOKS
THE JUNGLE AUDIOBOOK
READ BY A SELECTION OF TALKING ANIMALS
THE EGYPTIAN AUDIOBOOK OF THE DEAD
READ BY ANUBIS, WEIGHER OF SOULS
MAO'S LITTLE RED AUDIOBOOK
READ BY THE CENTRAL COMMITTEE OF THE CHINESE COMMUNIST PARTY
THE DOMESDAY AUDIOBOOK
READ BY THE GHOST OF A MEDIEVAL PEASANT
THE AUDIOBOOK OF KELLS
READ BY AN ENCHANTED SNAKE TIED IN AN ELABORATE KNOT

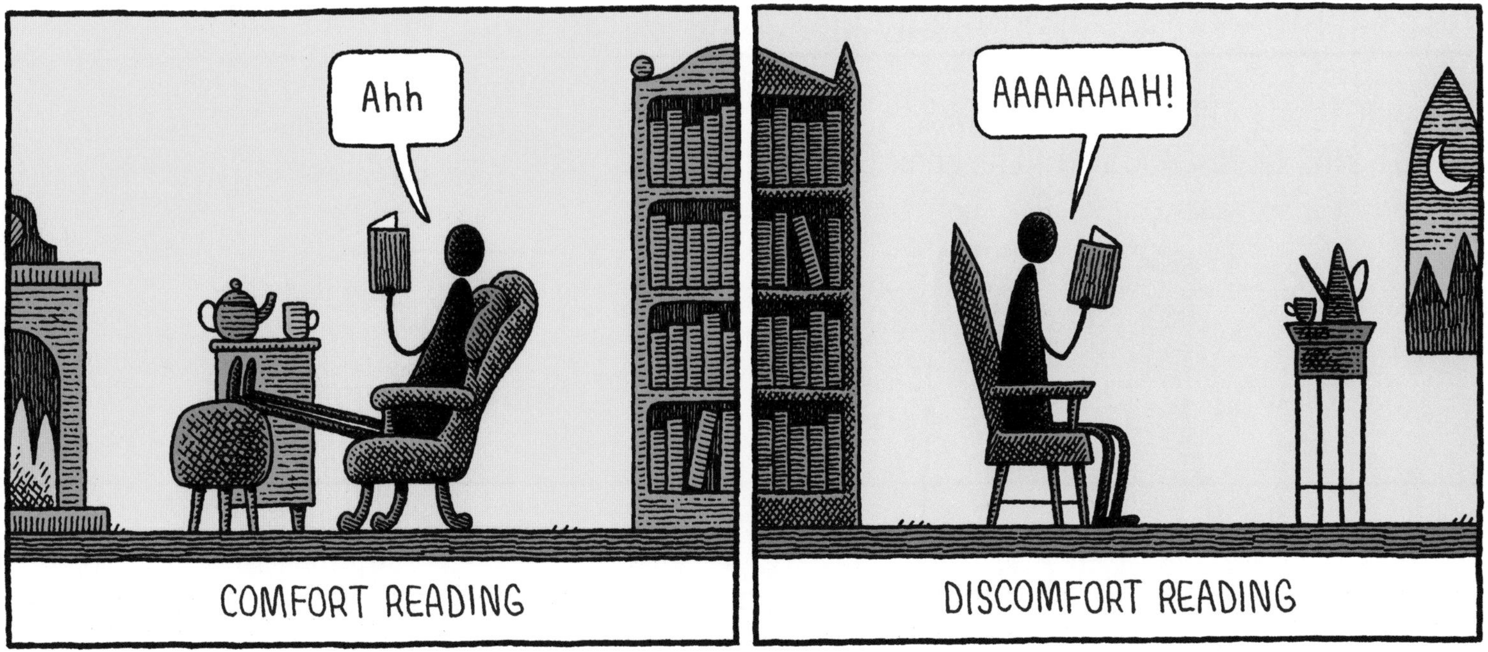
Ahh
COMFORT READING
AAAAAAAH!
DISCOMFORT READING

OUT THIS WEEK: TWO GROUNDBREAKING NEW BIOGRAPHIES OF GREAT WRITERS.

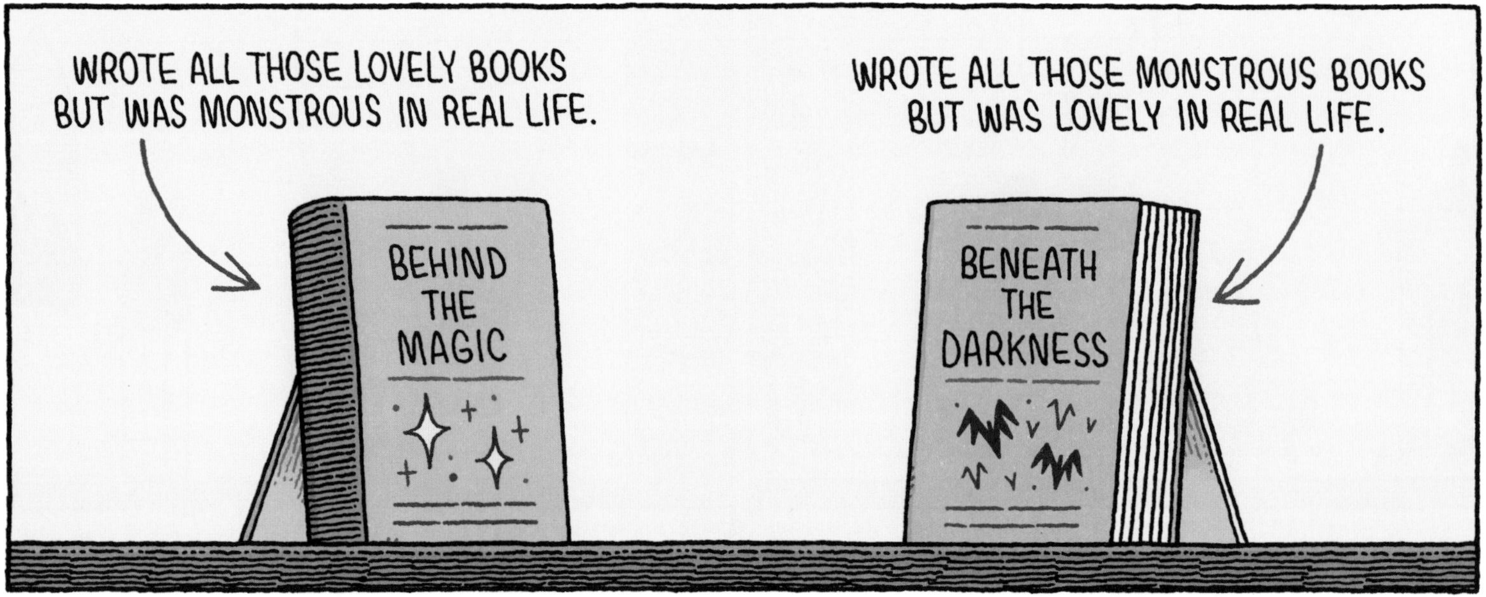
WROTE ALL THOSE LOVELY BOOKS BUT WAS MONSTROUS IN REAL LIFE.
BEHIND THE MAGIC
WROTE ALL THOSE MONSTROUS BOOKS BUT WAS LOVELY IN REAL LIFE.
BENEATH THE DARKNESS

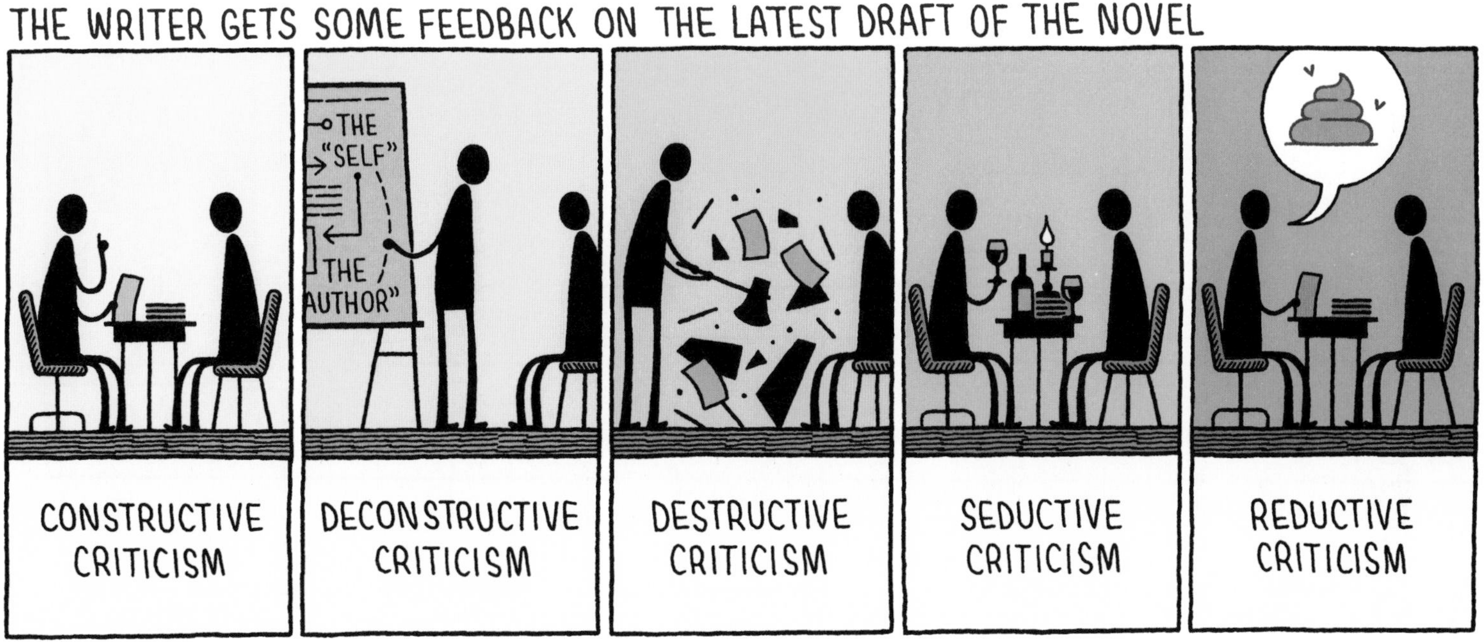
THE WRITER GETS SOME FEEDBACK ON THE LATEST DRAFT OF THE NOVEL
THE "SELF"
THE "AUTHOR"
CONSTRUCTIVE CRITICISM
DECONSTRUCTIVE CRITICISM
DESTRUCTIVE CRITICISM
SEDUCTIVE CRITICISM
REDUCTIVE CRITICISM

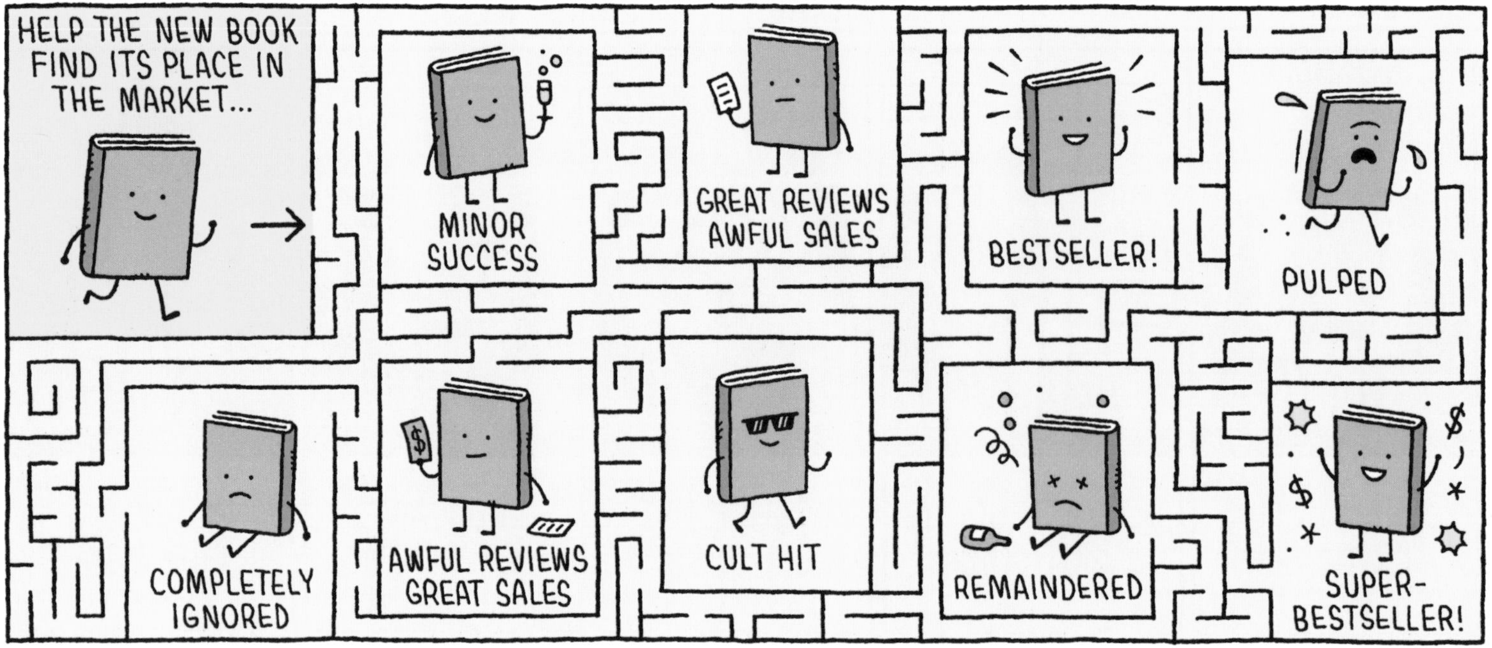

HELP THE NEW BOOK FIND ITS PLACE IN THE MARKET...
MINOR SUCCESS
GREAT REVIEWS AWFUL SALES
BESTSELLER!
PULPED
COMPLETELY IGNORED
AWFUL REVIEWS GREAT SALES
CULT HIT
REMAINDERED
SUPER-BESTSELLER!

COMMON MISTAKES MADE BY THE INEXPERIENCED ROMANCE NOVELIST

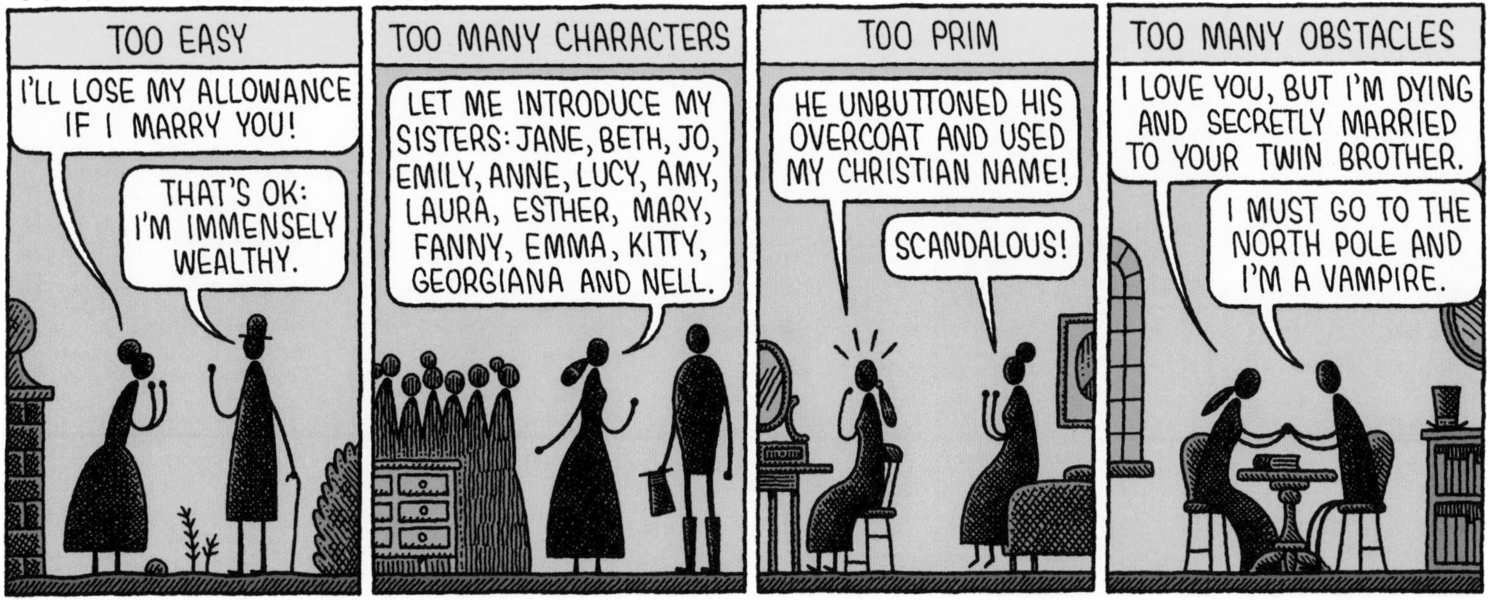

TOO EASY
I'LL LOSE MY ALLOWANCE IF I MARRY YOU!
THAT'S OK: I'M IMMENSELY WEALTHY.
TOO MANY CHARACTERS
LET ME INTRODUCE MY SISTERS: JANE, BETH, JO, EMILY, ANNE, LUCY, AMY, LAURA, ESTHER, MARY, FANNY, EMMA, KITTY, GEORGIANA AND NELL.
TOO PRIM
HE UNBUTTONED HIS OVERCOAT AND USED MY CHRISTIAN NAME!
SCANDALOUS!
TOO MANY OBSTACLES
I LOVE YOU, BUT I'M DYING AND SECRETLY MARRIED TO YOUR TWIN BROTHER.
I MUST GO TO THE NORTH POLE AND I'M A VAMPIRE.

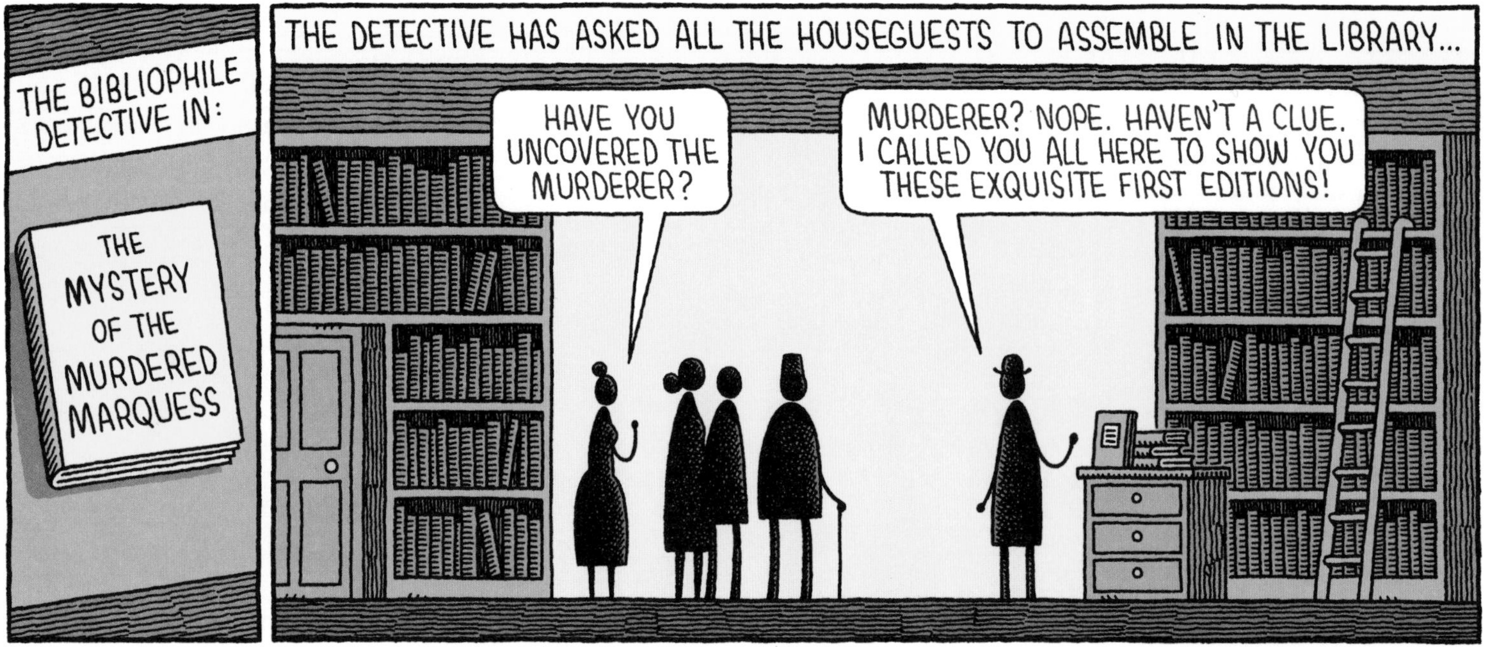

THE BIBLIOPHILE DETECTIVE IN:
THE MYSTERY OF THE MURDERED MARQUESS
THE DETECTIVE HAS ASKED ALL THE HOUSEGUESTS TO ASSEMBLE IN THE LIBRARY...
HAVE YOU UNCOVERED THE MURDERER?
MURDERER? NOPE. HAVEN'T A CLUE. I CALLED YOU ALL HERE TO SHOW YOU THESE EXQUISITE FIRST EDITIONS!

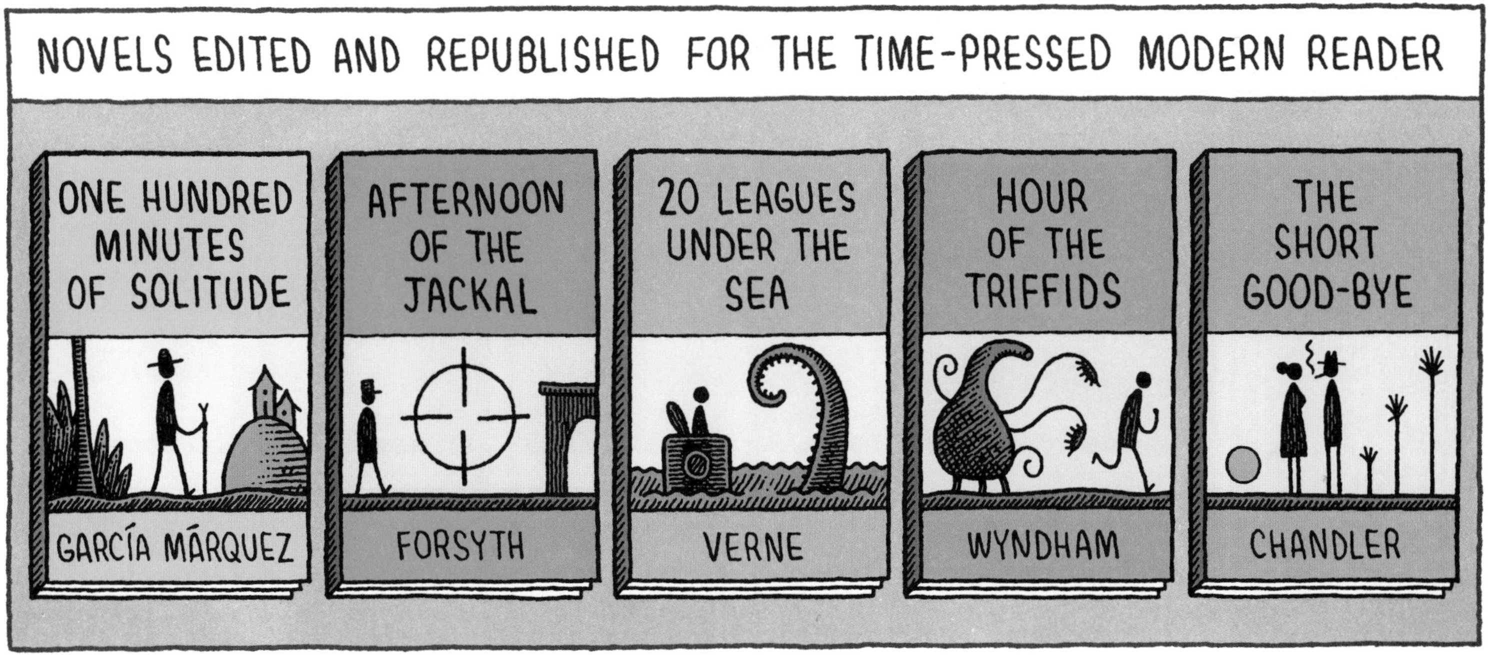
NOVELS EDITED AND REPUBLISHED FOR THE TIME-PRESSED MODERN READER
ONE HUNDRED MINUTES OF SOLITUDE
GARCÍA MÁRQUEZ
AFTERNOON OF THE JACKAL
FORSYTH
20 LEAGUES UNDER THE SEA
VERNE
HOUR OF THE TRIFFIDS
WYNDHAM
THE SHORT GOOD-BYE
CHANDLER

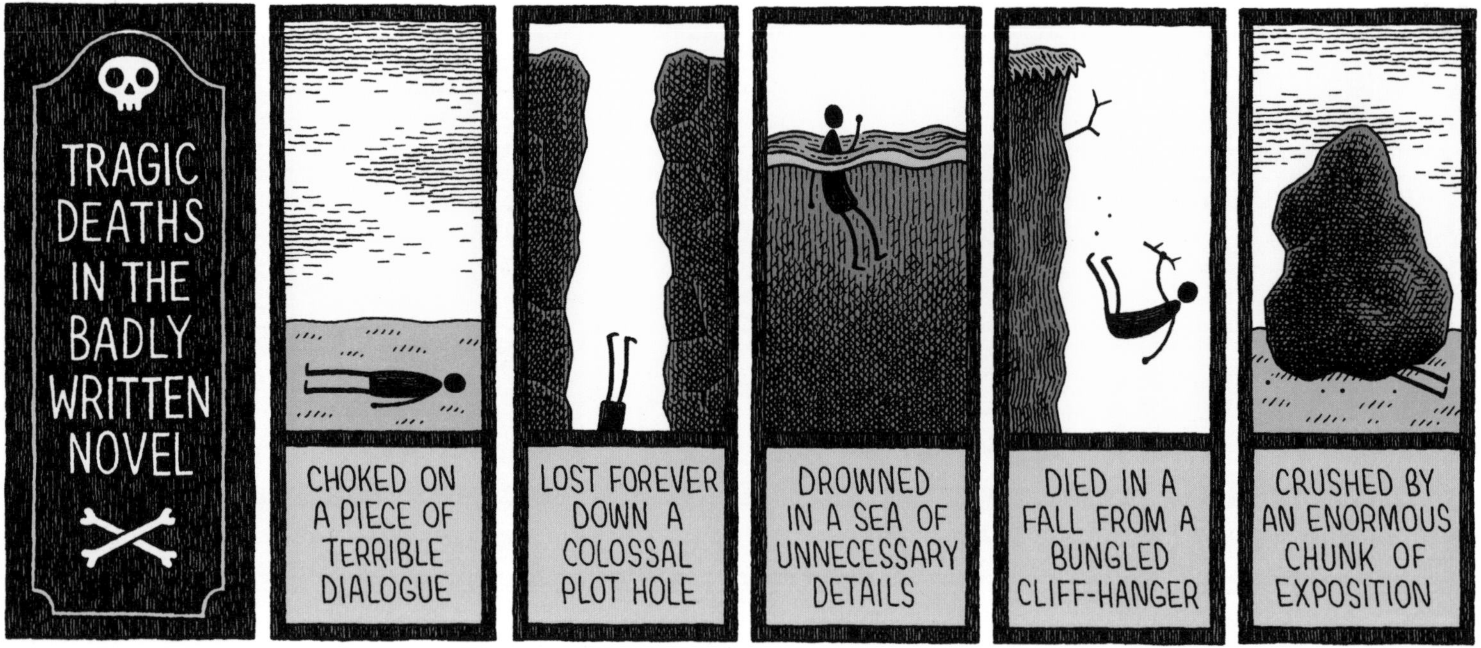
TRAGIC DEATHS IN THE BADLY WRITTEN NOVEL
CHOKED ON A PIECE OF TERRIBLE DIALOGUE
LOST FOREVER DOWN A COLOSSAL PLOT HOLE
DROWNED IN A SEA OF UNNECESSARY DETAILS
DIED IN A FALL FROM A BUNGLED CLIFF-HANGER
CRUSHED BY AN ENORMOUS CHUNK OF EXPOSITION

JO MARCH GETS SOME ADVICE FROM HER PUBLISHER

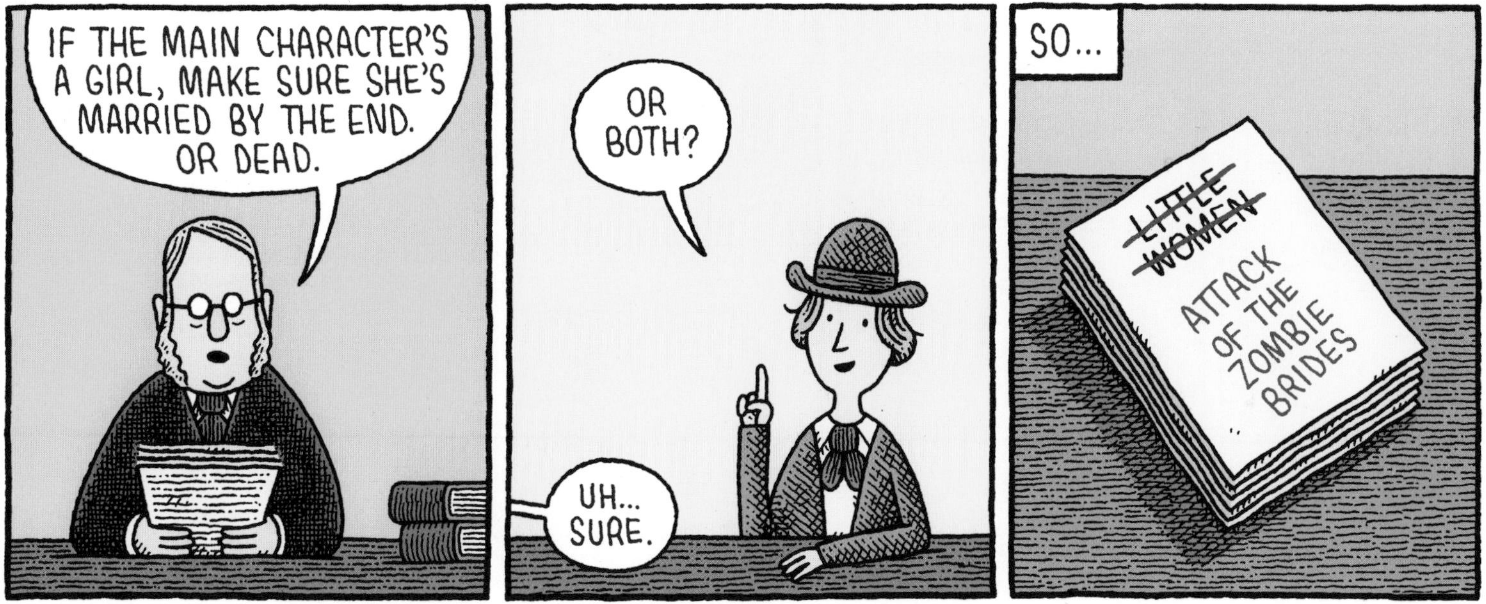
IF THE MAIN CHARACTER'S A GIRL, MAKE SURE SHE'S MARRIED BY THE END. OR DEAD.
OR BOTH?
UH... SURE.
SO...
LITTLE WOMEN
ATTACK OF THE ZOMBIE BRIDES

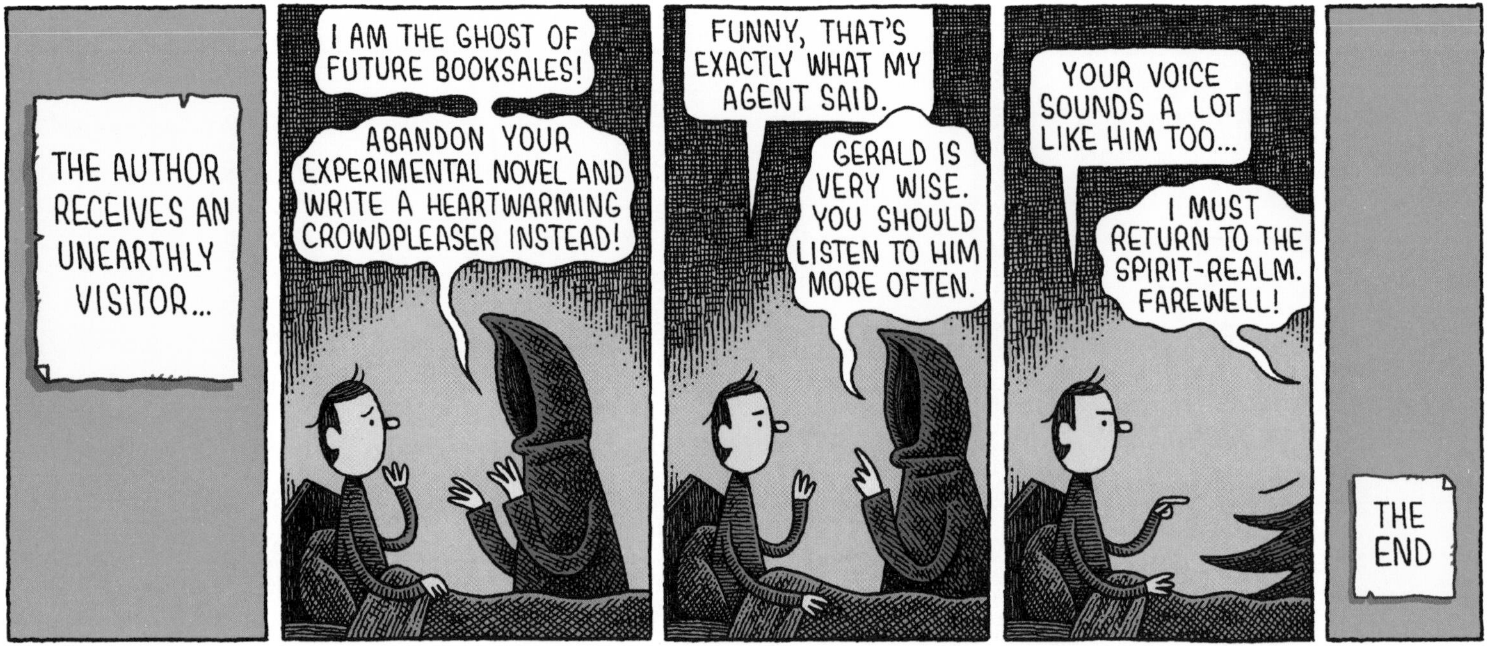
THE AUTHOR RECEIVES AN UNEARTHLY VISITOR...
I AM THE GHOST OF FUTURE BOOKSALES!
ABANDON YOUR EXPERIMENTAL NOVEL AND WRITE A HEARTWARMING CROWDPLEASER INSTEAD!
FUNNY, THAT'S EXACTLY WHAT MY AGENT SAID.
GERALD IS VERY WISE. YOU SHOULD LISTEN TO HIM MORE OFTEN.
YOUR VOICE SOUNDS A LOT LIKE HIM TOO...
I MUST RETURN TO THE SPIRIT-REALM. FAREWELL!
THE END

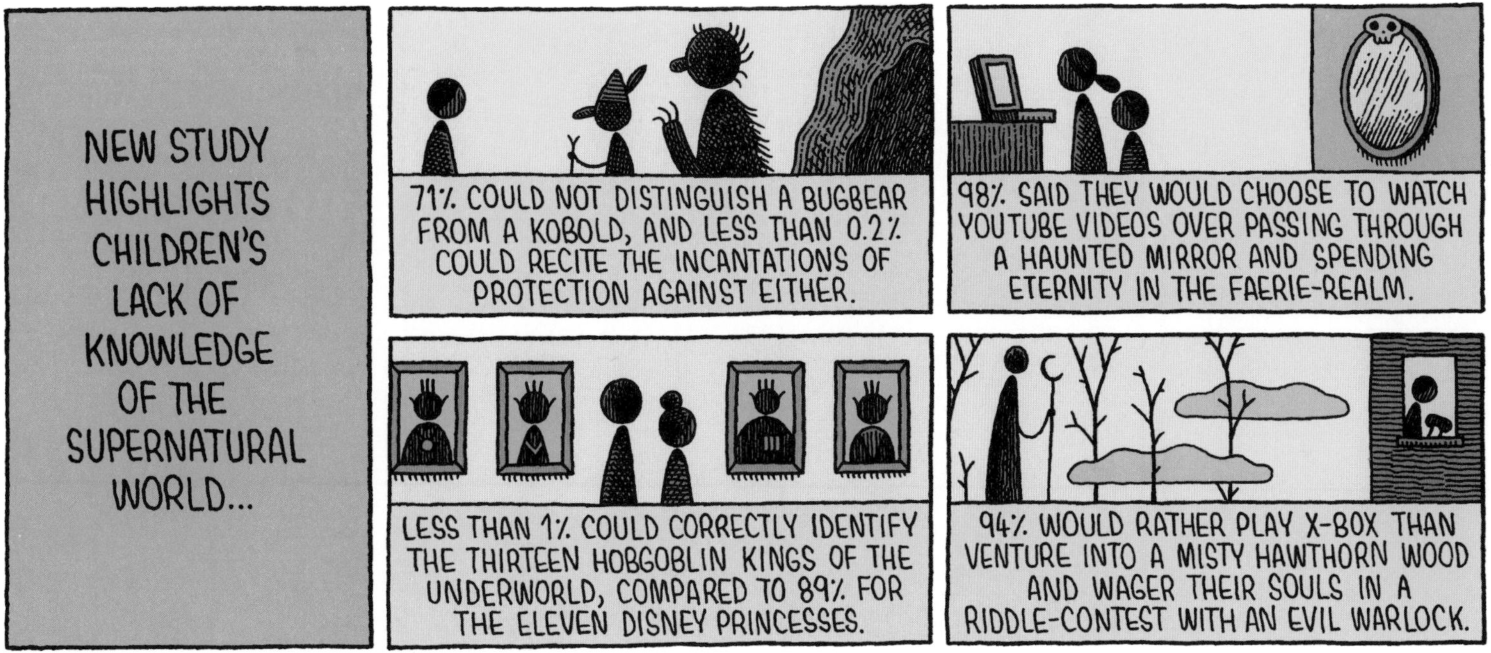
NEW STUDY HIGHLIGHTS CHILDREN'S LACK OF KNOWLEDGE OF THE SUPERNATURAL WORLD...
71% COULD NOT DISTINGUISH A BUGBEAR FROM A KOBOLD, AND LESS THAN 0.2% COULD RECITE THE INCANTATIONS OF PROTECTION AGAINST EITHER.
98% SAID THEY WOULD CHOOSE TO WATCH YOUTUBE VIDEOS OVER PASSING THROUGH A HAUNTED MIRROR AND SPENDING ETERNITY IN THE FAERIE-REALM.
LESS THAN 1% COULD CORRECTLY IDENTIFY THE THIRTEEN HOBGOBLIN KINGS OF THE UNDERWORLD, COMPARED TO 89% FOR THE ELEVEN DISNEY PRINCESSES.
94% WOULD RATHER PLAY X-BOX THAN VENTURE INTO A MISTY HAWTHORN WOOD AND WAGER THEIR SOULS IN A RIDDLE-CONTEST WITH AN EVIL WARLOCK.

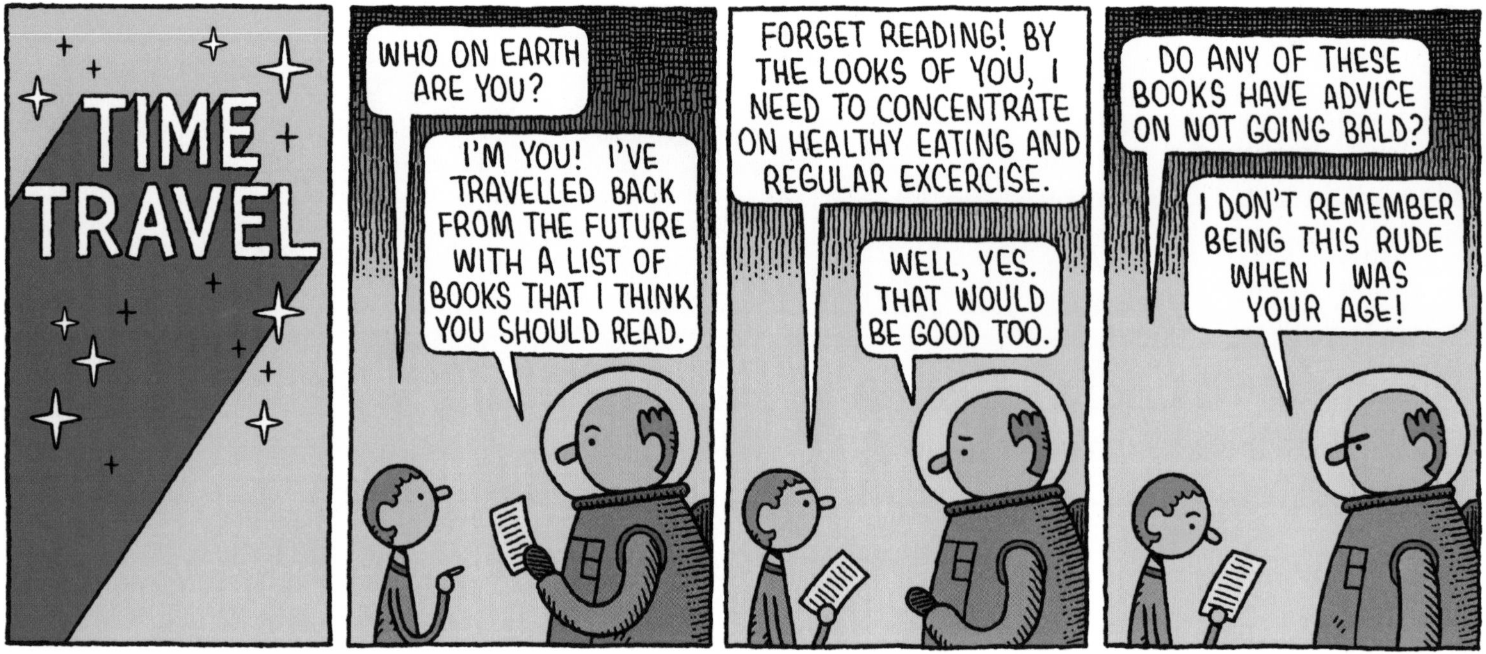
TIME TRAVEL
WHO ON EARTH ARE YOU?
I'M YOU! I'VE TRAVELLED BACK FROM THE FUTURE WITH A LIST OF BOOKS THAT I THINK YOU SHOULD READ.
FORGET READING! BY THE LOOKS OF YOU, I NEED TO CONCENTRATE ON HEALTHY EATING AND REGULAR EXCERCISE.
WELL, YES. THAT WOULD BE GOOD TOO.
DO ANY OF THESE BOOKS HAVE ADVICE ON NOT GOING BALD?
I DON'T REMEMBER BEING THIS RUDE WHEN I WAS YOUR AGE!

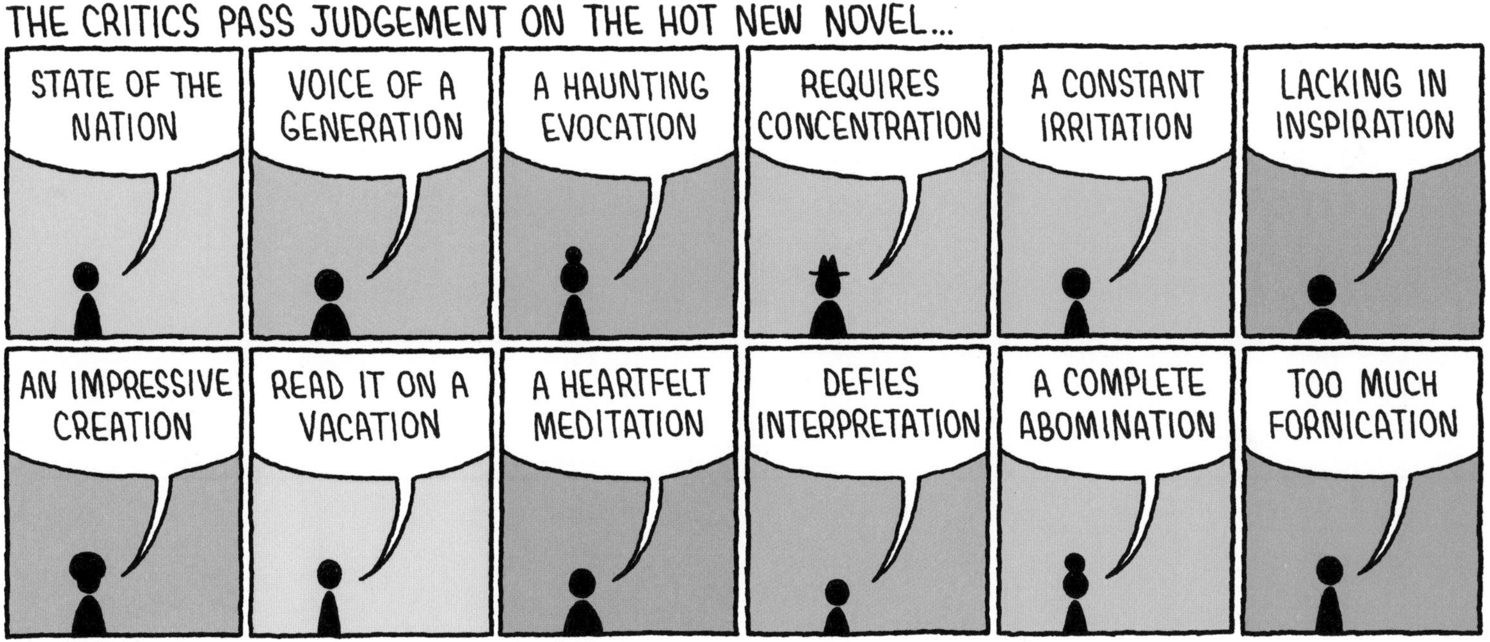
THE CRITICS PASS JUDGEMENT ON THE HOT NEW NOVEL...
STATE OF THE NATION
VOICE OF A GENERATION
A HAUNTING EVOCATION
REQUIRES CONCENTRATION
A CONSTANT IRRITATION
LACKING IN INSPIRATION
AN IMPRESSIVE CREATION
READ IT ON A VACATION
A HEARTFELT MEDITATION
DEFIES INTERPRETATION
A COMPLETE ABOMINATION
TOO MUCH FORNICATION

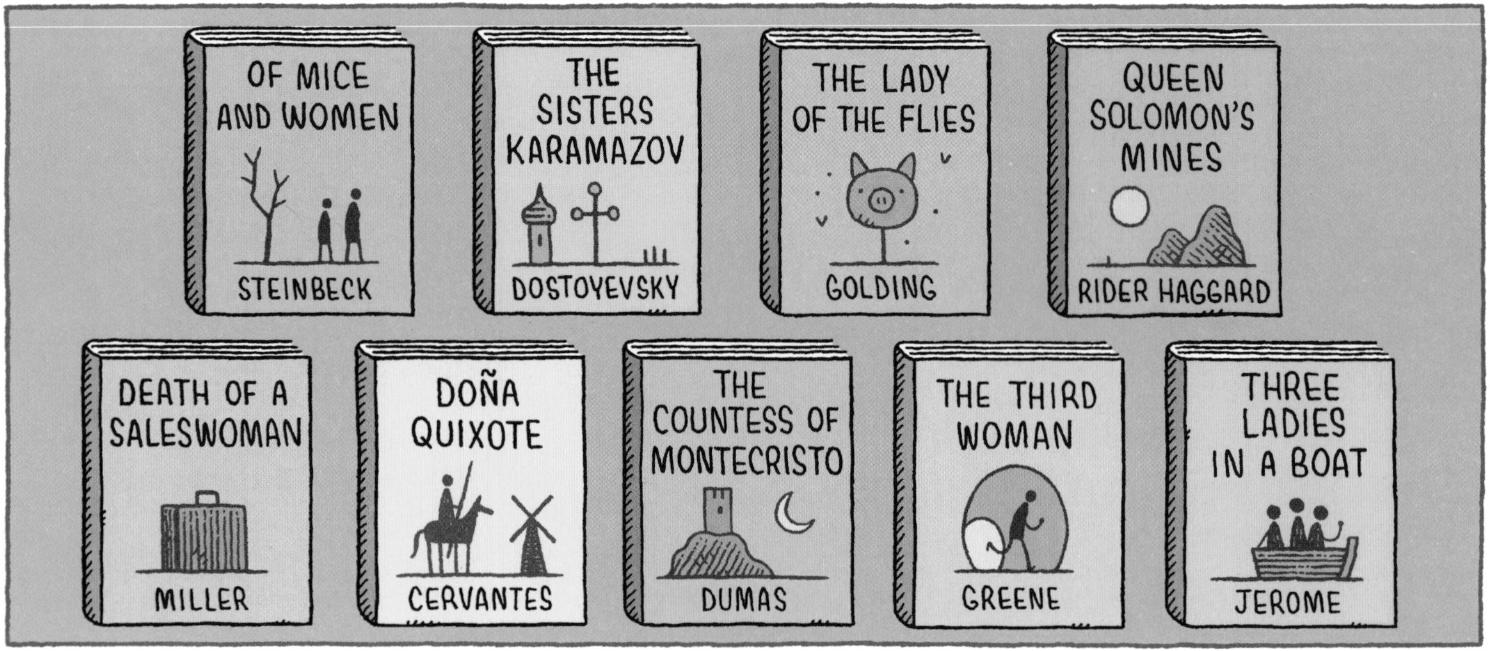
OF MICE AND WOMEN
STEINBECK
THE SISTERS KARAMAZOV
DOSTOYEVSKY
THE LADY OF THE FLIES
GOLDING
QUEEN SOLOMON'S MINES
RIDER HAGGARD
DEATH OF A SALESWOMAN
MILLER
DOÑA QUIXOTE
CERVANTES
THE COUNTESS OF MONTECRISTO
DUMAS
THE THIRD WOMAN
GREENE
THREE LADIES IN A BOAT
JEROME

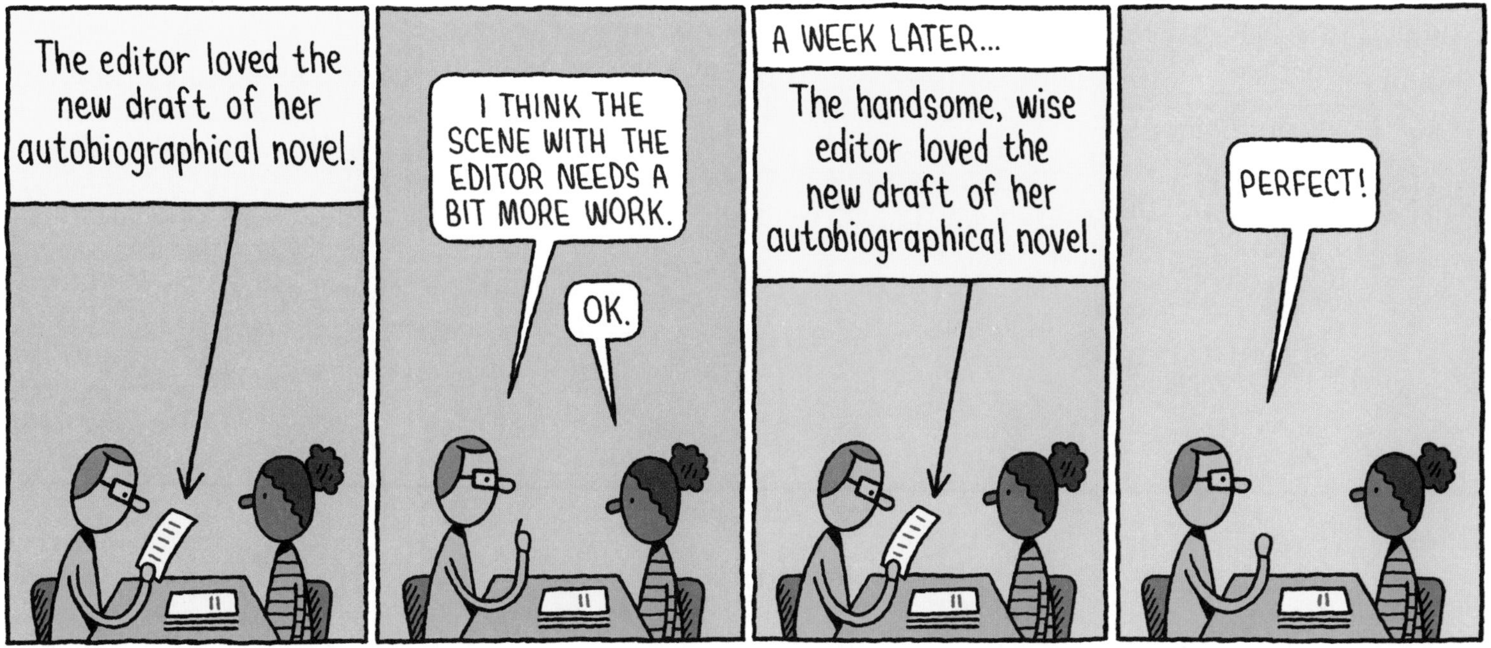
The editor loved the new draft of her autobiographical novel.
I THINK THE SCENE WITH THE EDITOR NEEDS A BIT MORE WORK.
OK.
A WEEK LATER...
The handsome, wise editor loved the new draft of her autobiographical novel.
PERFECT!

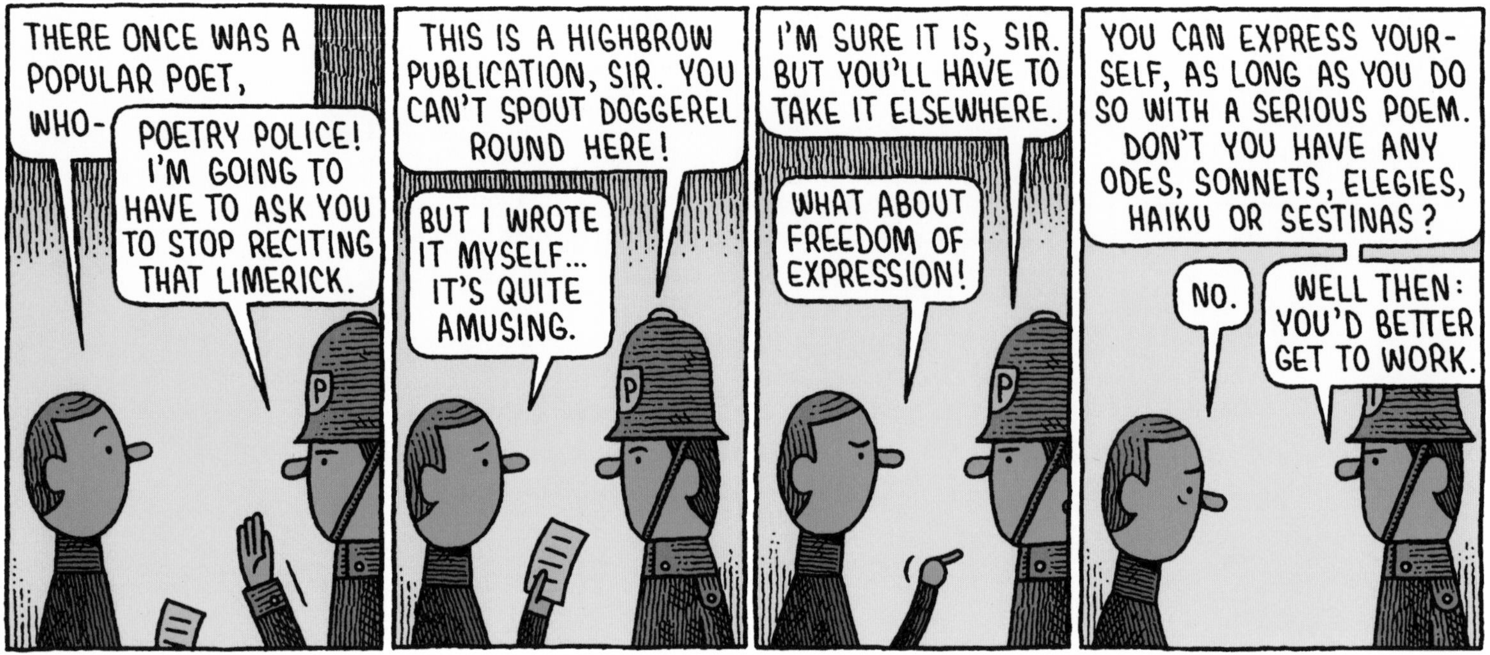

THERE ONCE WAS A POPULAR POET, WHO-
POETRY POLICE! I'M GOING TO HAVE TO ASK YOU TO STOP RECITING THAT LIMERICK.
THIS IS A HIGHBROW PUBLICATION, SIR. YOU CAN'T SPOUT DOGGEREL ROUND HERE!
BUT I WROTE IT MYSELF... IT'S QUITE AMUSING.
I'M SURE IT IS, SIR. BUT YOU'LL HAVE TO TAKE IT ELSEWHERE.
WHAT ABOUT FREEDOM OF EXPRESSION!
YOU CAN EXPRESS YOUR-SELF, AS LONG AS YOU DO SO WITH A SERIOUS POEM. DON'T YOU HAVE ANY ODES, SONNETS, ELEGIES, HAIKU OR SESTINAS?
NO.
WELL THEN: YOU'D BETTER GET TO WORK.

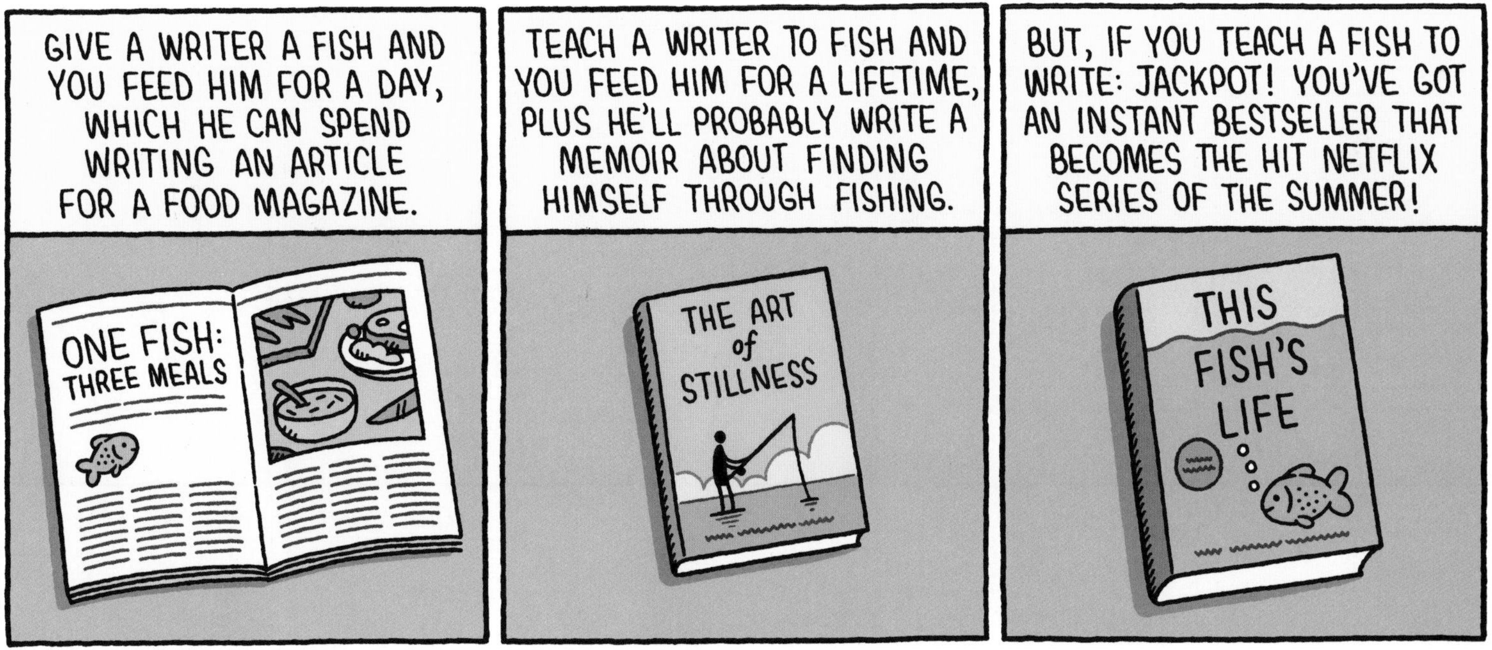
GIVE A WRITER A FISH AND YOU FEED HIM FOR A DAY, WHICH HE CAN SPEND WRITING AN ARTICLE FOR A FOOD MAGAZINE.
ONE FISH: THREE MEALS
TEACH A WRITER TO FISH AND YOU FEED HIM FOR A LIFETIME, PLUS HE'LL PROBABLY WRITE A MEMOIR ABOUT FINDING HIMSELF THROUGH FISHING.
THE ART of STILLNESS
BUT, IF YOU TEACH A FISH TO WRITE: JACKPOT! YOU'VE GOT AN INSTANT BESTSELLER THAT BECOMES THE HIT NETFLIX SERIES OF THE SUMMER!
THIS FISH'S LIFE

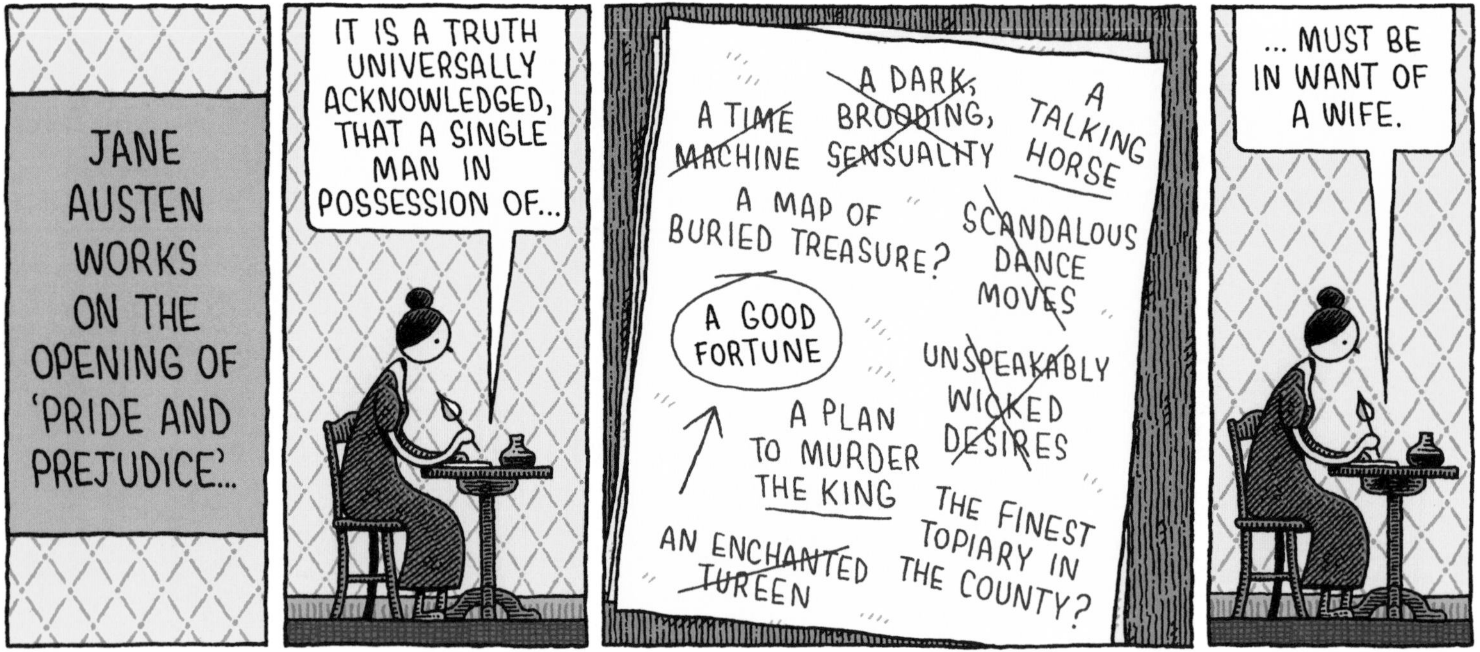

JANE AUSTEN WORKS ON THE OPENING OF 'PRIDE AND PREJUDICE'...
IT IS A TRUTH UNIVERSALLY ACKNOWLEDGED, THAT A SINGLE MAN IN POSSESSION OF...
A TIME MACHINE
A DARK, BROODING, SENSUALITY
A TALKING HORSE
A MAP OF BURIED TREASURE?
SCANDALOUS DANCE MOVES
A GOOD FORTUNE
UNSPEAKABLY WICKED DESIRES
A PLAN TO MURDER THE KING
THE FINEST TOPIARY IN THE COUNTY?
AN ENCHANTED TUREEN
... MUST BE IN WANT OF A WIFE.

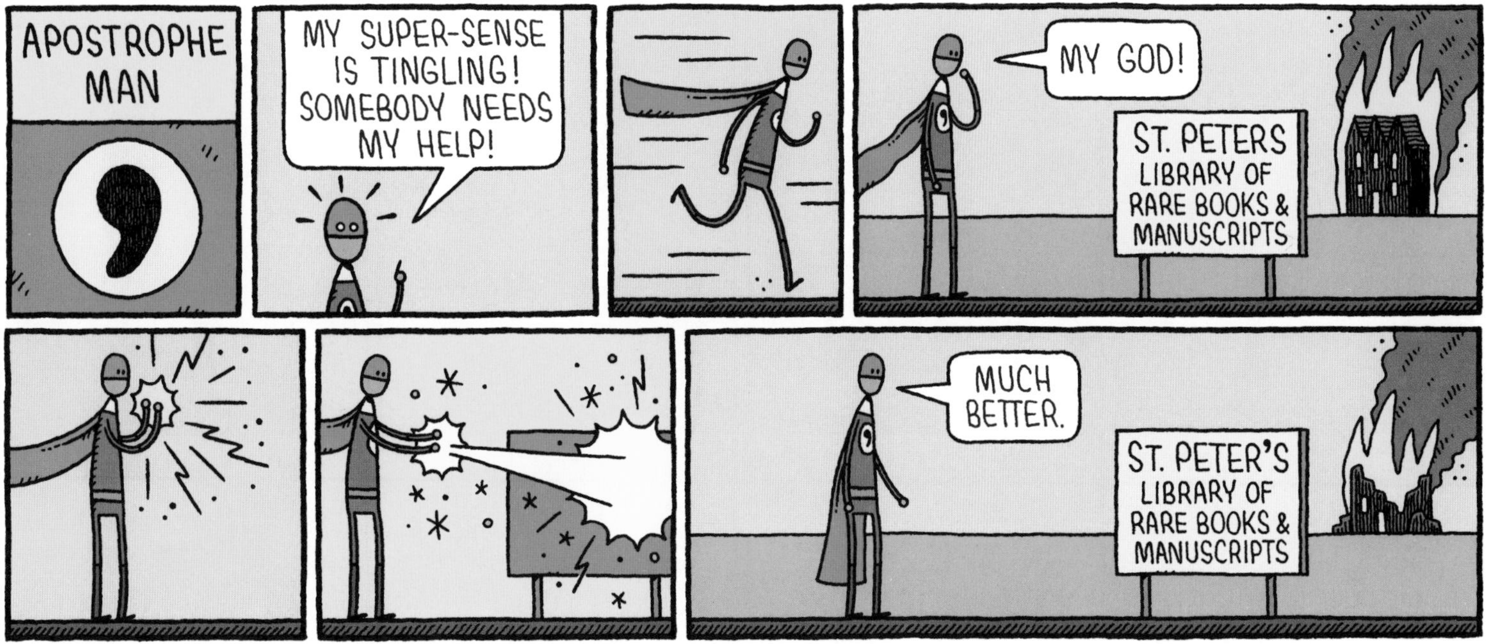
APOSTROPHE MAN
MY SUPER-SENSE IS TINGLING! SOMEBODY NEEDS MY HELP!
MY GOD!
ST. PETERS LIBRARY OF RARE BOOKS & MANUSCRIPTS
MUCH BETTER.
ST. PETER'S LIBRARY OF RARE BOOKS & MANUSCRIPTS

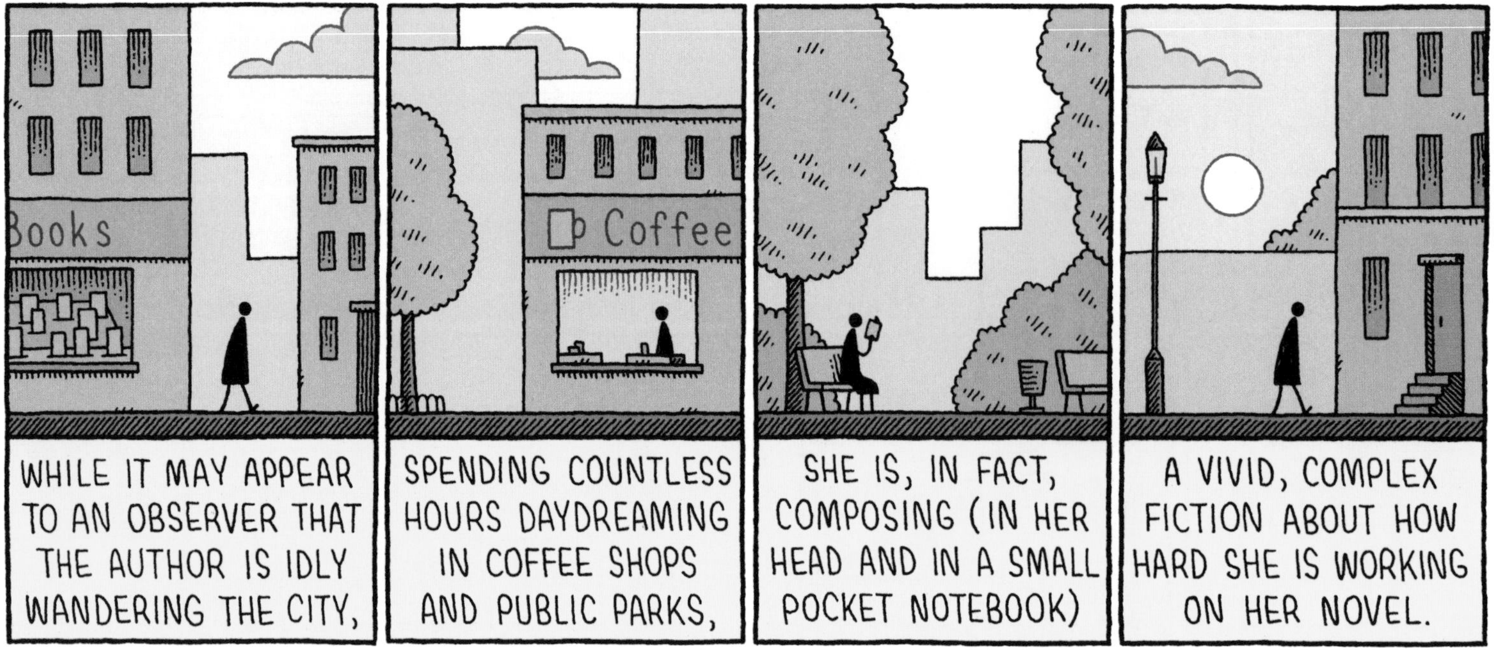
Books
WHILE IT MAY APPEAR TO AN OBSERVER THAT THE AUTHOR IS IDLY WANDERING THE CITY,
Coffee
SPENDING COUNTLESS HOURS DAYDREAMING IN COFFEE SHOPS AND PUBLIC PARKS,
SHE IS, IN FACT, COMPOSING (IN HER HEAD AND IN A SMALL POCKET NOTEBOOK)
A VIVID, COMPLEX FICTION ABOUT HOW HARD SHE IS WORKING ON HER NOVEL.

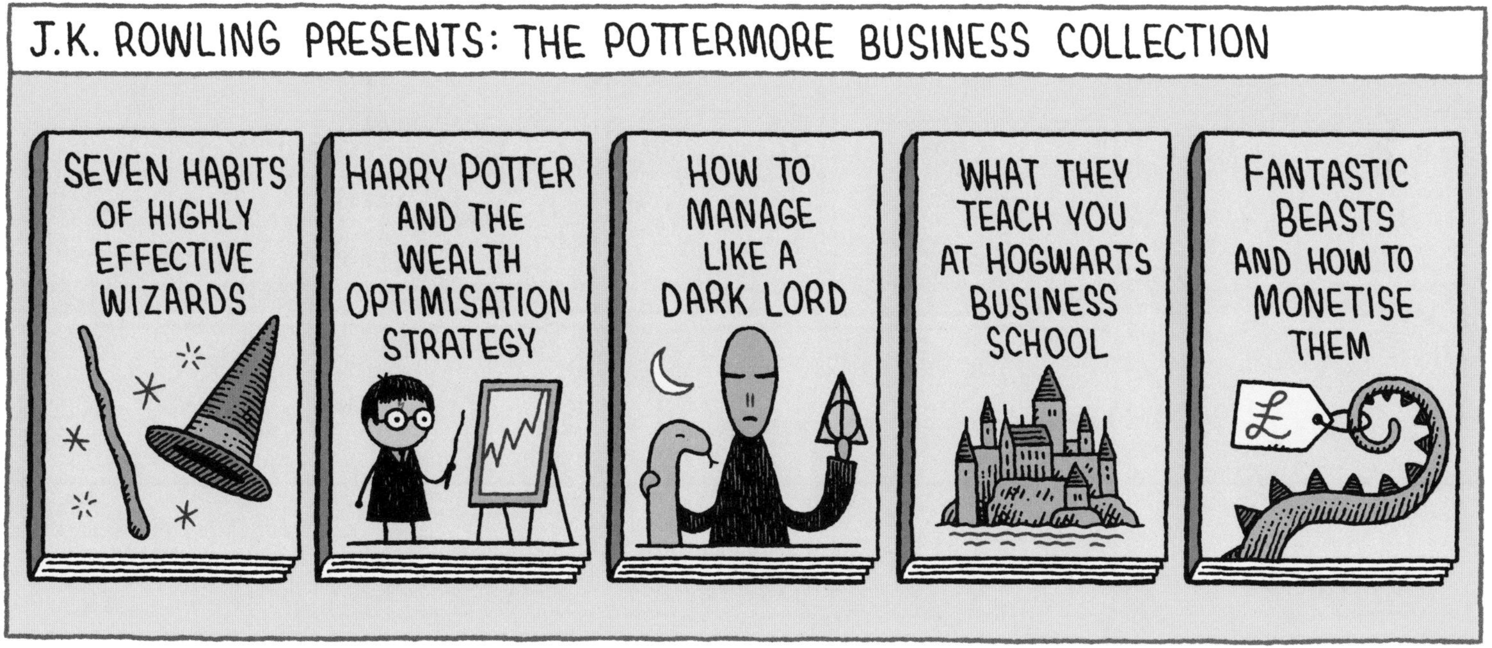
J.K. ROWLING PRESENTS: THE POTTERMORE BUSINESS COLLECTION
SEVEN HABITS OF HIGHLY EFFECTIVE WIZARDS
HARRY POTTER AND THE WEALTH OPTIMISATION STRATEGY
HOW TO MANAGE LIKE A DARK LORD
WHAT THEY TEACH YOU AT HOGWARTS BUSINESS SCHOOL
FANTASTIC BEASTS AND HOW TO MONETISE THEM
£

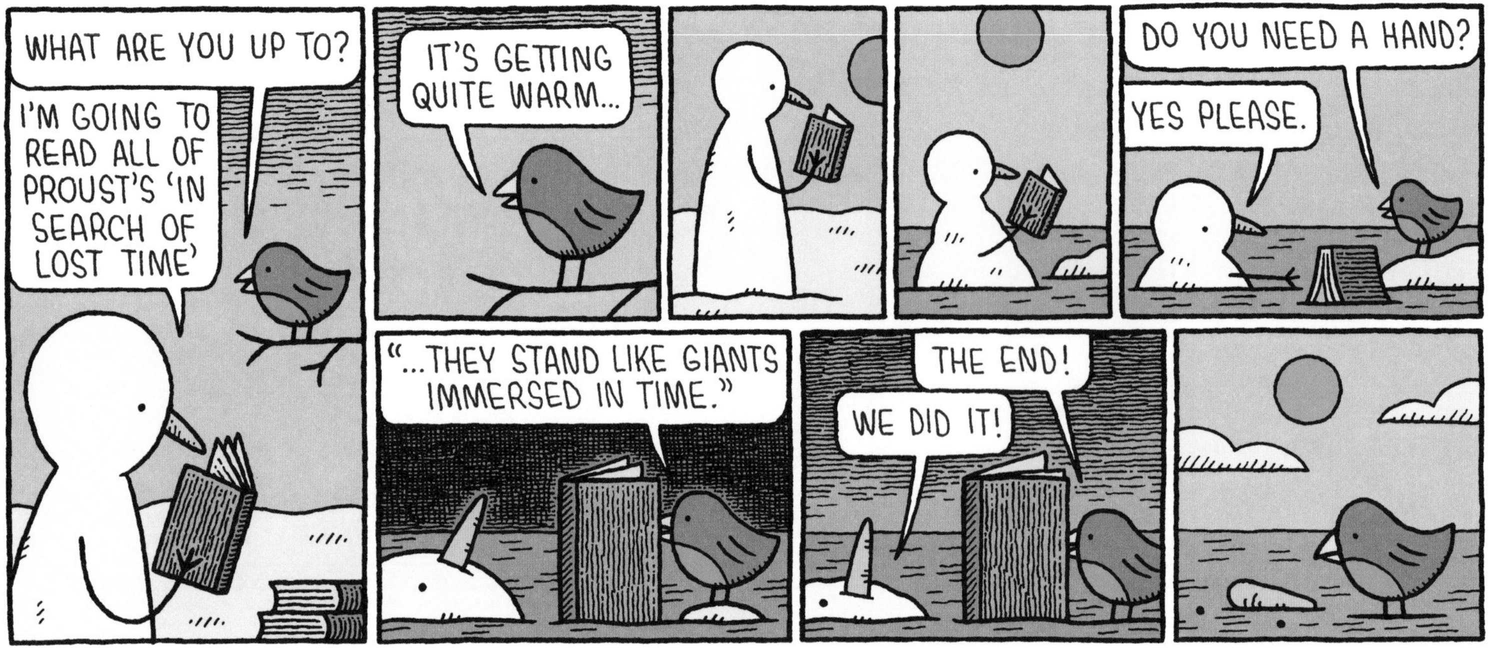
WHAT ARE YOU UP TO?
I'M GOING TO READ ALL OF PROUST'S 'IN SEARCH OF LOST TIME'
IT'S GETTING QUITE WARM...
DO YOU NEED A HAND?
YES PLEASE.
"...THEY STAND LIKE GIANTS IMMERSED IN TIME."
THE END!
WE DID IT!

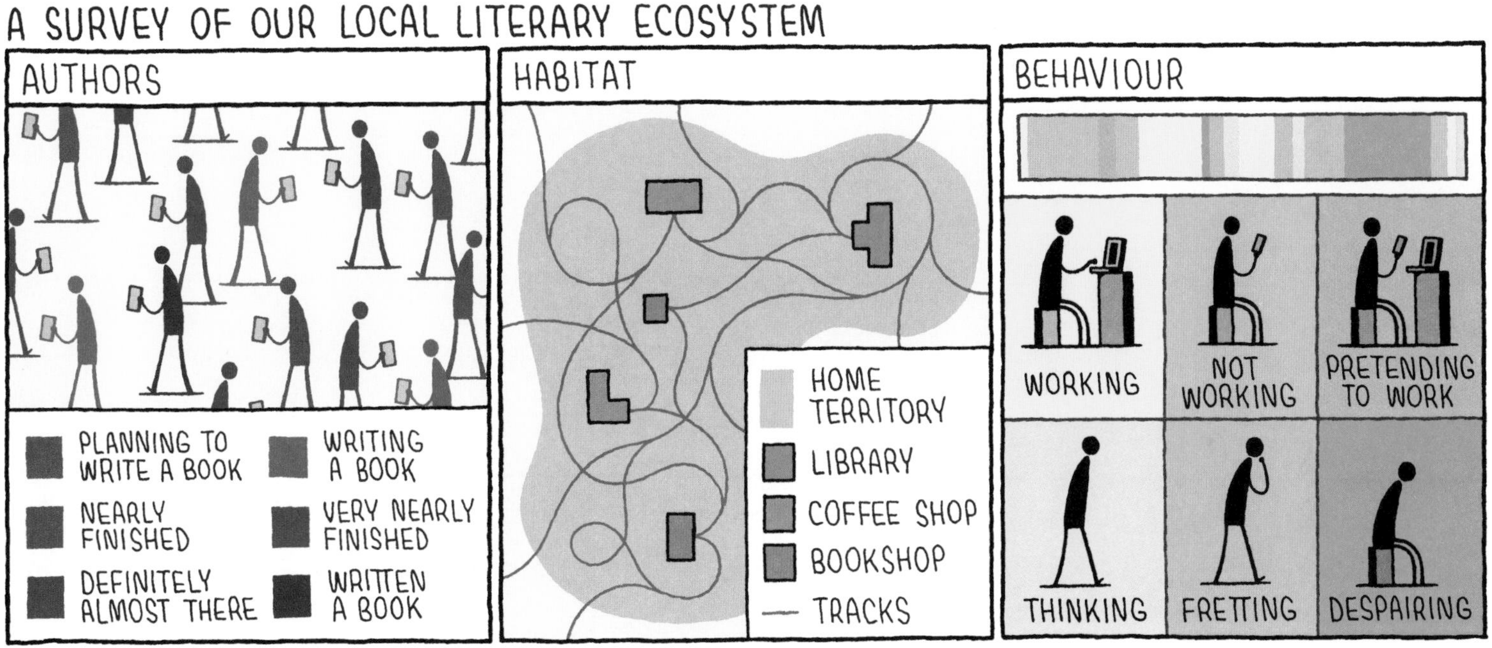
A SURVEY OF OUR LOCAL LITERARY ECOSYSTEM
AUTHORS
PLANNING TO WRITE A BOOK
WRITING A BOOK
NEARLY FINISHED
VERY NEARLY FINISHED
DEFINITELY ALMOST THERE
WRITTEN A BOOK
HABITAT
HOME TERRITORY
LIBRARY
COFFEE SHOP
BOOKSHOP
TRACKS
BEHAVIOUR
WORKING
NOT WORKING
PRETENDING TO WORK
THINKING
FRETTING
DESPAIRING

RECENTLY DISCOVERED ARTEFACTS SUGGEST THAT IN HOMER'S ORIGINAL VERSION OF 'THE ODYSSEY,' ODYSSEUS AND THE CYCLOPS MAY HAVE TEAMED UP FOR A SERIES OF EXCITING ADVENTURES...

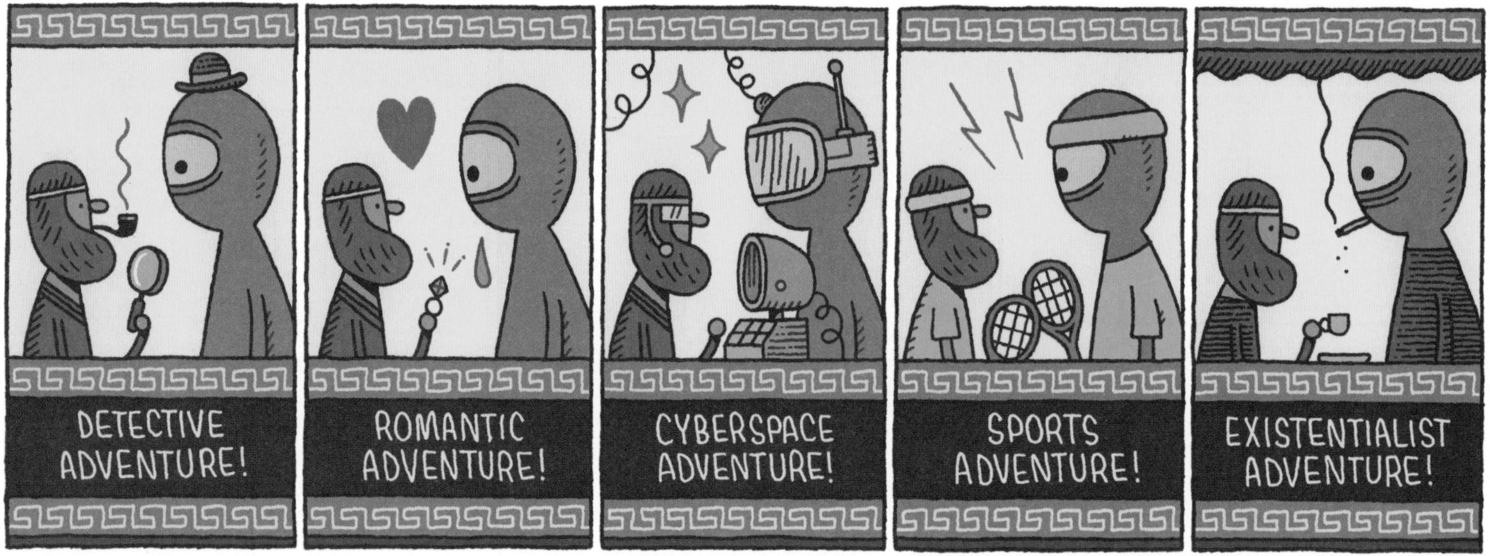
DETECTIVE ADVENTURE!
ROMANTIC ADVENTURE!
CYBERSPACE ADVENTURE!
SPORTS ADVENTURE!
EXISTENTIALIST ADVENTURE!

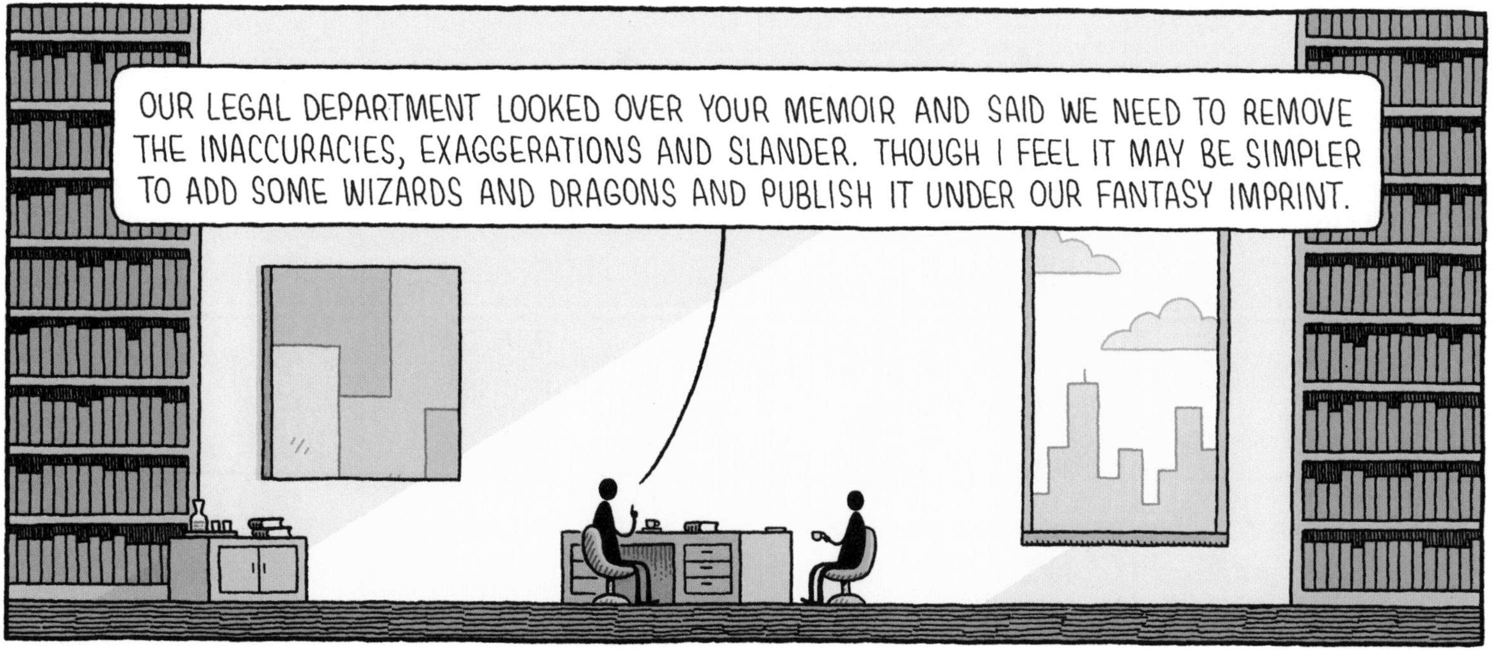
OUR LEGAL DEPARTMENT LOOKED OVER YOUR MEMOIR AND SAID WE NEED TO REMOVE THE INACCURACIES, EXAGGERATIONS AND SLANDER. THOUGH I FEEL IT MAY BE SIMPLER TO ADD SOME WIZARDS AND DRAGONS AND PUBLISH IT UNDER OUR FANTASY IMPRINT.

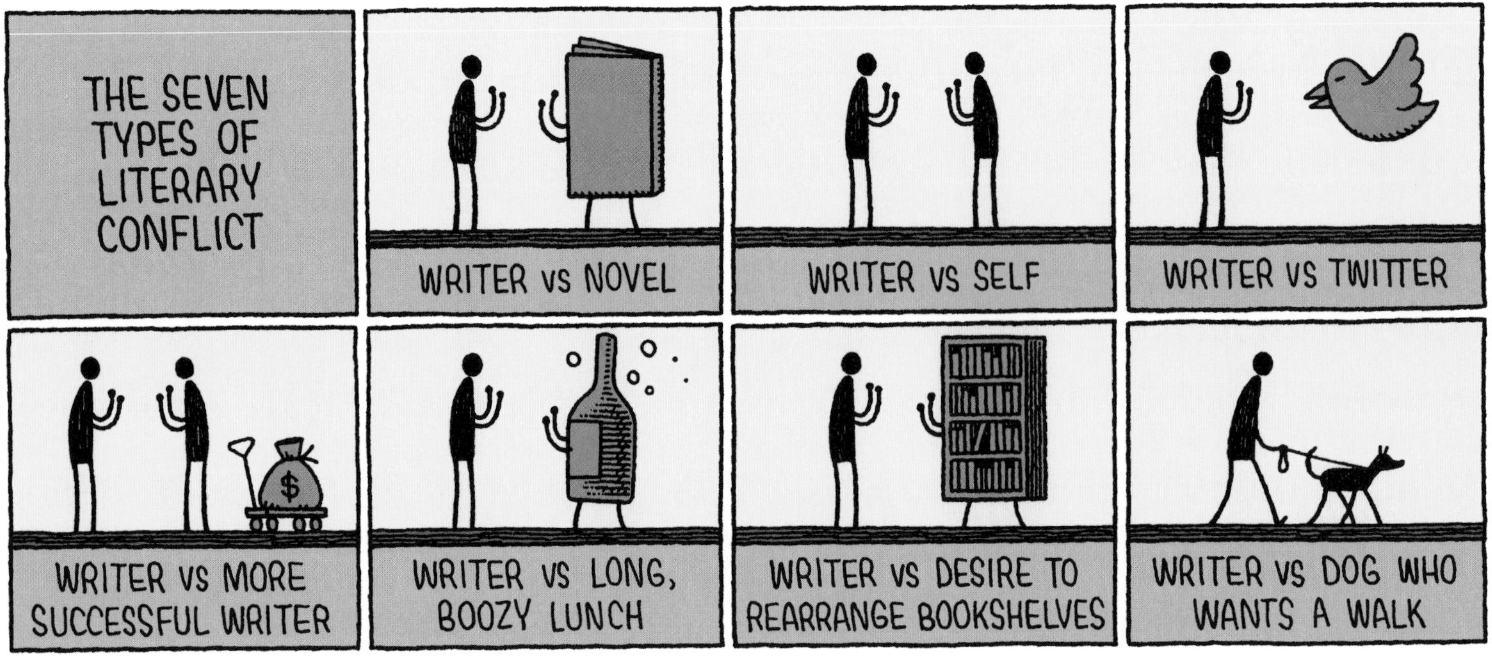
THE SEVEN TYPES OF LITERARY CONFLICT
WRITER vs NOVEL
WRITER vs SELF
WRITER vs TWITTER
WRITER vs MORE SUCCESSFUL WRITER
WRITER vs LONG, BOOZY LUNCH
WRITER vs DESIRE TO REARRANGE BOOKSHELVES
WRITER vs DOG WHO WANTS A WALK

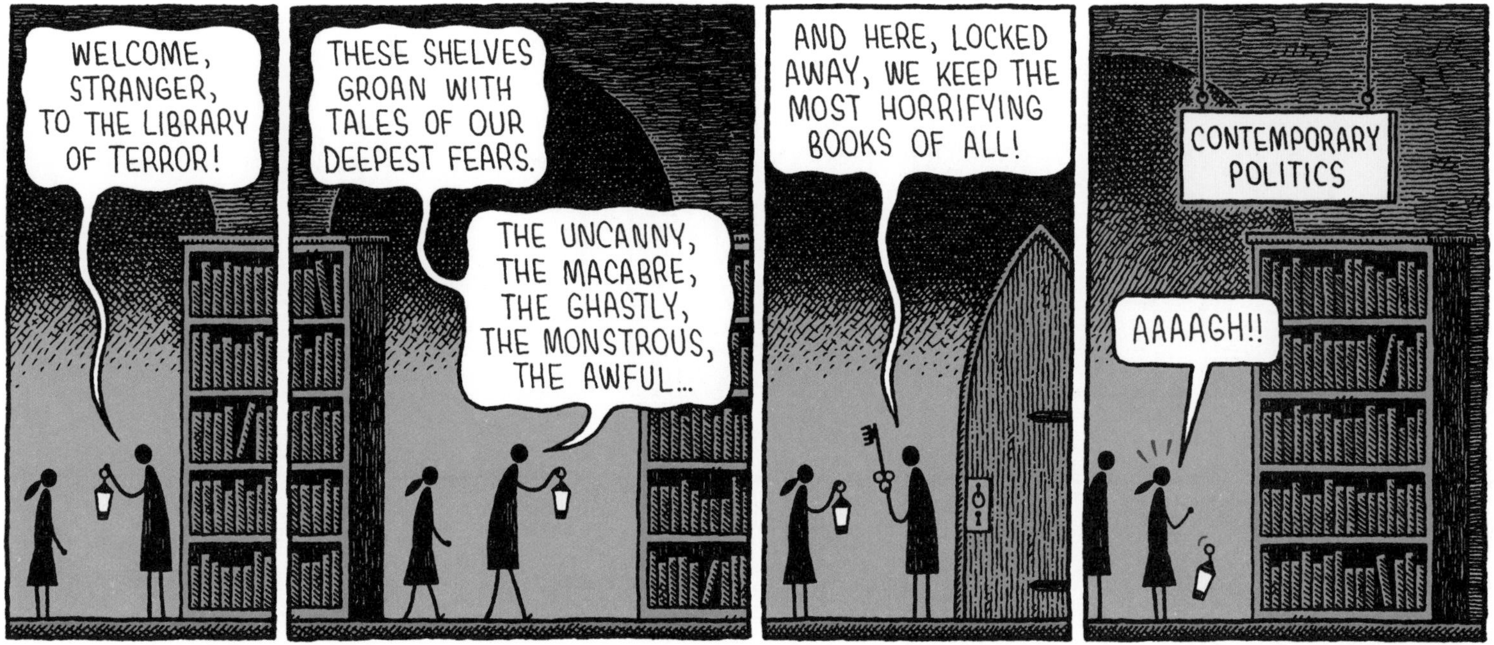
WELCOME, STRANGER, TO THE LIBRARY OF TERROR!
THESE SHELVES GROAN WITH TALES OF OUR DEEPEST FEARS.
THE UNCANNY, THE MACABRE, THE GHASTLY, THE MONSTROUS, THE AWFUL...
AND HERE, LOCKED AWAY, WE KEEP THE MOST HORRIFYING BOOKS OF ALL!
CONTEMPORARY POLITICS
AAAAGH!!

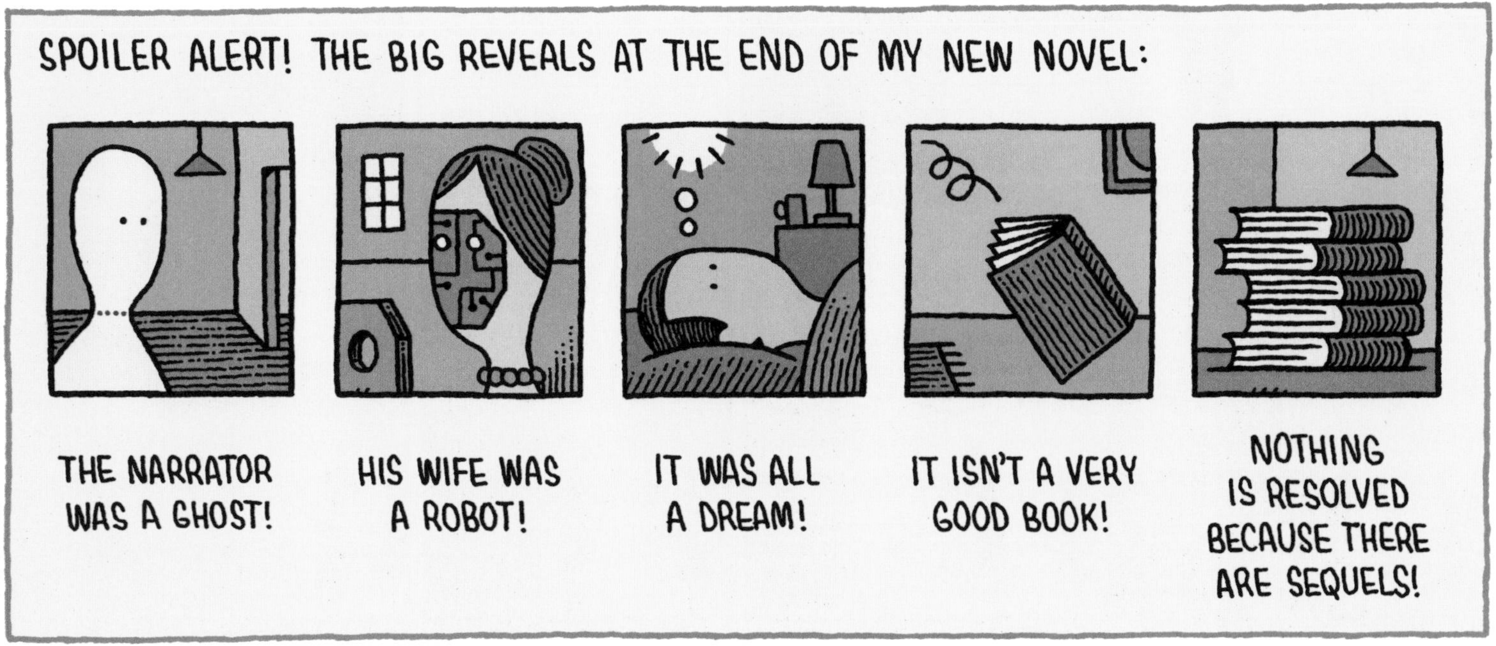
SPOILER ALERT! THE BIG REVEALS AT THE END OF MY NEW NOVEL:
THE NARRATOR WAS A GHOST!
HIS WIFE WAS A ROBOT!
IT WAS ALL A DREAM!
IT ISN'T A VERY GOOD BOOK!
NOTHING IS RESOLVED BECAUSE THERE ARE SEQUELS!

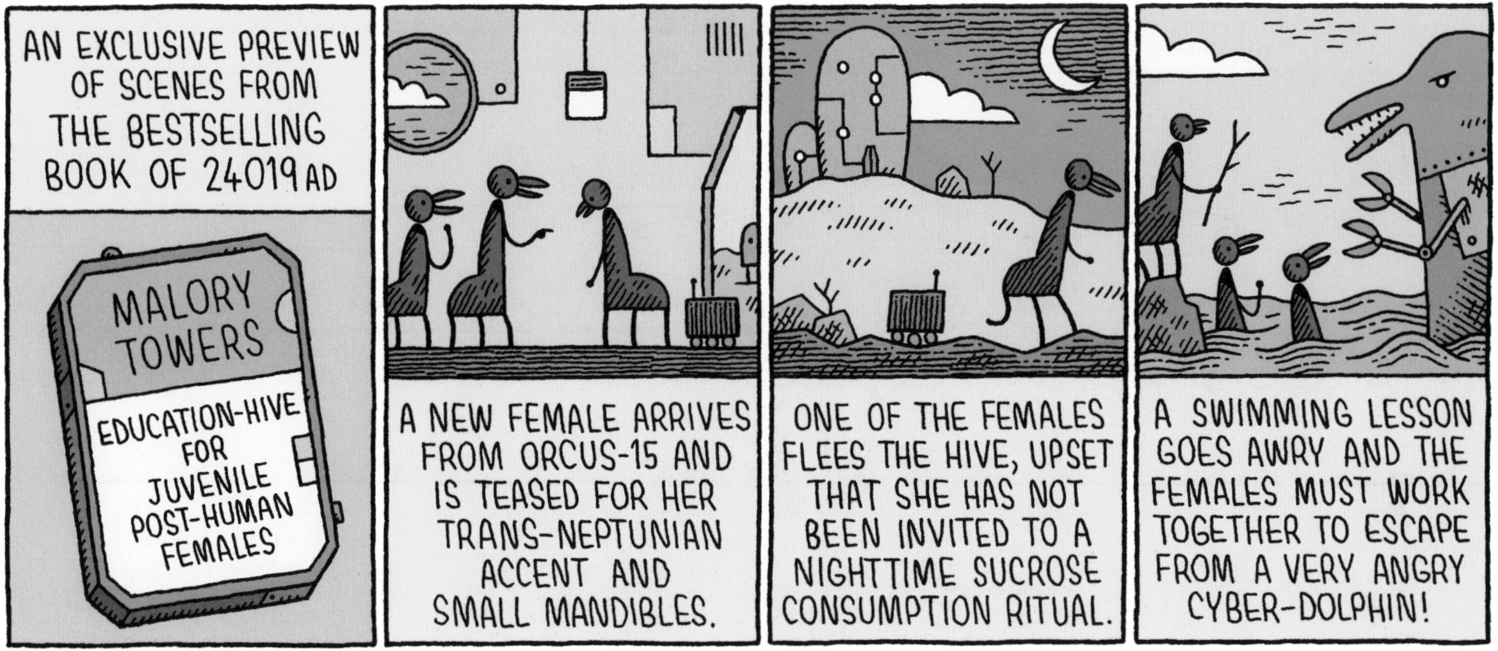
AN EXCLUSIVE PREVIEW OF SCENES FROM THE BESTSELLING BOOK OF 24019 AD
MALORY TOWERS
EDUCATION-HIVE FOR JUVENILE POST-HUMAN FEMALES
A NEW FEMALE ARRIVES FROM ORCUS-15 AND IS TEASED FOR HER TRANS-NEPTUNIAN ACCENT AND SMALL MANDIBLES.
ONE OF THE FEMALES FLEES THE HIVE, UPSET THAT SHE HAS NOT BEEN INVITED TO A NIGHTTIME SUCROSE CONSUMPTION RITUAL.
A SWIMMING LESSON GOES AWRY AND THE FEMALES MUST WORK TOGETHER TO ESCAPE FROM A VERY ANGRY CYBER-DOLPHIN!

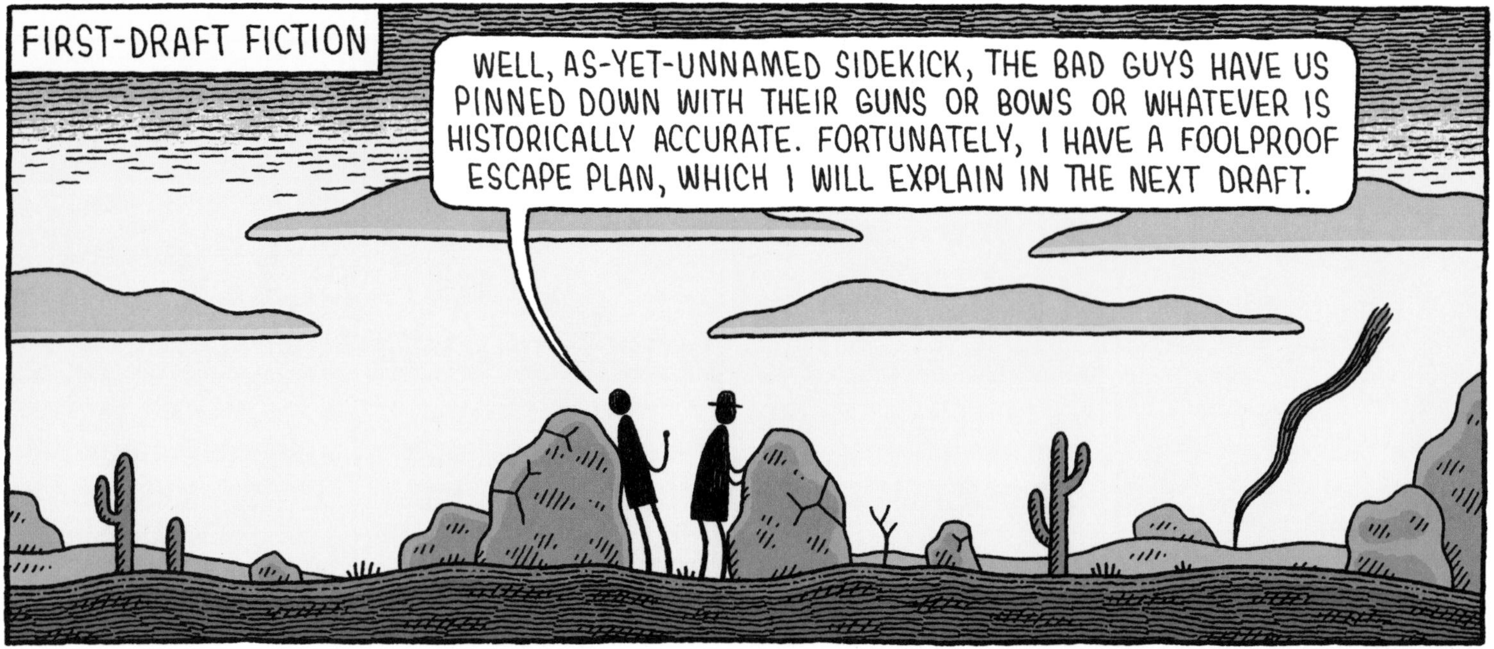
FIRST-DRAFT FICTION
WELL, AS-YET-UNNAMED SIDEKICK, THE BAD GUYS HAVE US PINNED DOWN WITH THEIR GUNS OR BOWS OR WHATEVER IS HISTORICALLY ACCURATE. FORTUNATELY, I HAVE A FOOLPROOF ESCAPE PLAN, WHICH I WILL EXPLAIN IN THE NEXT DRAFT.

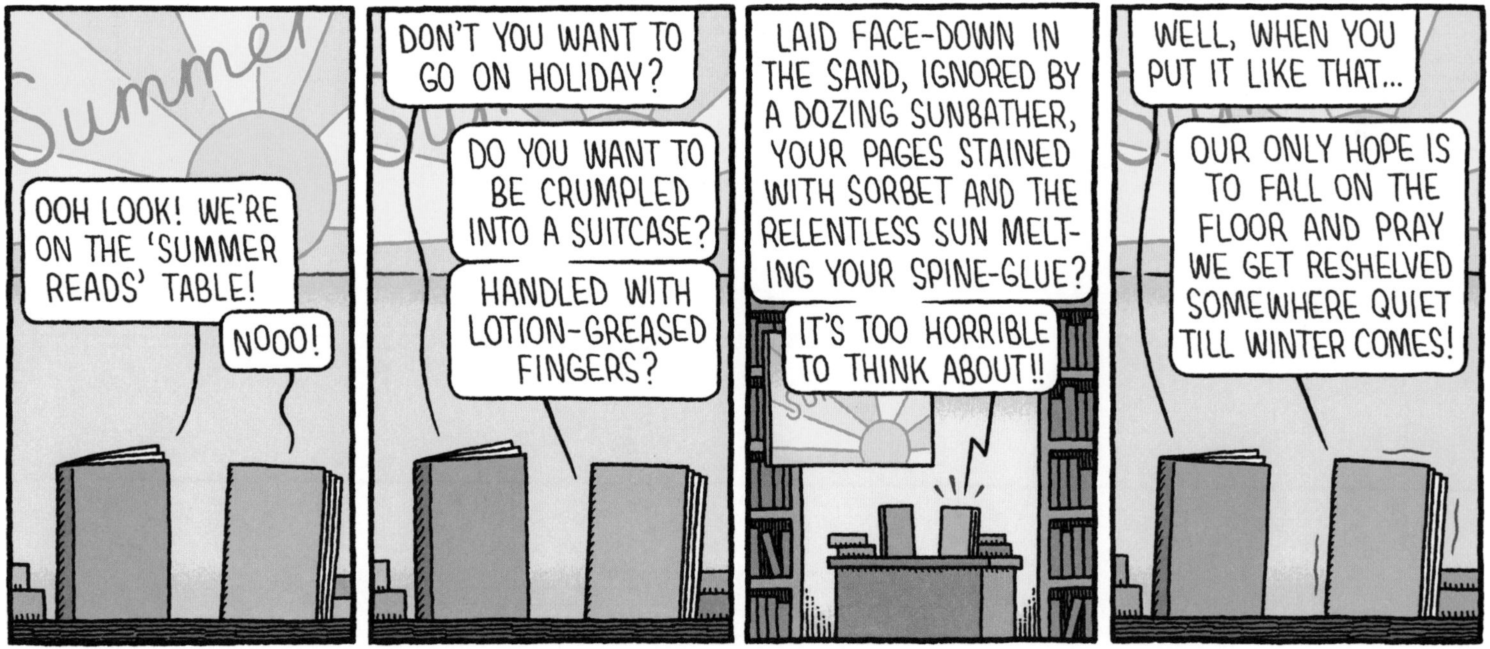
Summer
OOH LOOK! WE'RE ON THE 'SUMMER READS' TABLE!
NOOO!
DON'T YOU WANT TO GO ON HOLIDAY?
DO YOU WANT TO BE CRUMPLED INTO A SUITCASE?
HANDLED WITH LOTION-GREASED FINGERS?
LAID FACE-DOWN IN THE SAND, IGNORED BY A DOZING SUNBATHER, YOUR PAGES STAINED WITH SORBET AND THE RELENTLESS SUN MELTING YOUR SPINE-GLUE?
IT'S TOO HORRIBLE TO THINK ABOUT!!
WELL, WHEN YOU PUT IT LIKE THAT...
OUR ONLY HOPE IS TO FALL ON THE FLOOR AND PRAY WE GET RESHELVED SOMEWHERE QUIET TILL WINTER COMES!

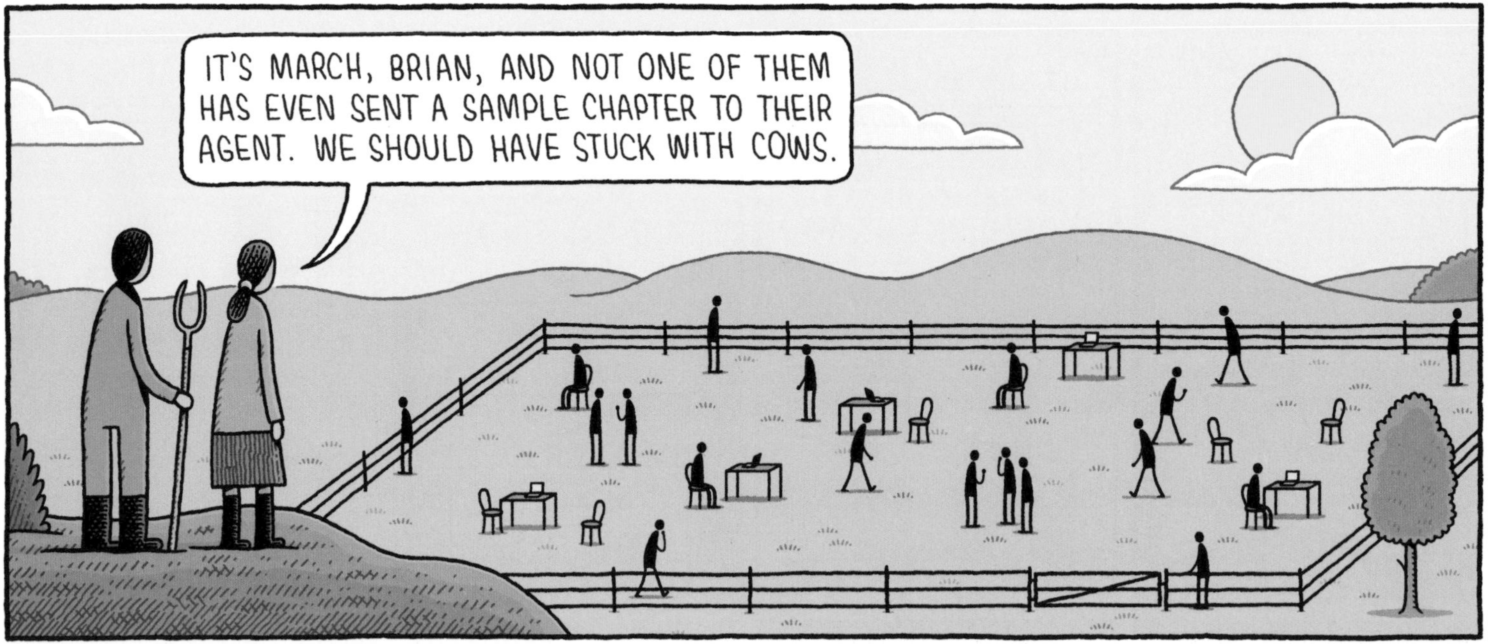
IT'S MARCH, BRIAN, AND NOT ONE OF THEM HAS EVEN SENT A SAMPLE CHAPTER TO THEIR AGENT. WE SHOULD HAVE STUCK WITH COWS.

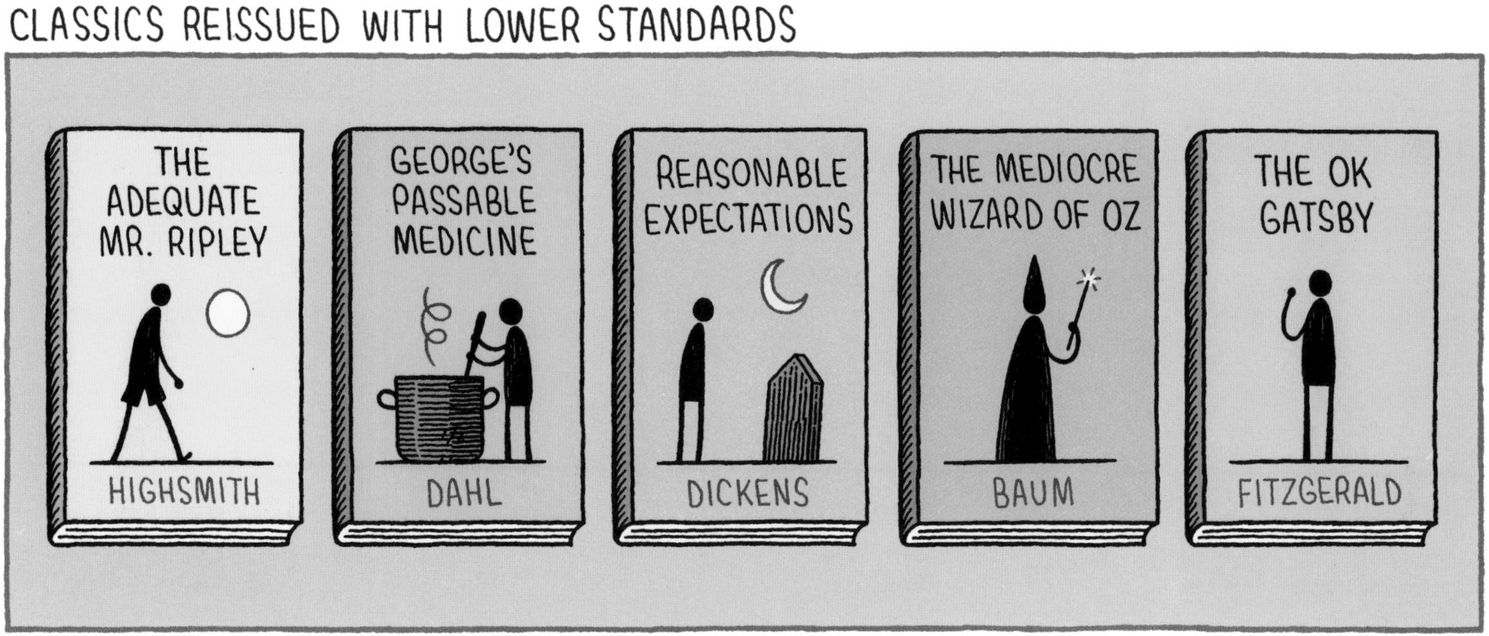
CLASSICS REISSUED WITH LOWER STANDARDS
THE ADEQUATE MR. RIPLEY
HIGHSMITH
GEORGE'S PASSABLE MEDICINE
DAHL
REASONABLE EXPECTATIONS
DICKENS
THE MEDIOCRE WIZARD OF OZ
BAUM
THE OK GATSBY
FITZGERALD

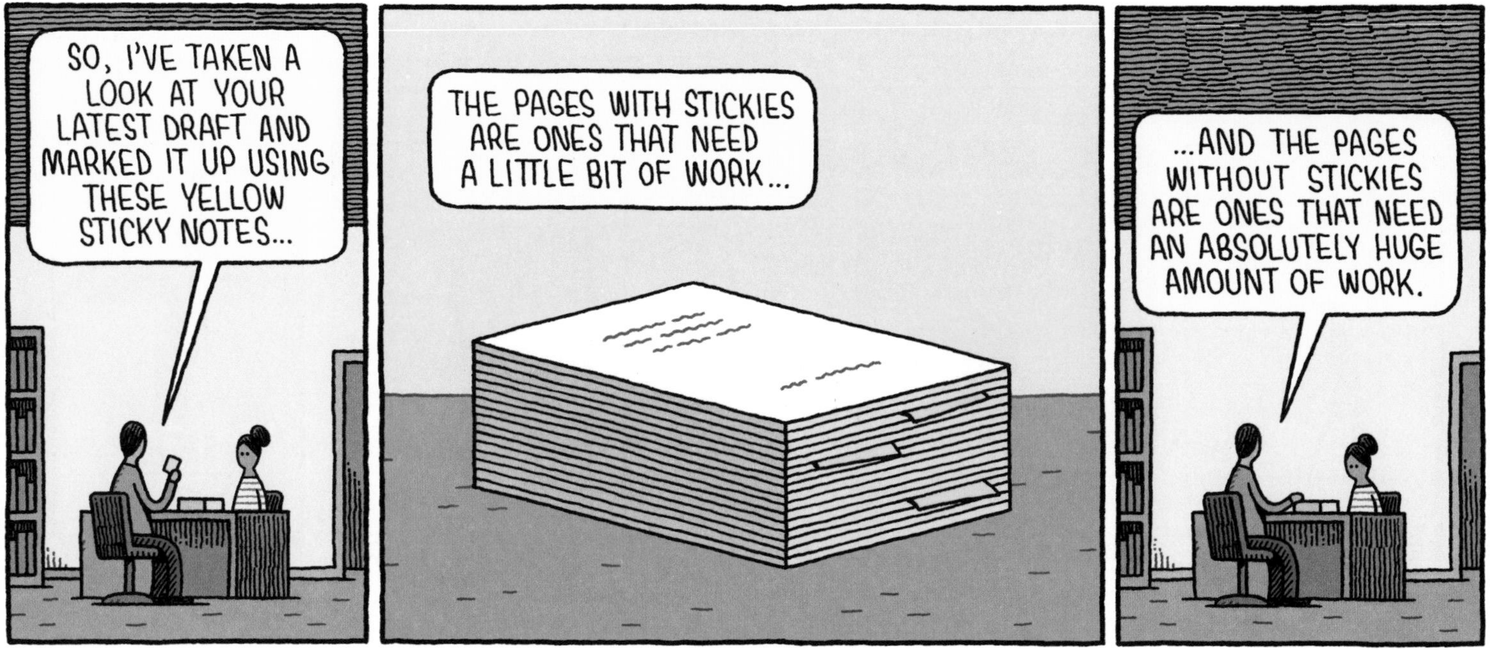
SO, I'VE TAKEN A LOOK AT YOUR LATEST DRAFT AND MARKED IT UP USING THESE YELLOW STICKY NOTES...
THE PAGES WITH STICKIES ARE ONES THAT NEED A LITTLE BIT OF WORK...
...AND THE PAGES WITHOUT STICKIES ARE ONES THAT NEED AN ABSOLUTELY HUGE AMOUNT OF WORK.

AN ALGORITHM THAT GENERATES IDEAS FOR STORIES ABOUT ARTIFICIAL INTELLIGENCE

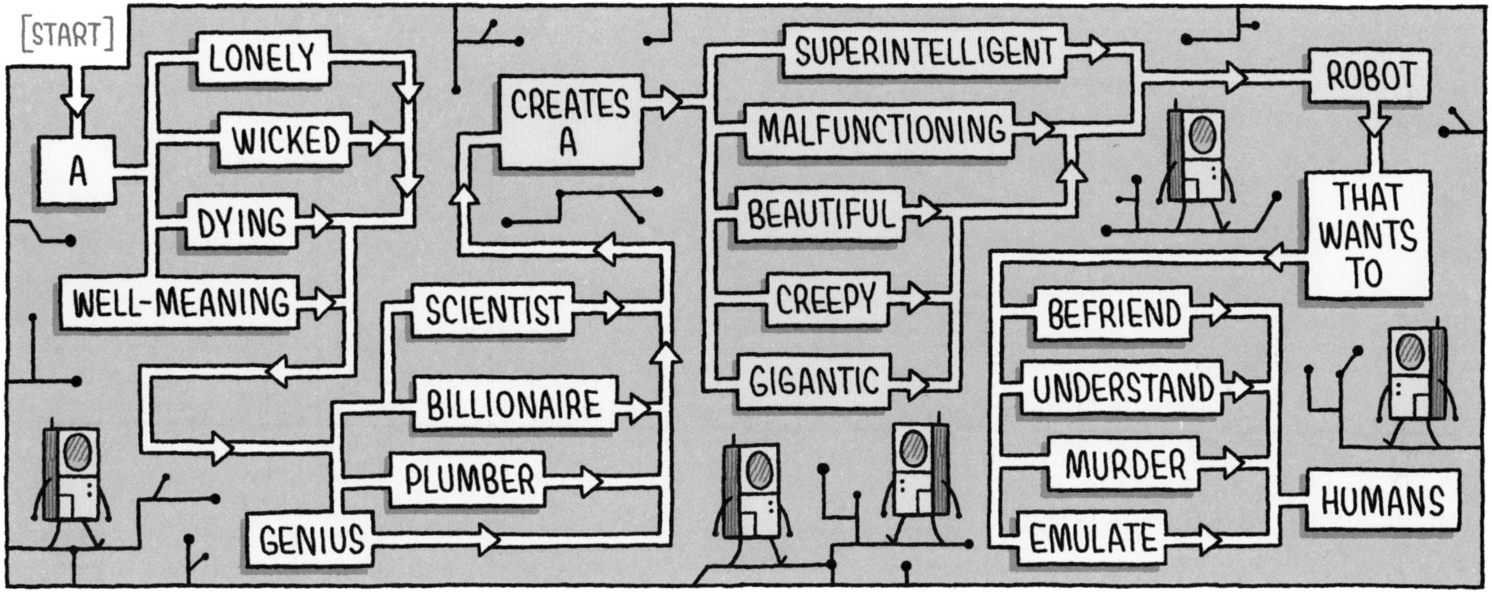
[START]
A
LONELY
WICKED
DYING
WELL-MEANING
GENIUS
SCIENTIST
BILLIONAIRE
PLUMBER
CREATES A
SUPERINTELLIGENT
MALFUNCTIONING
BEAUTIFUL
CREEPY
GIGANTIC
ROBOT
THAT WANTS TO
BEFRIEND
UNDERSTAND
MURDER
EMULATE
HUMANS

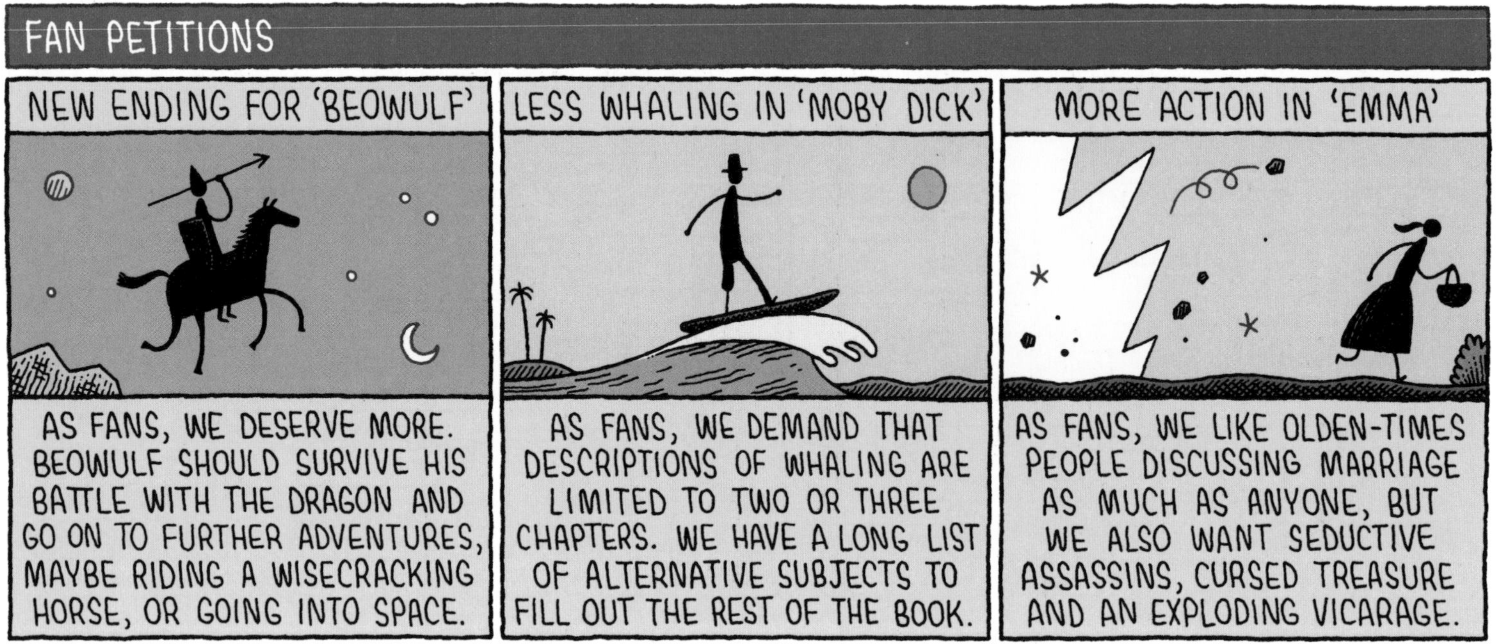
FAN PETITIONS
NEW ENDING FOR 'BEOWULF'
AS FANS, WE DESERVE MORE. BEOWULF SHOULD SURVIVE HIS BATTLE WITH THE DRAGON AND GO ON TO FURTHER ADVENTURES, MAYBE RIDING A WISECRACKING HORSE, OR GOING INTO SPACE.
LESS WHALING IN 'MOBY DICK'
AS FANS, WE DEMAND THAT DESCRIPTIONS OF WHALING ARE LIMITED TO TWO OR THREE CHAPTERS. WE HAVE A LONG LIST OF ALTERNATIVE SUBJECTS TO FILL OUT THE REST OF THE BOOK.
MORE ACTION IN 'EMMA'
AS FANS, WE LIKE OLDEN-TIMES PEOPLE DISCUSSING MARRIAGE AS MUCH AS ANYONE, BUT WE ALSO WANT SEDUCTIVE ASSASSINS, CURSED TREASURE AND AN EXPLODING VICARAGE.

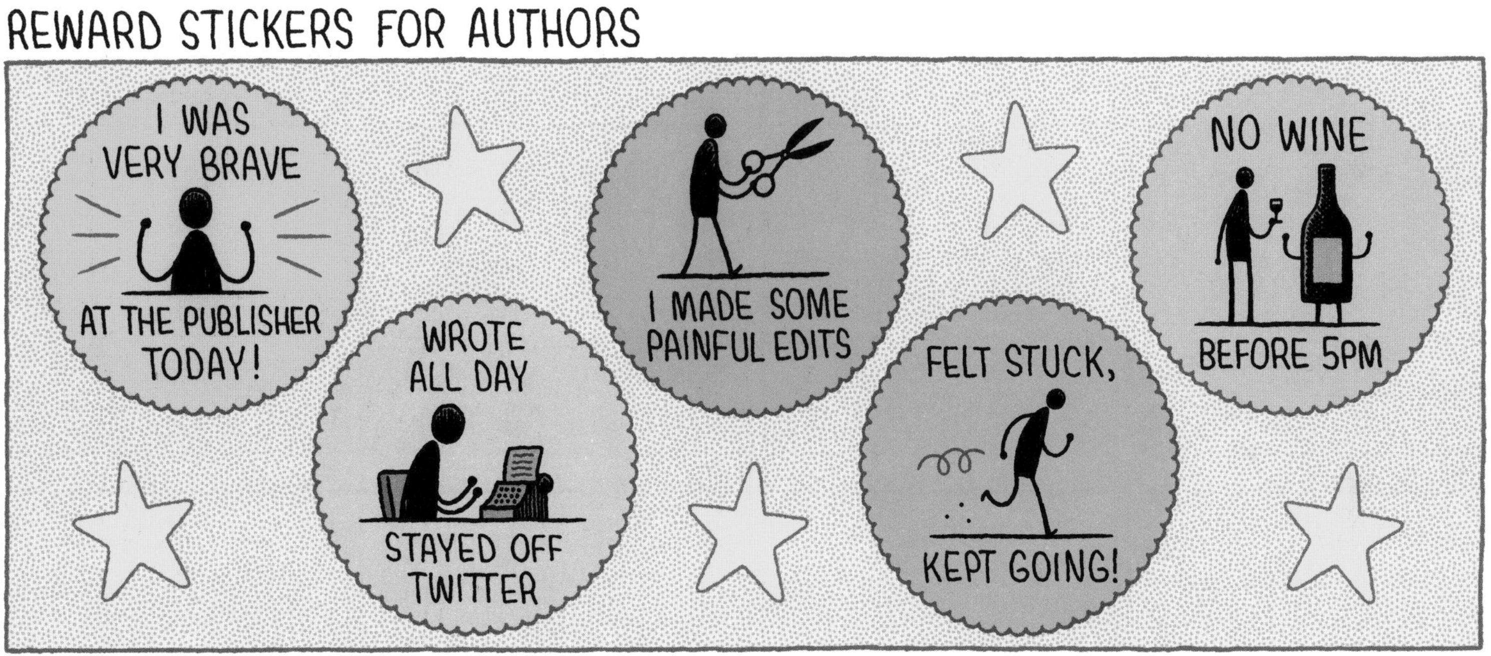
REWARD STICKERS FOR AUTHORS
I WAS VERY BRAVE
AT THE PUBLISHER TODAY!
WROTE ALL DAY
STAYED OFF TWITTER
I MADE SOME PAINFUL EDITS
FELT STUCK,
KEPT GOING!
NO WINE
BEFORE 5PM

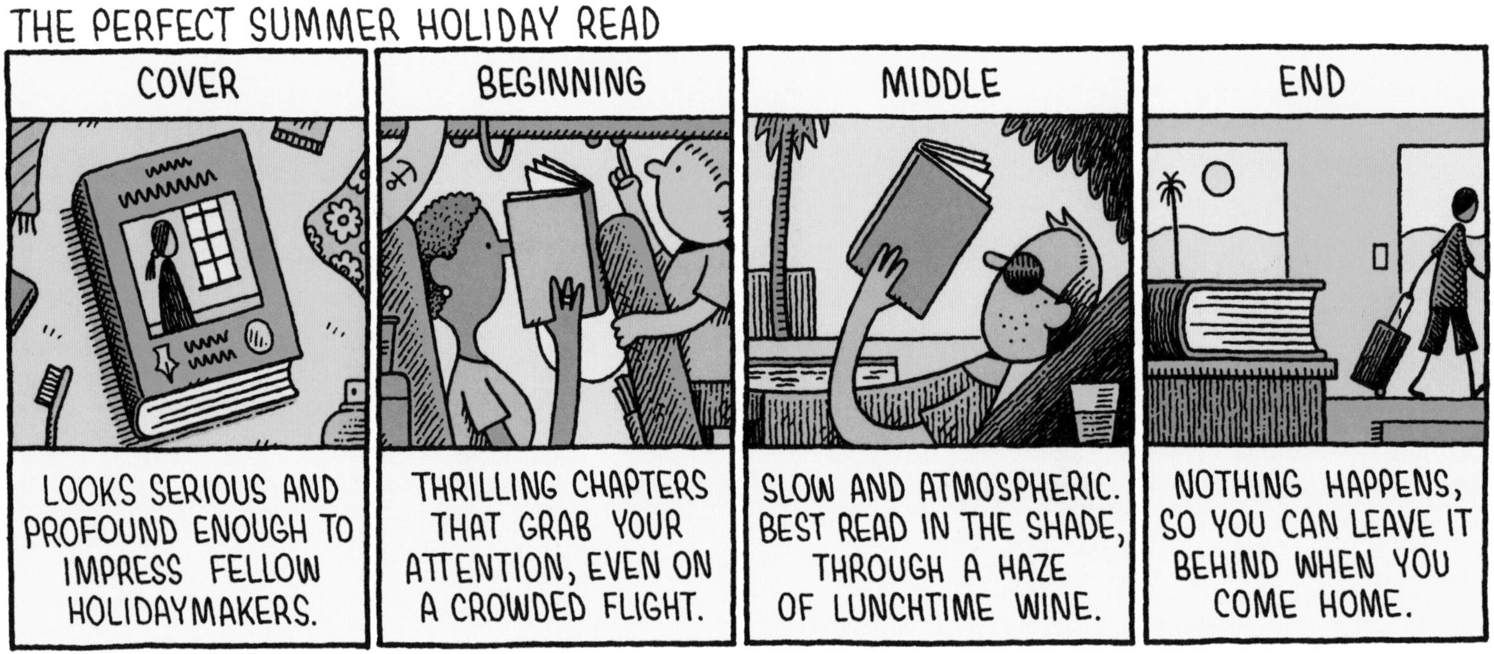
THE PERFECT SUMMER HOLIDAY READ
COVER
LOOKS SERIOUS AND PROFOUND ENOUGH TO IMPRESS FELLOW HOLIDAYMAKERS.
BEGINNING
THRILLING CHAPTERS THAT GRAB YOUR ATTENTION, EVEN ON A CROWDED FLIGHT.
MIDDLE
SLOW AND ATMOSPHERIC. BEST READ IN THE SHADE, THROUGH A HAZE OF LUNCHTIME WINE.
END
NOTHING HAPPENS, SO YOU CAN LEAVE IT BEHIND WHEN YOU COME HOME.

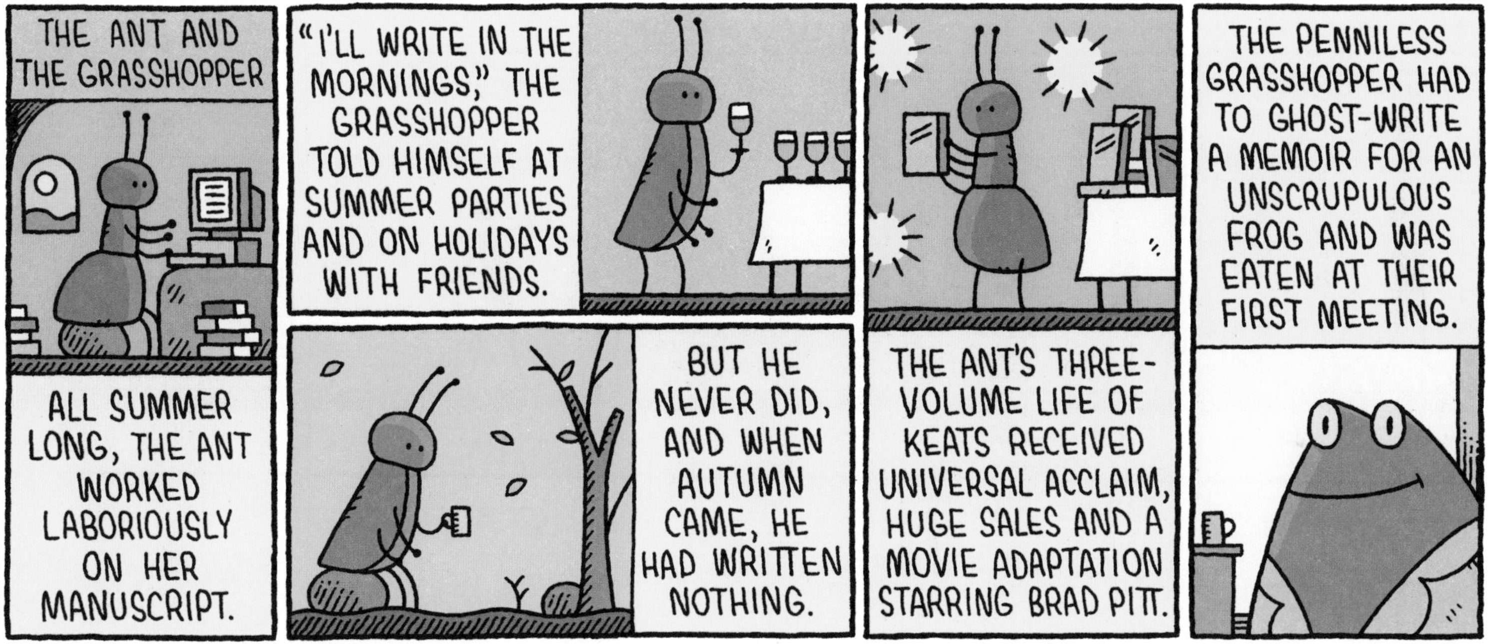
THE ANT AND THE GRASSHOPPER
ALL SUMMER LONG, THE ANT WORKED LABORIOUSLY ON HER MANUSCRIPT.
"I'LL WRITE IN THE MORNINGS," THE GRASSHOPPER TOLD HIMSELF AT SUMMER PARTIES AND ON HOLIDAYS WITH FRIENDS.
BUT HE NEVER DID, AND WHEN AUTUMN CAME, HE HAD WRITTEN NOTHING.
THE ANT'S THREE-VOLUME LIFE OF KEATS RECEIVED UNIVERSAL ACCLAIM, HUGE SALES AND A MOVIE ADAPTATION STARRING BRAD PITT.
THE PENNILESS GRASSHOPPER HAD TO GHOST-WRITE A MEMOIR FOR AN UNSCRUPULOUS FROG AND WAS EATEN AT THEIR FIRST MEETING.

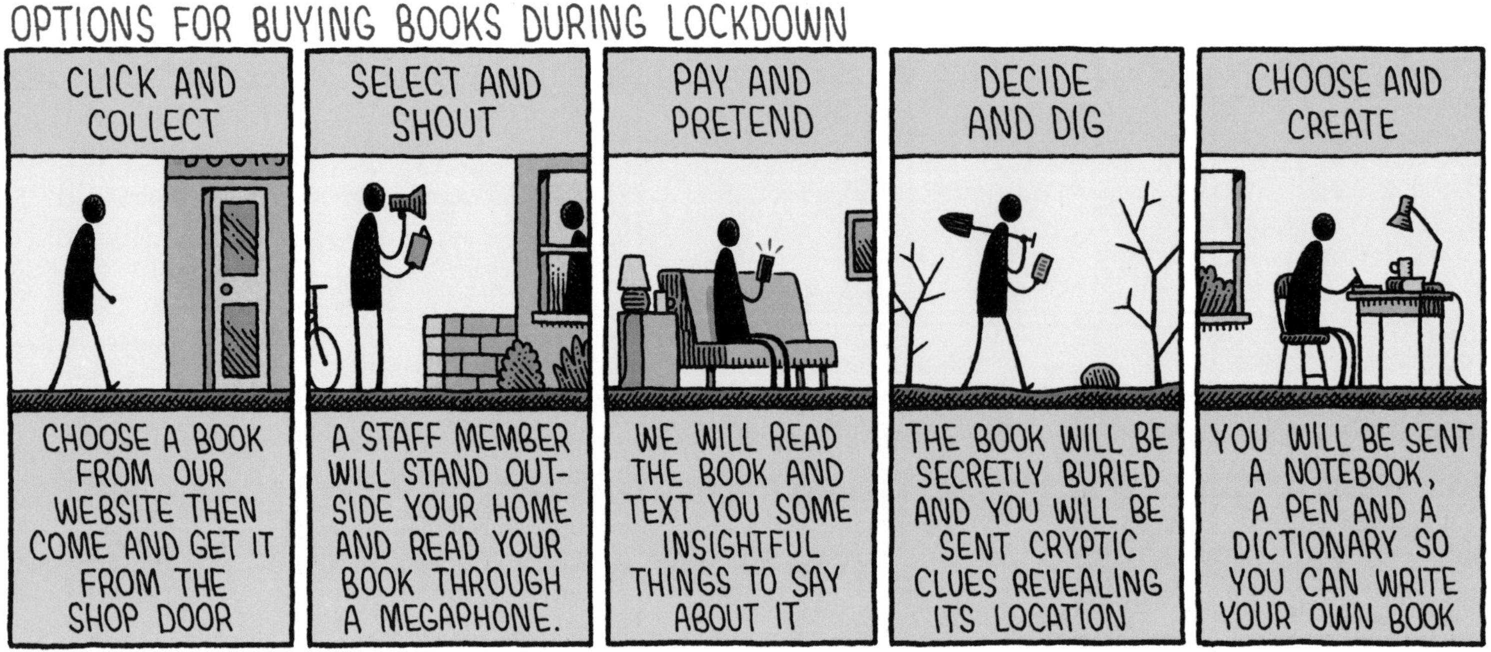
OPTIONS FOR BUYING BOOKS DURING LOCKDOWN
CLICK AND COLLECT
CHOOSE A BOOK FROM OUR WEBSITE THEN COME AND GET IT FROM THE SHOP DOOR
SELECT AND SHOUT
A STAFF MEMBER WILL STAND OUT-SIDE YOUR HOME AND READ YOUR BOOK THROUGH A MEGAPHONE.
PAY AND PRETEND
WE WILL READ THE BOOK AND TEXT YOU SOME INSIGHTFUL THINGS TO SAY ABOUT IT
DECIDE AND DIG
THE BOOK WILL BE SECRETLY BURIED AND YOU WILL BE SENT CRYPTIC CLUES REVEALING ITS LOCATION
CHOOSE AND CREATE
YOU WILL BE SENT A NOTEBOOK, A PEN AND A DICTIONARY SO YOU CAN WRITE YOUR OWN BOOK

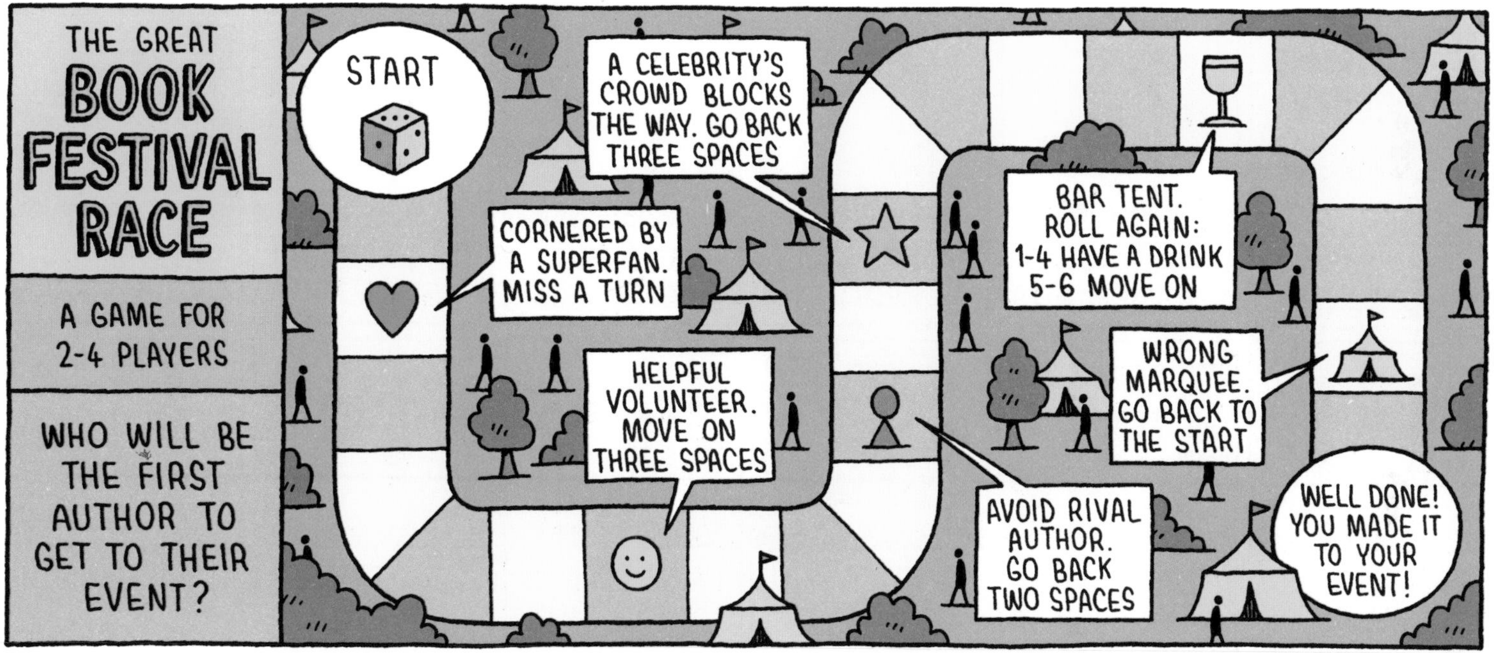
THE GREAT BOOK FESTIVAL RACE
A GAME FOR 2-4 PLAYERS
WHO WILL BE THE FIRST AUTHOR TO GET TO THEIR EVENT?
START
CORNERED BY A SUPERFAN. MISS A TURN
A CELEBRITY'S CROWD BLOCKS THE WAY. GO BACK THREE SPACES
HELPFUL VOLUNTEER. MOVE ON THREE SPACES
BAR TENT. ROLL AGAIN: 1-4 HAVE A DRINK 5-6 MOVE ON
AVOID RIVAL AUTHOR. GO BACK TWO SPACES
WRONG MARQUEE. GO BACK TO THE START
WELL DONE! YOU MADE IT TO YOUR EVENT!

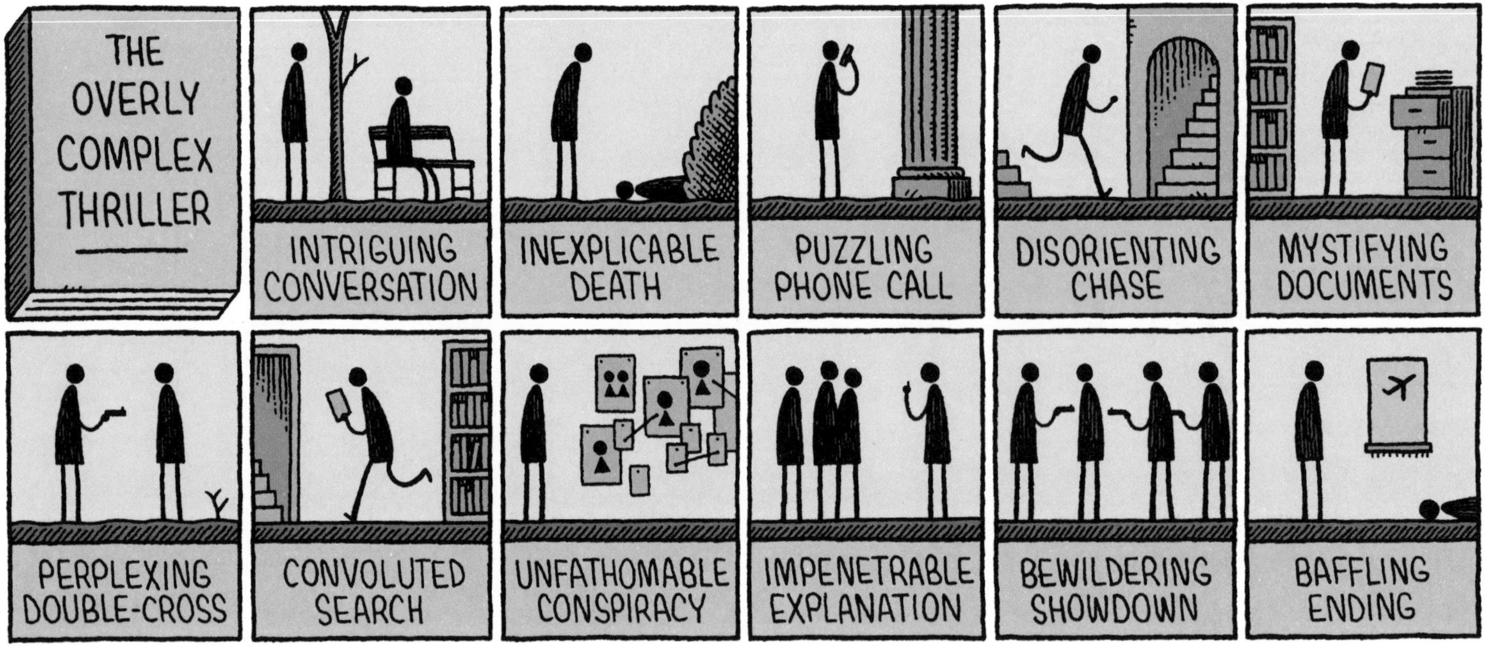
THE OVERLY COMPLEX THRILLER
INTRIGUING CONVERSATION
INEXPLICABLE DEATH
PUZZLING PHONE CALL
DISORIENTING CHASE
MYSTIFYING DOCUMENTS
PERPLEXING DOUBLE-CROSS
CONVOLUTED SEARCH
UNFATHOMABLE CONSPIRACY
IMPENETRABLE EXPLANATION
BEWILDERING SHOWDOWN
BAFFLING ENDING

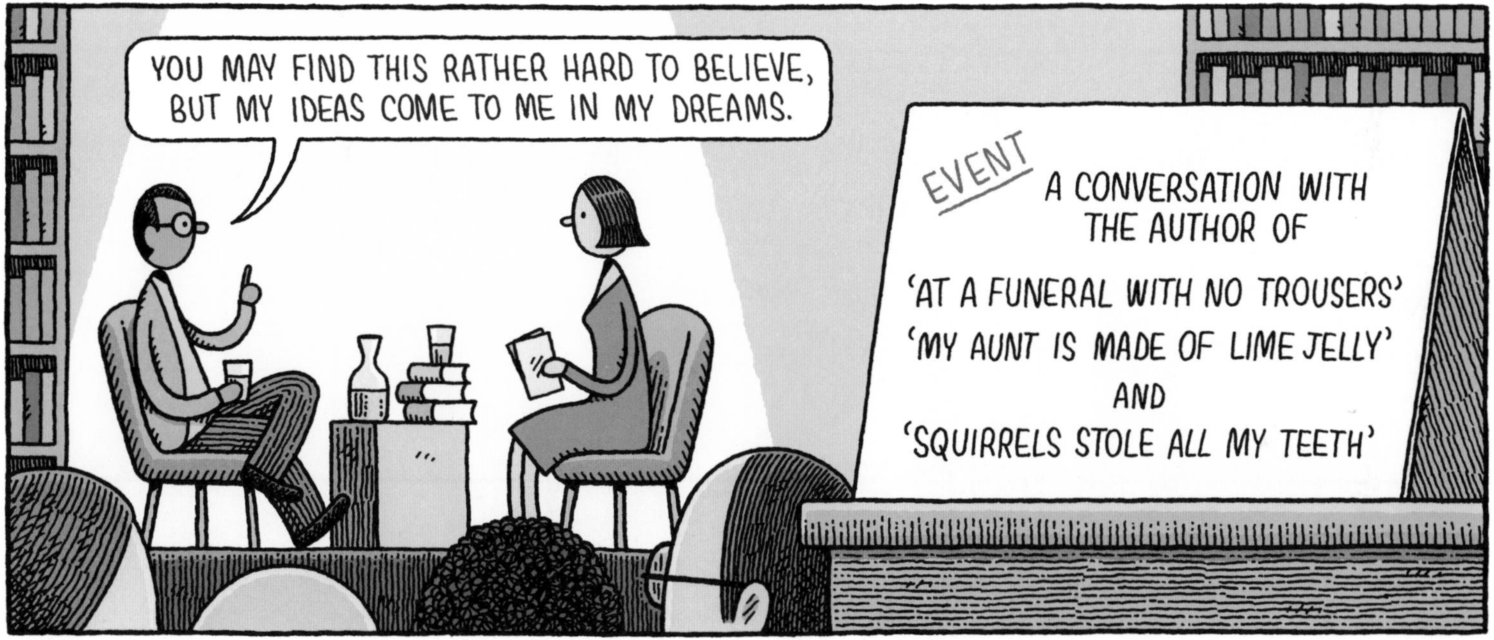
YOU MAY FIND THIS RATHER HARD TO BELIEVE, BUT MY IDEAS COME TO ME IN MY DREAMS.
EVENT
A CONVERSATION WITH THE AUTHOR OF
'AT A FUNERAL WITH NO TROUSERS'
'MY AUNT IS MADE OF LIME JELLY'
AND
'SQUIRRELS STOLE ALL MY TEETH'

VILLAGE MURDER MYSTERIES

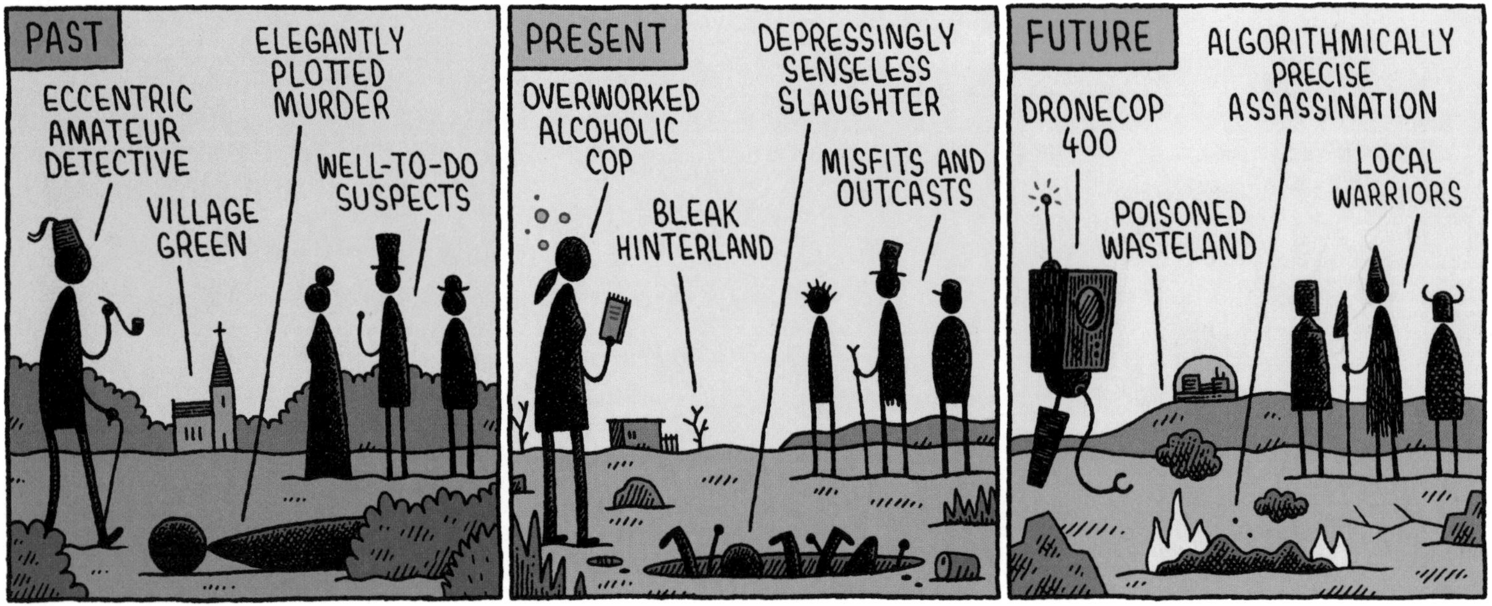

PAST
ECCENTRIC AMATEUR DETECTIVE
VILLAGE GREEN
ELEGANTLY PLOTTED MURDER
WELL-TO-DO SUSPECTS
PRESENT
OVERWORKED ALCOHOLIC COP
BLEAK HINTERLAND
DEPRESSINGLY SENSELESS SLAUGHTER
MISFITS AND OUTCASTS
FUTURE
DRONECOP 400
POISONED WASTELAND
ALGORITHMICALLY PRECISE ASSASSINATION
LOCAL WARRIORS

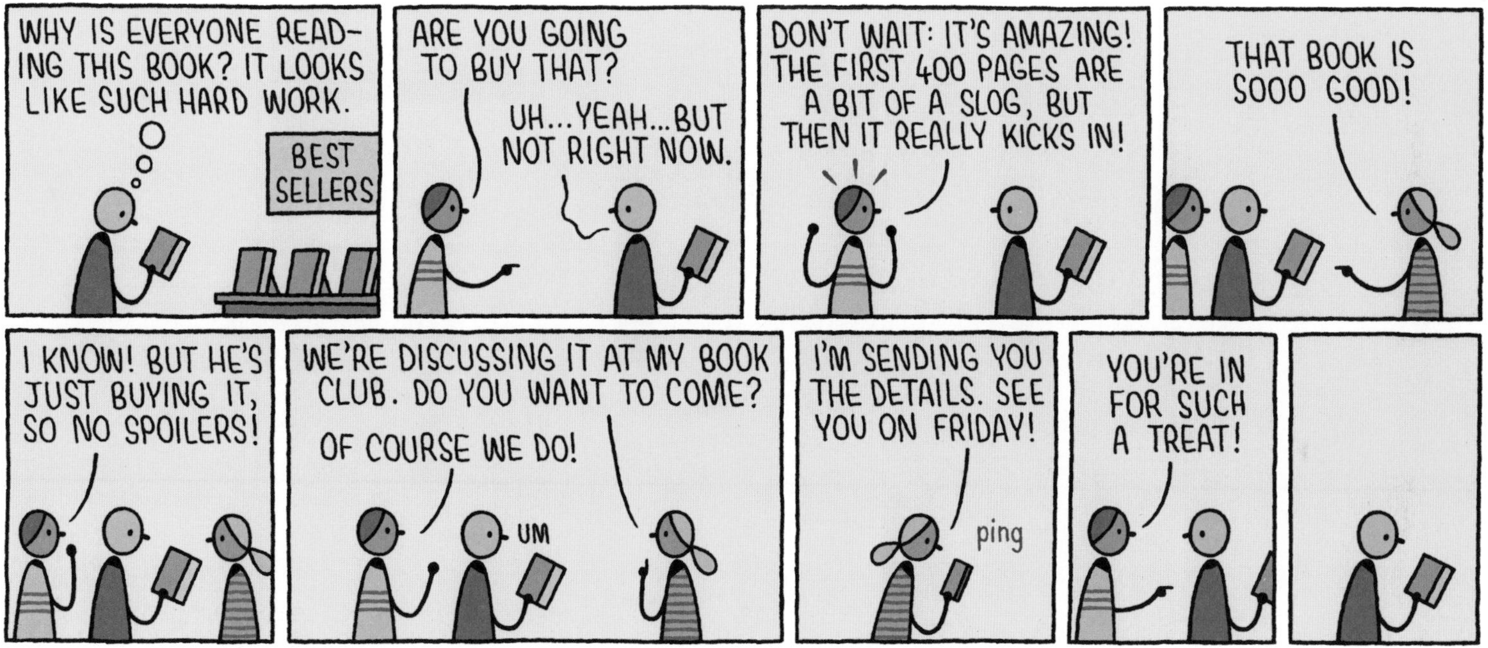
WHY IS EVERYONE READ-ING THIS BOOK? IT LOOKS LIKE SUCH HARD WORK.
BEST SELLERS
ARE YOU GOING TO BUY THAT?
UH... YEAH... BUT NOT RIGHT NOW.
DON'T WAIT: IT'S AMAZING! THE FIRST 400 PAGES ARE A BIT OF A SLOG, BUT THEN IT REALLY KICKS IN!
THAT BOOK IS SOOO GOOD!
I KNOW! BUT HE'S JUST BUYING IT, SO NO SPOILERS!
WE'RE DISCUSSING IT AT MY BOOK CLUB. DO YOU WANT TO COME?
OF COURSE WE DO!
UM
I'M SENDING YOU THE DETAILS. SEE YOU ON FRIDAY!
ping
YOU'RE IN FOR SUCH A TREAT!

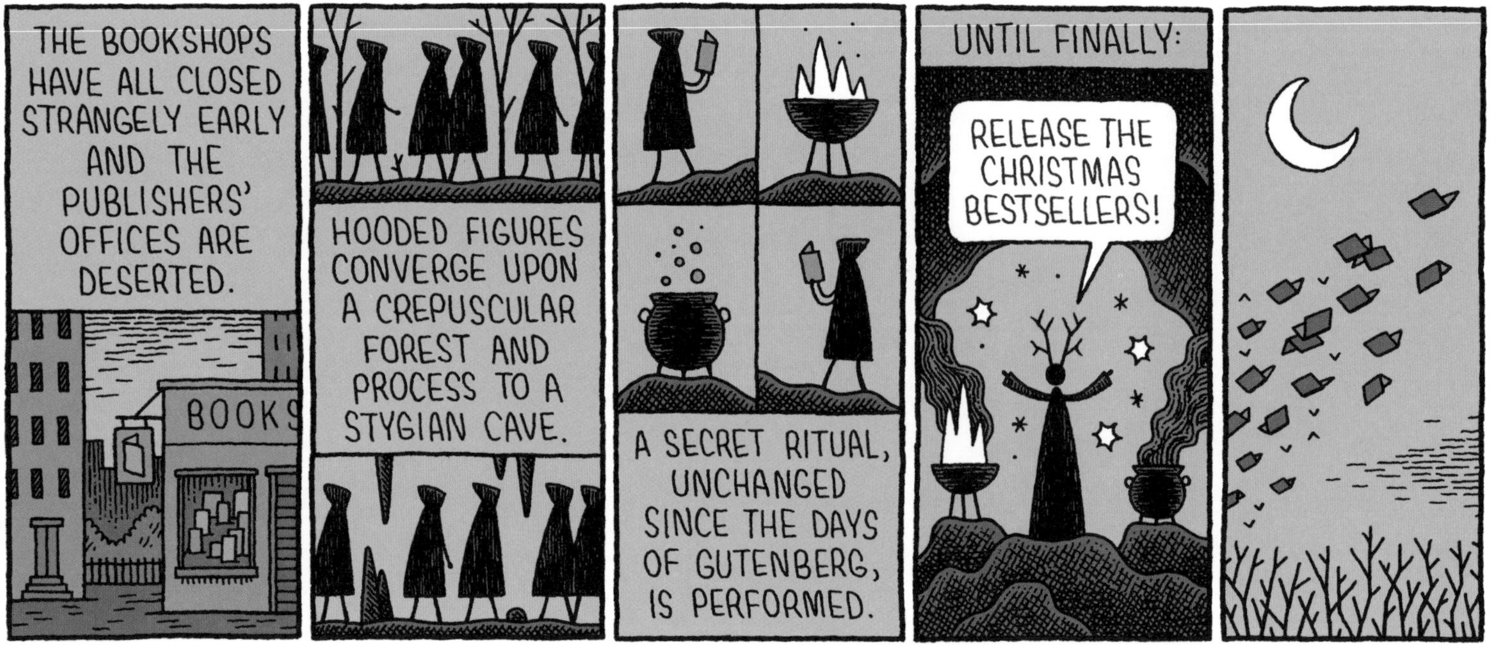
THE BOOKSHOPS HAVE ALL CLOSED STRANGELY EARLY AND THE PUBLISHERS' OFFICES ARE DESERTED.
BOOKS
HOODED FIGURES CONVERGE UPON A CREPUSCULAR FOREST AND PROCESS TO A STYGIAN CAVE.
A SECRET RITUAL, UNCHANGED SINCE THE DAYS OF GUTENBERG, IS PERFORMED.
UNTIL FINALLY:
RELEASE THE CHRISTMAS BESTSELLERS!

VIOLET FELT THAT HER CHRISTMAS SHOPPING WAS GOING RATHER WELL...

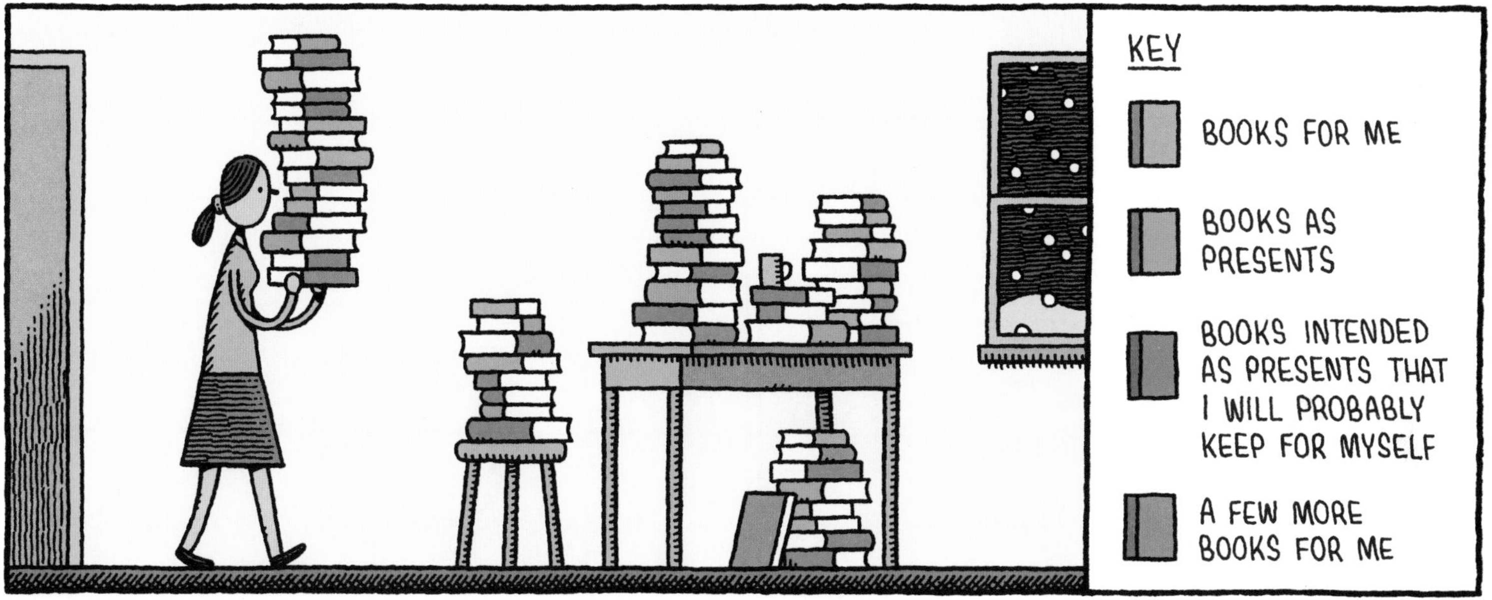
KEY
BOOKS FOR ME
BOOKS AS PRESENTS
BOOKS INTENDED AS PRESENTS THAT I WILL PROBABLY KEEP FOR MYSELF
A FEW MORE BOOKS FOR ME

JAMES JOYCE VISITS HIS PUBLISHER

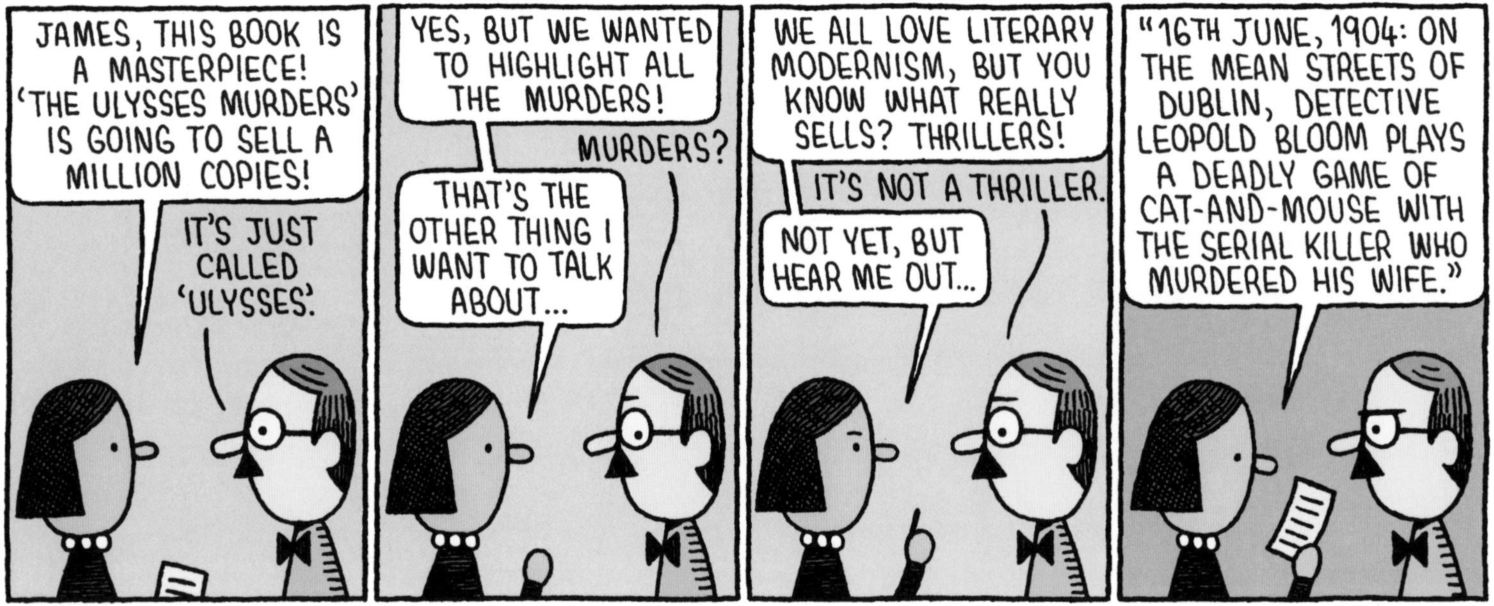

JAMES, THIS BOOK IS A MASTERPIECE! 'THE ULYSSES MURDERS' IS GOING TO SELL A MILLION COPIES!
IT'S JUST CALLED 'ULYSSES'.
YES, BUT WE WANTED TO HIGHLIGHT ALL THE MURDERS!
MURDERS?
THAT'S THE OTHER THING I WANT TO TALK ABOUT...
WE ALL LOVE LITERARY MODERNISM, BUT YOU KNOW WHAT REALLY SELLS? THRILLERS!
IT'S NOT A THRILLER.
NOT YET, BUT HEAR ME OUT...
"16TH JUNE, 1904: ON THE MEAN STREETS OF DUBLIN, DETECTIVE LEOPOLD BLOOM PLAYS A DEADLY GAME OF CAT-AND-MOUSE WITH THE SERIAL KILLER WHO MURDERED HIS WIFE."

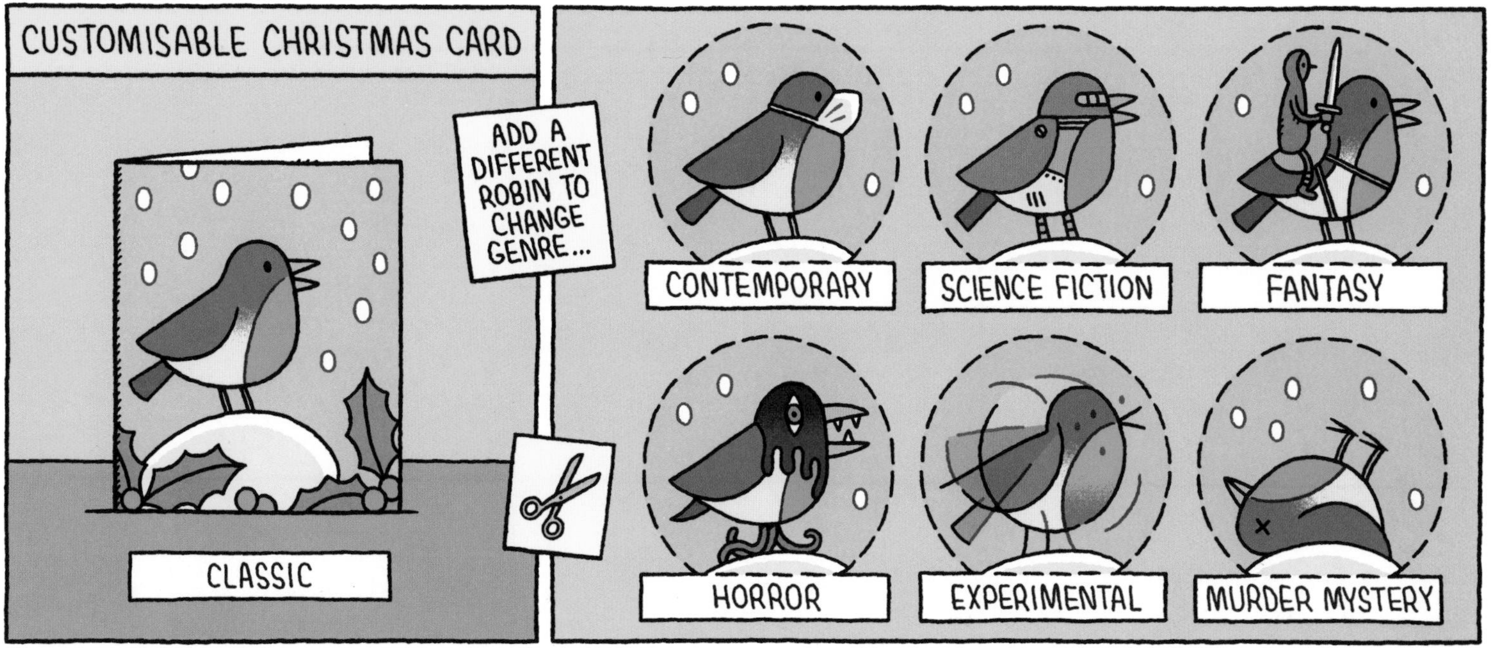
CUSTOMISABLE CHRISTMAS CARD
CLASSIC
ADD A DIFFERENT ROBIN TO CHANGE GENRE...
CONTEMPORARY
SCIENCE FICTION
FANTASY
HORROR
EXPERIMENTAL
MURDER MYSTERY

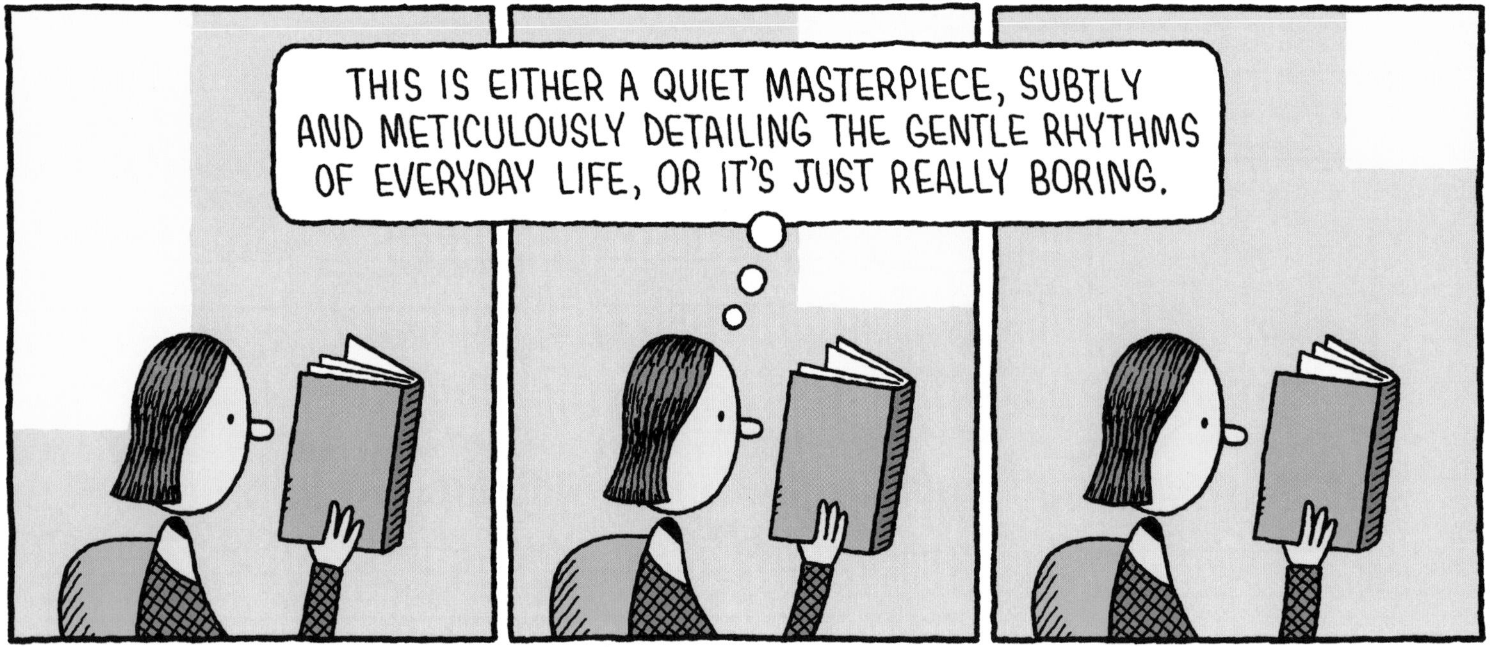
THIS IS EITHER A QUIET MASTERPIECE, SUBTLY AND METICULOUSLY DETAILING THE GENTLE RHYTHMS OF EVERYDAY LIFE, OR IT'S JUST REALLY BORING.

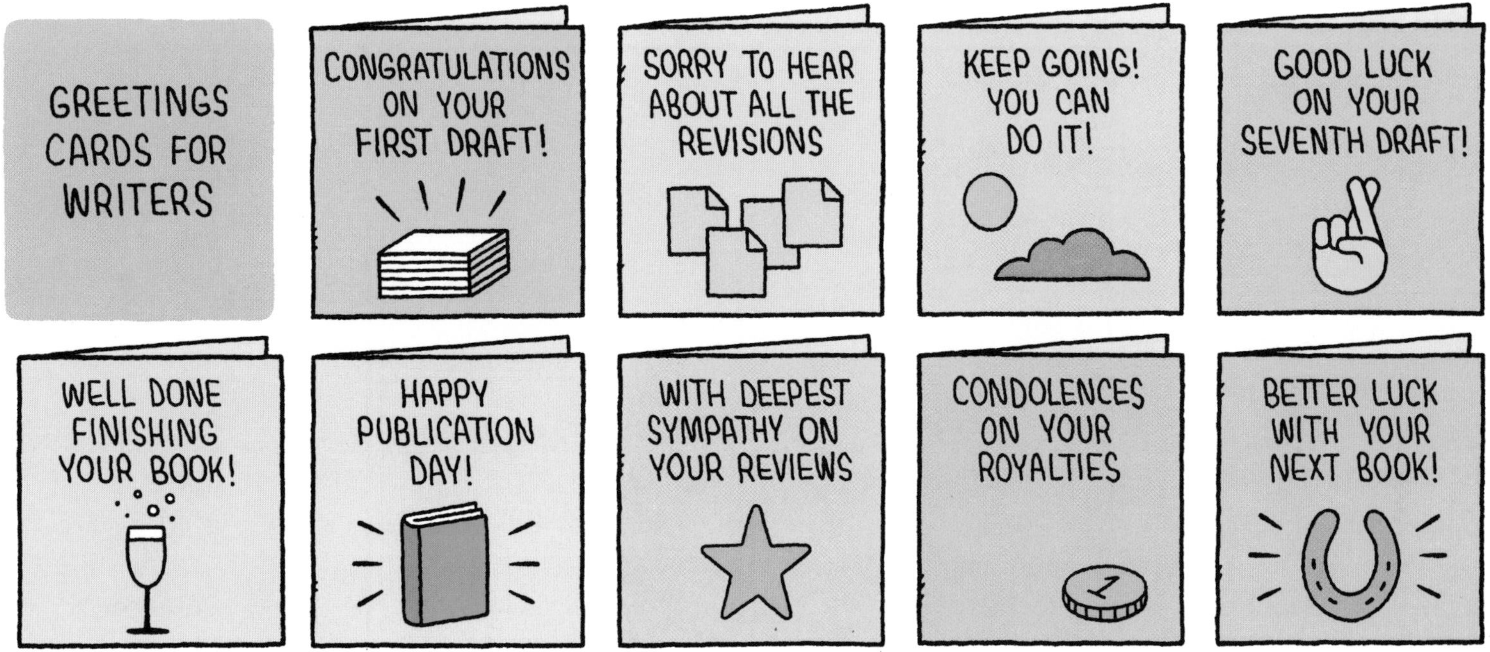

GREETINGS CARDS FOR WRITERS
CONGRATULATIONS ON YOUR FIRST DRAFT!
SORRY TO HEAR ABOUT ALL THE REVISIONS
KEEP GOING! YOU CAN DO IT!
GOOD LUCK ON YOUR SEVENTH DRAFT!
WELL DONE FINISHING YOUR BOOK!
HAPPY PUBLICATION DAY!
WITH DEEPEST SYMPATHY ON YOUR REVIEWS
CONDOLENCES ON YOUR ROYALTIES
BETTER LUCK WITH YOUR NEXT BOOK!

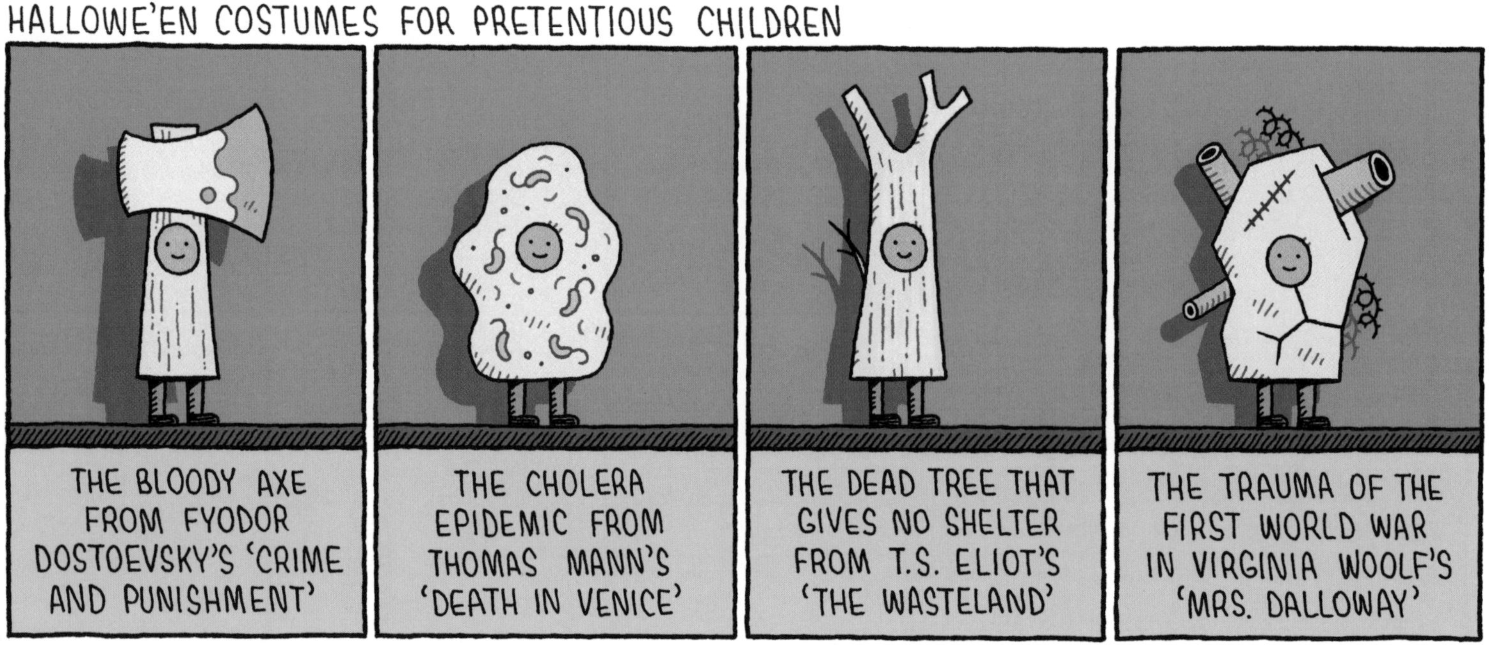
HALLOWE'EN COSTUMES FOR PRETENTIOUS CHILDREN
THE BLOODY AXE FROM FYODOR DOSTOEVSKY'S 'CRIME AND PUNISHMENT'
THE CHOLERA EPIDEMIC FROM THOMAS MANN'S 'DEATH IN VENICE'
THE DEAD TREE THAT GIVES NO SHELTER FROM T.S. ELIOT'S 'THE WASTELAND'
THE TRAUMA OF THE FIRST WORLD WAR IN VIRGINIA WOOLF'S 'MRS. DALLOWAY'

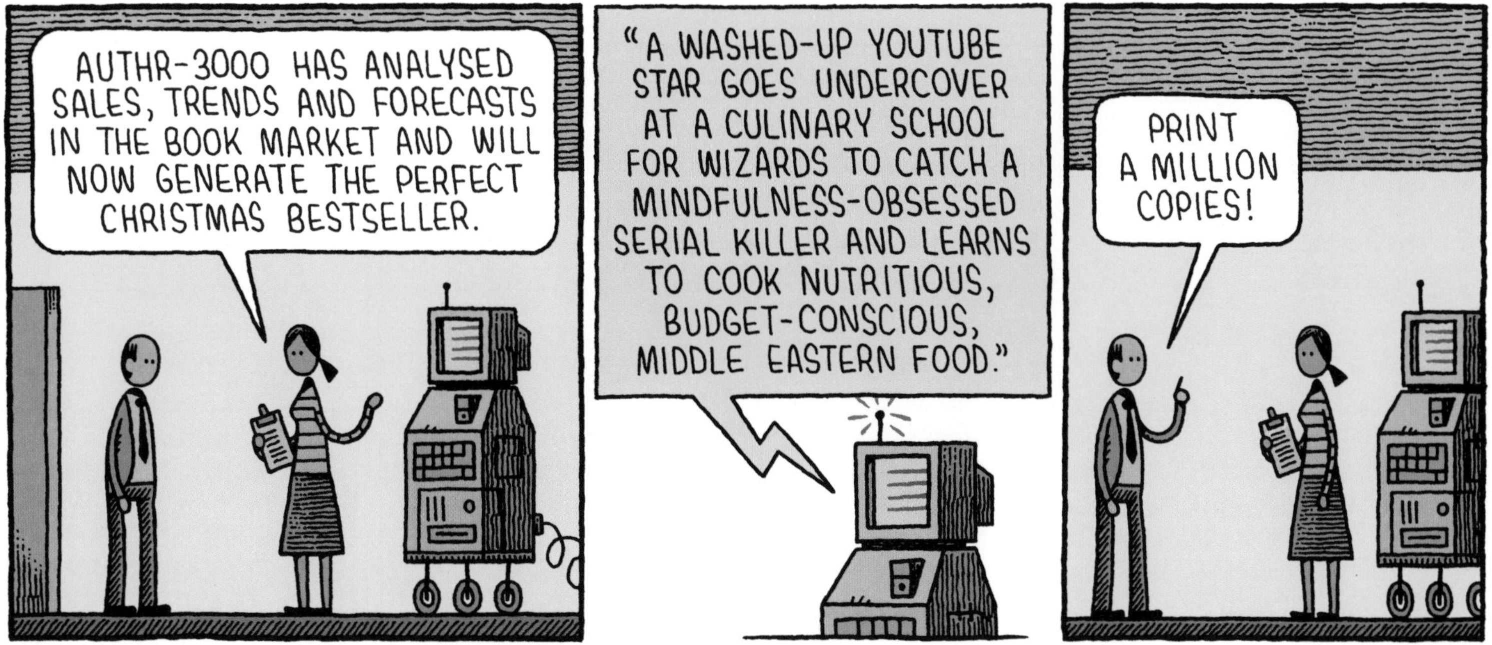
AUTHR-3000 HAS ANALYSED SALES, TRENDS AND FORECASTS IN THE BOOK MARKET AND WILL NOW GENERATE THE PERFECT CHRISTMAS BESTSELLER.
"A WASHED-UP YOUTUBE STAR GOES UNDERCOVER AT A CULINARY SCHOOL FOR WIZARDS TO CATCH A MINDFULNESS-OBSESSED SERIAL KILLER AND LEARNS TO COOK NUTRITIOUS, BUDGET-CONSCIOUS, MIDDLE EASTERN FOOD."
PRINT A MILLION COPIES!

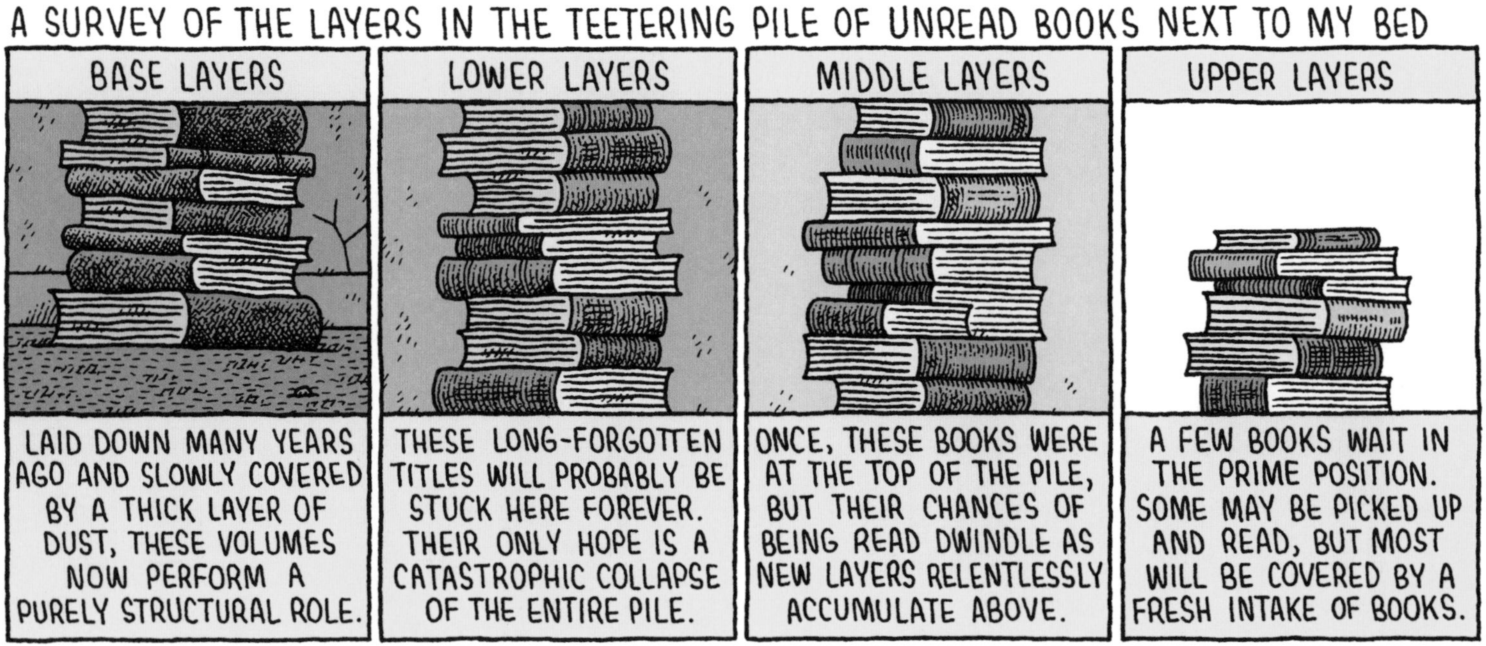
A SURVEY OF THE LAYERS IN THE TEETERING PILE OF UNREAD BOOKS NEXT TO MY BED
BASE LAYERS
LAID DOWN MANY YEARS AGO AND SLOWLY COVERED BY A THICK LAYER OF DUST, THESE VOLUMES NOW PERFORM A PURELY STRUCTURAL ROLE.
LOWER LAYERS
THESE LONG-FORGOTTEN TITLES WILL PROBABLY BE STUCK HERE FOREVER. THEIR ONLY HOPE IS A CATASTROPHIC COLLAPSE OF THE ENTIRE PILE.
MIDDLE LAYERS
ONCE, THESE BOOKS WERE AT THE TOP OF THE PILE, BUT THEIR CHANCES OF BEING READ DWINDLE AS NEW LAYERS RELENTLESSLY ACCUMULATE ABOVE.
UPPER LAYERS
A FEW BOOKS WAIT IN THE PRIME POSITION. SOME MAY BE PICKED UP AND READ, BUT MOST WILL BE COVERED BY A FRESH INTAKE OF BOOKS.

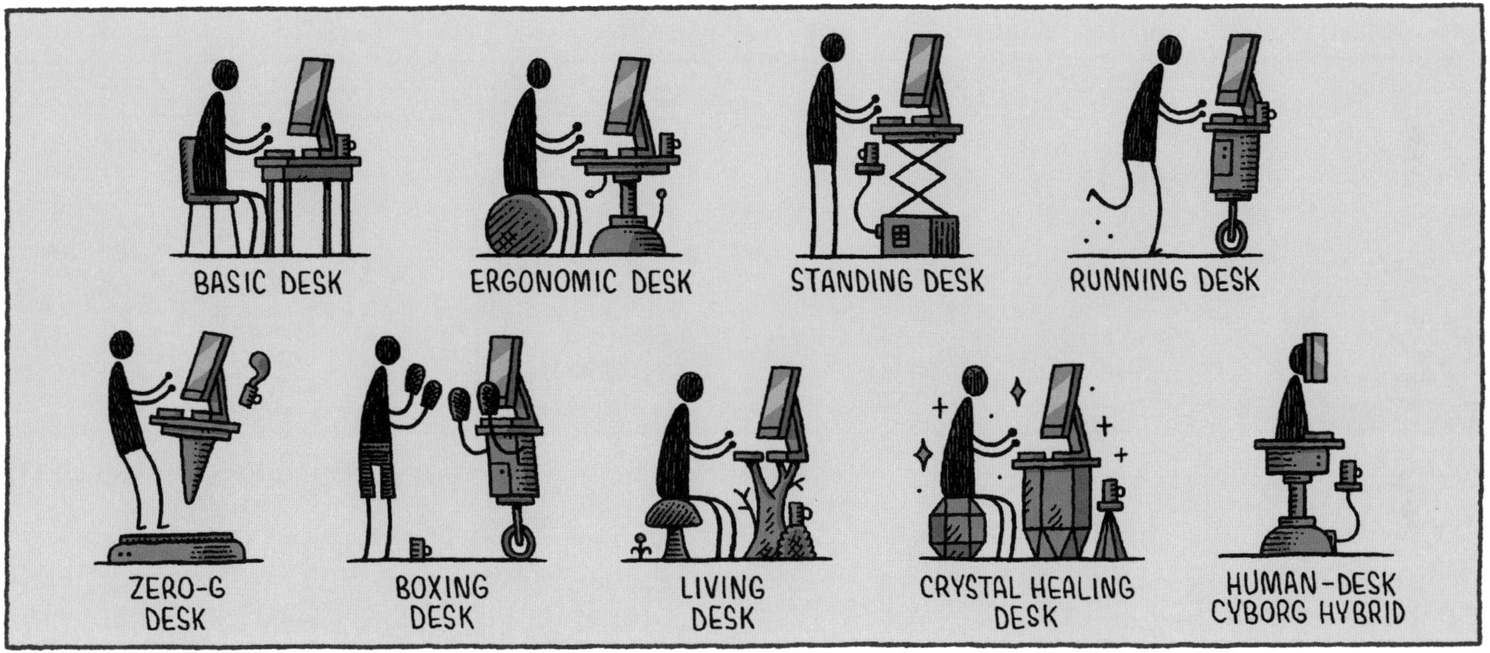
BASIC DESK
ERGONOMIC DESK
STANDING DESK
RUNNING DESK
ZERO-G DESK
BOXING DESK
LIVING DESK
CRYSTAL HEALING DESK
HUMAN-DESK CYBORG HYBRID

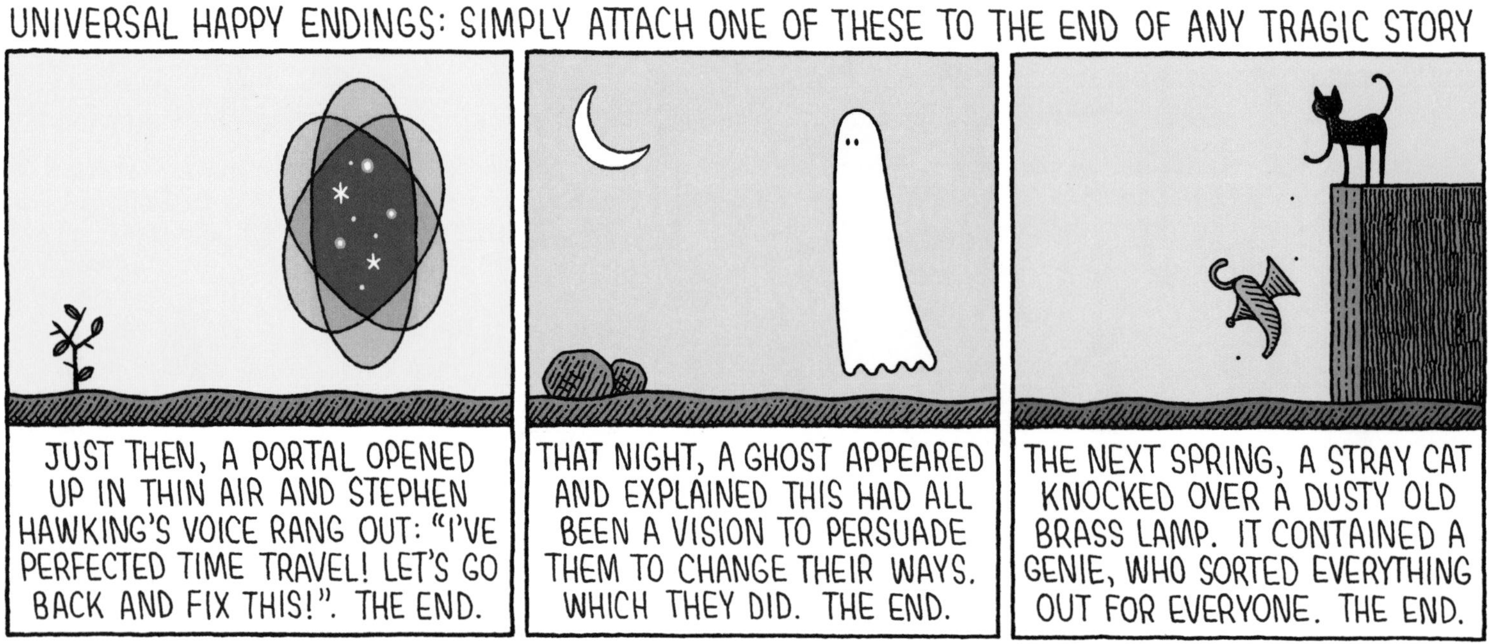
UNIVERSAL HAPPY ENDINGS: SIMPLY ATTACH ONE OF THESE TO THE END OF ANY TRAGIC STORY
JUST THEN, A PORTAL OPENED UP IN THIN AIR AND STEPHEN HAWKING'S VOICE RANG OUT: "I'VE PERFECTED TIME TRAVEL! LET'S GO BACK AND FIX THIS!". THE END.
THAT NIGHT, A GHOST APPEARED AND EXPLAINED THIS HAD ALL BEEN A VISION TO PERSUADE THEM TO CHANGE THEIR WAYS. WHICH THEY DID. THE END.
THE NEXT SPRING, A STRAY CAT KNOCKED OVER A DUSTY OLD BRASS LAMP. IT CONTAINED A GENIE, WHO SORTED EVERYTHING OUT FOR EVERYONE. THE END.

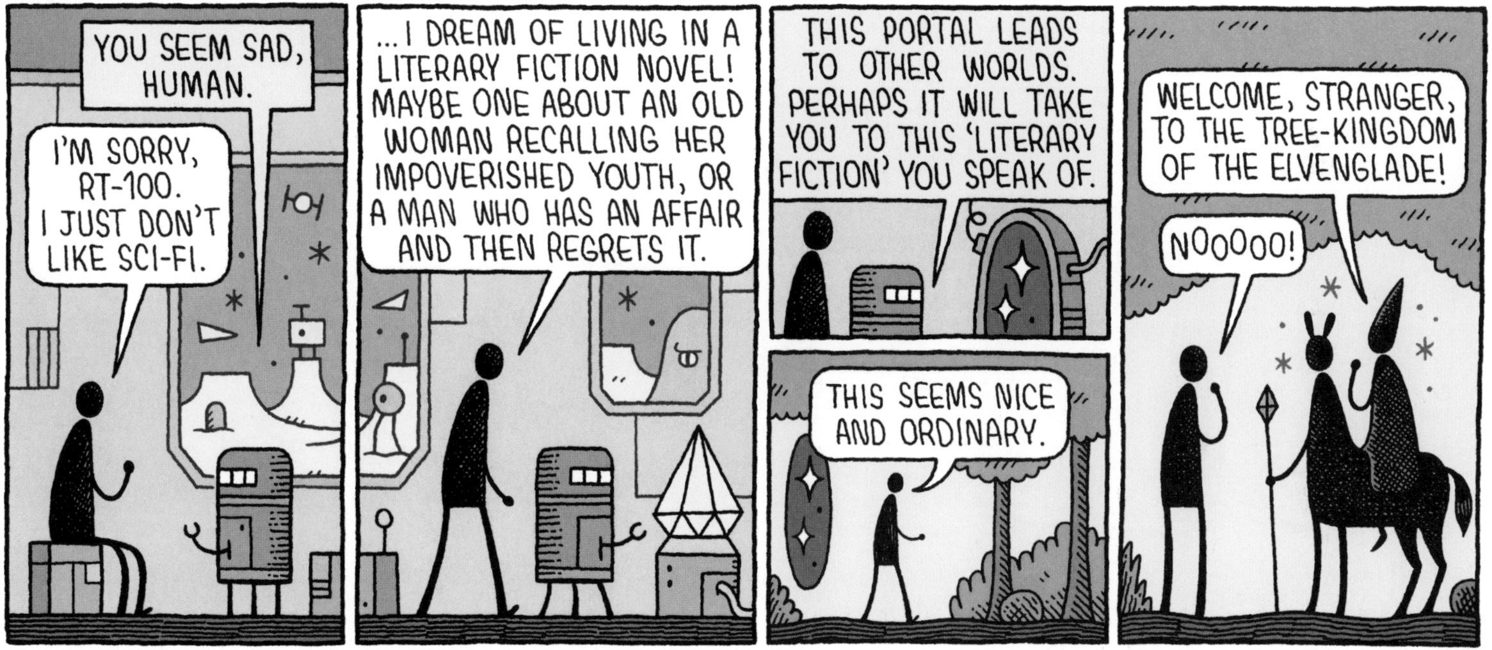
YOU SEEM SAD, HUMAN.
I'M SORRY, RT-100. I JUST DON'T LIKE SCI-FI.
...I DREAM OF LIVING IN A LITERARY FICTION NOVEL! MAYBE ONE ABOUT AN OLD WOMAN RECALLING HER IMPOVERISHED YOUTH, OR A MAN WHO HAS AN AFFAIR AND THEN REGRETS IT.
THIS PORTAL LEADS TO OTHER WORLDS. PERHAPS IT WILL TAKE YOU TO THIS 'LITERARY FICTION' YOU SPEAK OF.
THIS SEEMS NICE AND ORDINARY.
WELCOME, STRANGER, TO THE TREE-KINGDOM OF THE ELVENGLADE!
NOOOOO!

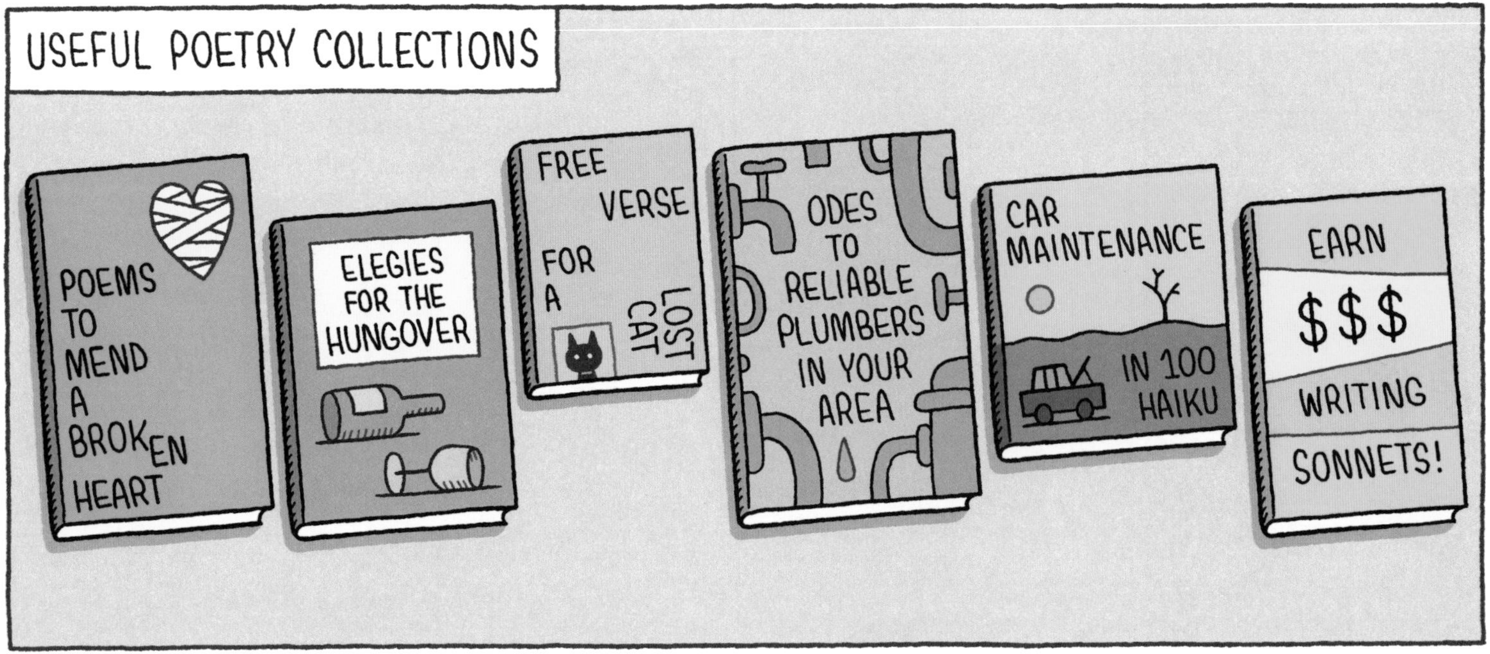

USEFUL POETRY COLLECTIONS
POEMS TO MEND A BROKEN HEART
ELEGIES FOR THE HUNGOVER
FREE VERSE FOR A LOST CAT
ODES TO RELIABLE PLUMBERS IN YOUR AREA
CAR MAINTENANCE IN 100 HAIKU
EARN $$$ WRITING SONNETS!

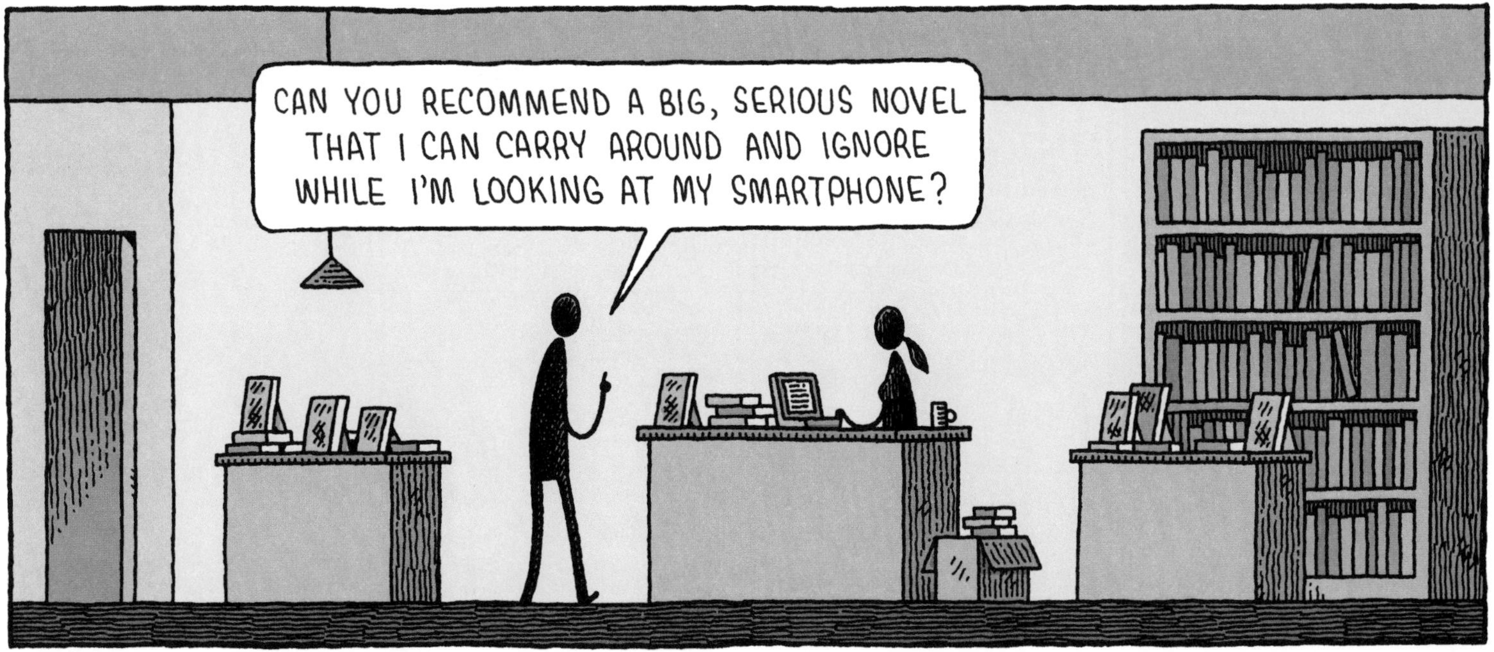
CAN YOU RECOMMEND A BIG, SERIOUS NOVEL THAT I CAN CARRY AROUND AND IGNORE WHILE I'M LOOKING AT MY SMARTPHONE?

LIFE FOR THE SCIENCE-FICTION WRITER

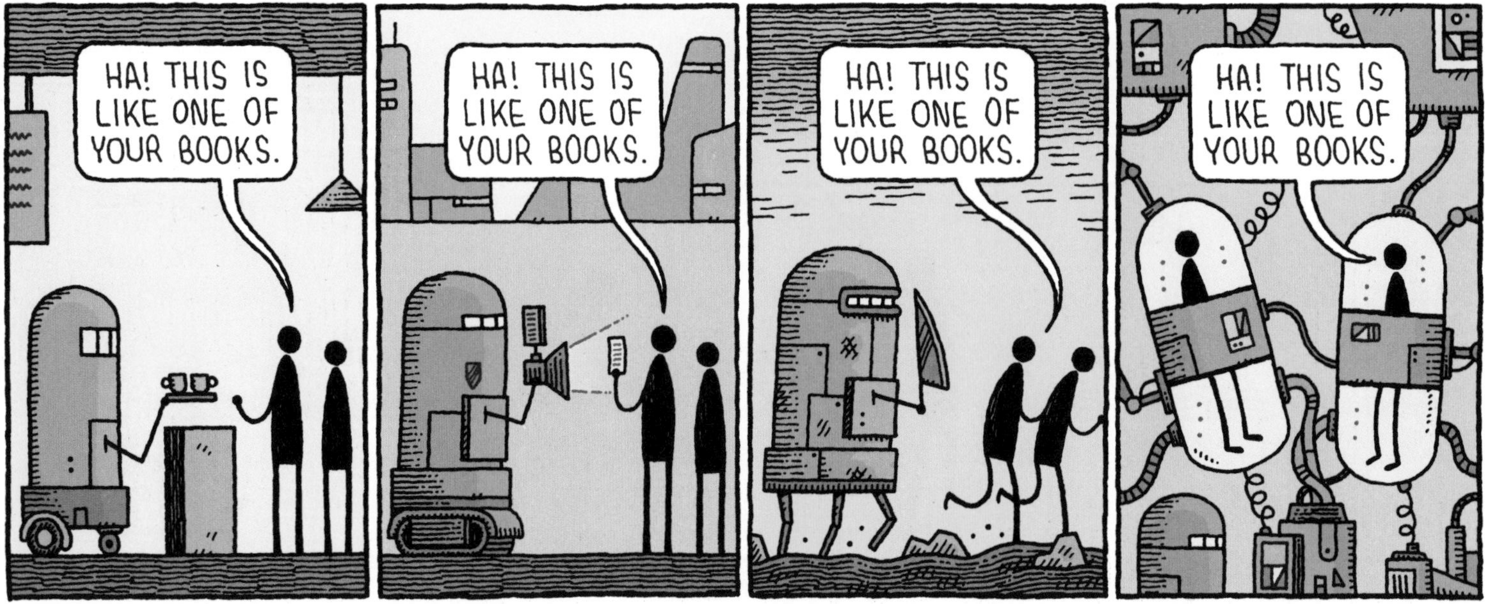
HA! THIS IS LIKE ONE OF YOUR BOOKS.
HA! THIS IS LIKE ONE OF YOUR BOOKS.
HA! THIS IS LIKE ONE OF YOUR BOOKS.
HA! THIS IS LIKE ONE OF YOUR BOOKS.

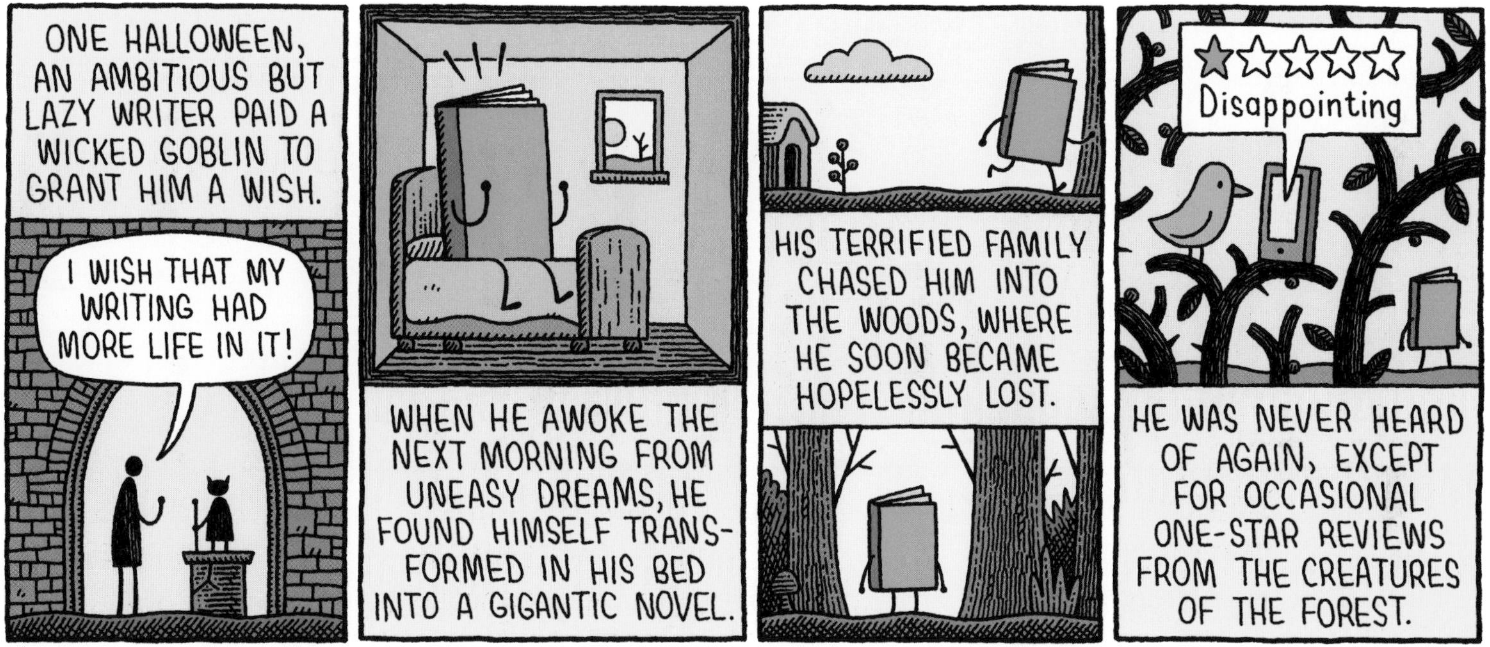
ONE HALLOWEEN, AN AMBITIOUS BUT LAZY WRITER PAID A WICKED GOBLIN TO GRANT HIM A WISH.
I WISH THAT MY WRITING HAD MORE LIFE IN IT!
WHEN HE AWOKE THE NEXT MORNING FROM UNEASY DREAMS, HE FOUND HIMSELF TRANS-FORMED IN HIS BED INTO A GIGANTIC NOVEL.
HIS TERRIFIED FAMILY CHASED HIM INTO THE WOODS, WHERE HE SOON BECAME HOPELESSLY LOST.
Disappointing
HE WAS NEVER HEARD OF AGAIN, EXCEPT FOR OCCASIONAL ONE-STAR REVIEWS FROM THE CREATURES OF THE FOREST.

YOU ARE CORDIALLY INVITED TO THE SOCIETY OF LITERARY FEUDS SUMMER PARTY

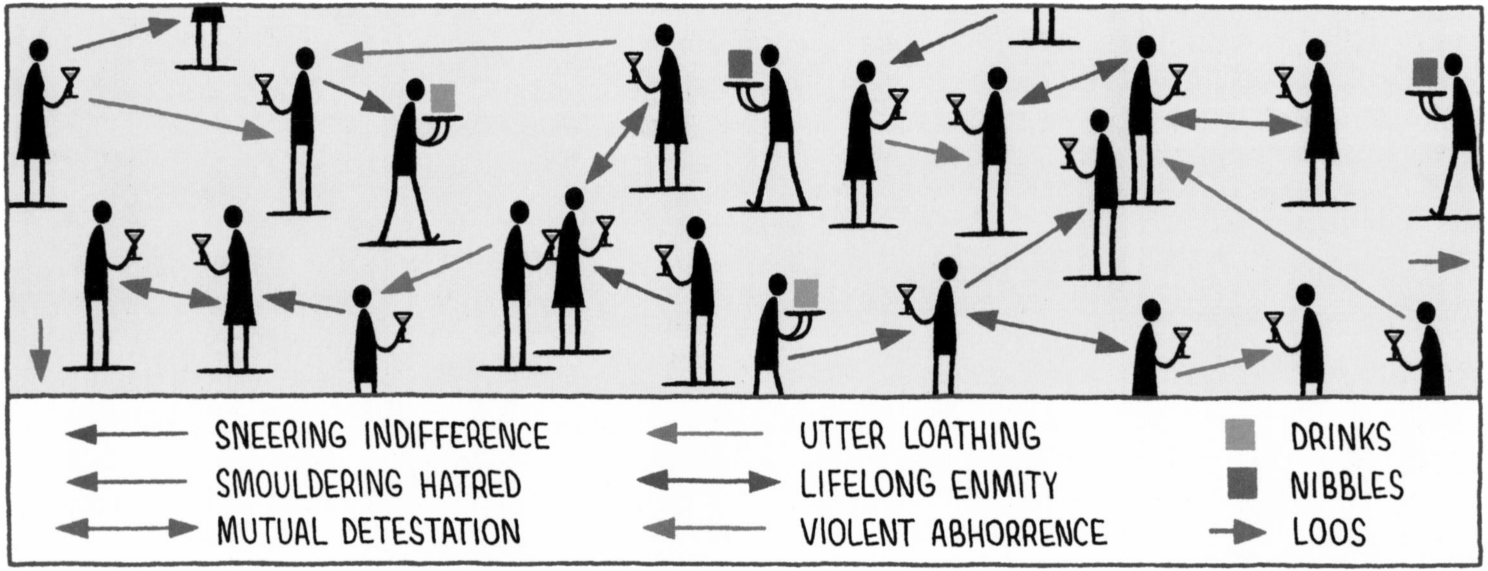
SNEERING INDIFFERENCE
SMOULDERING HATRED
MUTUAL DETESTATION
UTTER LOATHING
LIFELONG ENMITY
VIOLENT ABHORRENCE
DRINKS
NIBBLES
LOOS

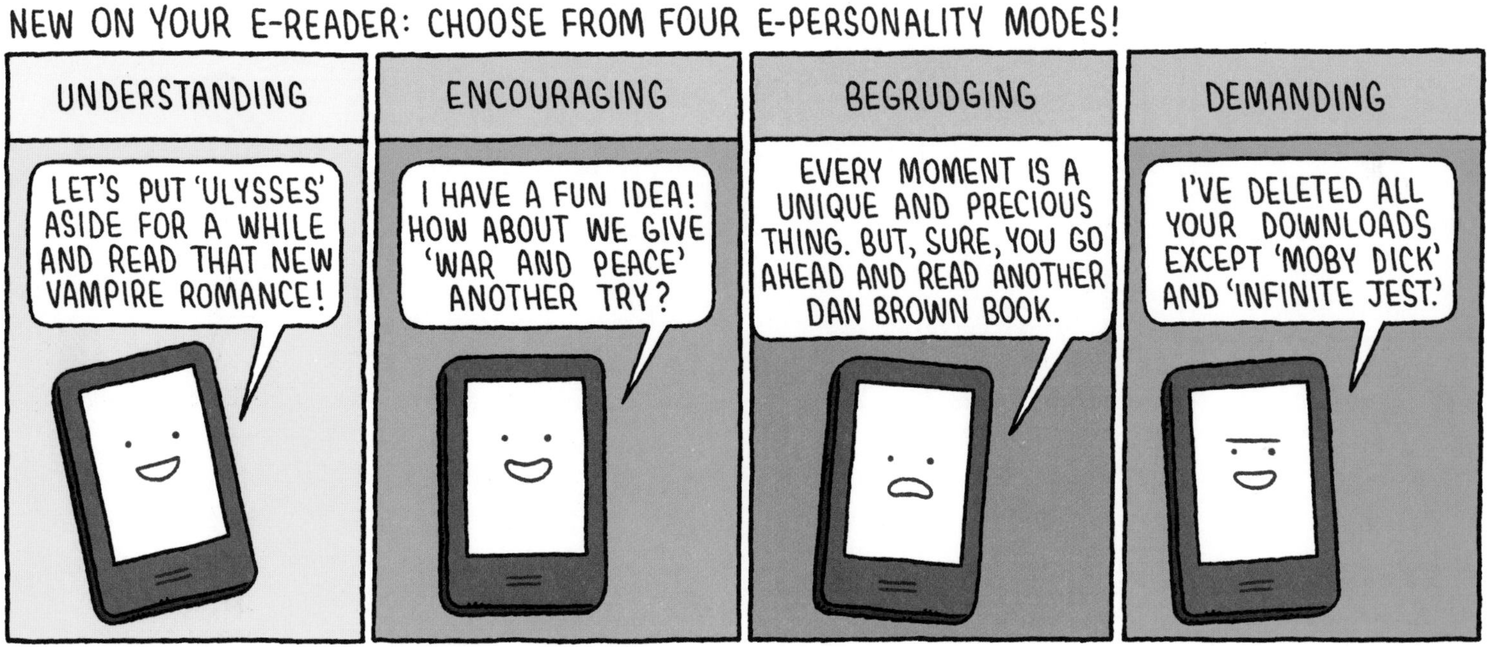
NEW ON YOUR E-READER: CHOOSE FROM FOUR E-PERSONALITY MODES!
UNDERSTANDING
LET'S PUT 'ULYSSES' ASIDE FOR A WHILE AND READ THAT NEW VAMPIRE ROMANCE!
ENCOURAGING
I HAVE A FUN IDEA! HOW ABOUT WE GIVE 'WAR AND PEACE' ANOTHER TRY?
BEGRUDGING
EVERY MOMENT IS A UNIQUE AND PRECIOUS THING. BUT, SURE, YOU GO AHEAD AND READ ANOTHER DAN BROWN BOOK.
DEMANDING
I'VE DELETED ALL YOUR DOWNLOADS EXCEPT 'MOBY DICK' AND 'INFINITE JEST.'

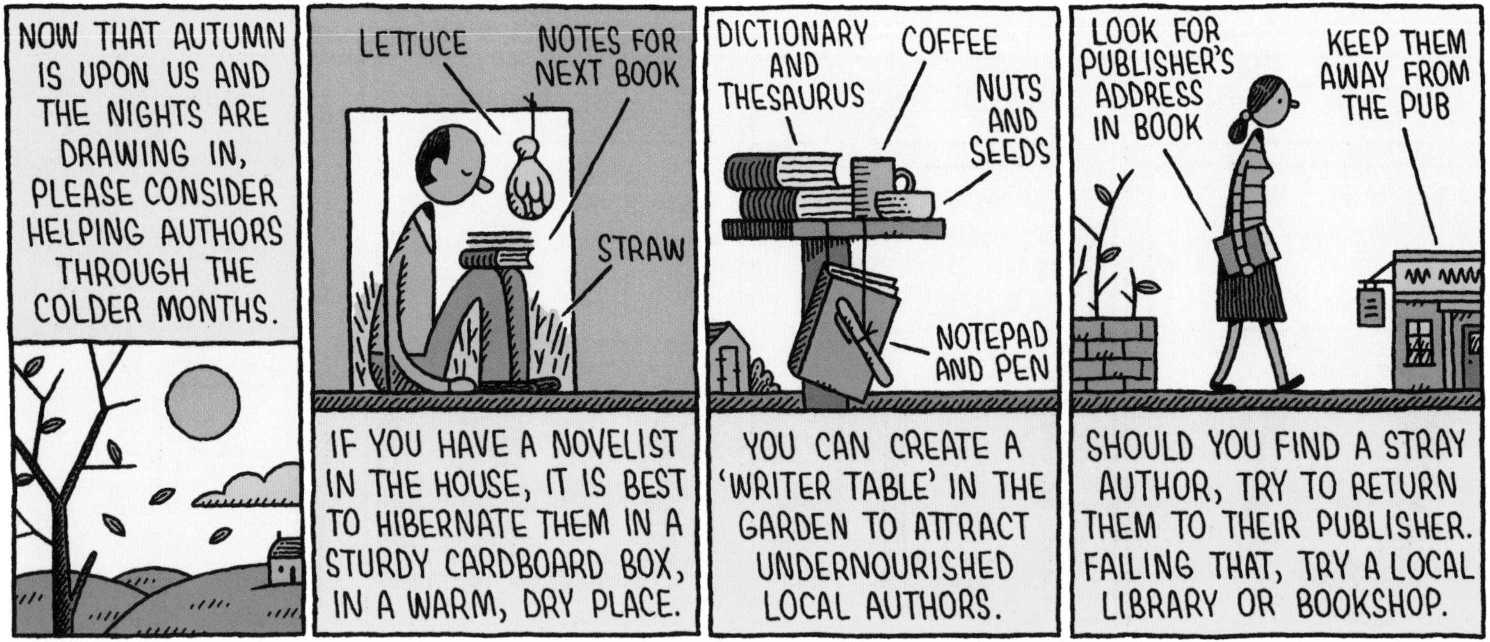
NOW THAT AUTUMN IS UPON US AND THE NIGHTS ARE DRAWING IN, PLEASE CONSIDER HELPING AUTHORS THROUGH THE COLDER MONTHS.
LETTUCE
NOTES FOR NEXT BOOK
STRAW
IF YOU HAVE A NOVELIST IN THE HOUSE, IT IS BEST TO HIBERNATE THEM IN A STURDY CARDBOARD BOX, IN A WARM, DRY PLACE.
DICTIONARY AND THESAURUS
COFFEE
NUTS AND SEEDS
NOTEPAD AND PEN
YOU CAN CREATE A 'WRITER TABLE' IN THE GARDEN TO ATTRACT UNDERNOURISHED LOCAL AUTHORS.
LOOK FOR PUBLISHER'S ADDRESS IN BOOK
KEEP THEM AWAY FROM THE PUB
SHOULD YOU FIND A STRAY AUTHOR, TRY TO RETURN THEM TO THEIR PUBLISHER. FAILING THAT, TRY A LOCAL LIBRARY OR BOOKSHOP.

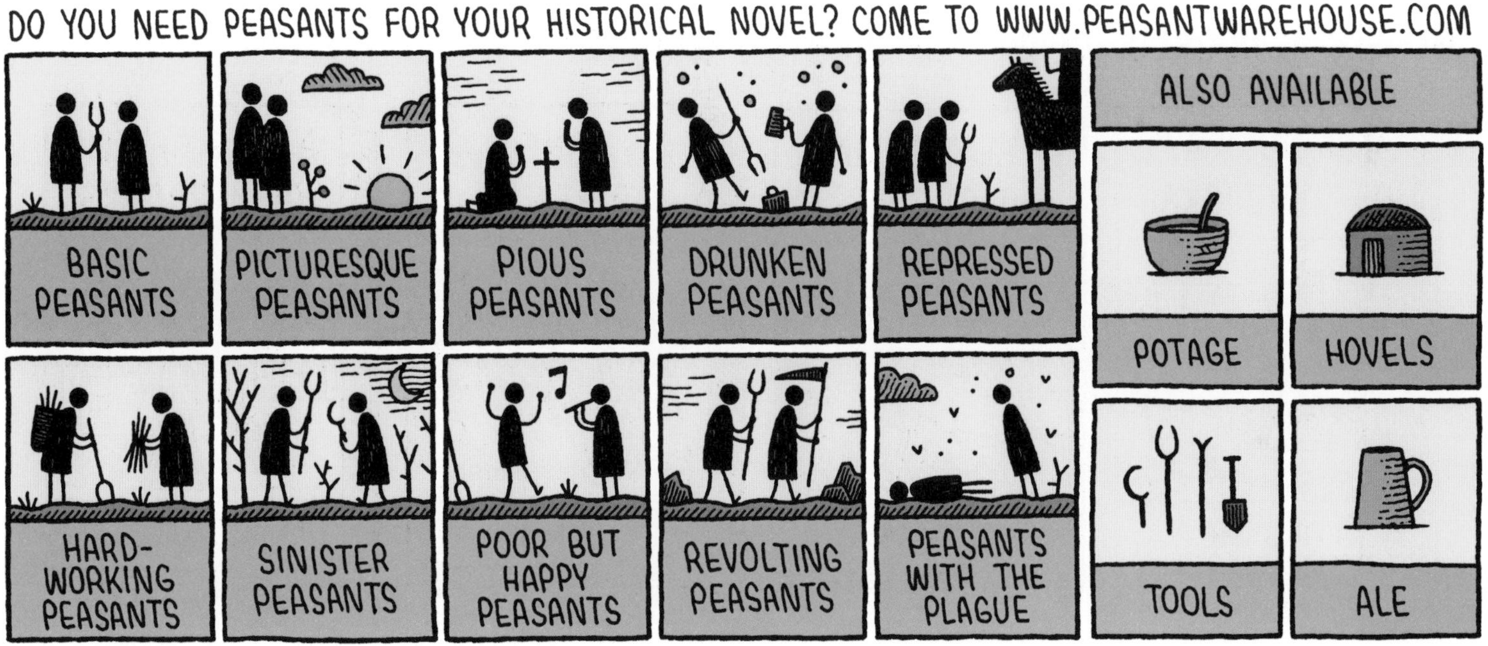
DO YOU NEED PEASANTS FOR YOUR HISTORICAL NOVEL? COME TO WWW.PEASANTWAREHOUSE.COM
BASIC PEASANTS
PICTURESQUE PEASANTS
PIOUS PEASANTS
DRUNKEN PEASANTS
REPRESSED PEASANTS
ALSO AVAILABLE
POTAGE
HOVELS
HARD-WORKING PEASANTS
SINISTER PEASANTS
POOR BUT HAPPY PEASANTS
REVOLTING PEASANTS
PEASANTS WITH THE PLAGUE
TOOLS
ALE

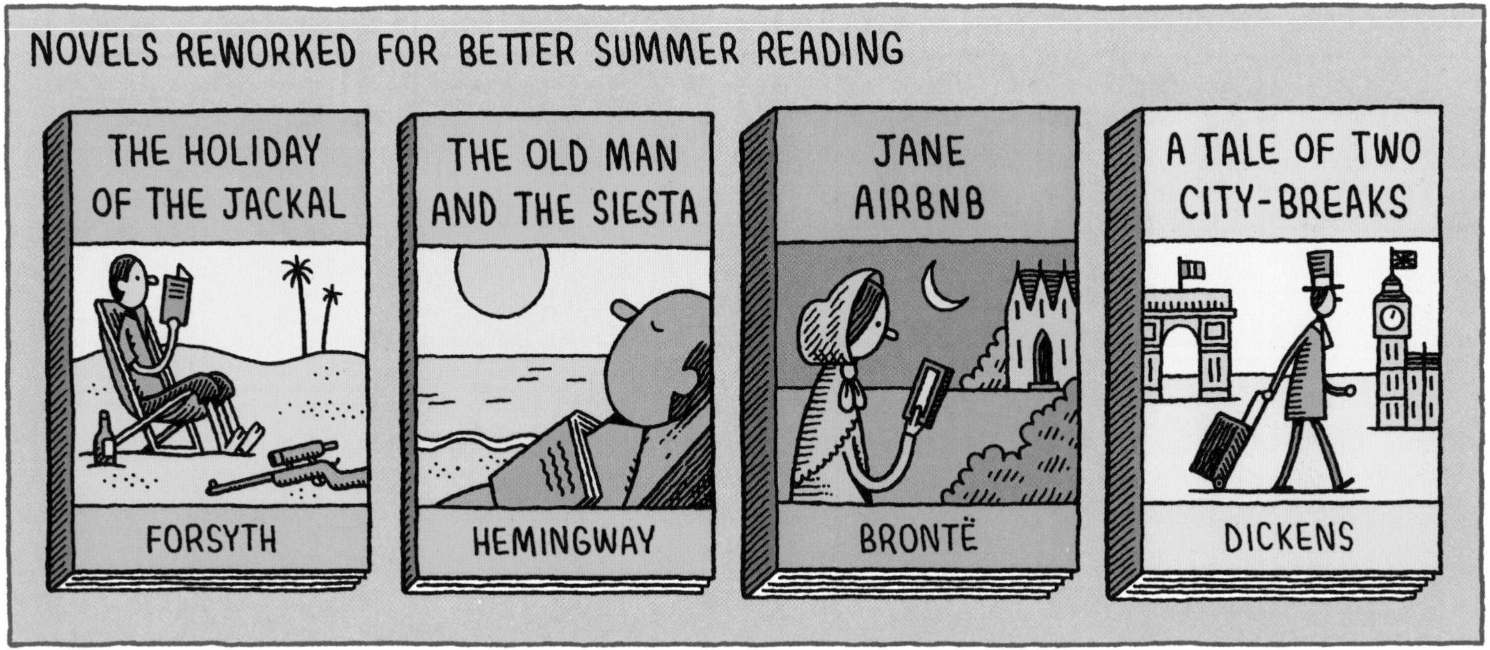

NOVELS REWORKED FOR BETTER SUMMER READING
THE HOLIDAY OF THE JACKAL
FORSYTH
THE OLD MAN AND THE SIESTA
HEMINGWAY
JANE AIRBNB
BRONTË
A TALE OF TWO CITY-BREAKS
DICKENS

MARKETING PLAN FOR THE MEMOIR:

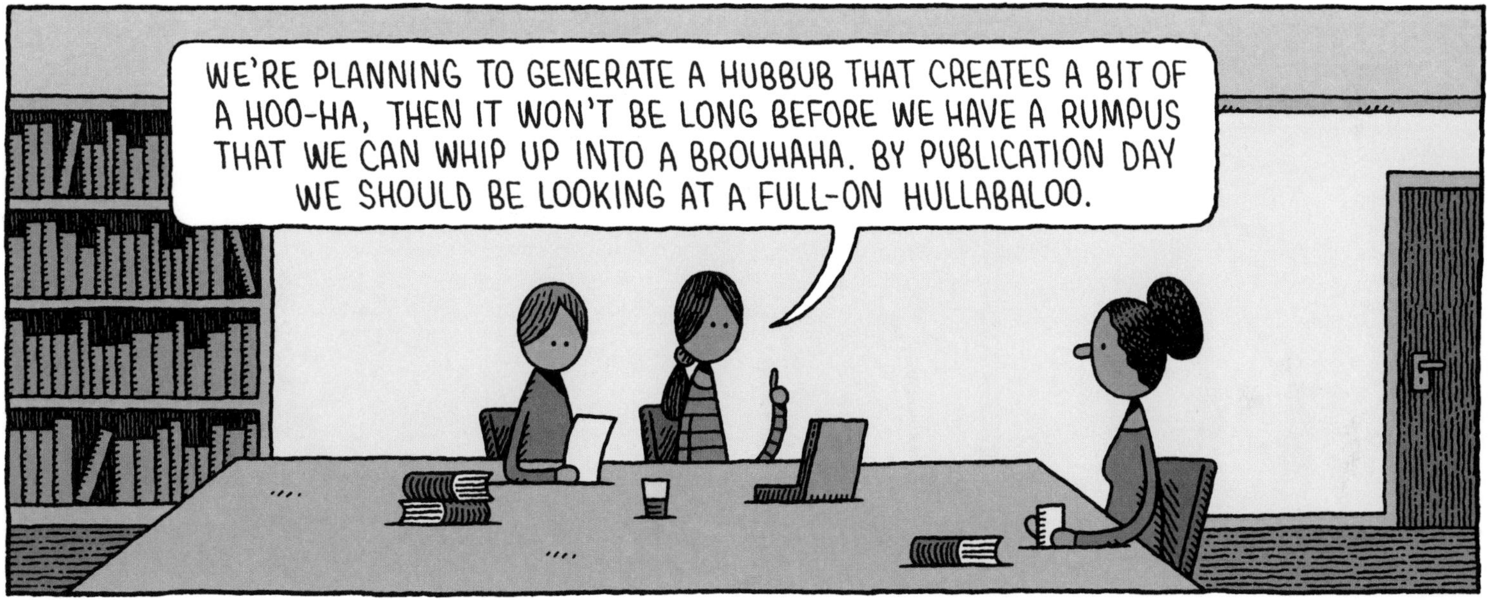
WE'RE PLANNING TO GENERATE A HUBBUB THAT CREATES A BIT OF A HOO-HA, THEN IT WON'T BE LONG BEFORE WE HAVE A RUMPUS THAT WE CAN WHIP UP INTO A BROUHAHA. BY PUBLICATION DAY WE SHOULD BE LOOKING AT A FULL-ON HULLABALOO.

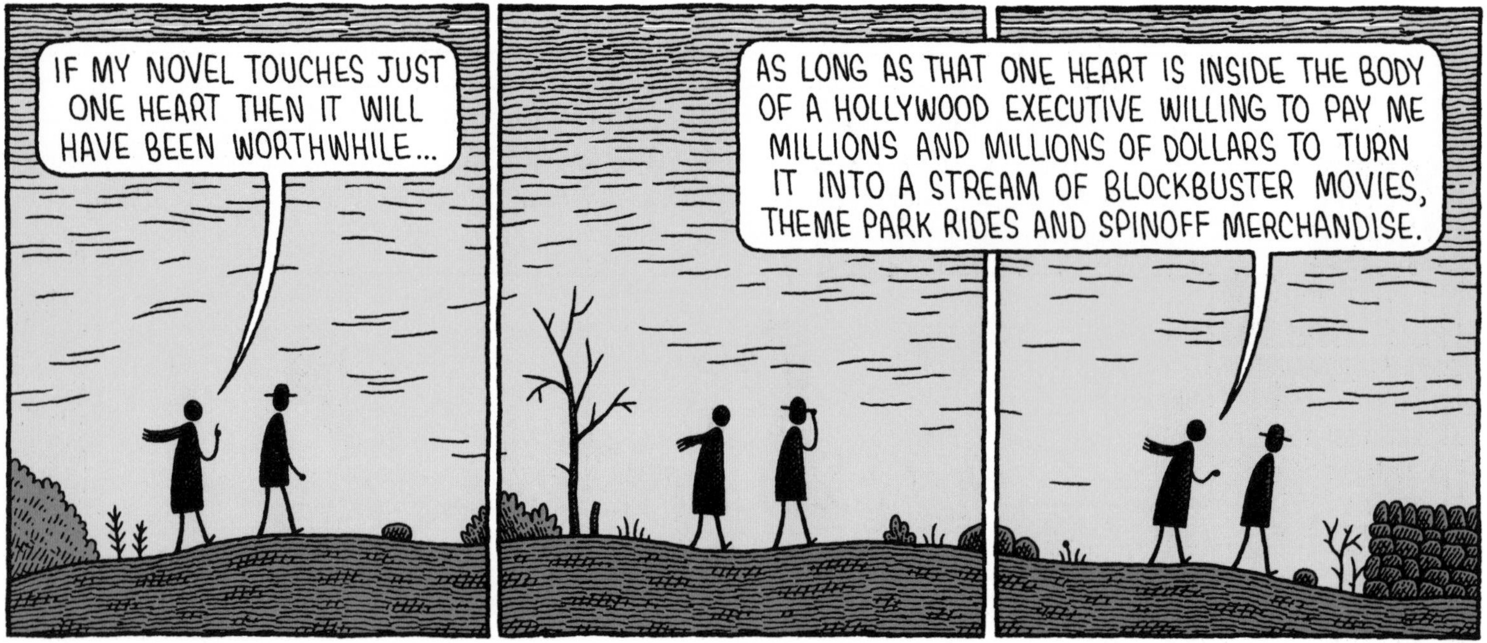
IF MY NOVEL TOUCHES JUST ONE HEART THEN IT WILL HAVE BEEN WORTHWHILE...
AS LONG AS THAT ONE HEART IS INSIDE THE BODY OF A HOLLYWOOD EXECUTIVE WILLING TO PAY ME MILLIONS AND MILLIONS OF DOLLARS TO TURN IT INTO A STREAM OF BLOCKBUSTER MOVIES, THEME PARK RIDES AND SPINOFF MERCHANDISE.

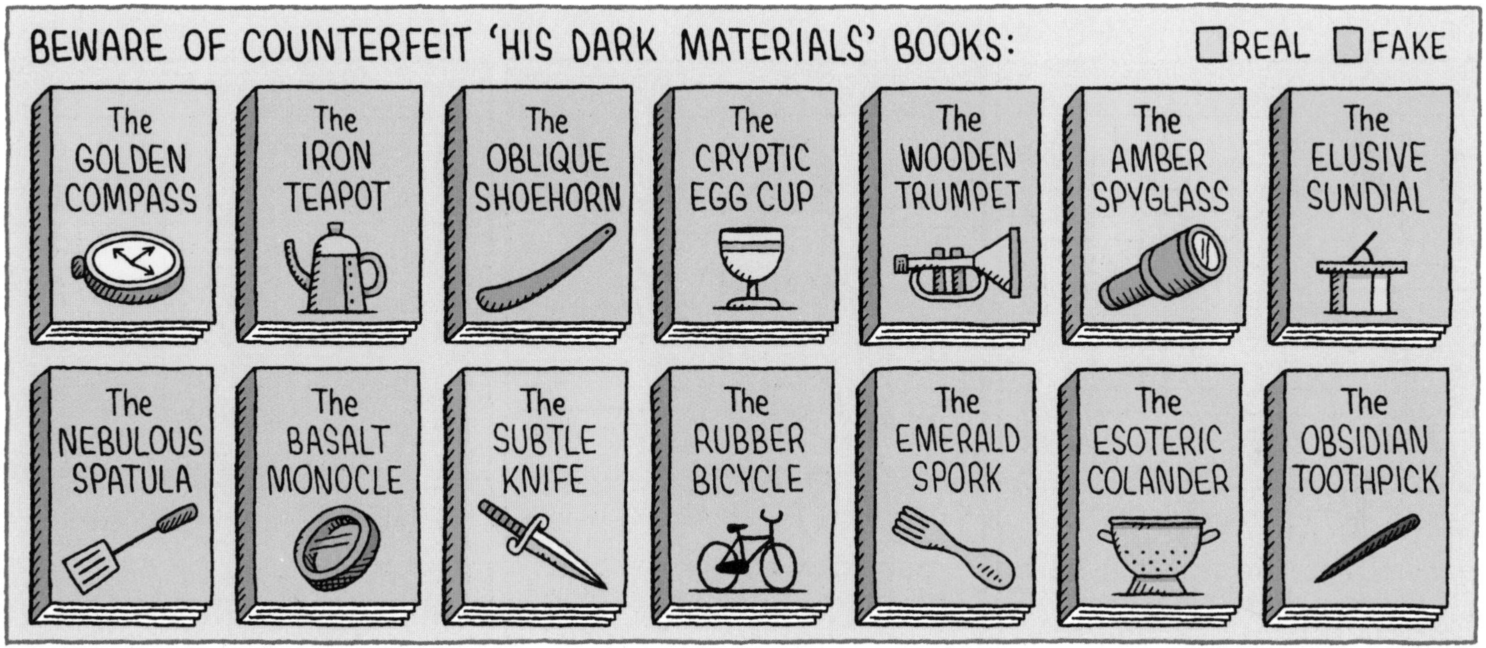

BEWARE OF COUNTERFEIT 'HIS DARK MATERIALS' BOOKS:
REAL
FAKE
The GOLDEN COMPASS
The IRON TEAPOT
The OBLIQUE SHOEHORN
The CRYPTIC EGG CUP
The WOODEN TRUMPET
The AMBER SPYGLASS
The ELUSIVE SUNDIAL
The NEBULOUS SPATULA
The BASALT MONOCLE
The SUBTLE KNIFE
The RUBBER BICYCLE
The EMERALD SPORK
The ESOTERIC COLANDER
The OBSIDIAN TOOTHPICK

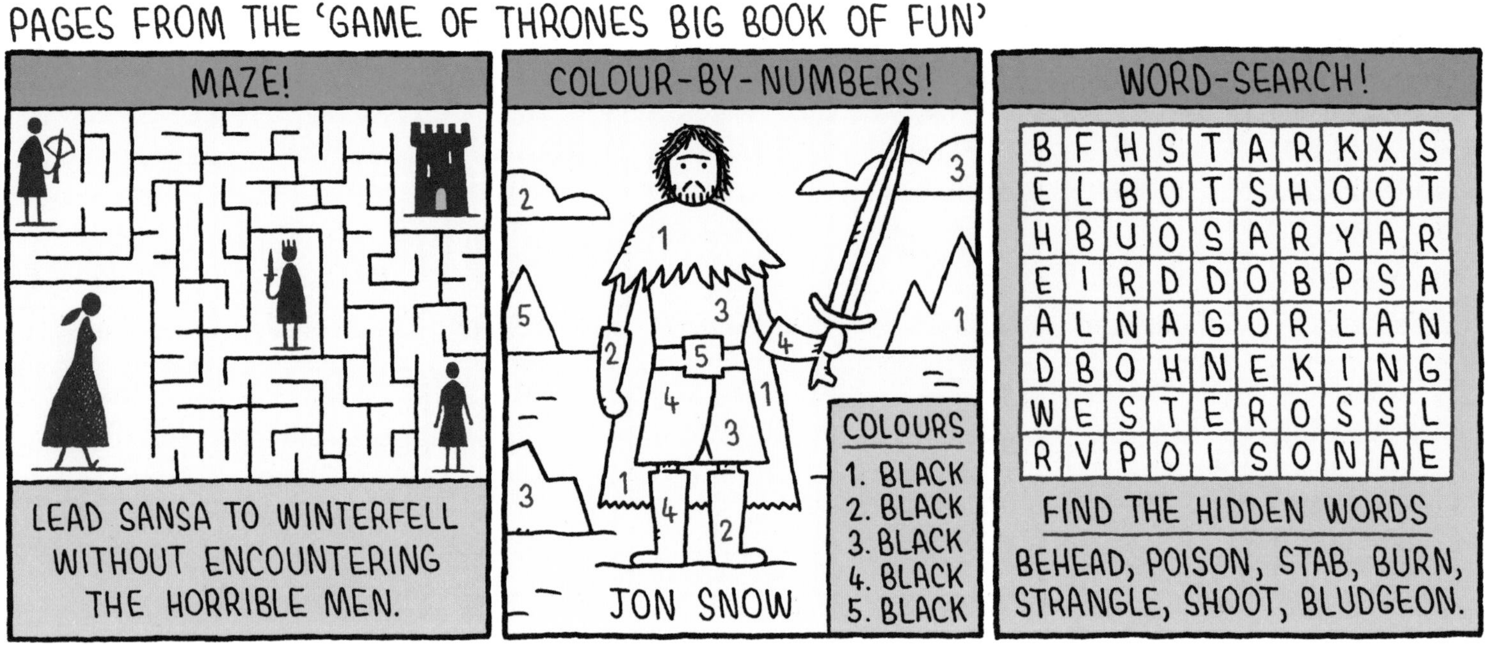
PAGES FROM THE 'GAME OF THRONES BIG BOOK OF FUN'
MAZE!
LEAD SANSA TO WINTERFELL WITHOUT ENCOUNTERING THE HORRIBLE MEN.
COLOUR-BY-NUMBERS!
JON SNOW
COLOURS
1. BLACK
2. BLACK
3. BLACK
4. BLACK
5. BLACK
WORD-SEARCH!
B F H S T A R K X S
E L B O T S H O O T
H B U O S A R Y A R
E I R D D O B P S A
A L N A G O R L A N
D B O H N E K I N G
W E S T E R O S S L
R V P O I S O N A E
FIND THE HIDDEN WORDS
BEHEAD, POISON, STAB, BURN, STRANGLE, SHOOT, BLUDGEON.

AT MISS CROQUEMBOUCHE'S FINISHING SCHOOL FOR ELEGANT YOUNG WRITERS

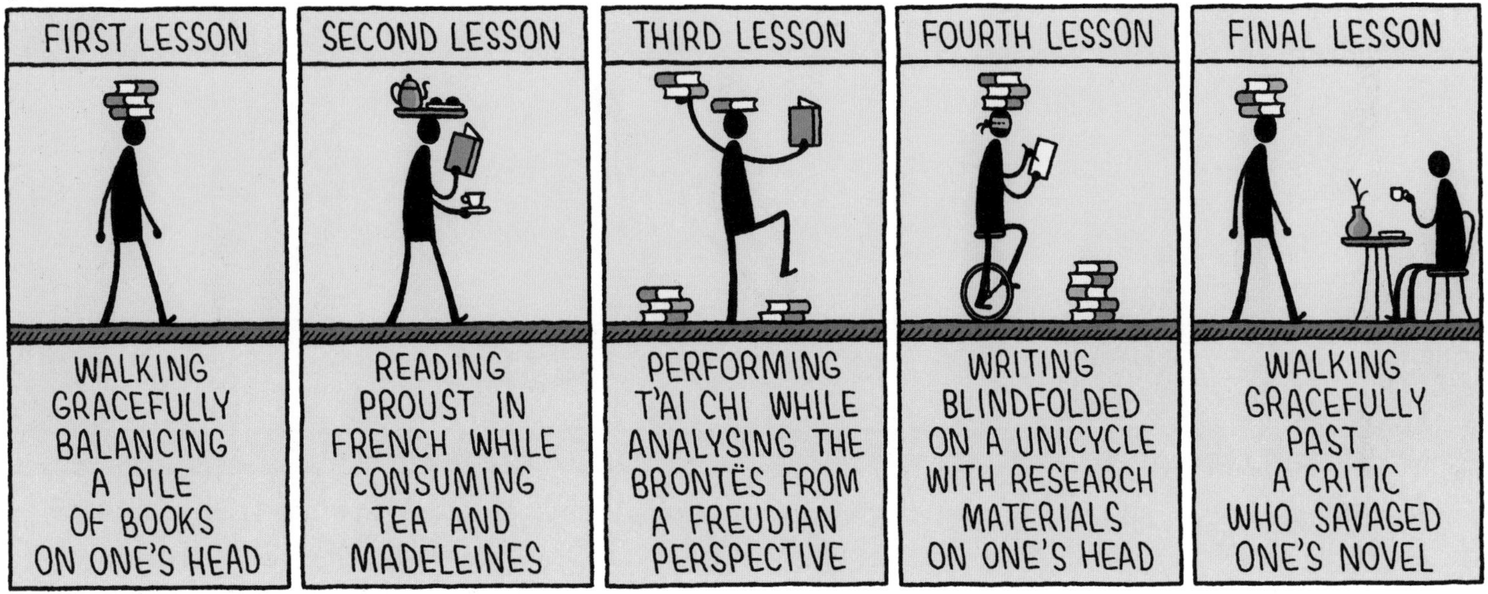
FIRST LESSON
WALKING GRACEFULLY BALANCING A PILE OF BOOKS ON ONE'S HEAD
SECOND LESSON
READING PROUST IN FRENCH WHILE CONSUMING TEA AND MADELEINES
THIRD LESSON
PERFORMING T'AI CHI WHILE ANALYSING THE BRONTËS FROM A FREUDIAN PERSPECTIVE
FOURTH LESSON
WRITING BLINDFOLDED ON A UNICYCLE WITH RESEARCH MATERIALS ON ONE'S HEAD
FINAL LESSON
WALKING GRACEFULLY PAST A CRITIC WHO SAVAGED ONE'S NOVEL

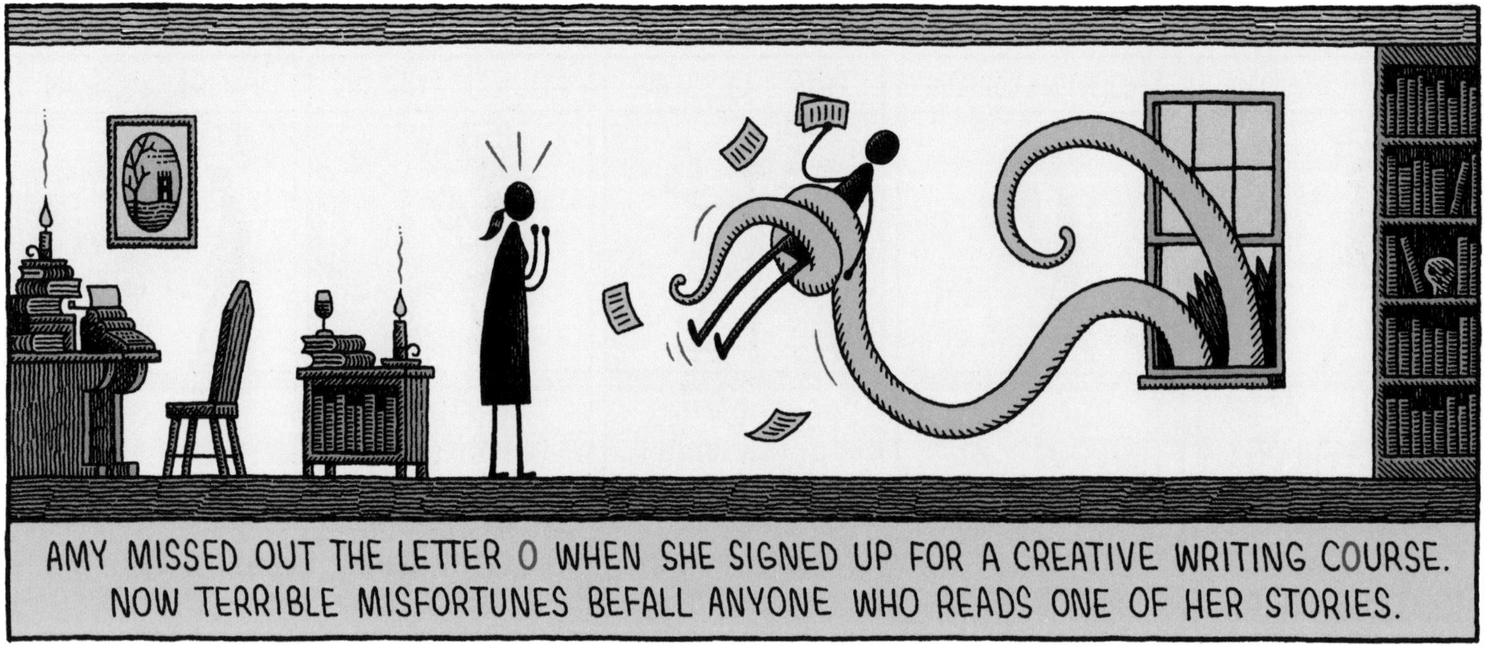
AMY MISSED OUT THE LETTER O WHEN SHE SIGNED UP FOR A CREATIVE WRITING COURSE.
NOW TERRIBLE MISFORTUNES BEFALL ANYONE WHO READS ONE OF HER STORIES.

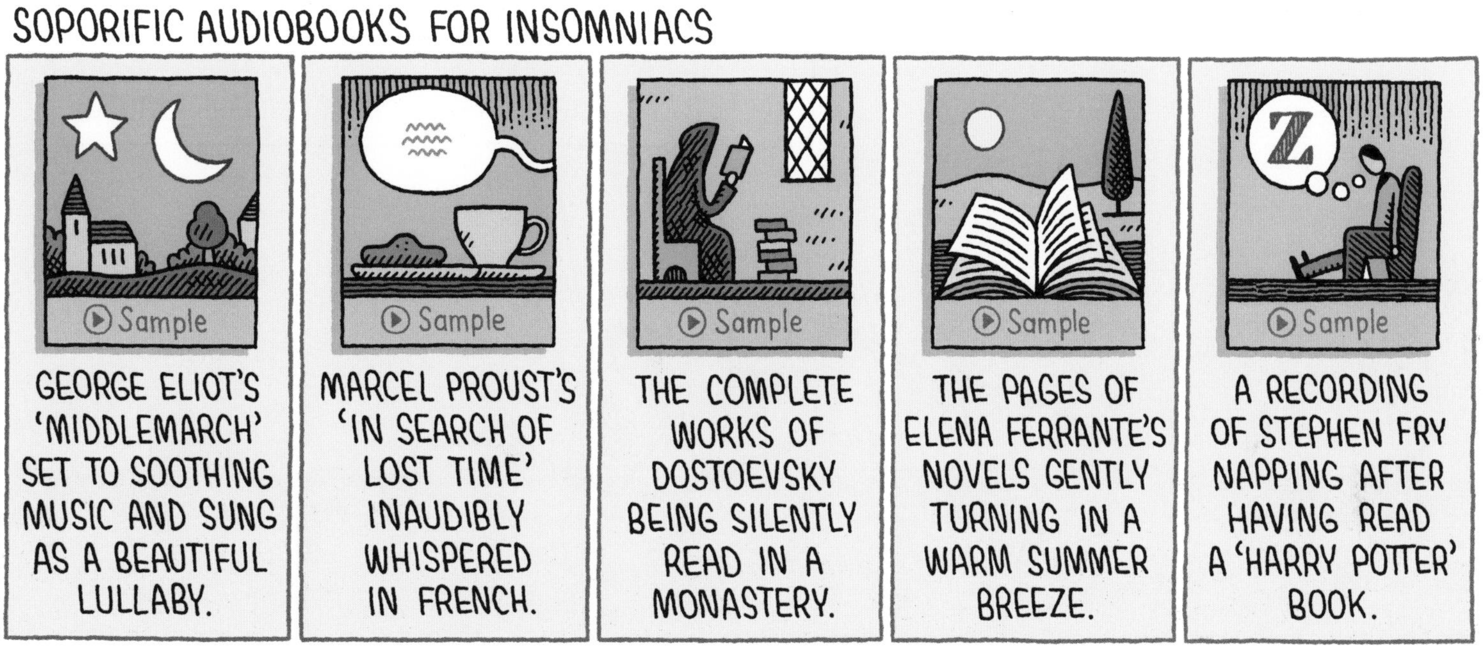
SOPORIFIC AUDIOBOOKS FOR INSOMNIACS
Sample
GEORGE ELIOT'S 'MIDDLEMARCH' SET TO SOOTHING MUSIC AND SUNG AS A BEAUTIFUL LULLABY.
Sample
MARCEL PROUST'S 'IN SEARCH OF LOST TIME' INAUDIBLY WHISPERED IN FRENCH.
Sample
THE COMPLETE WORKS OF DOSTOEVSKY BEING SILENTLY READ IN A MONASTERY.
Sample
THE PAGES OF ELENA FERRANTE'S NOVELS GENTLY TURNING IN A WARM SUMMER BREEZE.
Z
Sample
A RECORDING OF STEPHEN FRY NAPPING AFTER HAVING READ A 'HARRY POTTER' BOOK.

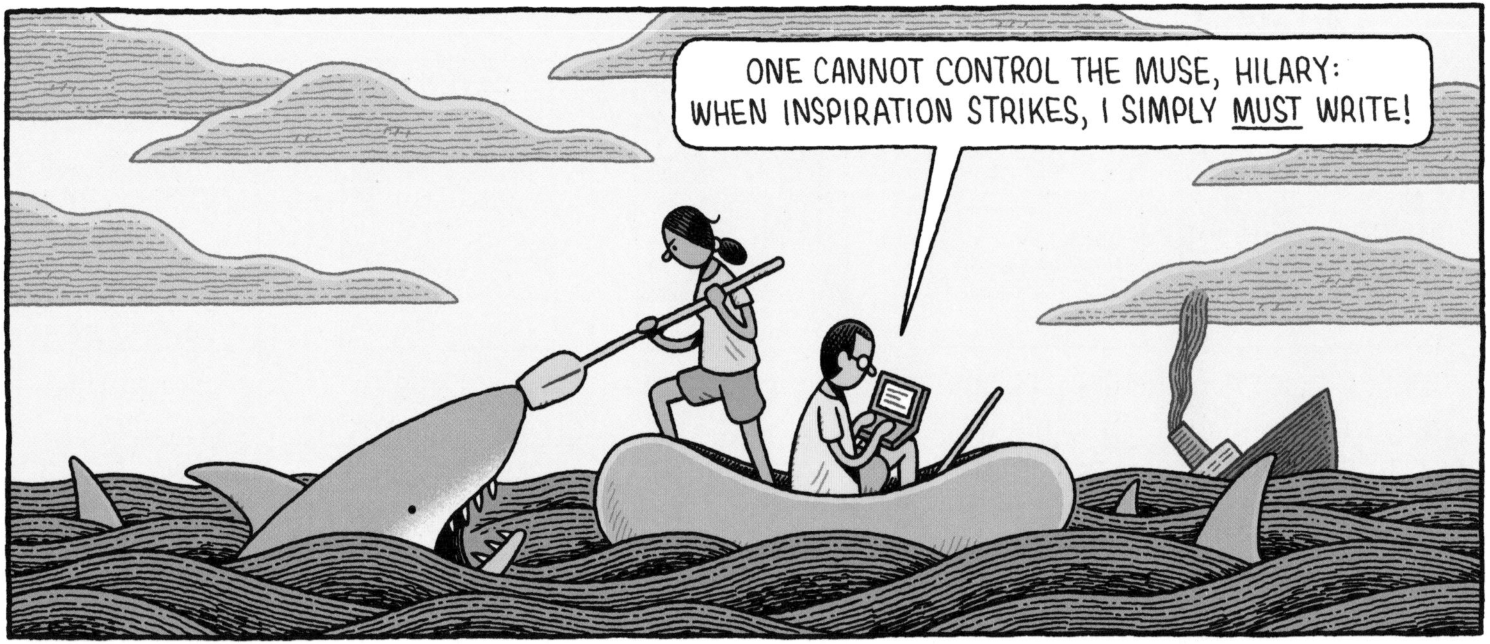
ONE CANNOT CONTROL THE MUSE, HILARY: WHEN INSPIRATION STRIKES, I SIMPLY MUST WRITE!

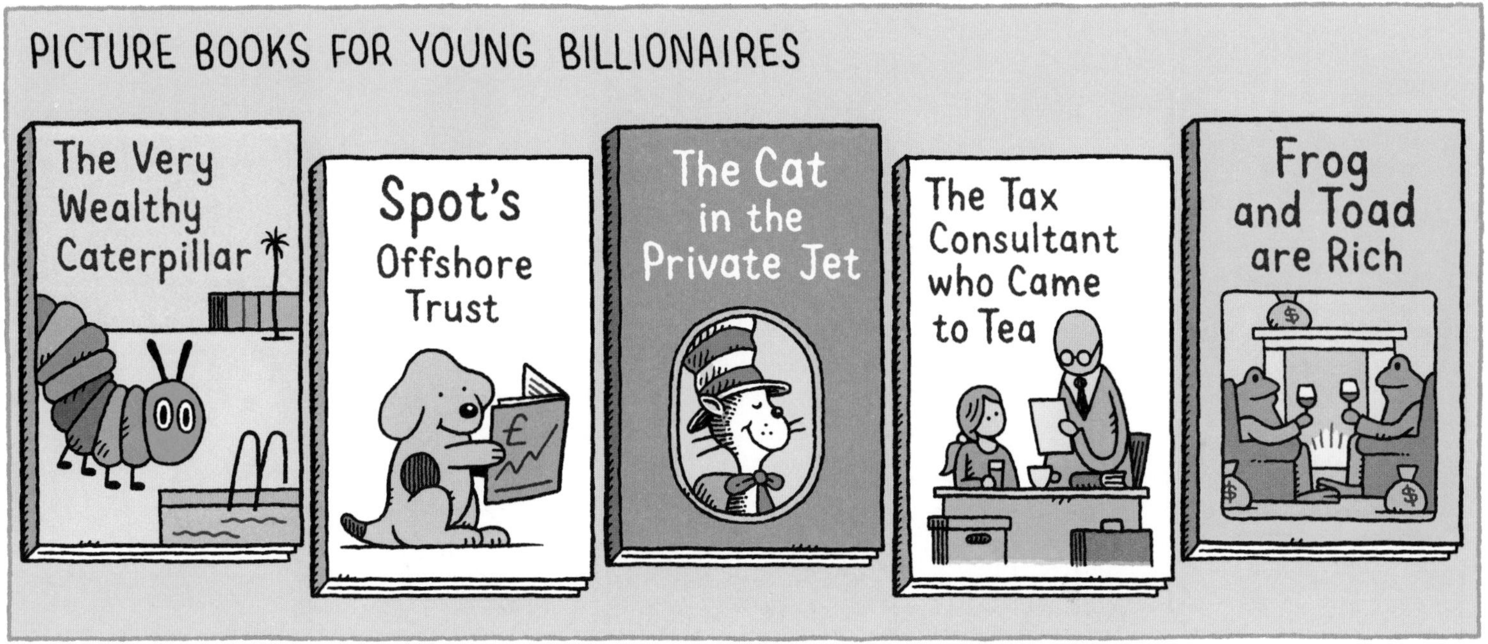
PICTURE BOOKS FOR YOUNG BILLIONAIRES
The Very Wealthy Caterpillar
Spot's Offshore Trust
£
The Cat in the Private Jet
The Tax Consultant who Came to Tea
Frog and Toad are Rich
$
$
$

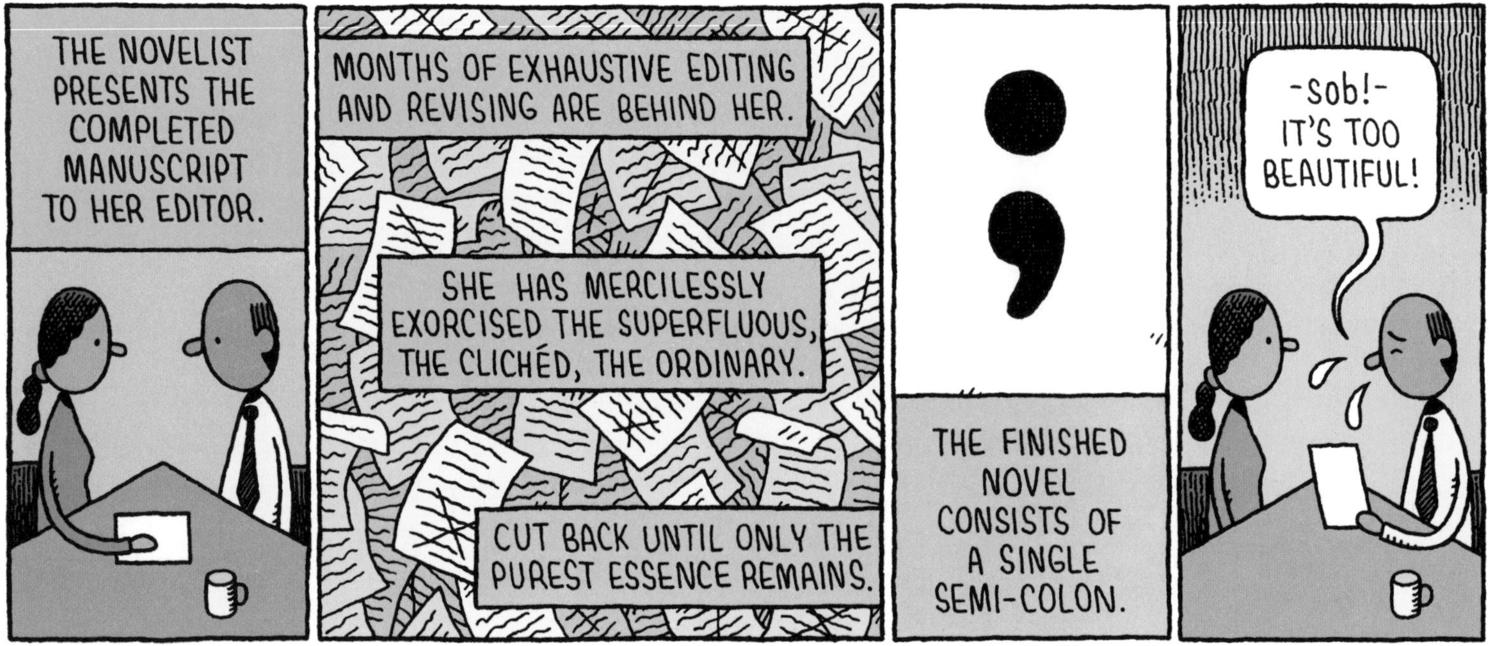

THE NOVELIST PRESENTS THE COMPLETED MANUSCRIPT TO HER EDITOR.
MONTHS OF EXHAUSTIVE EDITING AND REVISING ARE BEHIND HER.
SHE HAS MERCILESSLY EXORCISED THE SUPERFLUOUS, THE CLICHÉD, THE ORDINARY.
CUT BACK UNTIL ONLY THE PUREST ESSENCE REMAINS.
;
THE FINISHED NOVEL CONSISTS OF A SINGLE SEMI-COLON.
-sob!- IT'S TOO BEAUTIFUL!

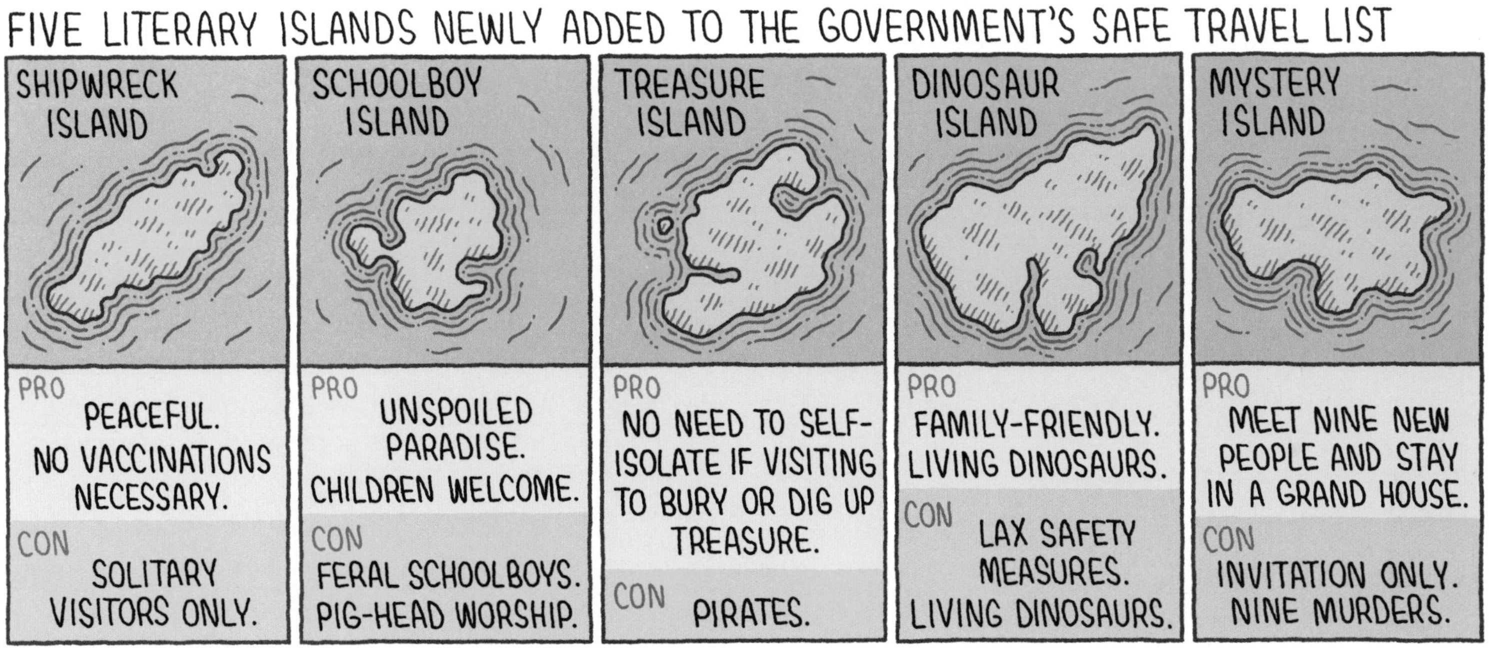

FIVE LITERARY ISLANDS NEWLY ADDED TO THE GOVERNMENT'S SAFE TRAVEL LIST
SHIPWRECK ISLAND
PRO
PEACEFUL. NO VACCINATIONS NECESSARY.
CON
SOLITARY VISITORS ONLY.
SCHOOLBOY ISLAND
PRO
UNSPOILED PARADISE. CHILDREN WELCOME.
CON
FERAL SCHOOLBOYS. PIG-HEAD WORSHIP.
TREASURE ISLAND
PRO
NO NEED TO SELF-ISOLATE IF VISITING TO BURY OR DIG UP TREASURE.
CON
PIRATES.
DINOSAUR ISLAND
PRO
FAMILY-FRIENDLY. LIVING DINOSAURS.
CON
LAX SAFETY MEASURES. LIVING DINOSAURS.
MYSTERY ISLAND
PRO
MEET NINE NEW PEOPLE AND STAY IN A GRAND HOUSE.
CON
INVITATION ONLY. NINE MURDERS.

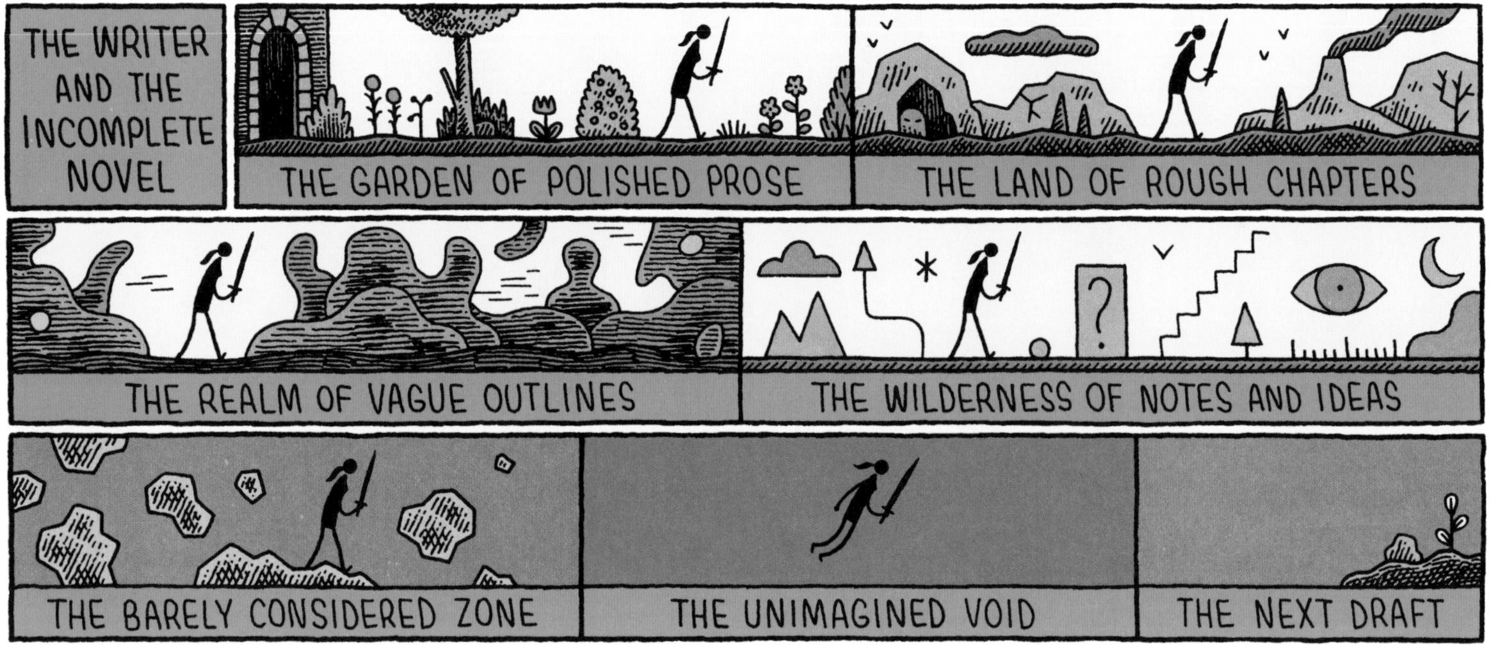

THE WRITER AND THE INCOMPLETE NOVEL
THE GARDEN OF POLISHED PROSE
THE LAND OF ROUGH CHAPTERS
THE REALM OF VAGUE OUTLINES
THE WILDERNESS OF NOTES AND IDEAS
?
THE BARELY CONSIDERED ZONE
THE UNIMAGINED VOID
THE NEXT DRAFT

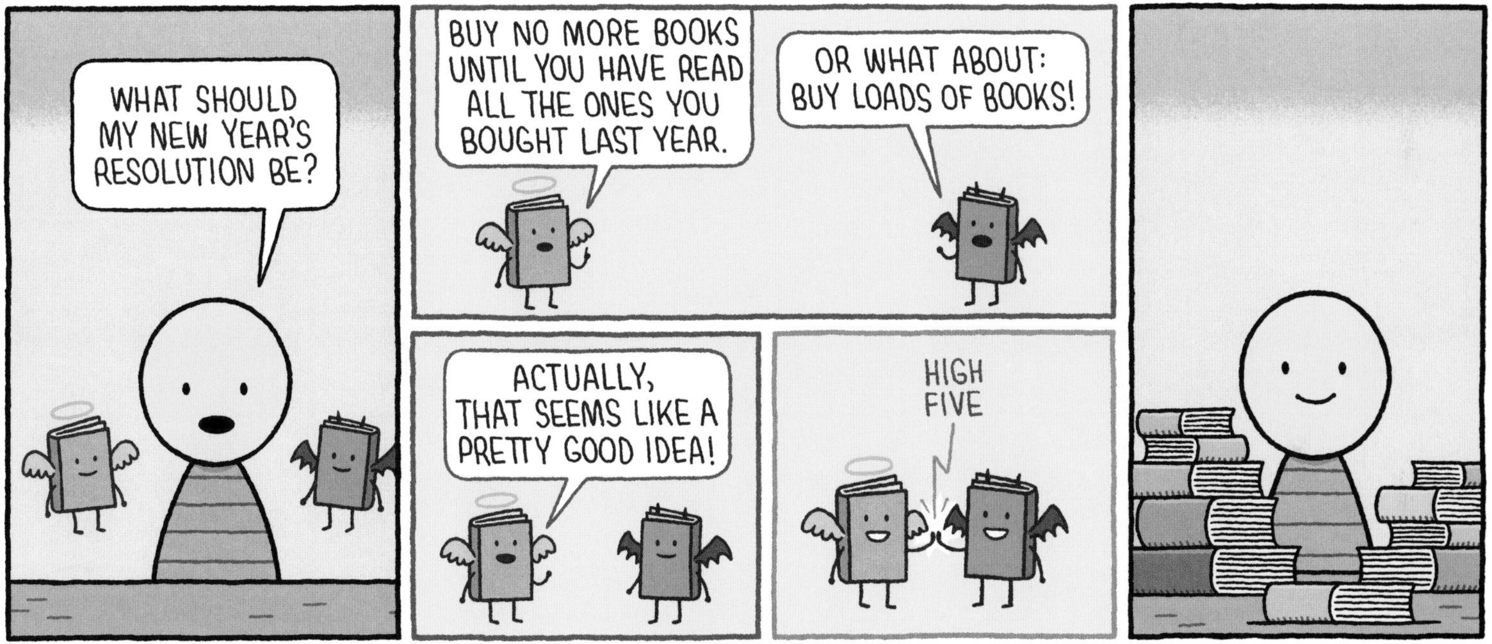
WHAT SHOULD MY NEW YEAR'S RESOLUTION BE?
BUY NO MORE BOOKS UNTIL YOU HAVE READ ALL THE ONES YOU BOUGHT LAST YEAR.
OR WHAT ABOUT: BUY LOADS OF BOOKS!
ACTUALLY, THAT SEEMS LIKE A PRETTY GOOD IDEA!
HIGH FIVE

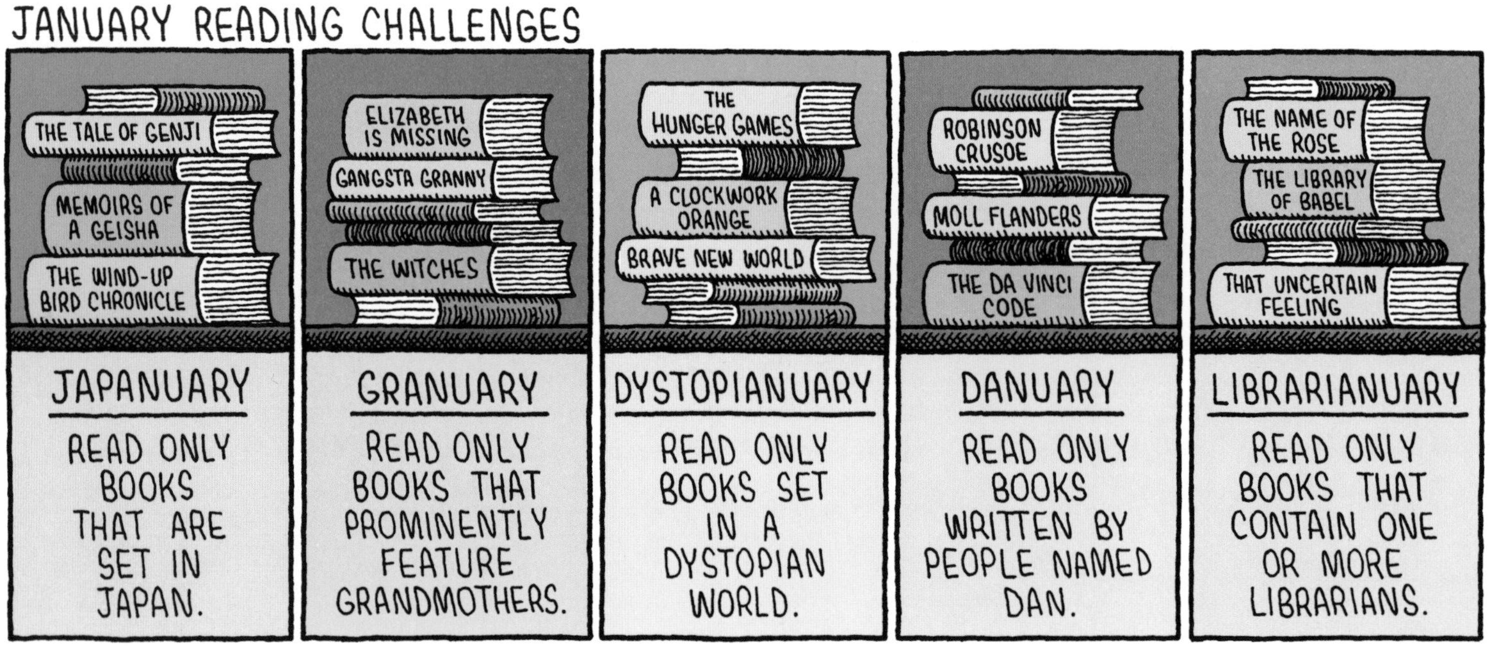
JANUARY READING CHALLENGES
THE TALE OF GENJI
MEMOIRS OF A GEISHA
THE WIND-UP BIRD CHRONICLE
JAPANUARY
READ ONLY BOOKS THAT ARE SET IN JAPAN.
ELIZABETH IS MISSING
GANGSTA GRANNY
THE WITCHES
GRANUARY
READ ONLY BOOKS THAT PROMINENTLY FEATURE GRANDMOTHERS.
THE HUNGER GAMES
A CLOCKWORK ORANGE
BRAVE NEW WORLD
DYSTOPIANUARY
READ ONLY BOOKS SET IN A DYSTOPIAN WORLD.
ROBINSON CRUSOE
MOLL FLANDERS
THE DA VINCI CODE
DANUARY
READ ONLY BOOKS WRITTEN BY PEOPLE NAMED DAN.
THE NAME OF THE ROSE
THE LIBRARY OF BABEL
THAT UNCERTAIN FEELING
LIBRARIANUARY
READ ONLY BOOKS THAT CONTAIN ONE OR MORE LIBRARIANS.

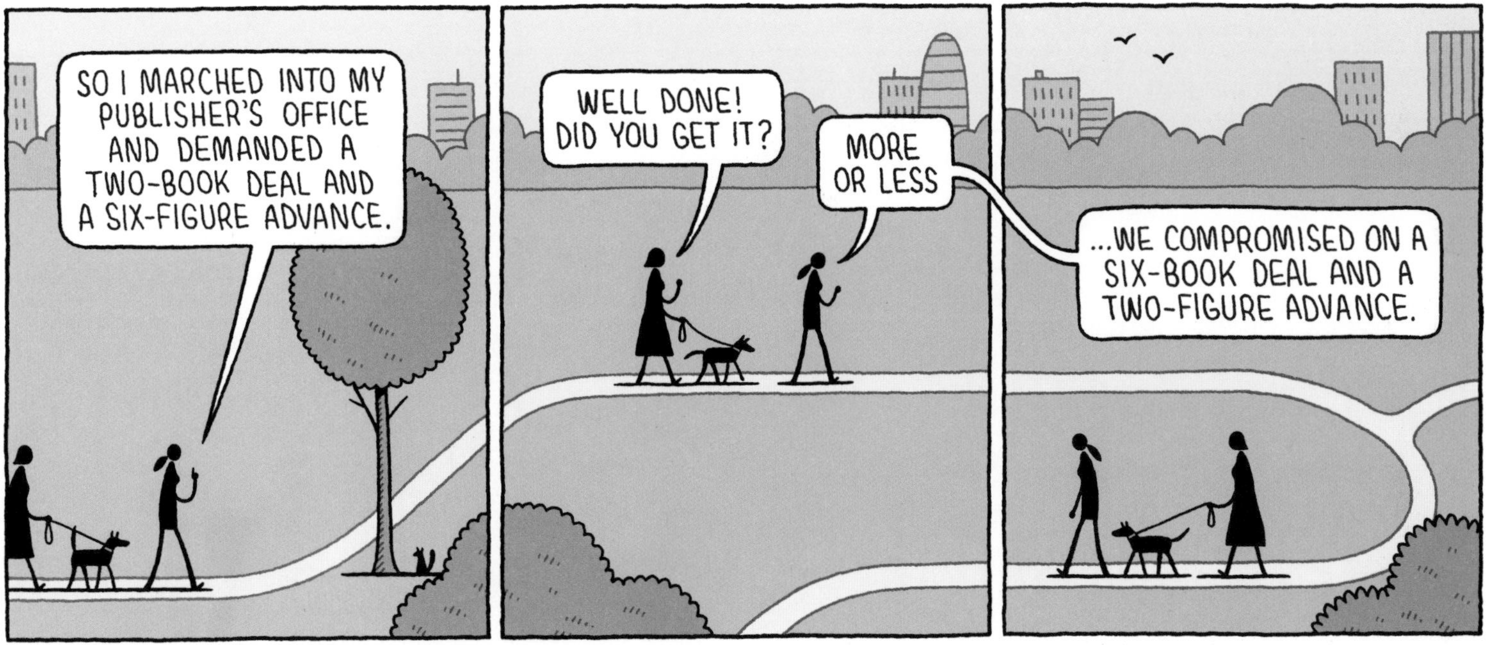
SO I MARCHED INTO MY PUBLISHER'S OFFICE AND DEMANDED A TWO-BOOK DEAL AND A SIX-FIGURE ADVANCE.
WELL DONE! DID YOU GET IT?
MORE OR LESS
...WE COMPROMISED ON A SIX-BOOK DEAL AND A TWO-FIGURE ADVANCE.

HOW DO YOU TAKE REVENGE ON YOUR CRITICS?

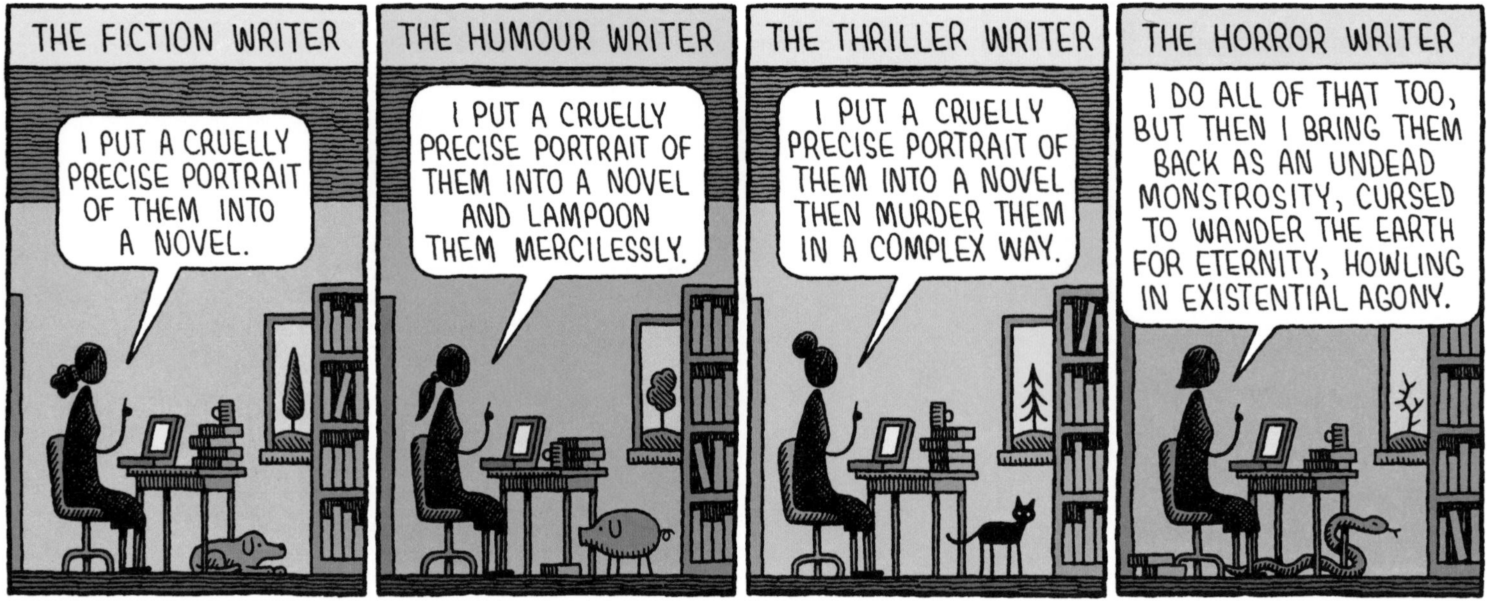
THE FICTION WRITER
I PUT A CRUELLY PRECISE PORTRAIT OF THEM INTO A NOVEL.
THE HUMOUR WRITER
I PUT A CRUELLY PRECISE PORTRAIT OF THEM INTO A NOVEL AND LAMPOON THEM MERCILESSLY.
THE THRILLER WRITER
I PUT A CRUELLY PRECISE PORTRAIT OF THEM INTO A NOVEL THEN MURDER THEM IN A COMPLEX WAY.
THE HORROR WRITER
I DO ALL OF THAT TOO, BUT THEN I BRING THEM BACK AS AN UNDEAD MONSTROSITY, CURSED TO WANDER THE EARTH FOR ETERNITY, HOWLING IN EXISTENTIAL AGONY.

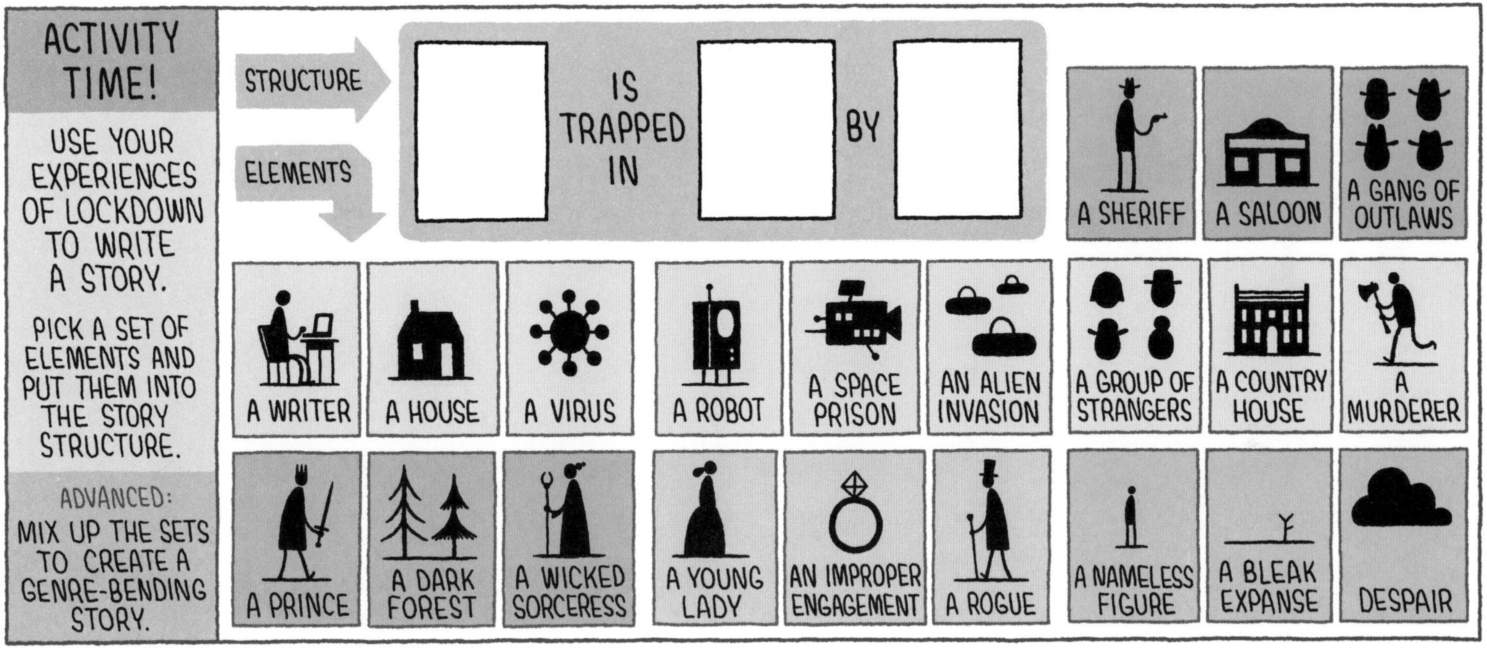
ACTIVITY TIME!
USE YOUR EXPERIENCES OF LOCKDOWN TO WRITE A STORY.
PICK A SET OF ELEMENTS AND PUT THEM INTO THE STORY STRUCTURE.
ADVANCED:
MIX UP THE SETS TO CREATE A GENRE-BENDING STORY.
STRUCTURE
ELEMENTS
IS TRAPPED IN
BY
A SHERIFF
A SALOON
A GANG OF OUTLAWS
A WRITER
A HOUSE
A VIRUS
A ROBOT
A SPACE PRISON
AN ALIEN INVASION
A GROUP OF STRANGERS
A COUNTRY HOUSE
A MURDERER
A PRINCE
A DARK FOREST
A WICKED SORCERESS
A YOUNG LADY
AN IMPROPER ENGAGEMENT
A ROGUE
A NAMELESS FIGURE
A BLEAK EXPANSE
DESPAIR

READING SUGGESTIONS FOR SUMMER 2020

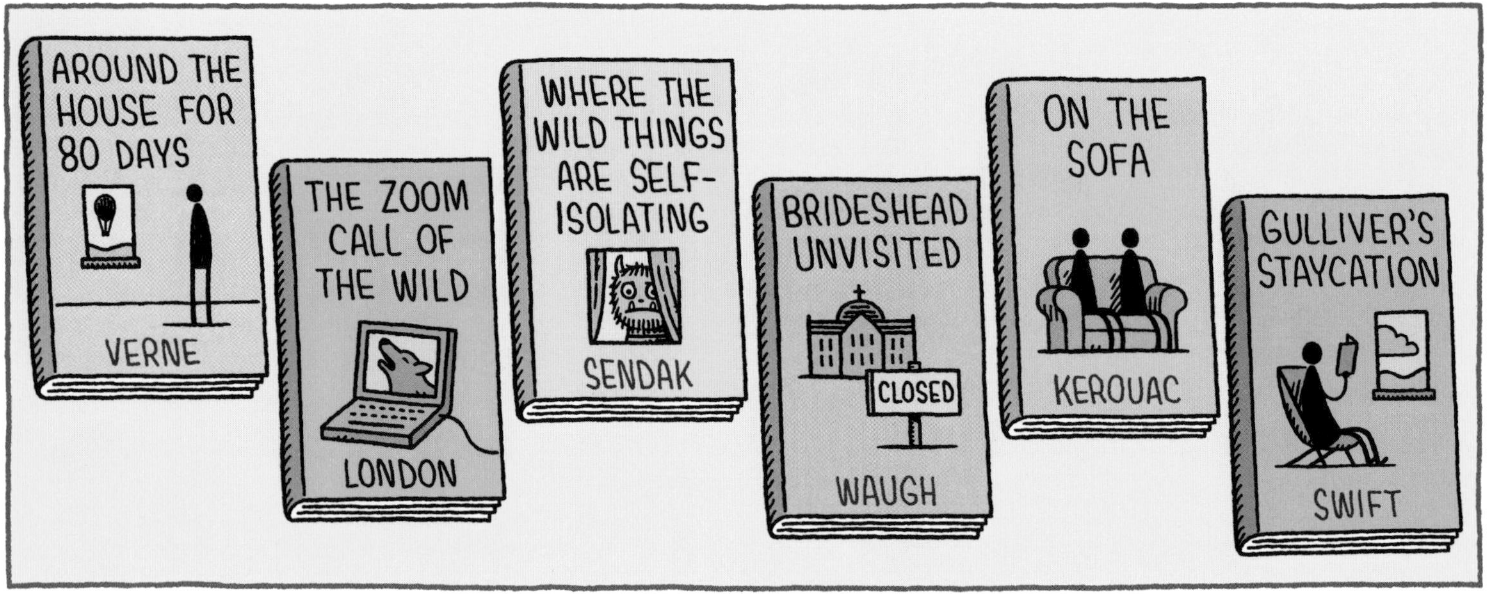

AROUND THE HOUSE FOR 80 DAYS
VERNE
THE ZOOM CALL OF THE WILD
LONDON
WHERE THE WILD THINGS ARE SELF-ISOLATING
SENDAK
BRIDESHEAD UNVISITED
CLOSED
WAUGH
ON THE SOFA
KEROUAC
GULLIVER'S STAYCATION
SWIFT

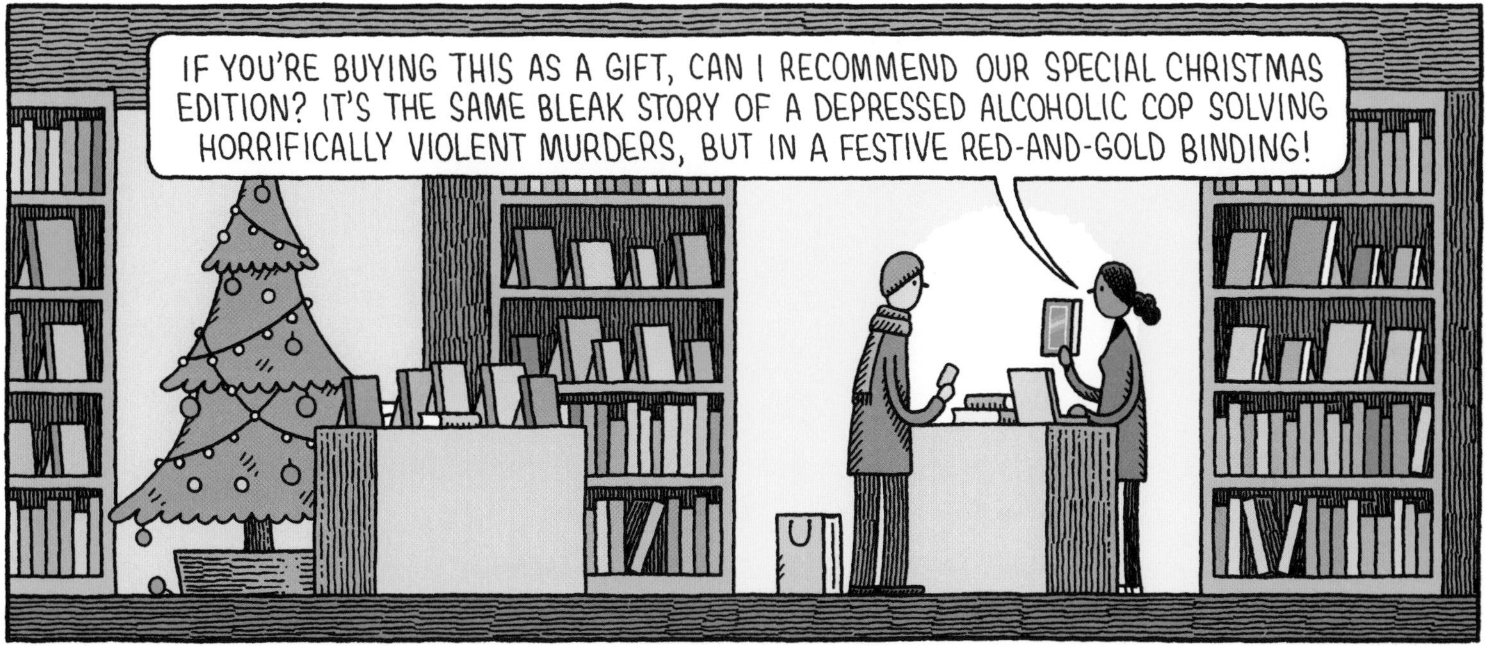
IF YOU'RE BUYING THIS AS A GIFT, CAN I RECOMMEND OUR SPECIAL CHRISTMAS EDITION? IT'S THE SAME BLEAK STORY OF A DEPRESSED ALCOHOLIC COP SOLVING HORRIFICALLY VIOLENT MURDERS, BUT IN A FESTIVE RED-AND-GOLD BINDING!

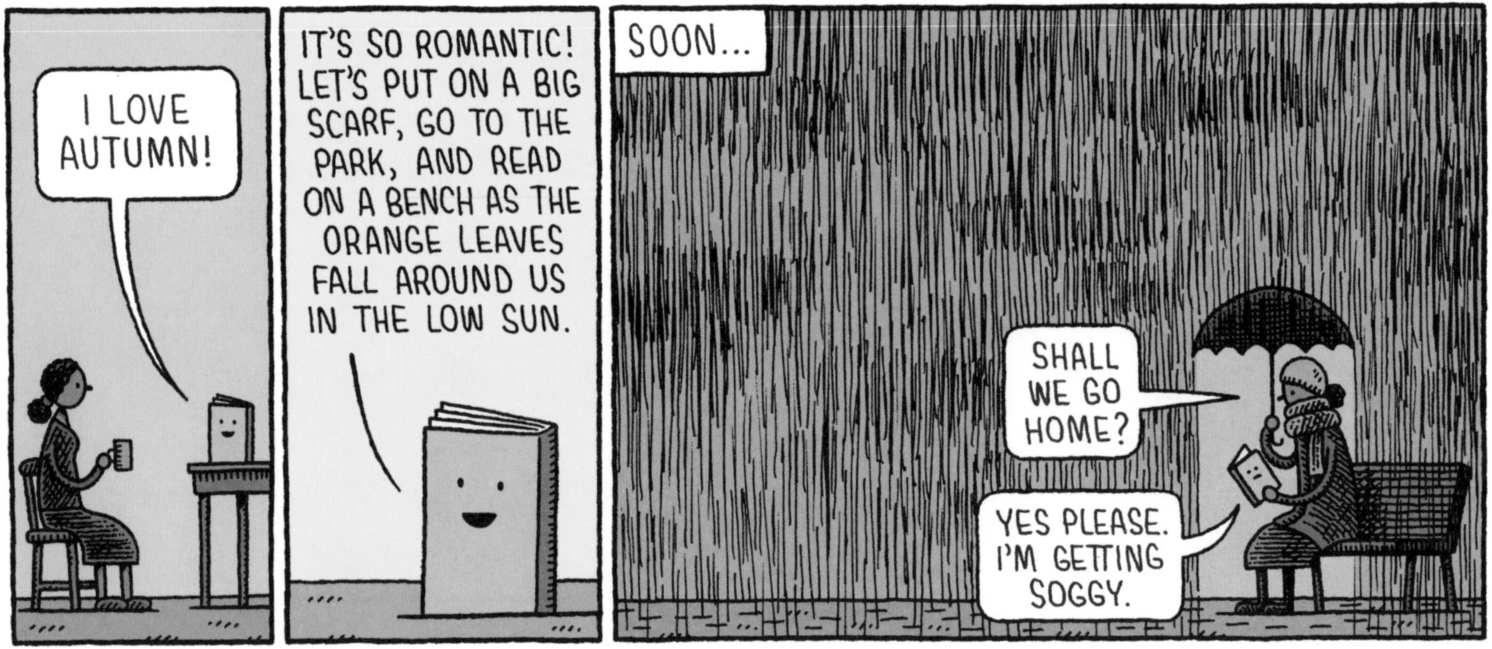
I LOVE AUTUMN!
IT'S SO ROMANTIC! LET'S PUT ON A BIG SCARF, GO TO THE PARK, AND READ ON A BENCH AS THE ORANGE LEAVES FALL AROUND US IN THE LOW SUN.
SOON...
SHALL WE GO HOME?
YES PLEASE. I'M GETTING SOGGY.

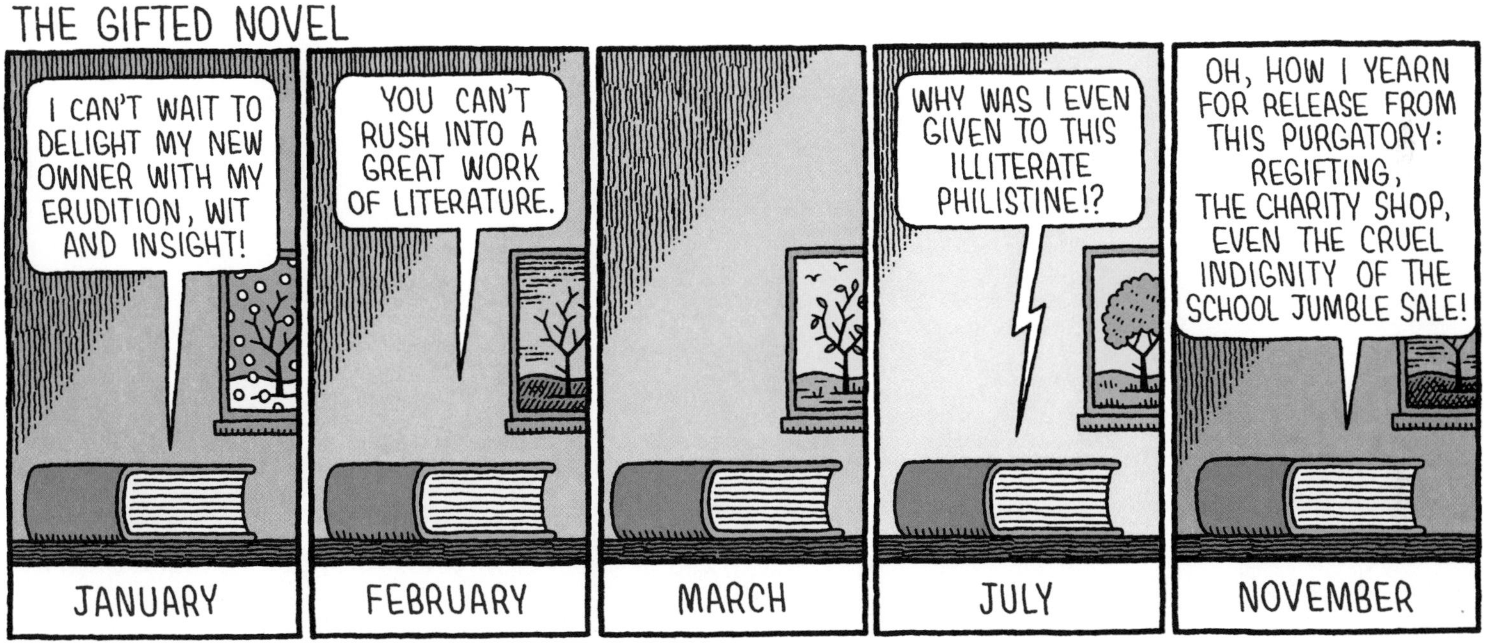
THE GIFTED NOVEL
I CAN'T WAIT TO DELIGHT MY NEW OWNER WITH MY ERUDITION, WIT AND INSIGHT!
JANUARY
YOU CAN'T RUSH INTO A GREAT WORK OF LITERATURE.
FEBRUARY
MARCH
WHY WAS I EVEN GIVEN TO THIS ILLITERATE PHILISTINE!?
JULY
OH, HOW I YEARN FOR RELEASE FROM THIS PURGATORY: REGIFTING, THE CHARITY SHOP, EVEN THE CRUEL INDIGNITY OF THE SCHOOL JUMBLE SALE!
NOVEMBER

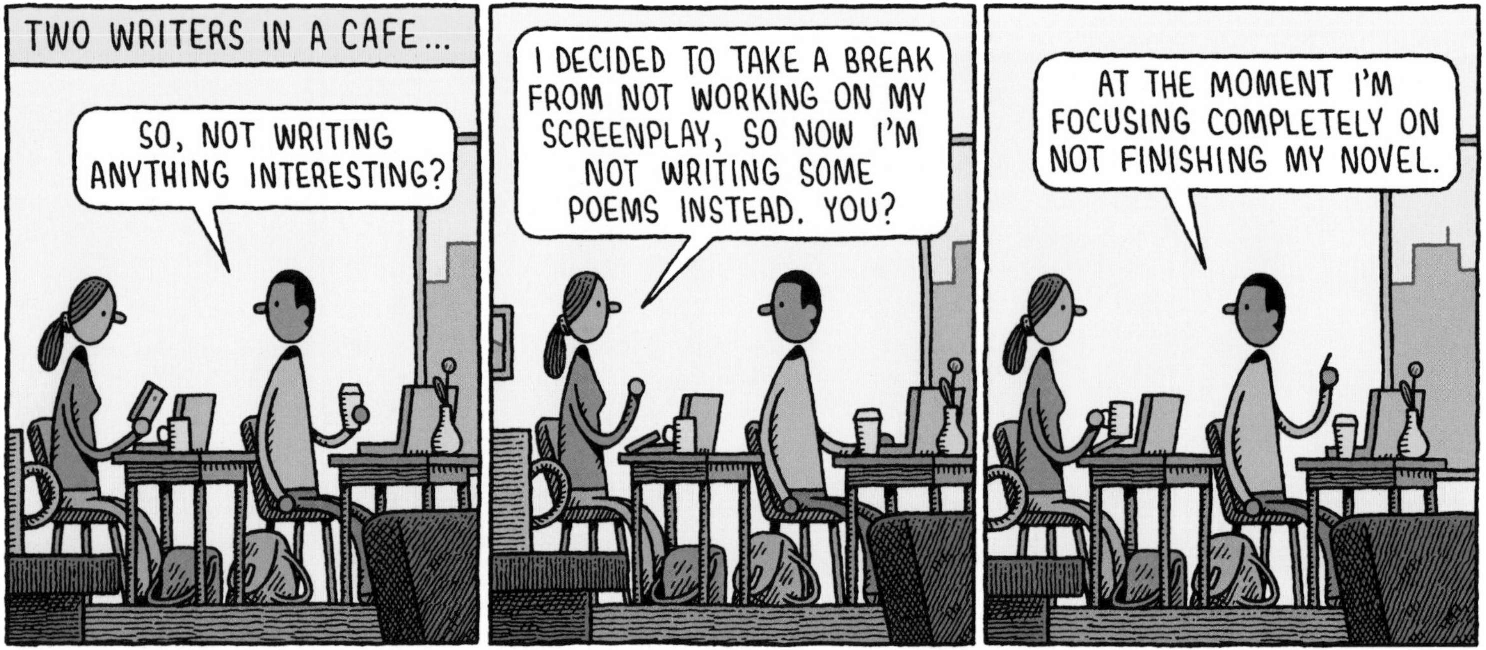
TWO WRITERS IN A CAFE...
SO, NOT WRITING ANYTHING INTERESTING?
I DECIDED TO TAKE A BREAK FROM NOT WORKING ON MY SCREENPLAY, SO NOW I'M NOT WRITING SOME POEMS INSTEAD. YOU?
AT THE MOMENT I'M FOCUSING COMPLETELY ON NOT FINISHING MY NOVEL.

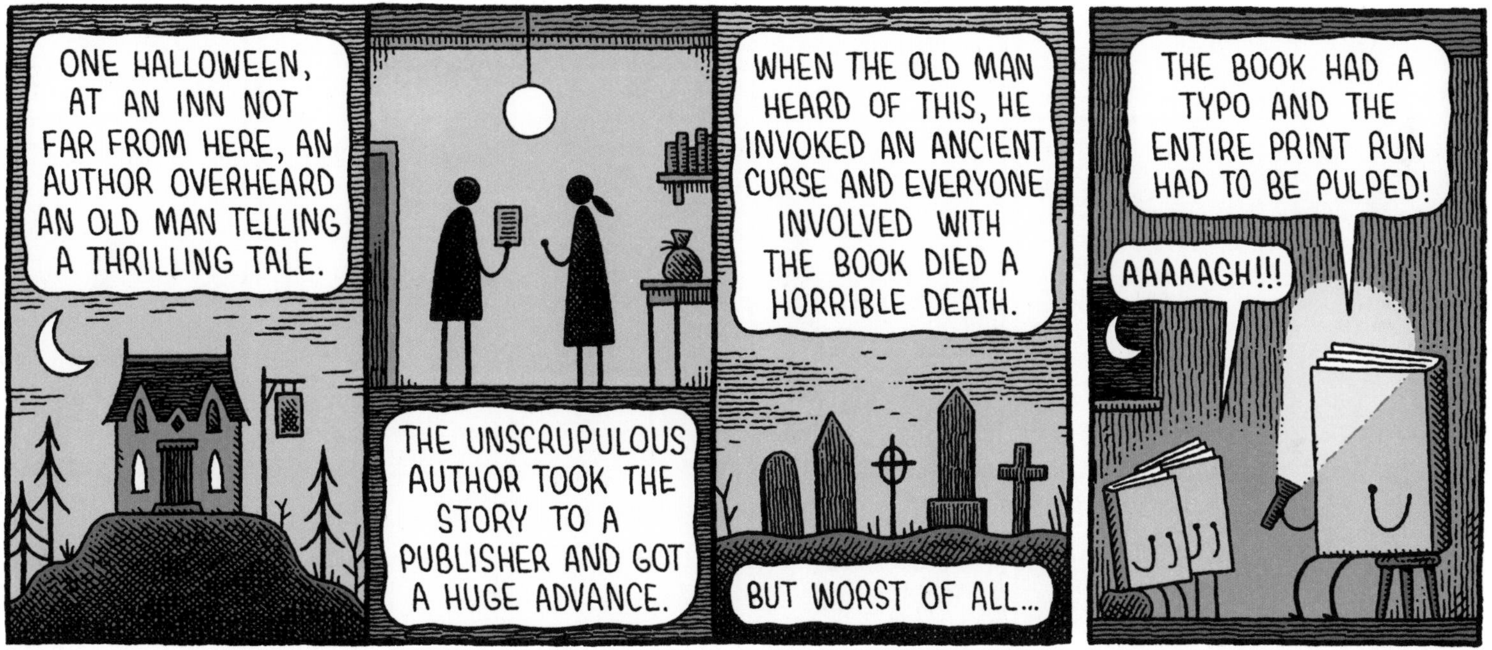
ONE HALLOWEEN, AT AN INN NOT FAR FROM HERE, AN AUTHOR OVERHEARD AN OLD MAN TELLING A THRILLING TALE.
THE UNSCRUPULOUS AUTHOR TOOK THE STORY TO A PUBLISHER AND GOT A HUGE ADVANCE.
WHEN THE OLD MAN HEARD OF THIS, HE INVOKED AN ANCIENT CURSE AND EVERYONE INVOLVED WITH THE BOOK DIED A HORRIBLE DEATH.
BUT WORST OF ALL...
THE BOOK HAD A TYPO AND THE ENTIRE PRINT RUN HAD TO BE PULPED!
AAAAAGH!!!

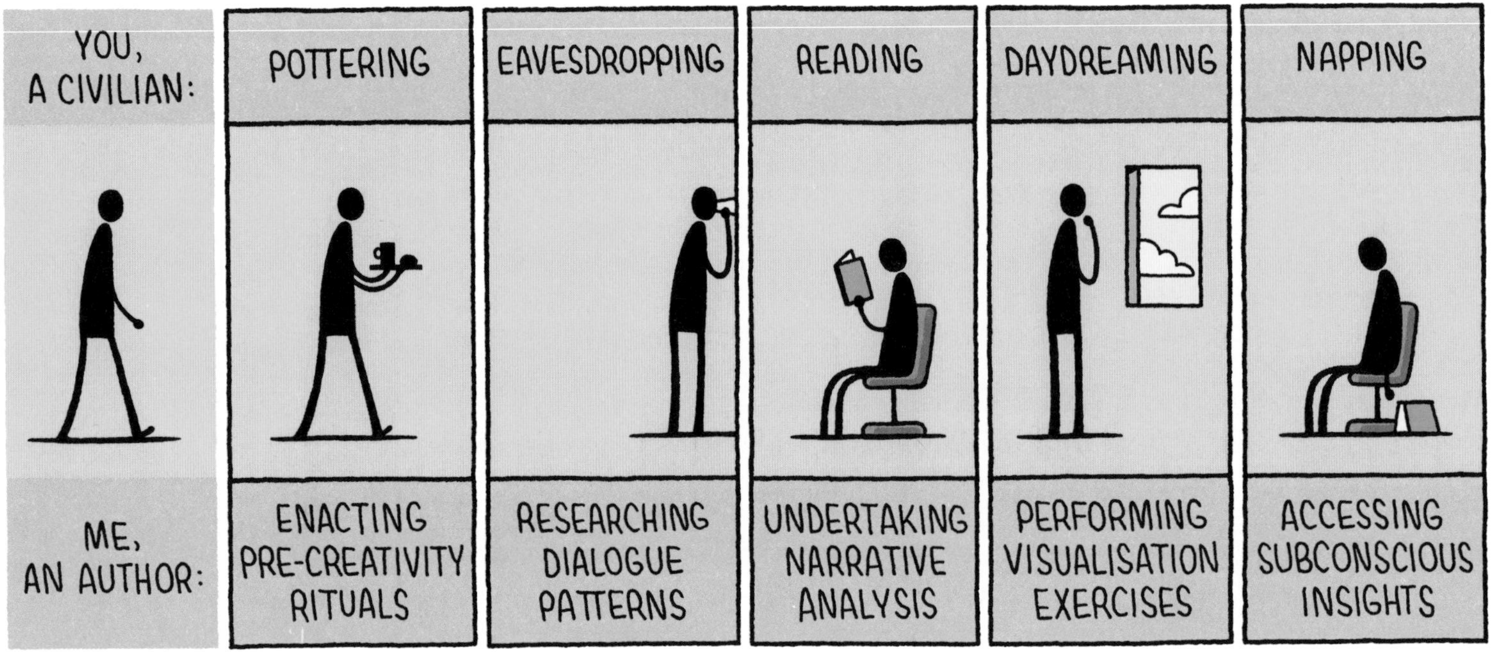
YOU, A CIVILIAN:
ME, AN AUTHOR:
POTTERING
ENACTING PRE-CREATIVITY RITUALS
EAVESDROPPING
RESEARCHING DIALOGUE PATTERNS
READING
UNDERTAKING NARRATIVE ANALYSIS
DAYDREAMING
PERFORMING VISUALISATION EXERCISES
NAPPING
ACCESSING SUBCONSCIOUS INSIGHTS

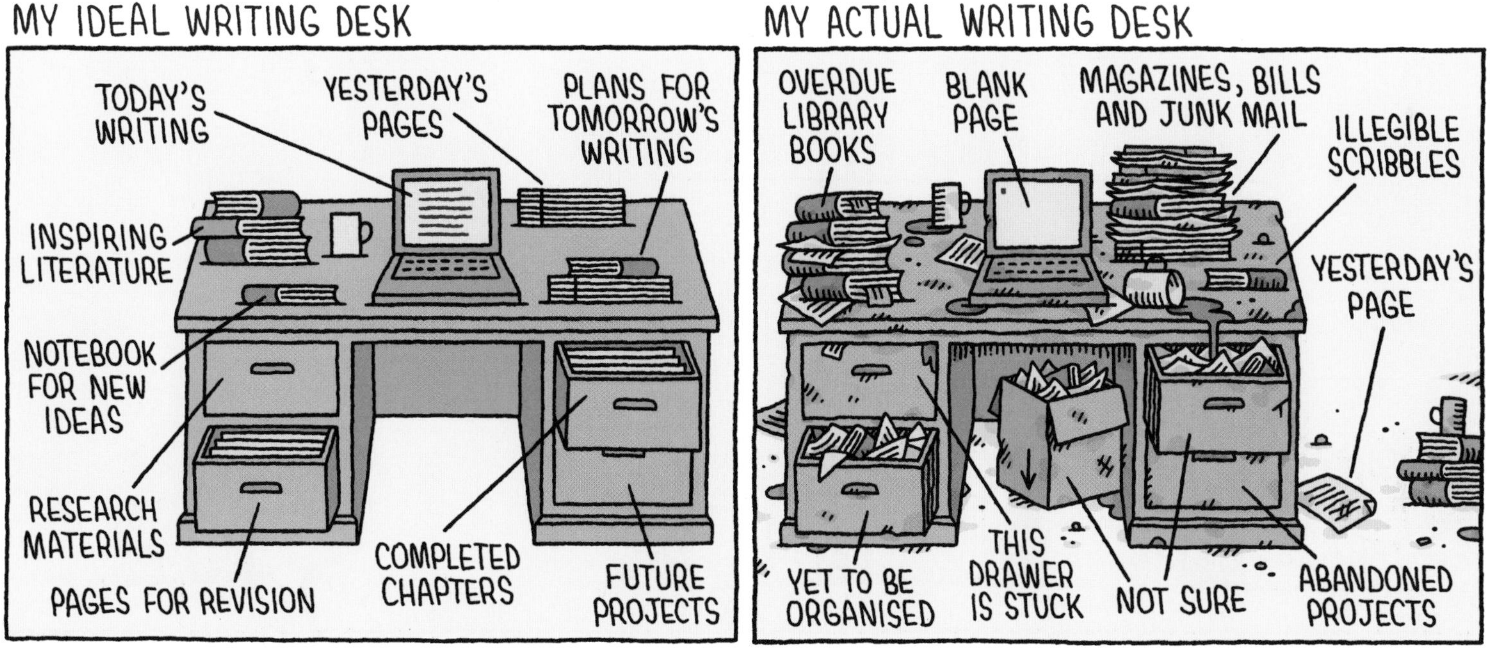
MY IDEAL WRITING DESK
TODAY'S WRITING
YESTERDAY'S PAGES
PLANS FOR TOMORROW'S WRITING
INSPIRING LITERATURE
NOTEBOOK FOR NEW IDEAS
RESEARCH MATERIALS
PAGES FOR REVISION
COMPLETED CHAPTERS
FUTURE PROJECTS
MY ACTUAL WRITING DESK
OVERDUE LIBRARY BOOKS
BLANK PAGE
MAGAZINES, BILLS AND JUNK MAIL
ILLEGIBLE SCRIBBLES
YESTERDAY'S PAGE
YET TO BE ORGANISED
THIS DRAWER IS STUCK
NOT SURE
ABANDONED PROJECTS

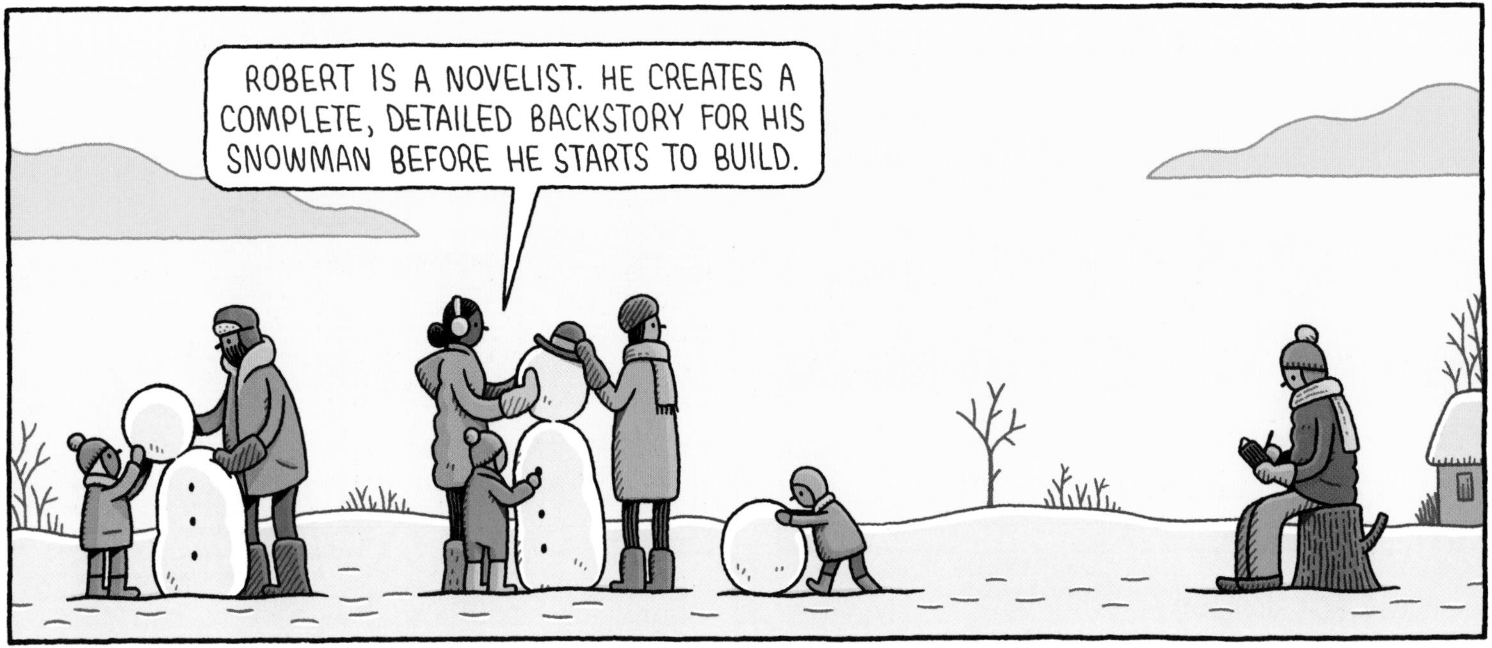
ROBERT IS A NOVELIST. HE CREATES A COMPLETE, DETAILED BACKSTORY FOR HIS SNOWMAN BEFORE HE STARTS TO BUILD.

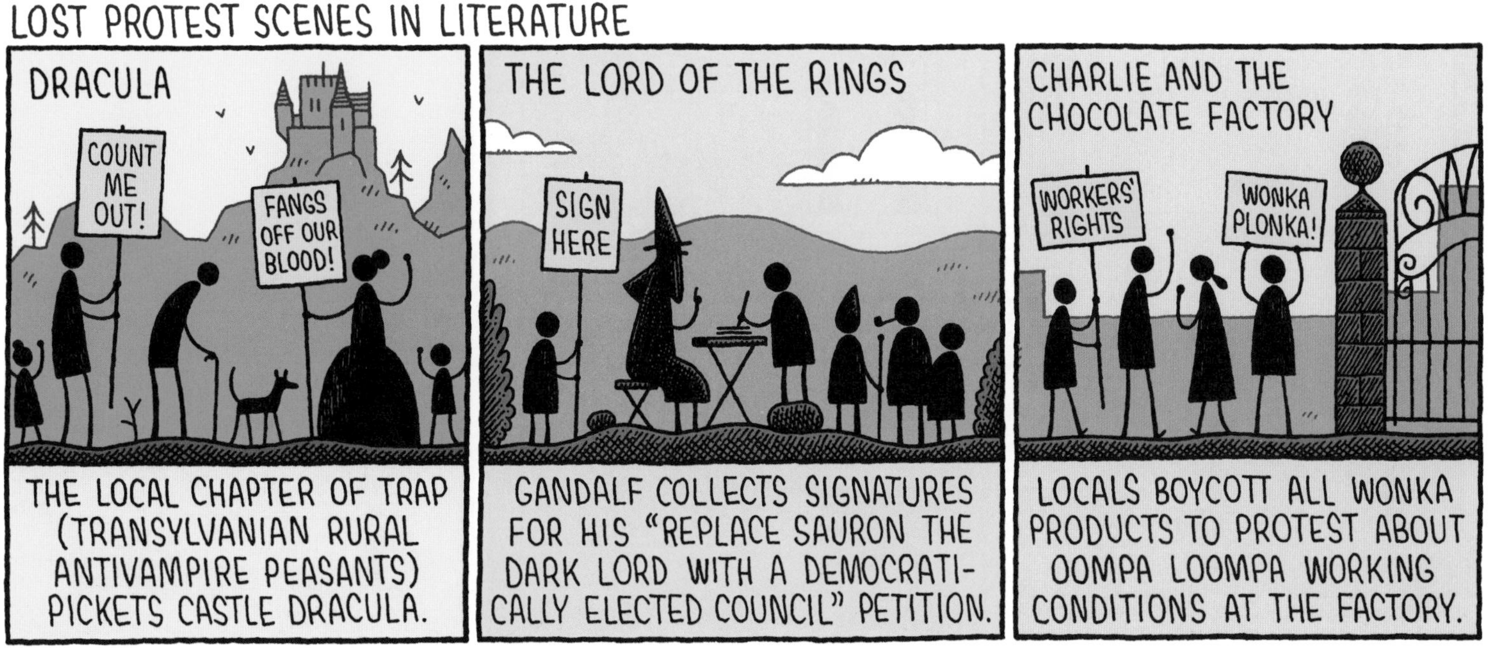
LOST PROTEST SCENES IN LITERATURE
DRACULA
COUNT ME OUT!
FANGS OFF OUR BLOOD!
THE LOCAL CHAPTER OF TRAP (TRANSYLVANIAN RURAL ANTIVAMPIRE PEASANTS) PICKETS CASTLE DRACULA.
THE LORD OF THE RINGS
SIGN HERE
GANDALF COLLECTS SIGNATURES FOR HIS "REPLACE SAURON THE DARK LORD WITH A DEMOCRATICALLY ELECTED COUNCIL" PETITION.
CHARLIE AND THE CHOCOLATE FACTORY
WORKERS' RIGHTS
WONKA PLONKA!
LOCALS BOYCOTT ALL WONKA PRODUCTS TO PROTEST ABOUT OOMPA LOOMPA WORKING CONDITIONS AT THE FACTORY.

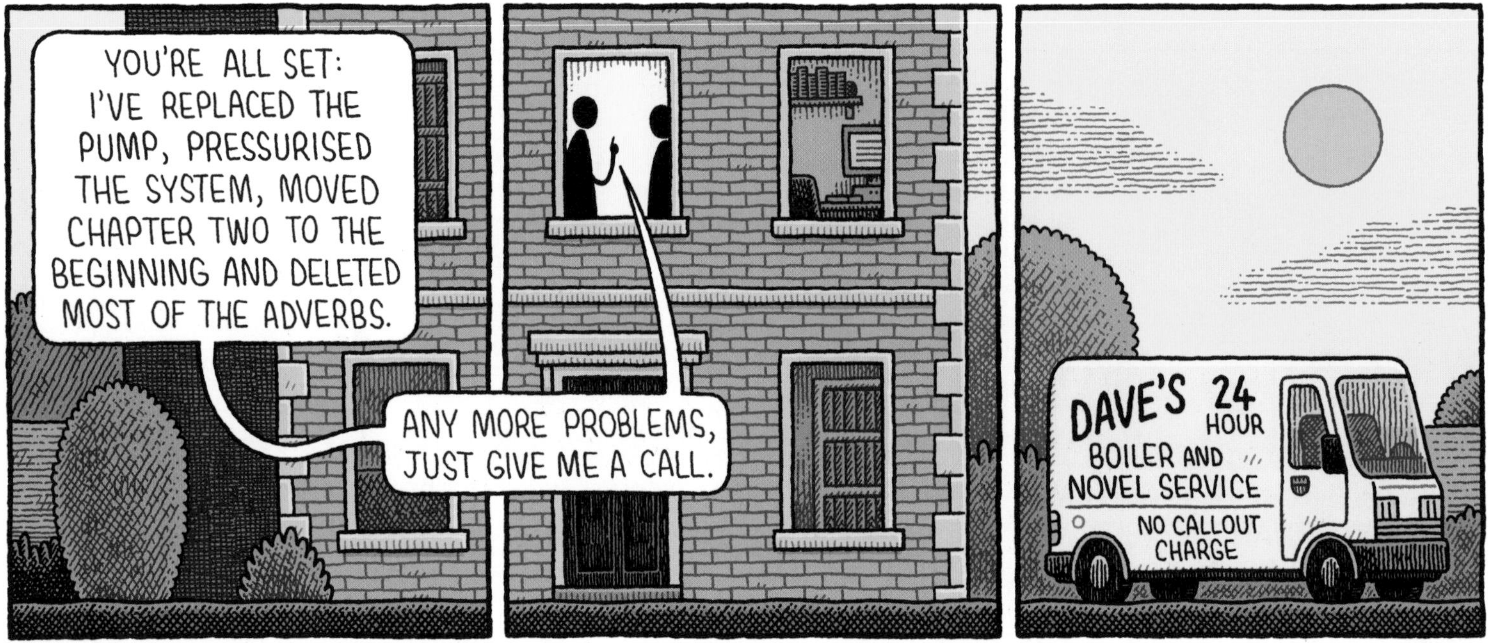
YOU'RE ALL SET: I'VE REPLACED THE PUMP, PRESSURISED THE SYSTEM, MOVED CHAPTER TWO TO THE BEGINNING AND DELETED MOST OF THE ADVERBS.
ANY MORE PROBLEMS, JUST GIVE ME A CALL.
DAVE'S 24 HOUR
BOILER AND NOVEL SERVICE
NO CALLOUT CHARGE

ANALYSIS OF AN ACCEPTABLE READING SPOT IN THE PARK

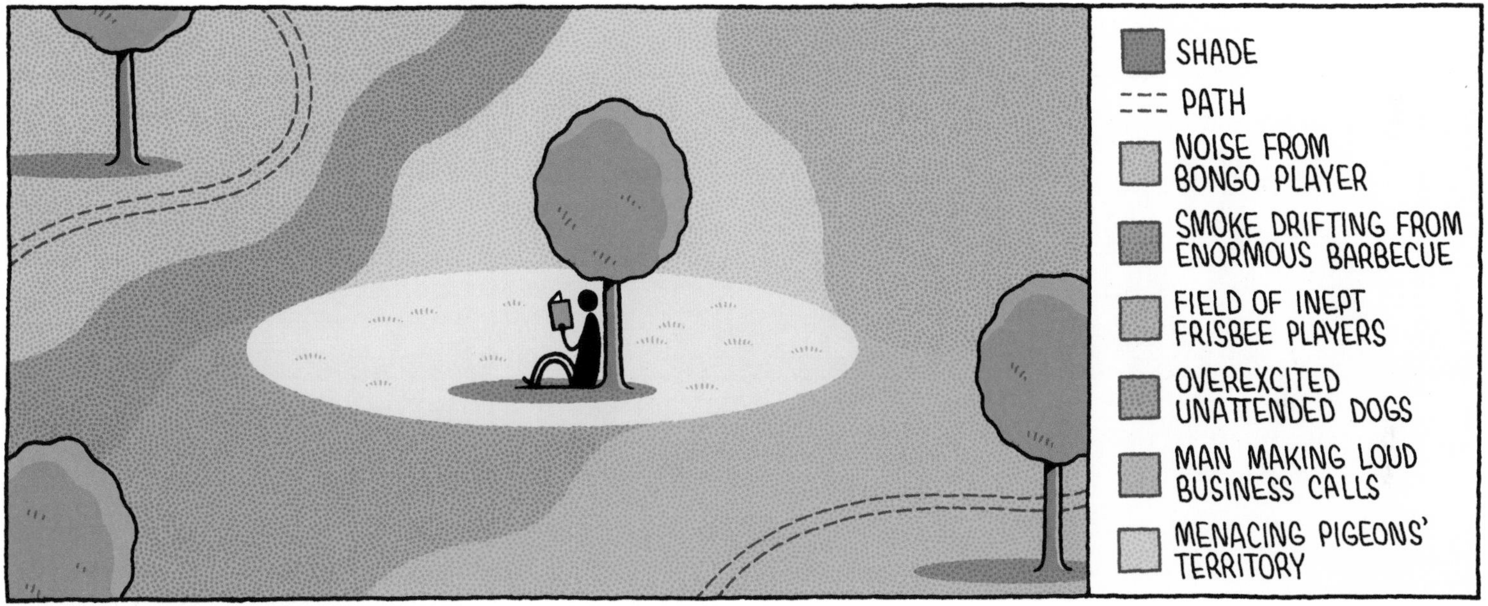
SHADE
PATH
NOISE FROM BONGO PLAYER
SMOKE DRIFTING FROM ENORMOUS BARBECUE
FIELD OF INEPT FRISBEE PLAYERS
OVEREXCITED UNATTENDED DOGS
MAN MAKING LOUD BUSINESS CALLS
MENACING PIGEONS' TERRITORY

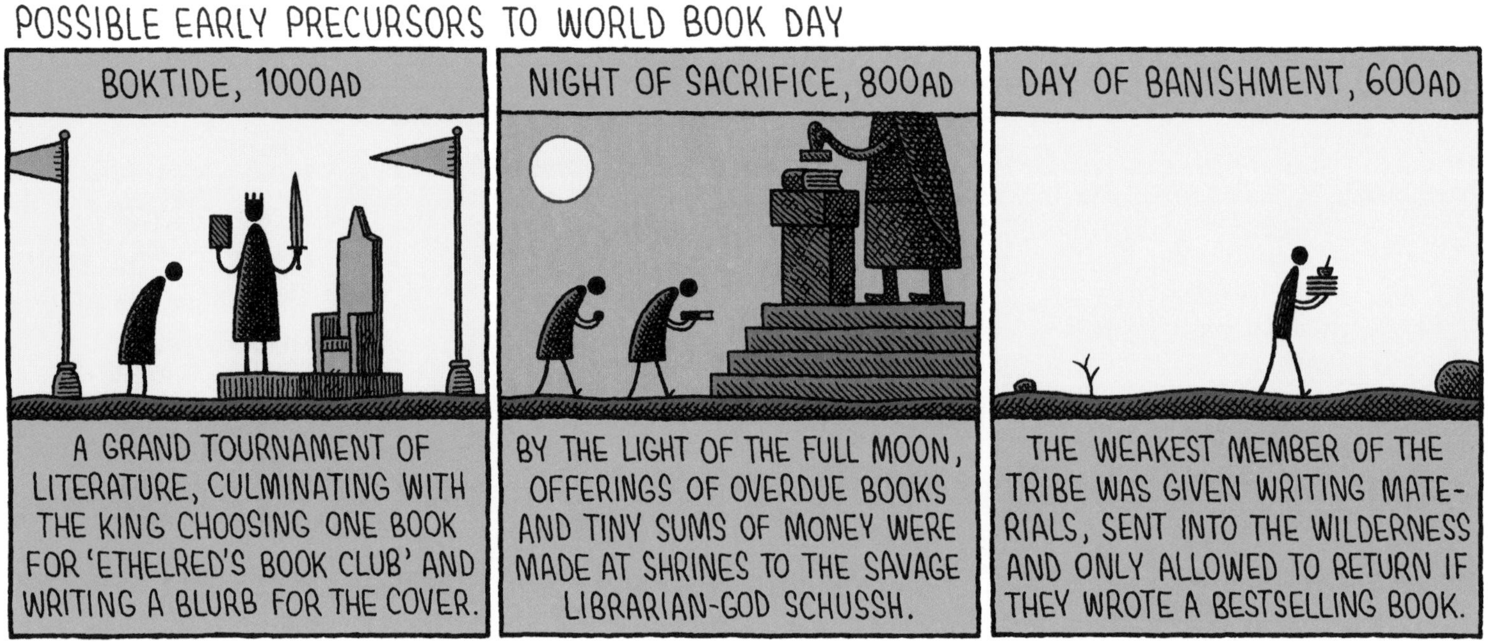
POSSIBLE EARLY PRECURSORS TO WORLD BOOK DAY
BOKTIDE, 1000AD
A GRAND TOURNAMENT OF LITERATURE, CULMINATING WITH THE KING CHOOSING ONE BOOK FOR 'ETHELRED'S BOOK CLUB' AND WRITING A BLURB FOR THE COVER.
NIGHT OF SACRIFICE, 800AD
BY THE LIGHT OF THE FULL MOON, OFFERINGS OF OVERDUE BOOKS AND TINY SUMS OF MONEY WERE MADE AT SHRINES TO THE SAVAGE LIBRARIAN-GOD SCHUSSH.
DAY OF BANISHMENT, 600AD
THE WEAKEST MEMBER OF THE TRIBE WAS GIVEN WRITING MATERIALS, SENT INTO THE WILDERNESS AND ONLY ALLOWED TO RETURN IF THEY WROTE A BESTSELLING BOOK.

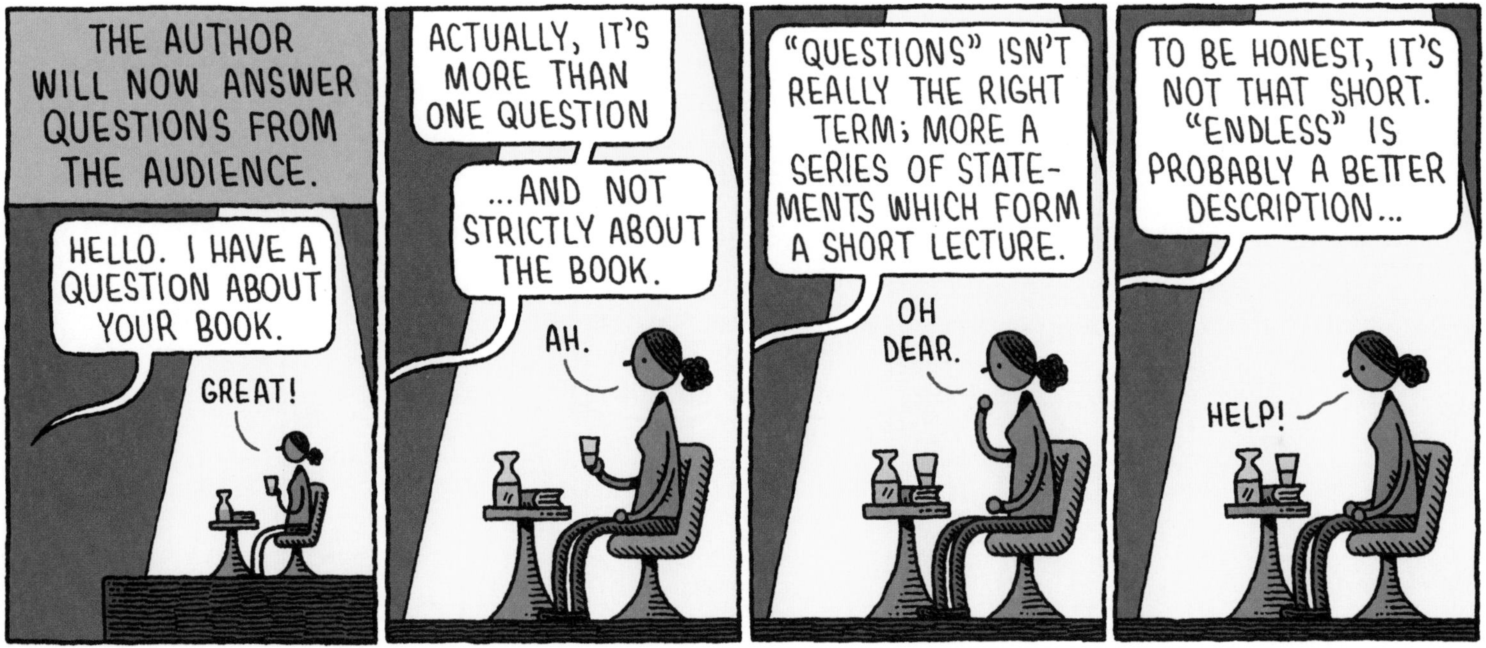
THE AUTHOR WILL NOW ANSWER QUESTIONS FROM THE AUDIENCE.
HELLO. I HAVE A QUESTION ABOUT YOUR BOOK.
GREAT!
ACTUALLY, IT'S MORE THAN ONE QUESTION
...AND NOT STRICTLY ABOUT THE BOOK.
AH.
"QUESTIONS" ISN'T REALLY THE RIGHT TERM; MORE A SERIES OF STATE-MENTS WHICH FORM A SHORT LECTURE.
OH DEAR.
TO BE HONEST, IT'S NOT THAT SHORT. "ENDLESS" IS PROBABLY A BETTER DESCRIPTION...
HELP!

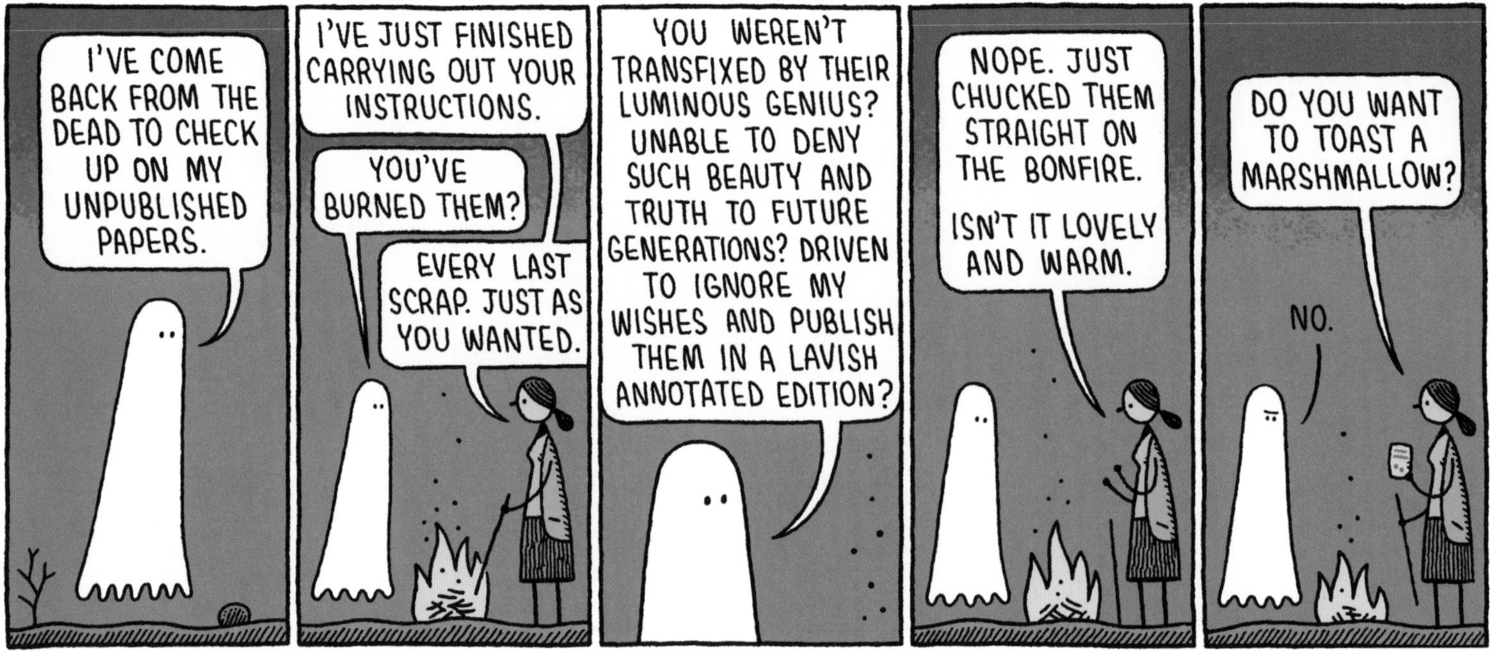
I'VE COME BACK FROM THE DEAD TO CHECK UP ON MY UNPUBLISHED PAPERS.
I'VE JUST FINISHED CARRYING OUT YOUR INSTRUCTIONS.
YOU'VE BURNED THEM?
EVERY LAST SCRAP. JUST AS YOU WANTED.
YOU WEREN'T TRANSFIXED BY THEIR LUMINOUS GENIUS? UNABLE TO DENY SUCH BEAUTY AND TRUTH TO FUTURE GENERATIONS? DRIVEN TO IGNORE MY WISHES AND PUBLISH THEM IN A LAVISH ANNOTATED EDITION?
NOPE. JUST CHUCKED THEM STRAIGHT ON THE BONFIRE.
ISN'T IT LOVELY AND WARM.
DO YOU WANT TO TOAST A MARSHMALLOW?
NO.

REARRANGING MY BOOKSHELVES

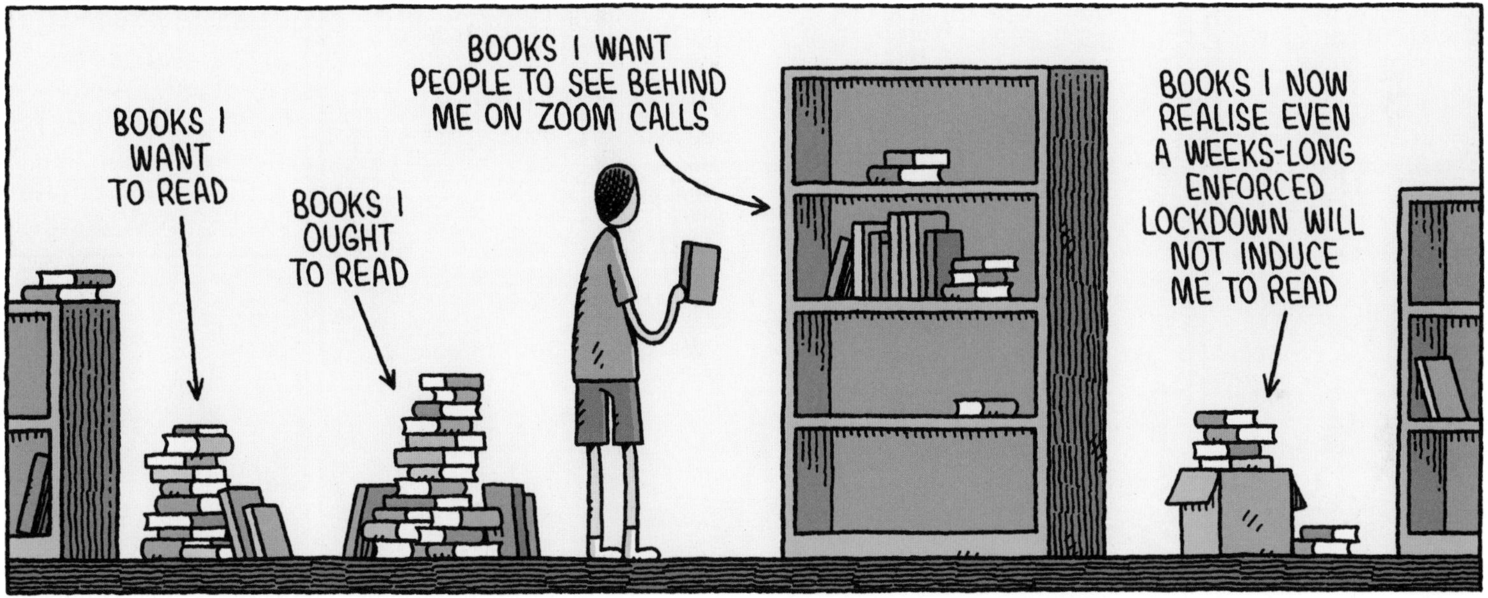
BOOKS I WANT TO READ
BOOKS I OUGHT TO READ
BOOKS I WANT PEOPLE TO SEE BEHIND ME ON ZOOM CALLS
BOOKS I NOW REALISE EVEN A WEEKS-LONG ENFORCED LOCKDOWN WILL NOT INDUCE ME TO READ

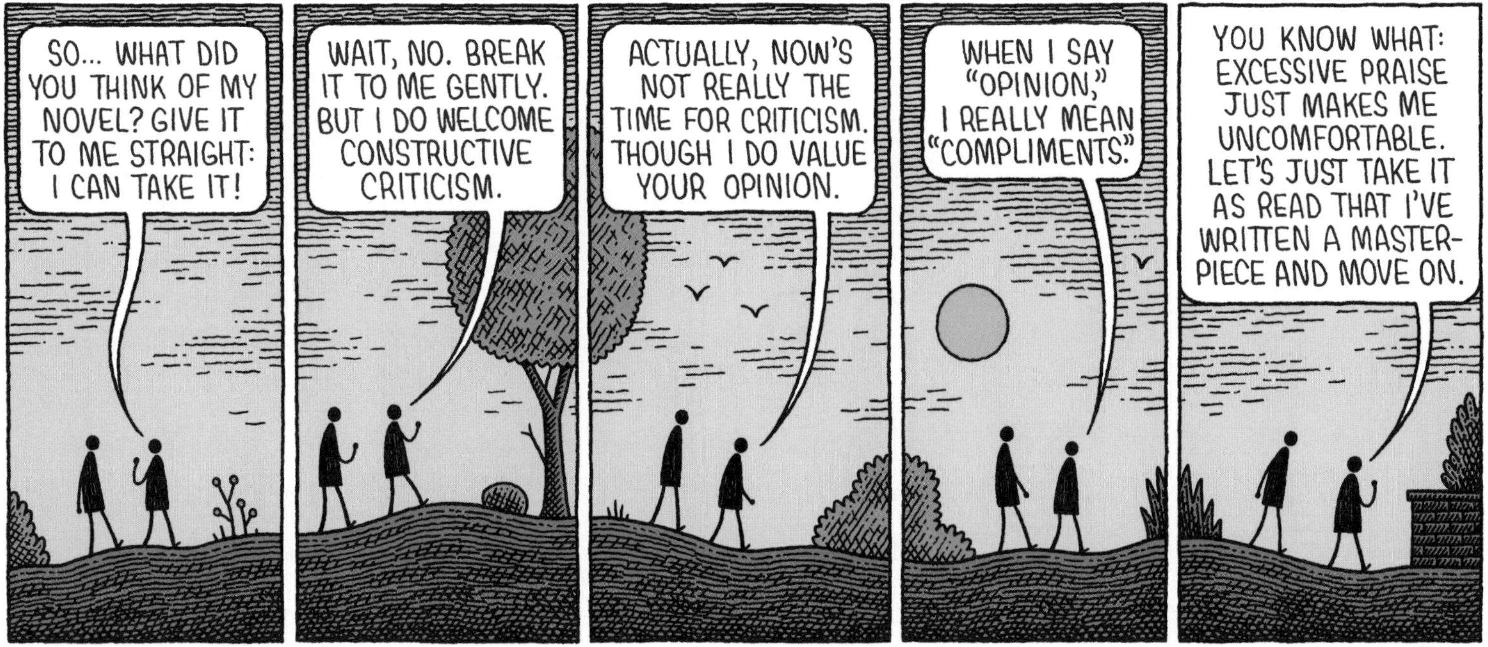
SO... WHAT DID YOU THINK OF MY NOVEL? GIVE IT TO ME STRAIGHT: I CAN TAKE IT!
WAIT, NO. BREAK IT TO ME GENTLY. BUT I DO WELCOME CONSTRUCTIVE CRITICISM.
ACTUALLY, NOW'S NOT REALLY THE TIME FOR CRITICISM. THOUGH I DO VALUE YOUR OPINION.
WHEN I SAY "OPINION," I REALLY MEAN "COMPLIMENTS."
YOU KNOW WHAT: EXCESSIVE PRAISE JUST MAKES ME UNCOMFORTABLE. LET'S JUST TAKE IT AS READ THAT I'VE WRITTEN A MASTER-PIECE AND MOVE ON.

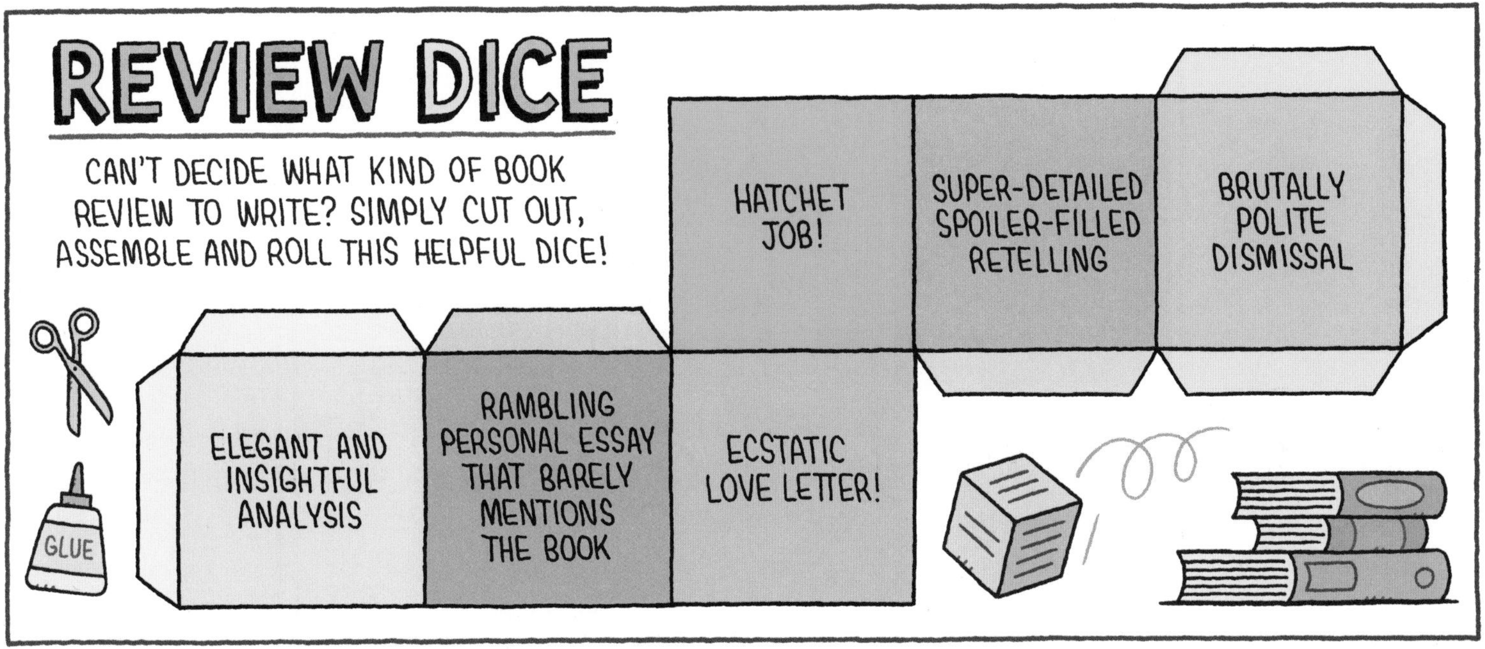
REVIEW DICE
CAN'T DECIDE WHAT KIND OF BOOK REVIEW TO WRITE? SIMPLY CUT OUT, ASSEMBLE AND ROLL THIS HELPFUL DICE!
HATCHET JOB!
SUPER-DETAILED SPOILER-FILLED RETELLING
BRUTALLY POLITE DISMISSAL
ELEGANT AND INSIGHTFUL ANALYSIS
RAMBLING PERSONAL ESSAY THAT BARELY MENTIONS THE BOOK
ECSTATIC LOVE LETTER!
GLUE

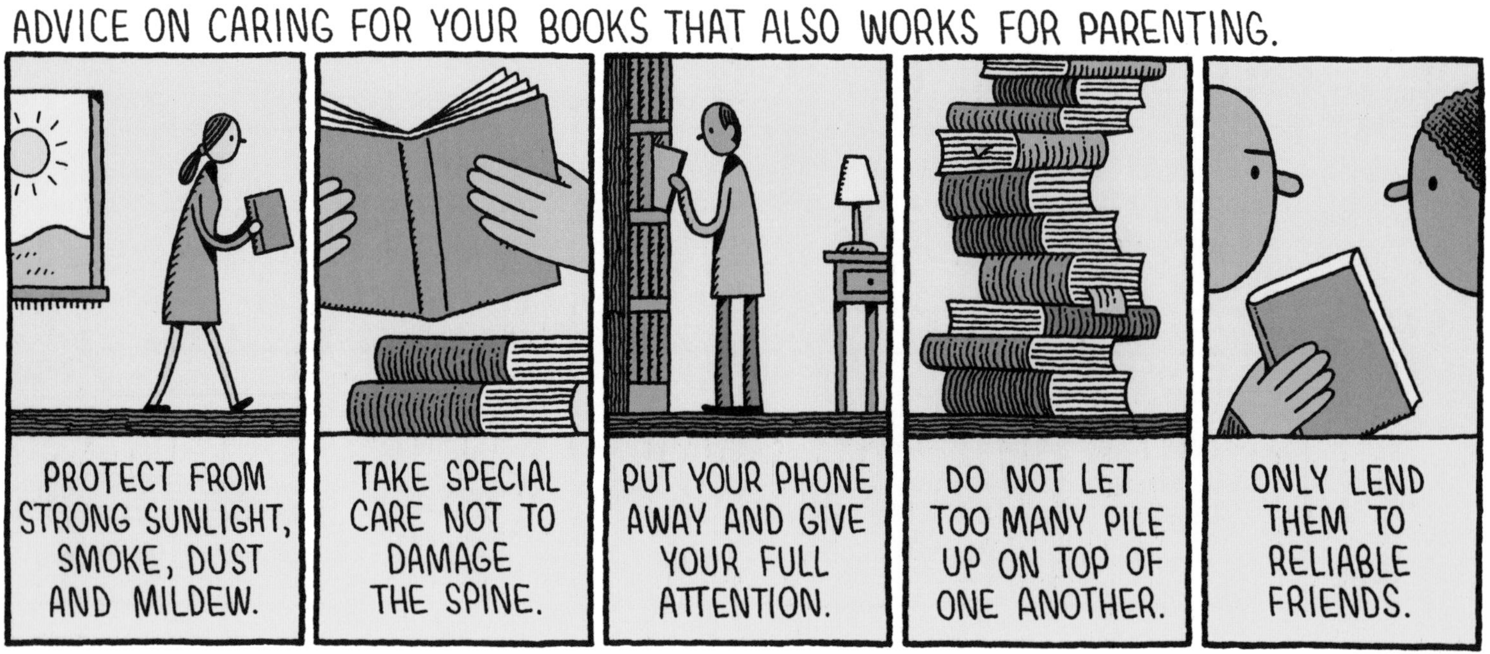
ADVICE ON CARING FOR YOUR BOOKS THAT ALSO WORKS FOR PARENTING.
PROTECT FROM STRONG SUNLIGHT, SMOKE, DUST AND MILDEW.
TAKE SPECIAL CARE NOT TO DAMAGE THE SPINE.
PUT YOUR PHONE AWAY AND GIVE YOUR FULL ATTENTION.
DO NOT LET TOO MANY PILE UP ON TOP OF ONE ANOTHER.
ONLY LEND THEM TO RELIABLE FRIENDS.

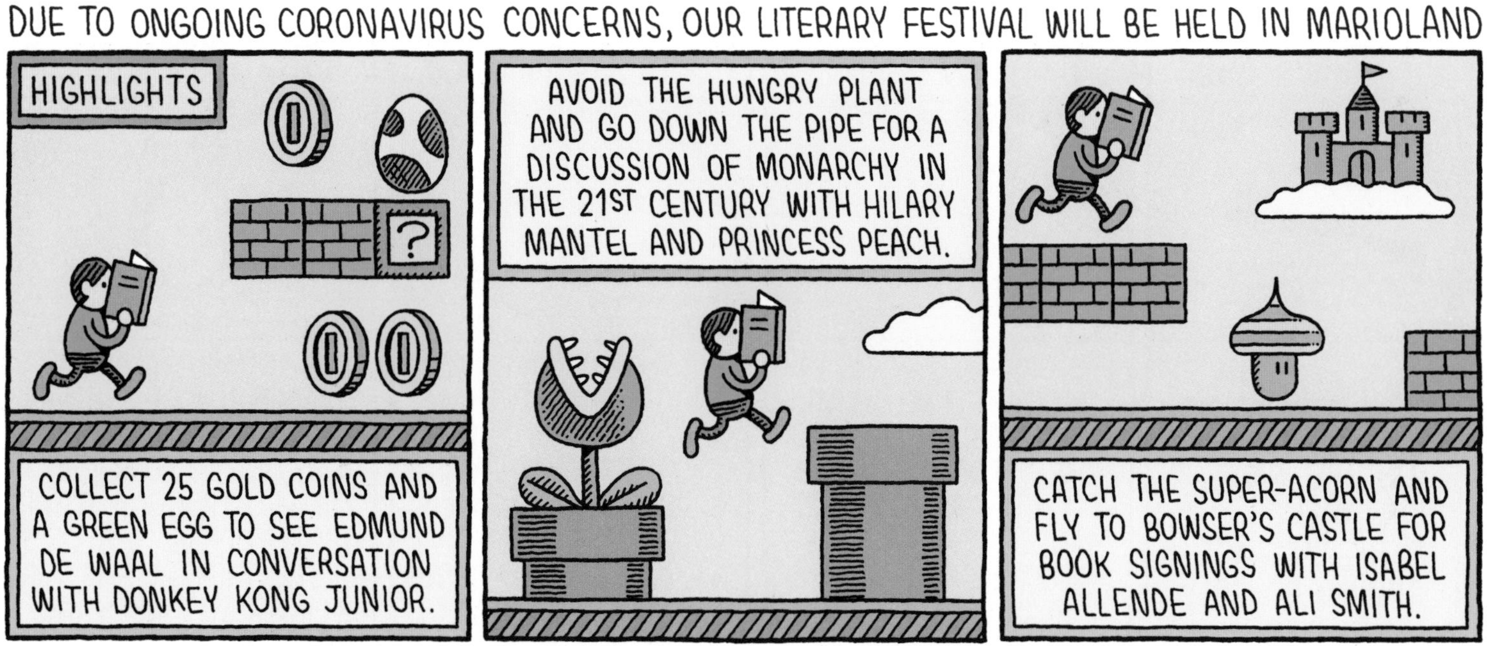

DUE TO ONGOING CORONAVIRUS CONCERNS, OUR LITERARY FESTIVAL WILL BE HELD IN MARIOLAND
HIGHLIGHTS
?
COLLECT 25 GOLD COINS AND A GREEN EGG TO SEE EDMUND DE WAAL IN CONVERSATION WITH DONKEY KONG JUNIOR.
AVOID THE HUNGRY PLANT AND GO DOWN THE PIPE FOR A DISCUSSION OF MONARCHY IN THE 21ST CENTURY WITH HILARY MANTEL AND PRINCESS PEACH.
CATCH THE SUPER-ACORN AND FLY TO BOWSER'S CASTLE FOR BOOK SIGNINGS WITH ISABEL ALLENDE AND ALI SMITH.

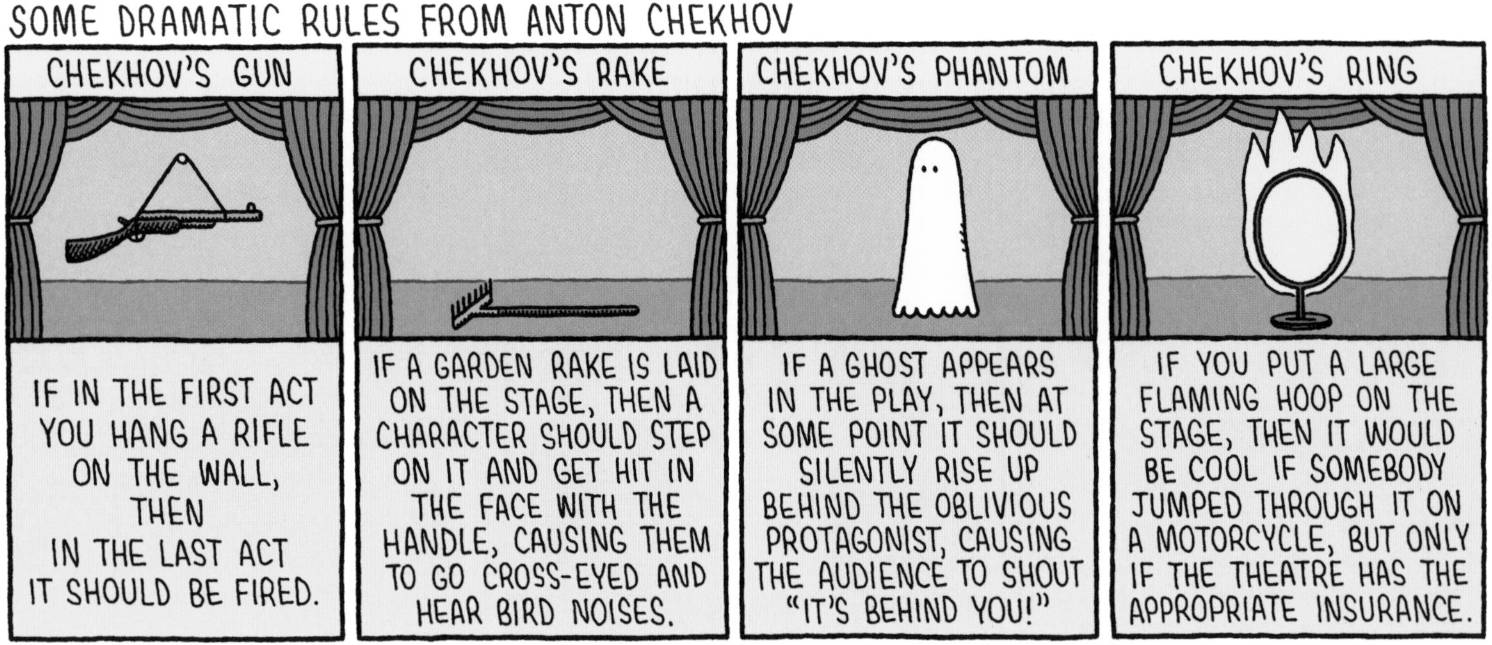
SOME DRAMATIC RULES FROM ANTON CHEKHOV
CHEKHOV'S GUN
IF IN THE FIRST ACT YOU HANG A RIFLE ON THE WALL, THEN IN THE LAST ACT IT SHOULD BE FIRED.
CHEKHOV'S RAKE
IF A GARDEN RAKE IS LAID ON THE STAGE, THEN A CHARACTER SHOULD STEP ON IT AND GET HIT IN THE FACE WITH THE HANDLE, CAUSING THEM TO GO CROSS-EYED AND HEAR BIRD NOISES.
CHEKHOV'S PHANTOM
IF A GHOST APPEARS IN THE PLAY, THEN AT SOME POINT IT SHOULD SILENTLY RISE UP BEHIND THE OBLIVIOUS PROTAGONIST, CAUSING THE AUDIENCE TO SHOUT "IT'S BEHIND YOU!"
CHEKHOV'S RING
IF YOU PUT A LARGE FLAMING HOOP ON THE STAGE, THEN IT WOULD BE COOL IF SOMEBODY JUMPED THROUGH IT ON A MOTORCYCLE, BUT ONLY IF THE THEATRE HAS THE APPROPRIATE INSURANCE.

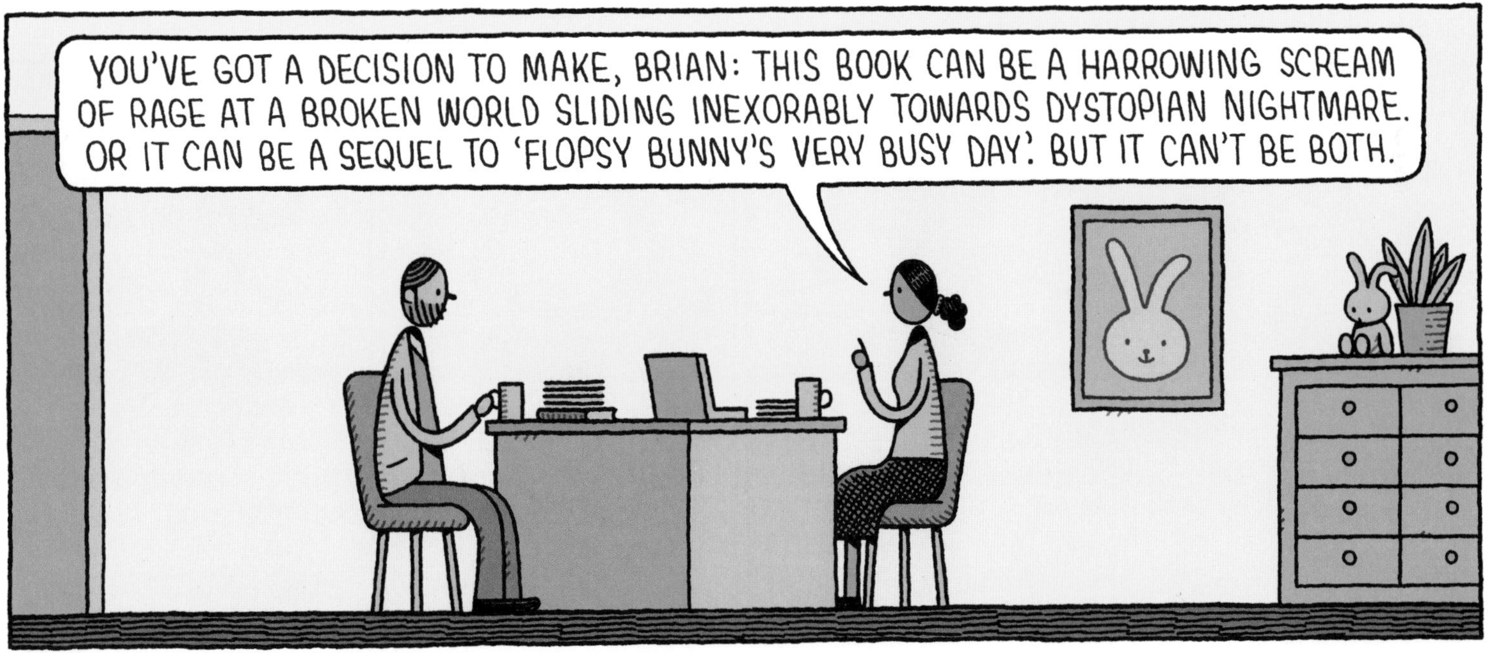
YOU'VE GOT A DECISION TO MAKE, BRIAN: THIS BOOK CAN BE A HARROWING SCREAM OF RAGE AT A BROKEN WORLD SLIDING INEXORABLY TOWARDS DYSTOPIAN NIGHTMARE. OR IT CAN BE A SEQUEL TO 'FLOPSY BUNNY'S VERY BUSY DAY'. BUT IT CAN'T BE BOTH.

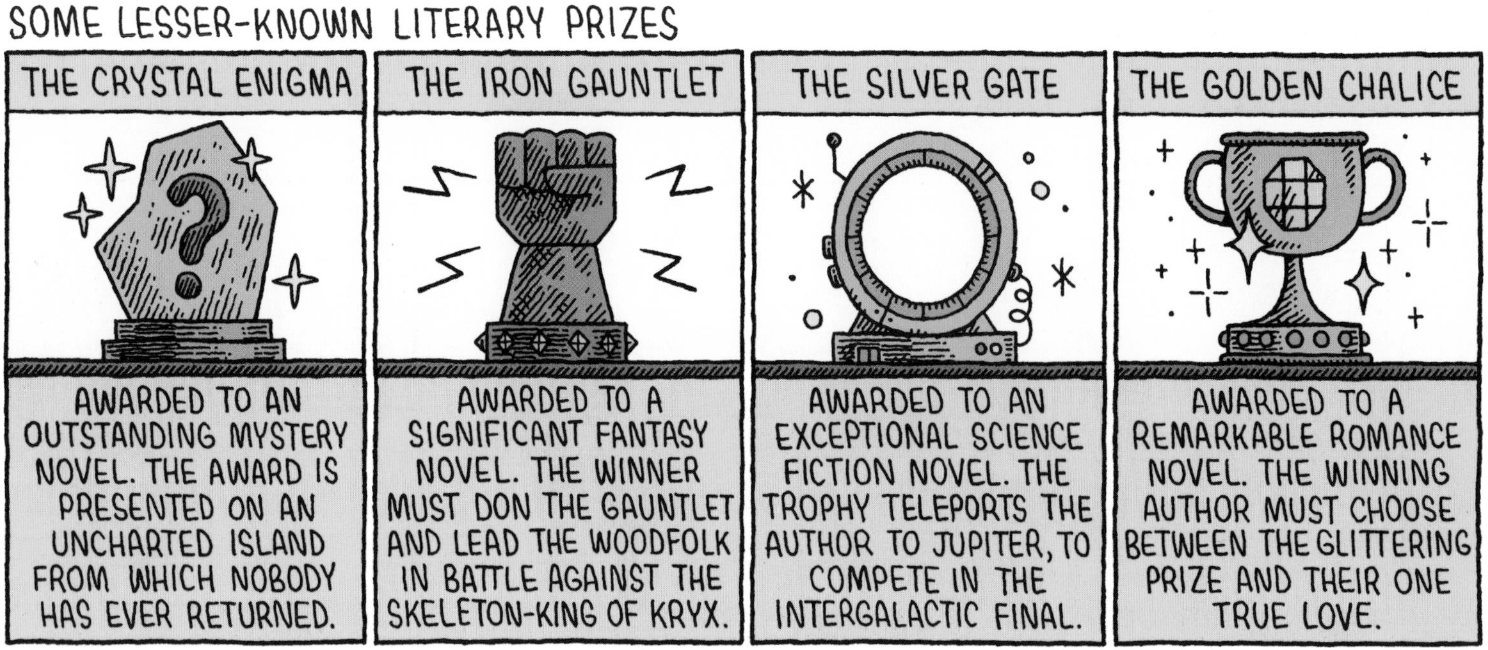
SOME LESSER-KNOWN LITERARY PRIZES
THE CRYSTAL ENIGMA
AWARDED TO AN OUTSTANDING MYSTERY NOVEL. THE AWARD IS PRESENTED ON AN UNCHARTED ISLAND FROM WHICH NOBODY HAS EVER RETURNED.
THE IRON GAUNTLET
AWARDED TO A SIGNIFICANT FANTASY NOVEL. THE WINNER MUST DON THE GAUNTLET AND LEAD THE WOODFOLK IN BATTLE AGAINST THE SKELETON-KING OF KRYX.
THE SILVER GATE
AWARDED TO AN EXCEPTIONAL SCIENCE FICTION NOVEL. THE TROPHY TELEPORTS THE AUTHOR TO JUPITER, TO COMPETE IN THE INTERGALACTIC FINAL.
THE GOLDEN CHALICE
AWARDED TO A REMARKABLE ROMANCE NOVEL. THE WINNING AUTHOR MUST CHOOSE BETWEEN THE GLITTERING PRIZE AND THEIR ONE TRUE LOVE.

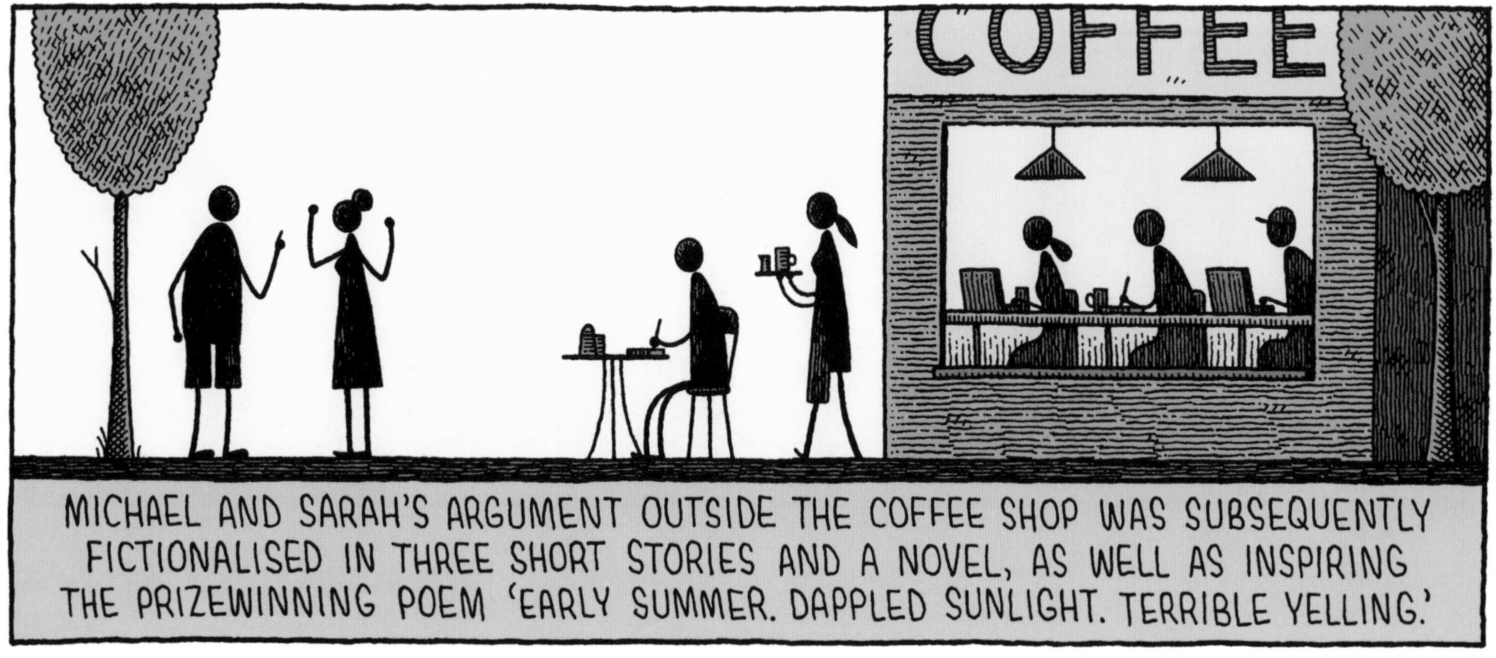
COFFEE

MICHAEL AND SARAH'S ARGUMENT OUTSIDE THE COFFEE SHOP WAS SUBSEQUENTLY FICTIONALISED IN THREE SHORT STORIES AND A NOVEL, AS WELL AS INSPIRING THE PRIZEWINNING POEM 'EARLY SUMMER. DAPPLED SUNLIGHT. TERRIBLE YELLING.'

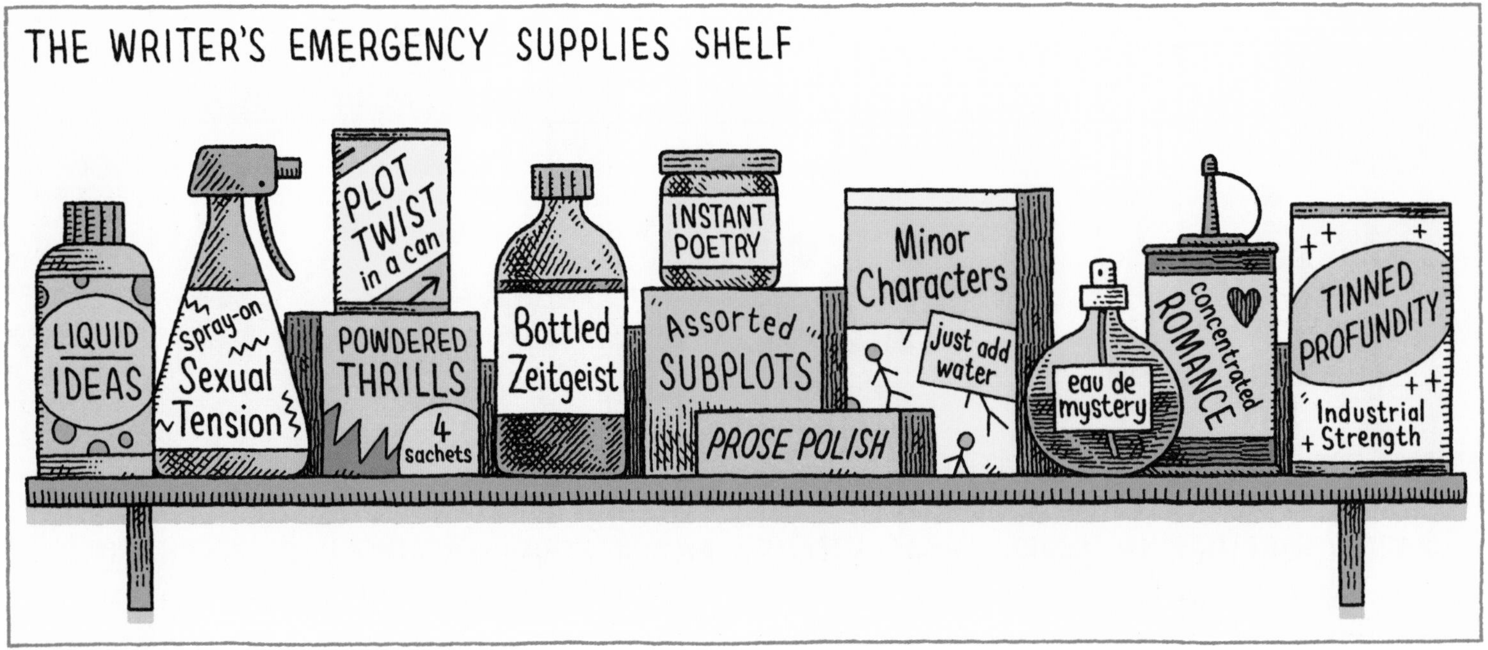
THE WRITER'S EMERGENCY SUPPLIES SHELF
LIQUID IDEAS
Spray-on Sexual Tension
PLOT TWIST in a can
POWDERED THRILLS
4 sachets
Bottled Zeitgeist
INSTANT POETRY
Assorted SUBPLOTS
PROSE POLISH
Minor Characters
just add water
eau de mystery
concentrated ROMANCE
TINNED PROFUNDITY
Industrial Strength

THE ARMY OF RONNODIR RIDES NORTH TO BATTLE THE SKELETON QUEEN...

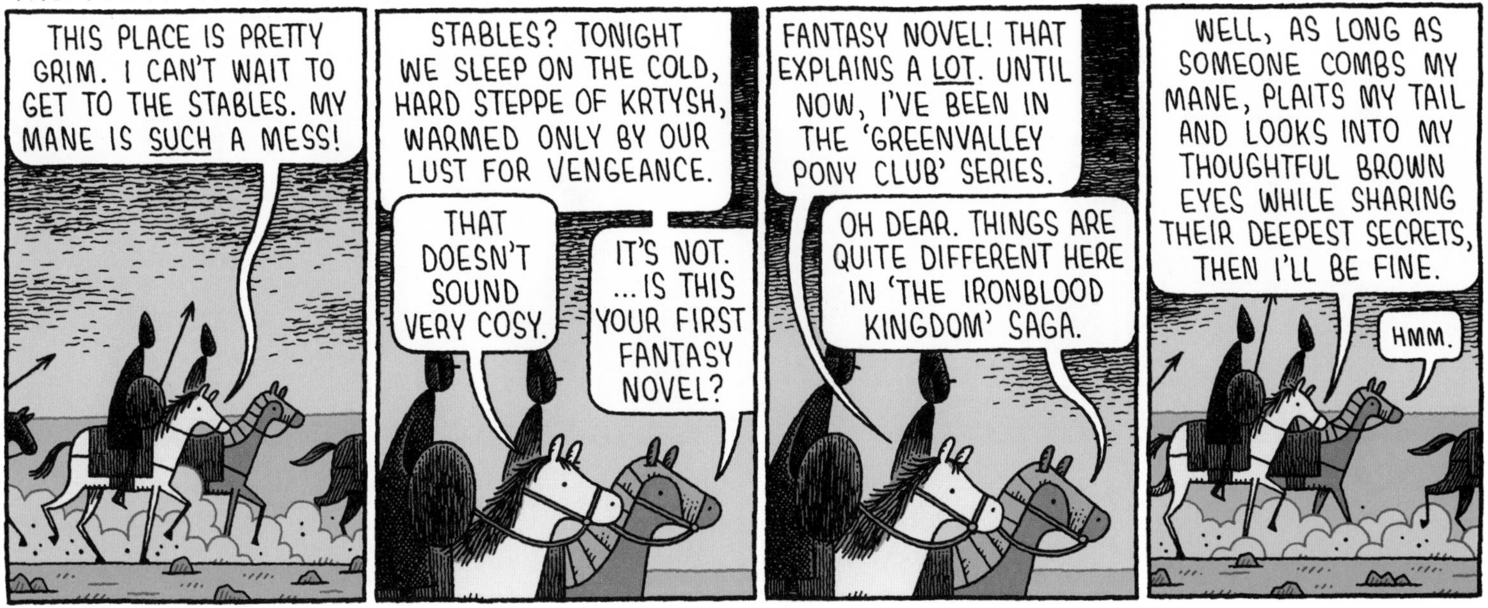
THIS PLACE IS PRETTY GRIM. I CAN'T WAIT TO GET TO THE STABLES. MY MANE IS SUCH A MESS!
STABLES? TONIGHT WE SLEEP ON THE COLD, HARD STEPPE OF KRTYSH, WARMED ONLY BY OUR LUST FOR VENGEANCE.
THAT DOESN'T SOUND VERY COSY.
IT'S NOT. ...IS THIS YOUR FIRST FANTASY NOVEL?
FANTASY NOVEL! THAT EXPLAINS A LOT. UNTIL NOW, I'VE BEEN IN THE 'GREENVALLEY PONY CLUB' SERIES.
OH DEAR. THINGS ARE QUITE DIFFERENT HERE IN 'THE IRONBLOOD KINGDOM' SAGA.
WELL, AS LONG AS SOMEONE COMBS MY MANE, PLAITS MY TAIL AND LOOKS INTO MY THOUGHTFUL BROWN EYES WHILE SHARING THEIR DEEPEST SECRETS, THEN I'LL BE FINE.
HMM.

CORONAVIRUS ADVICE FROM A REGENCY NOVEL

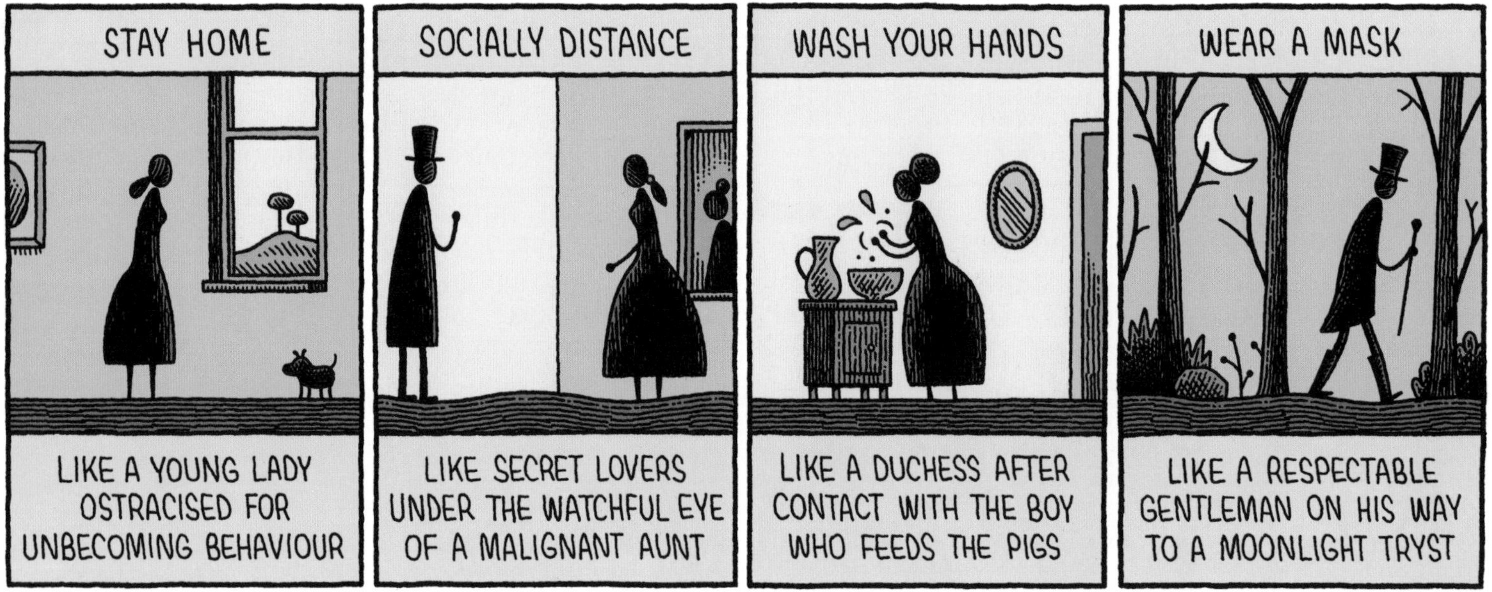
STAY HOME
LIKE A YOUNG LADY OSTRACISED FOR UNBECOMING BEHAVIOUR
SOCIALLY DISTANCE
LIKE SECRET LOVERS UNDER THE WATCHFUL EYE OF A MALIGNANT AUNT
WASH YOUR HANDS
LIKE A DUCHESS AFTER CONTACT WITH THE BOY WHO FEEDS THE PIGS
WEAR A MASK
LIKE A RESPECTABLE GENTLEMAN ON HIS WAY TO A MOONLIGHT TRYST

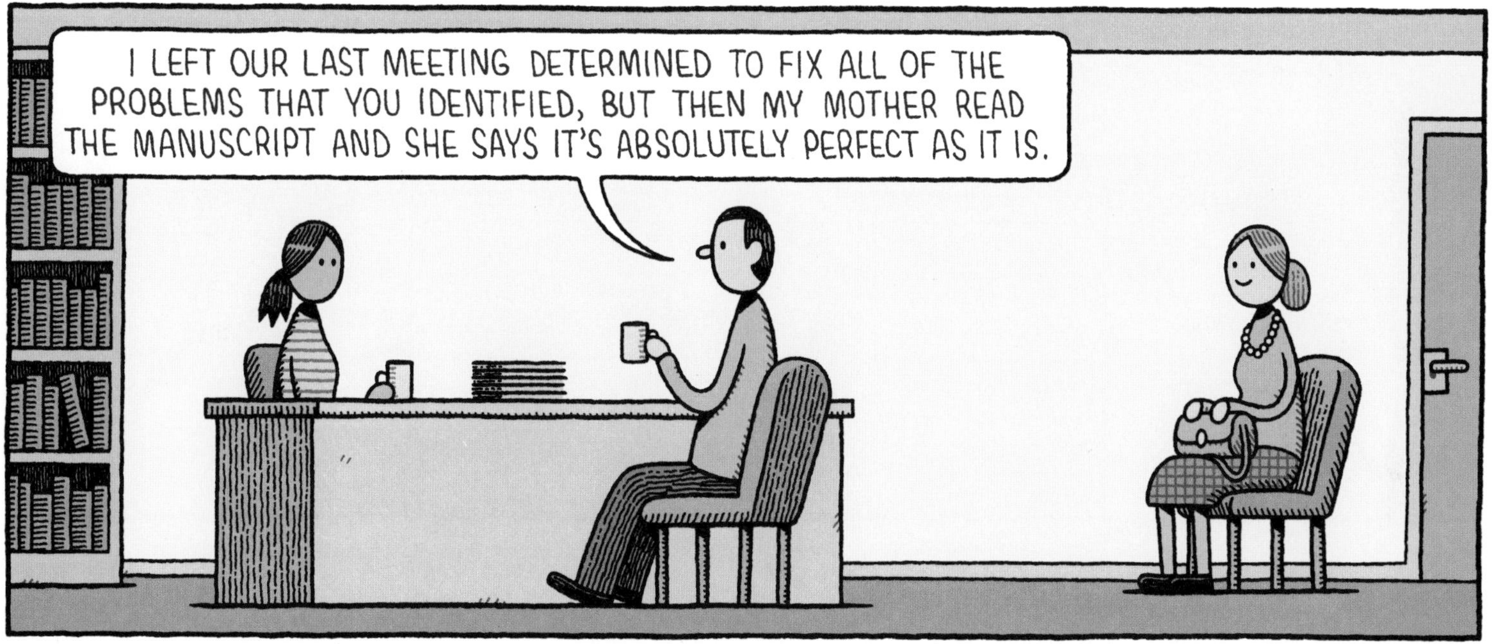
I LEFT OUR LAST MEETING DETERMINED TO FIX ALL OF THE PROBLEMS THAT YOU IDENTIFIED, BUT THEN MY MOTHER READ THE MANUSCRIPT AND SHE SAYS IT'S ABSOLUTELY PERFECT AS IT IS.

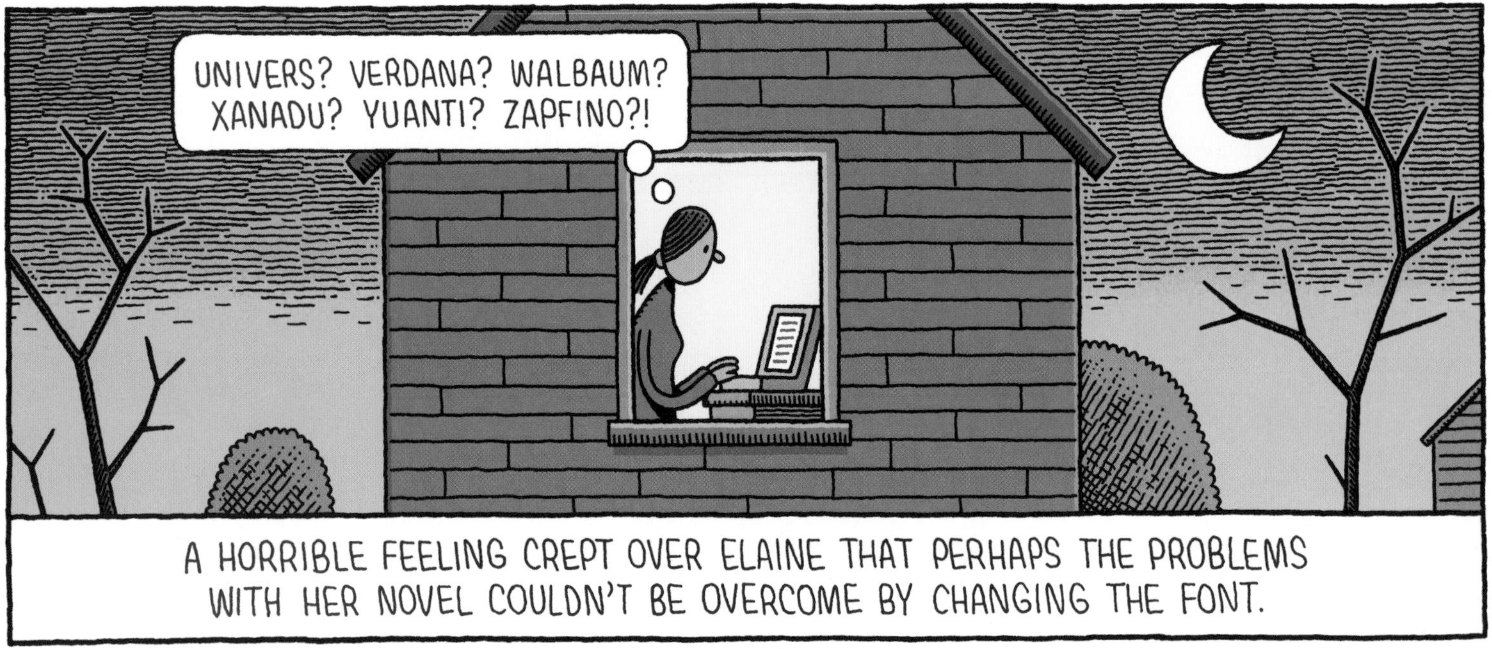
UNIVERS? VERDANA? WALBAUM? XANADU? YUANTI? ZAPFINO?!
A HORRIBLE FEELING CREPT OVER ELAINE THAT PERHAPS THE PROBLEMS WITH HER NOVEL COULDN'T BE OVERCOME BY CHANGING THE FONT.

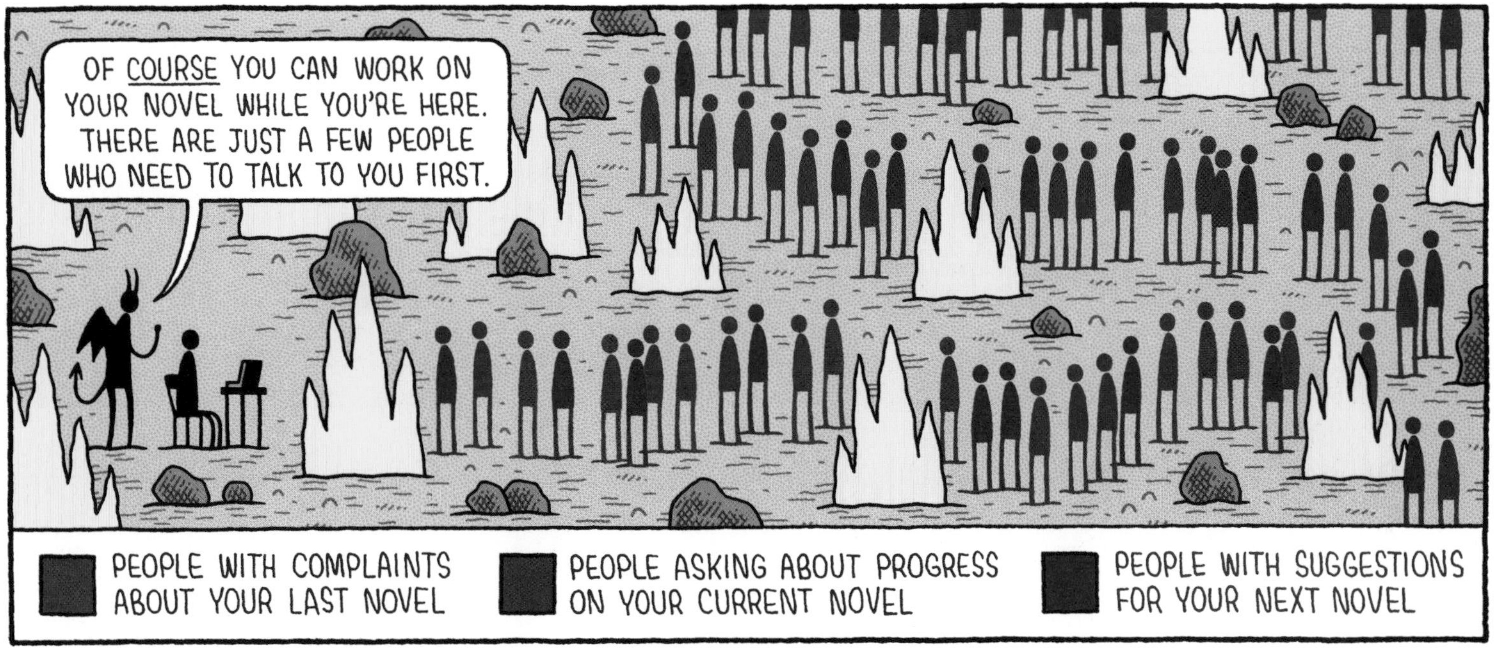
OF COURSE YOU CAN WORK ON YOUR NOVEL WHILE YOU'RE HERE. THERE ARE JUST A FEW PEOPLE WHO NEED TO TALK TO YOU FIRST.
PEOPLE WITH COMPLAINTS ABOUT YOUR LAST NOVEL
PEOPLE ASKING ABOUT PROGRESS ON YOUR CURRENT NOVEL
PEOPLE WITH SUGGESTIONS FOR YOUR NEXT NOVEL

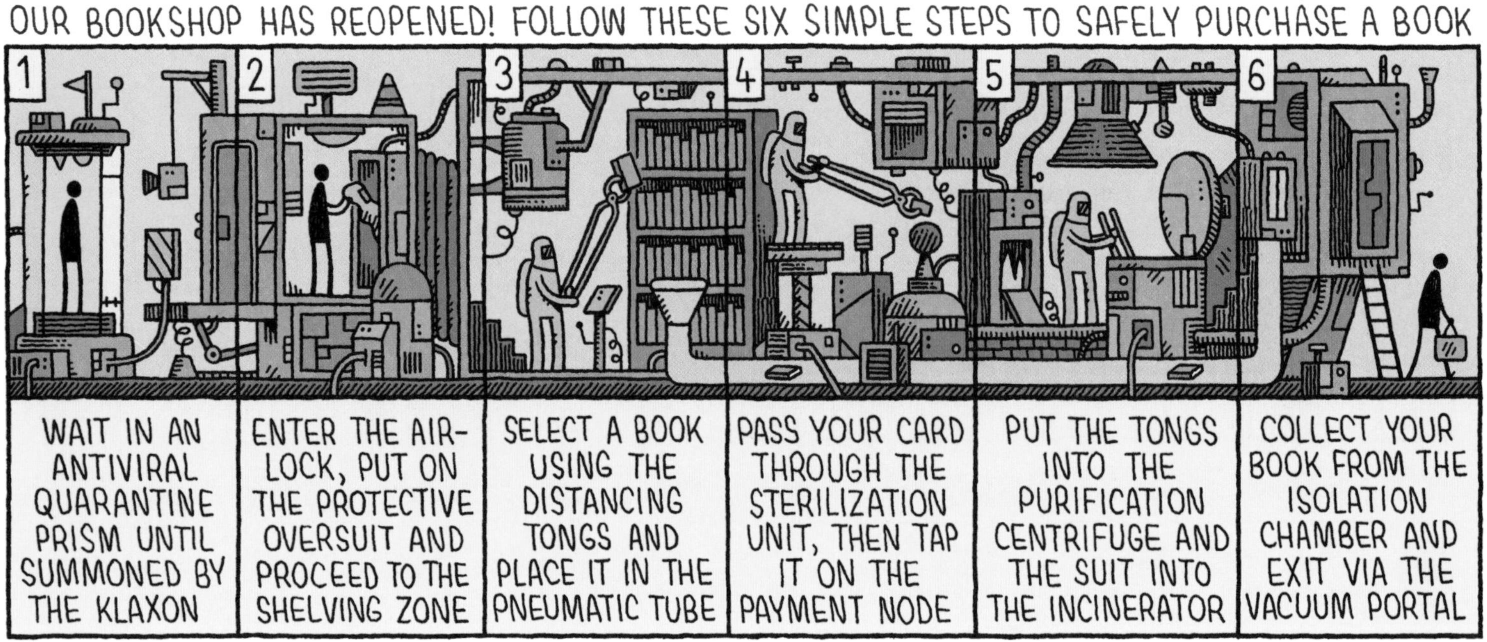
OUR BOOKSHOP HAS REOPENED! FOLLOW THESE SIX SIMPLE STEPS TO SAFELY PURCHASE A BOOK
1
WAIT IN AN ANTIVIRAL QUARANTINE PRISM UNTIL SUMMONED BY THE KLAXON
2
ENTER THE AIR-LOCK, PUT ON THE PROTECTIVE OVERSUIT AND PROCEED TO THE SHELVING ZONE
3
SELECT A BOOK USING THE DISTANCING TONGS AND PLACE IT IN THE PNEUMATIC TUBE
4
PASS YOUR CARD THROUGH THE STERILIZATION UNIT, THEN TAP IT ON THE PAYMENT NODE
5
PUT THE TONGS INTO THE PURIFICATION CENTRIFUGE AND THE SUIT INTO THE INCINERATOR
6
COLLECT YOUR BOOK FROM THE ISOLATION CHAMBER AND EXIT VIA THE VACUUM PORTAL

COMING SOON! CLASSIC NOVELS WITH ADDED POSITIVITY...

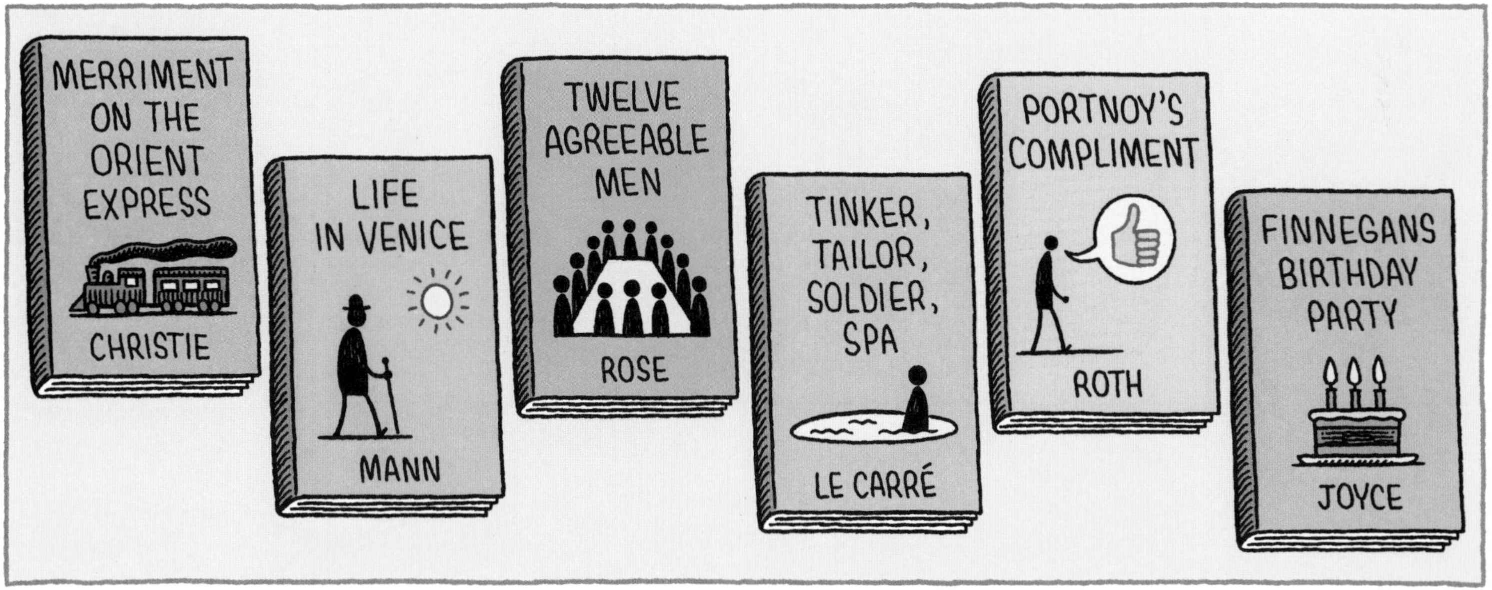
MERRIMENT ON THE ORIENT EXPRESS
CHRISTIE
LIFE IN VENICE
MANN
TWELVE AGREEABLE MEN
ROSE
TINKER, TAILOR, SOLDIER, SPA
LE CARRÉ
PORTNOY'S COMPLIMENT
ROTH
FINNEGANS BIRTHDAY PARTY
JOYCE

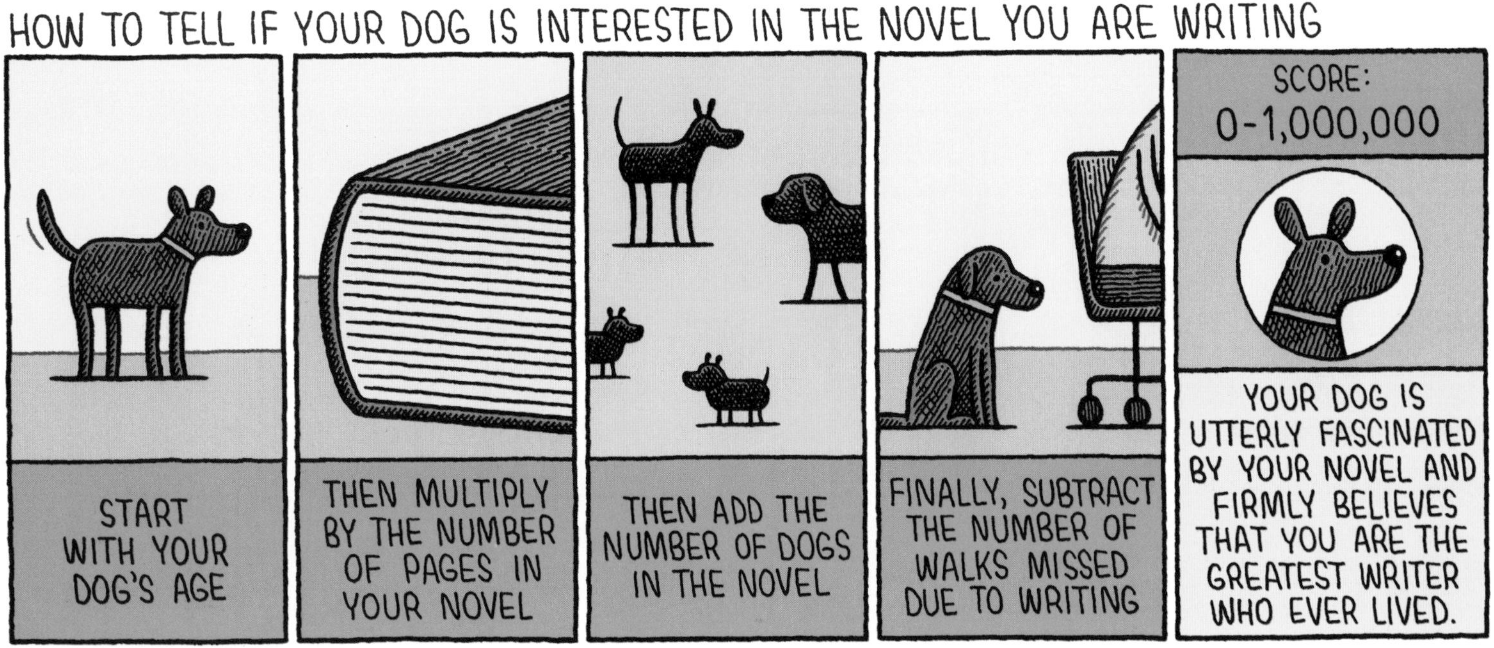
HOW TO TELL IF YOUR DOG IS INTERESTED IN THE NOVEL YOU ARE WRITING
START WITH YOUR DOG'S AGE
THEN MULTIPLY BY THE NUMBER OF PAGES IN YOUR NOVEL
THEN ADD THE NUMBER OF DOGS IN THE NOVEL
FINALLY, SUBTRACT THE NUMBER OF WALKS MISSED DUE TO WRITING
SCORE: 0-1,000,000
YOUR DOG IS UTTERLY FASCINATED BY YOUR NOVEL AND FIRMLY BELIEVES THAT YOU ARE THE GREATEST WRITER WHO EVER LIVED.

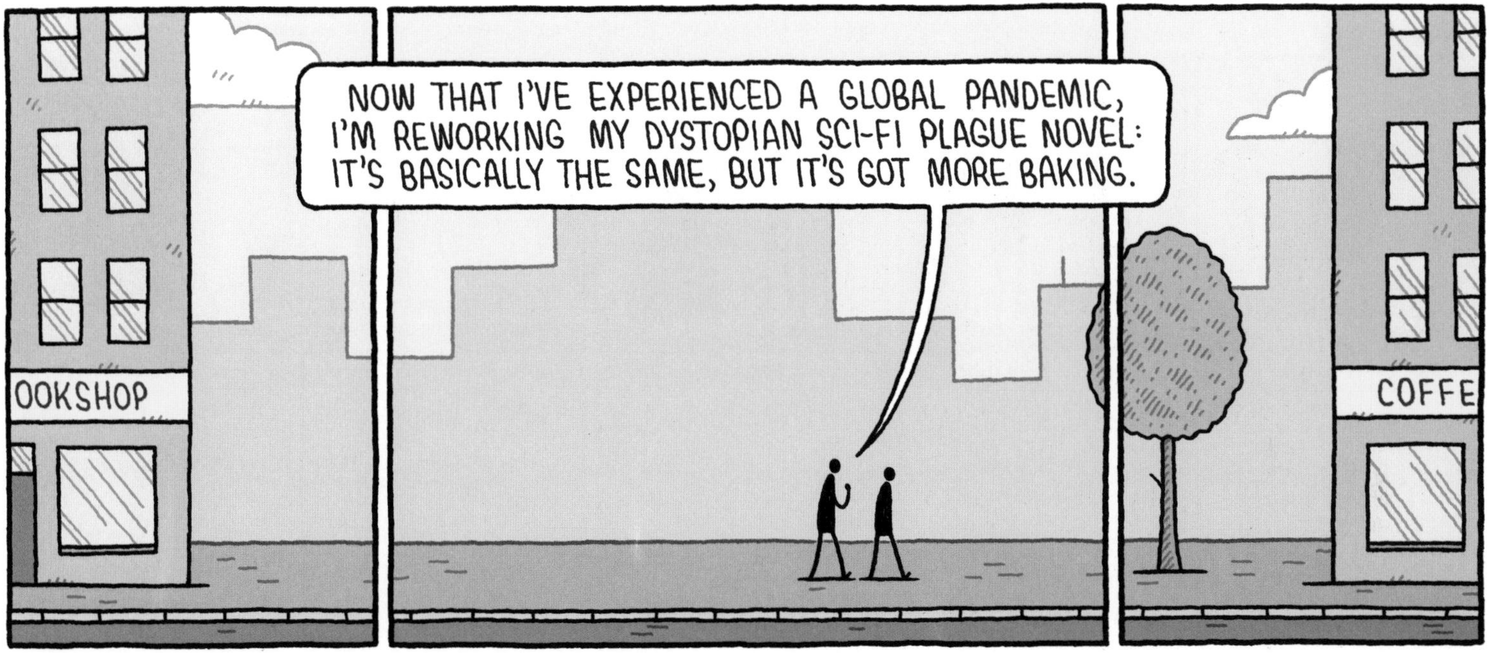
OOKSHOP
NOW THAT I'VE EXPERIENCED A GLOBAL PANDEMIC, I'M REWORKING MY DYSTOPIAN SCI-FI PLAGUE NOVEL: IT'S BASICALLY THE SAME, BUT IT'S GOT MORE BAKING.
COFFE

SOME ENDINGS FOR A JANE AUSTEN CHOOSE-YOUR-OWN-ADVENTURE BOOK

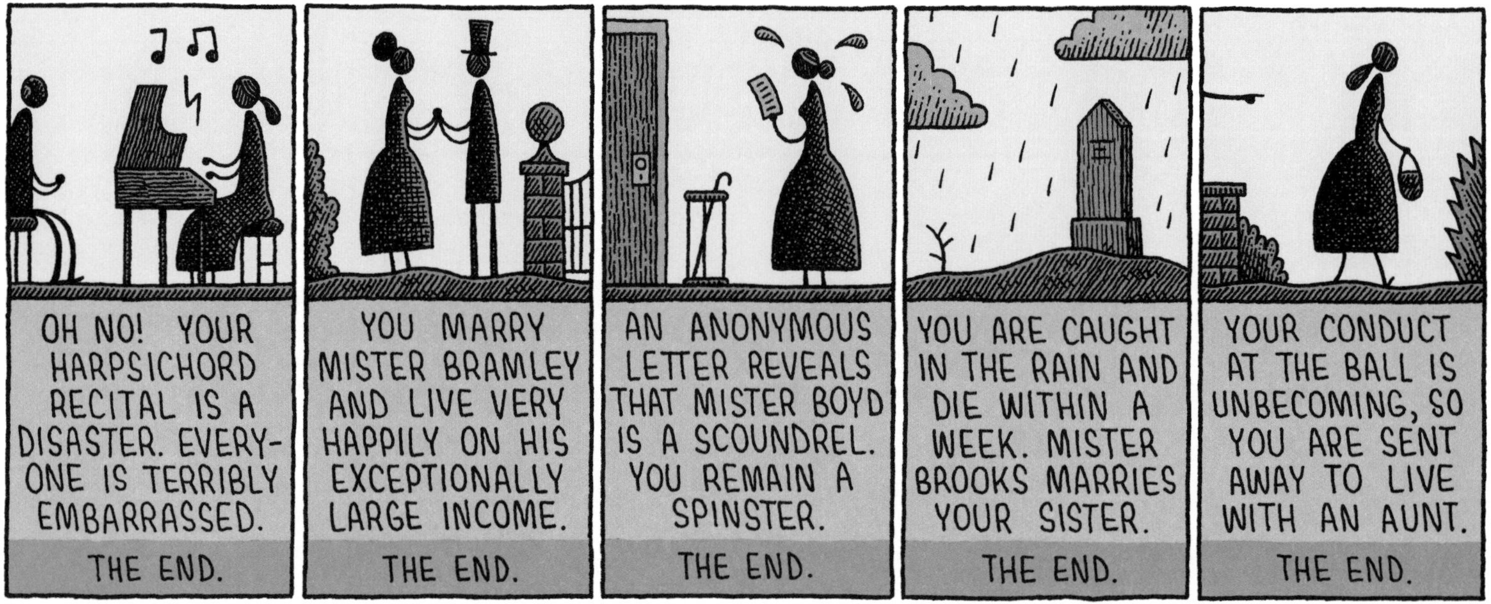
OH NO! YOUR HARPSICHORD RECITAL IS A DISASTER. EVERY-ONE IS TERRIBLY EMBARRASSED.
THE END.
YOU MARRY MISTER BRAMLEY AND LIVE VERY HAPPILY ON HIS EXCEPTIONALLY LARGE INCOME.
THE END.
AN ANONYMOUS LETTER REVEALS THAT MISTER BOYD IS A SCOUNDREL. YOU REMAIN A SPINSTER.
THE END.
YOU ARE CAUGHT IN THE RAIN AND DIE WITHIN A WEEK. MISTER BROOKS MARRIES YOUR SISTER.
THE END.
YOUR CONDUCT AT THE BALL IS UNBECOMING, SO YOU ARE SENT AWAY TO LIVE WITH AN AUNT.
THE END.

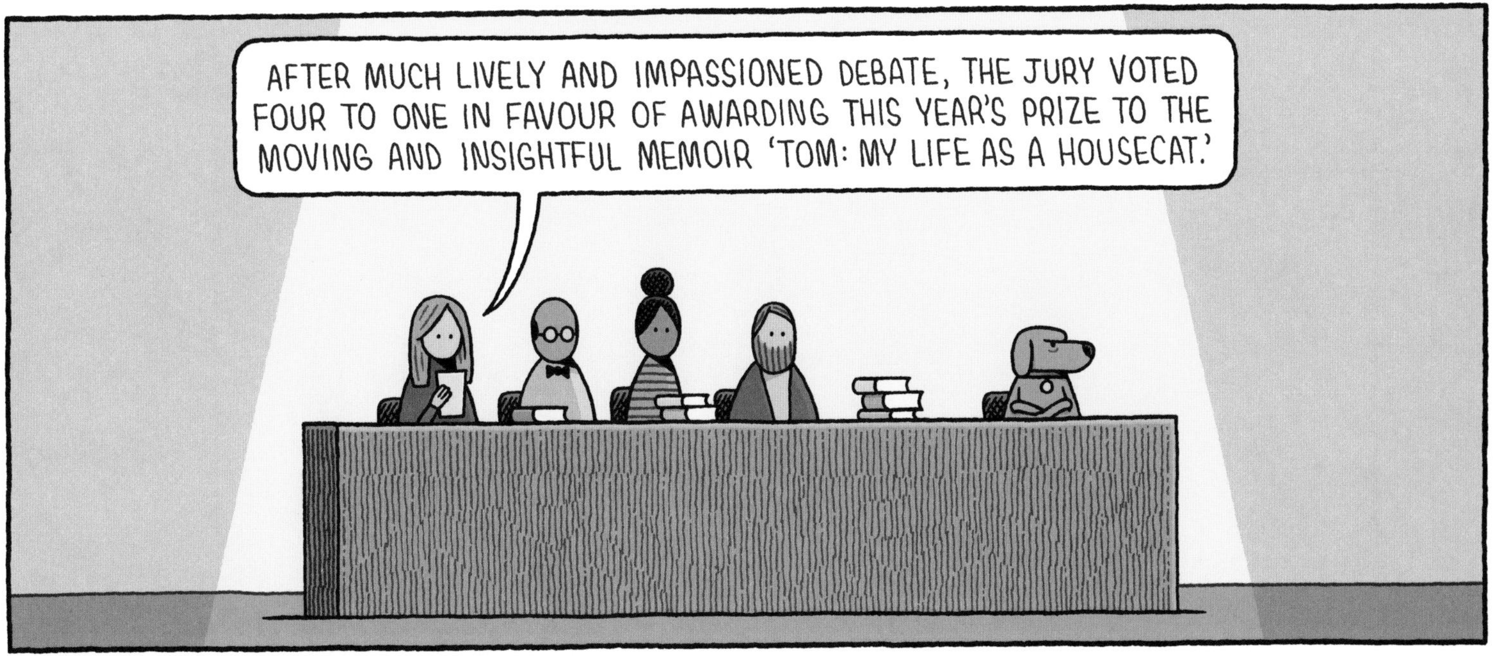
AFTER MUCH LIVELY AND IMPASSIONED DEBATE, THE JURY VOTED FOUR TO ONE IN FAVOUR OF AWARDING THIS YEAR'S PRIZE TO THE MOVING AND INSIGHTFUL MEMOIR 'TOM: MY LIFE AS A HOUSECAT.'

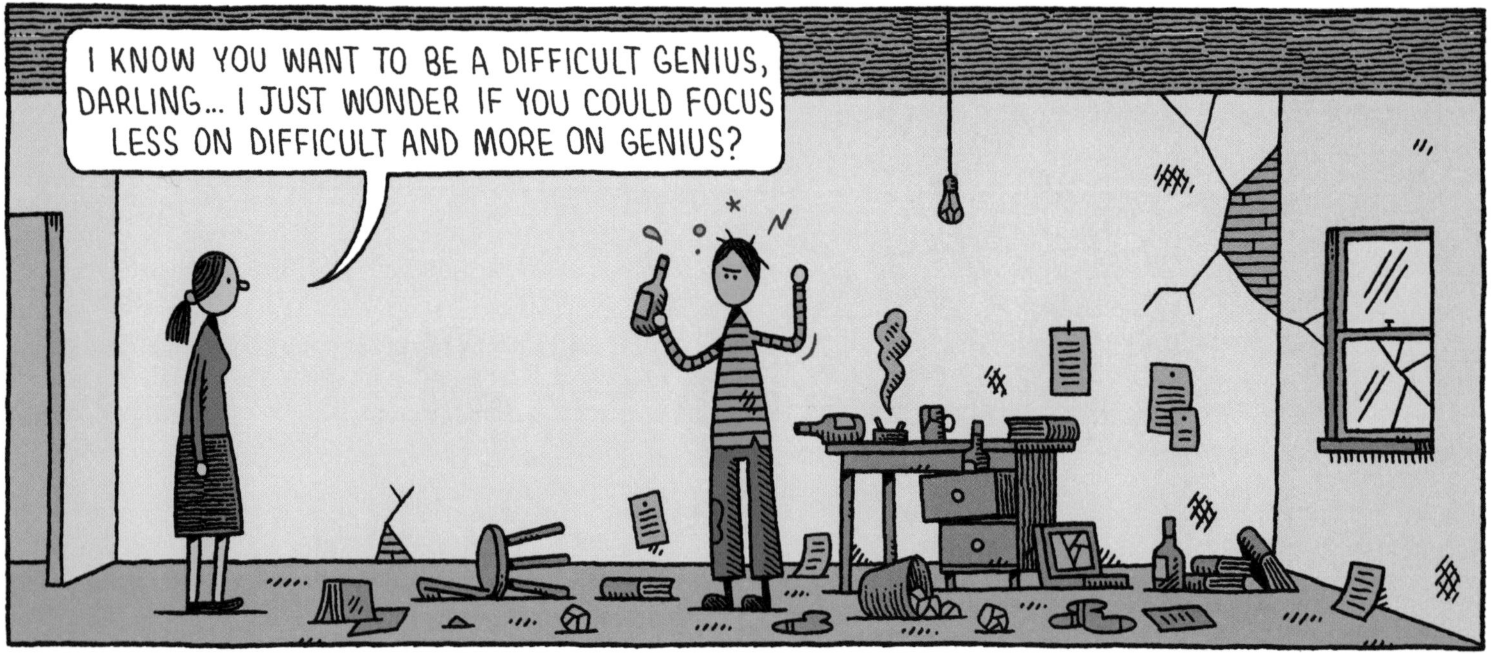
I KNOW YOU WANT TO BE A DIFFICULT GENIUS, DARLING... I JUST WONDER IF YOU COULD FOCUS LESS ON DIFFICULT AND MORE ON GENIUS?

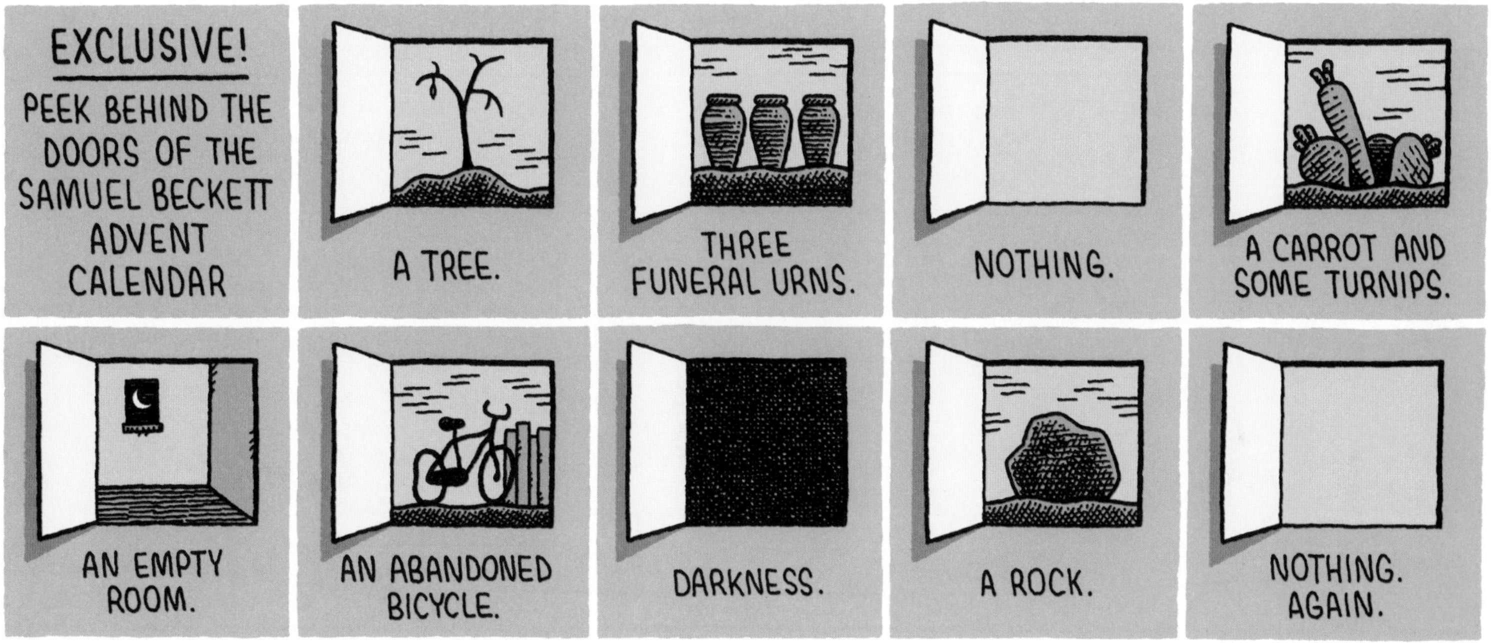
EXCLUSIVE!
PEEK BEHIND THE DOORS OF THE SAMUEL BECKETT ADVENT CALENDAR
A TREE.
THREE FUNERAL URNS.
NOTHING.
A CARROT AND SOME TURNIPS.
AN EMPTY ROOM.
AN ABANDONED BICYCLE.
DARKNESS.
A ROCK.
NOTHING. AGAIN.

BABY BOOK CLUB

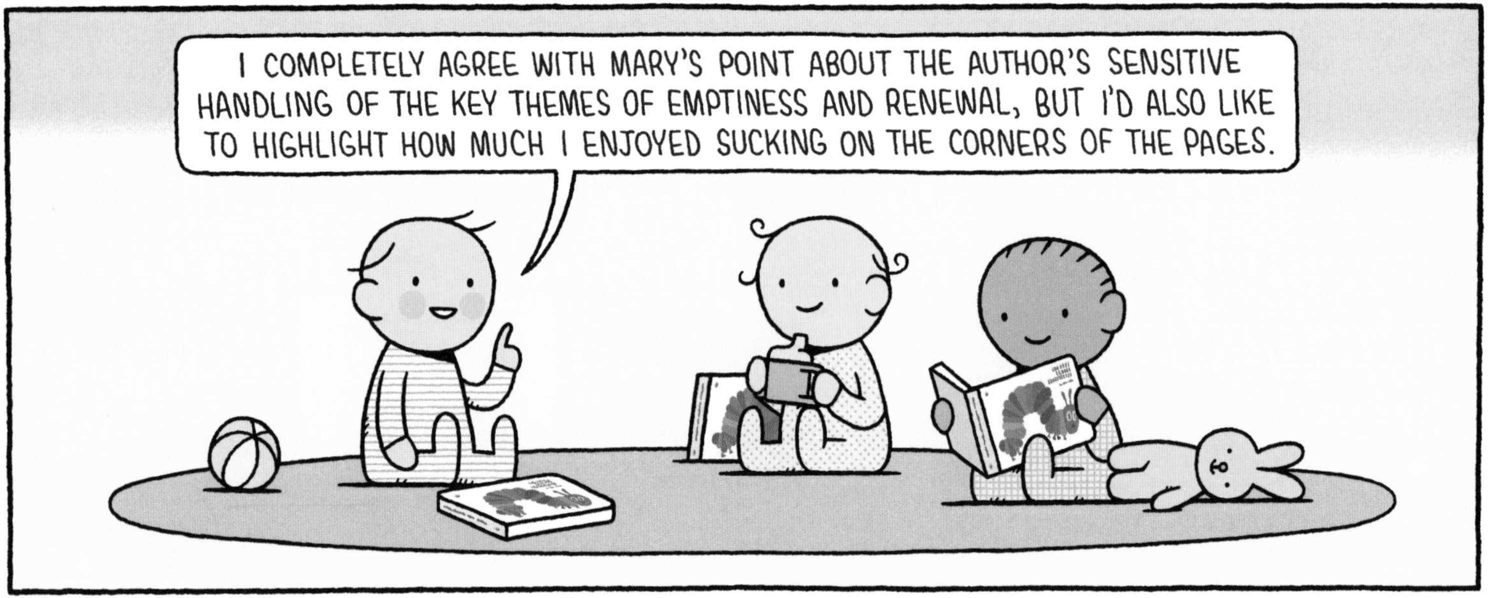
I COMPLETELY AGREE WITH MARY'S POINT ABOUT THE AUTHOR'S SENSITIVE HANDLING OF THE KEY THEMES OF EMPTINESS AND RENEWAL, BUT I'D ALSO LIKE TO HIGHLIGHT HOW MUCH I ENJOYED SUCKING ON THE CORNERS OF THE PAGES.

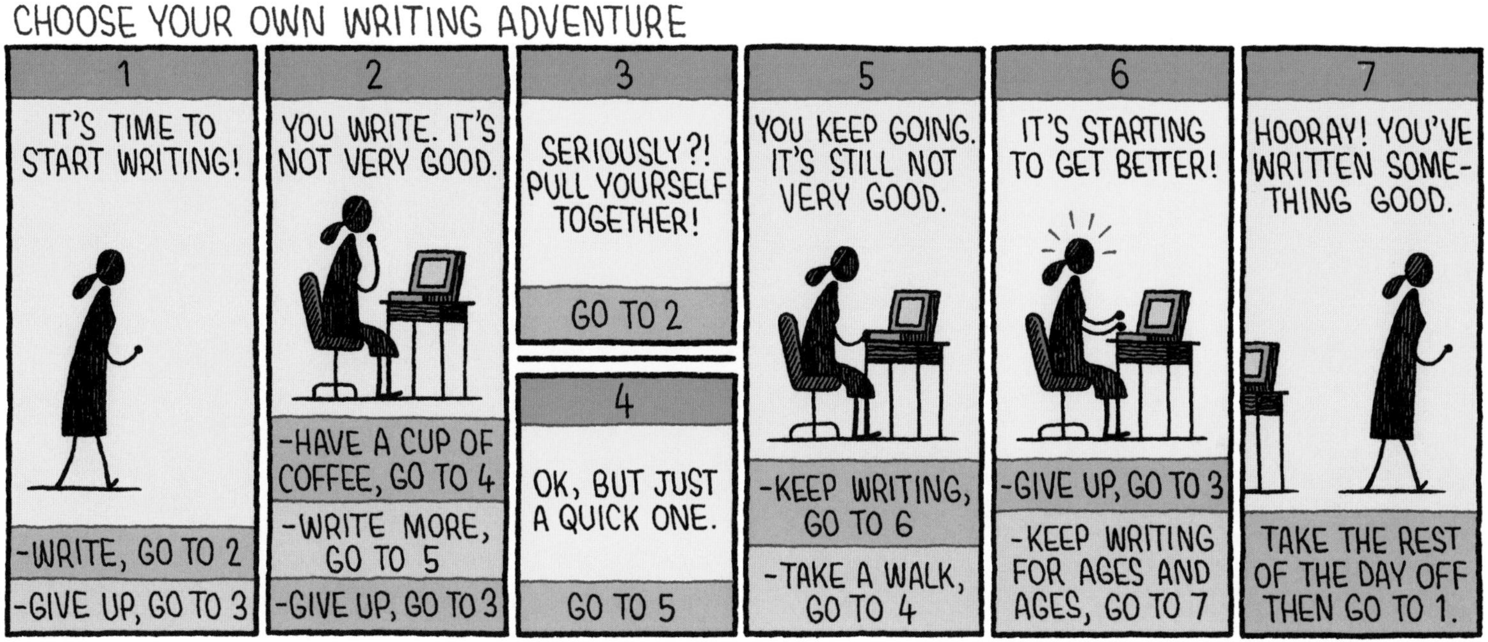
CHOOSE YOUR OWN WRITING ADVENTURE
1
IT'S TIME TO START WRITING!
-WRITE, GO TO 2
-GIVE UP, GO TO 3
2
YOU WRITE. IT'S NOT VERY GOOD.
-HAVE A CUP OF COFFEE, GO TO 4
-WRITE MORE, GO TO 5
-GIVE UP, GO TO 3
3
SERIOUSLY?! PULL YOURSELF TOGETHER!
GO TO 2
4
OK, BUT JUST A QUICK ONE.
GO TO 5
5
YOU KEEP GOING. IT'S STILL NOT VERY GOOD.
-KEEP WRITING, GO TO 6
-TAKE A WALK, GO TO 4
6
IT'S STARTING TO GET BETTER!
-GIVE UP, GO TO 3
-KEEP WRITING FOR AGES AND AGES, GO TO 7
7
HOORAY! YOU'VE WRITTEN SOME-THING GOOD.
TAKE THE REST OF THE DAY OFF THEN GO TO 1.

AN ANONYMOUS LETTER ARRIVES AT THE HALL...

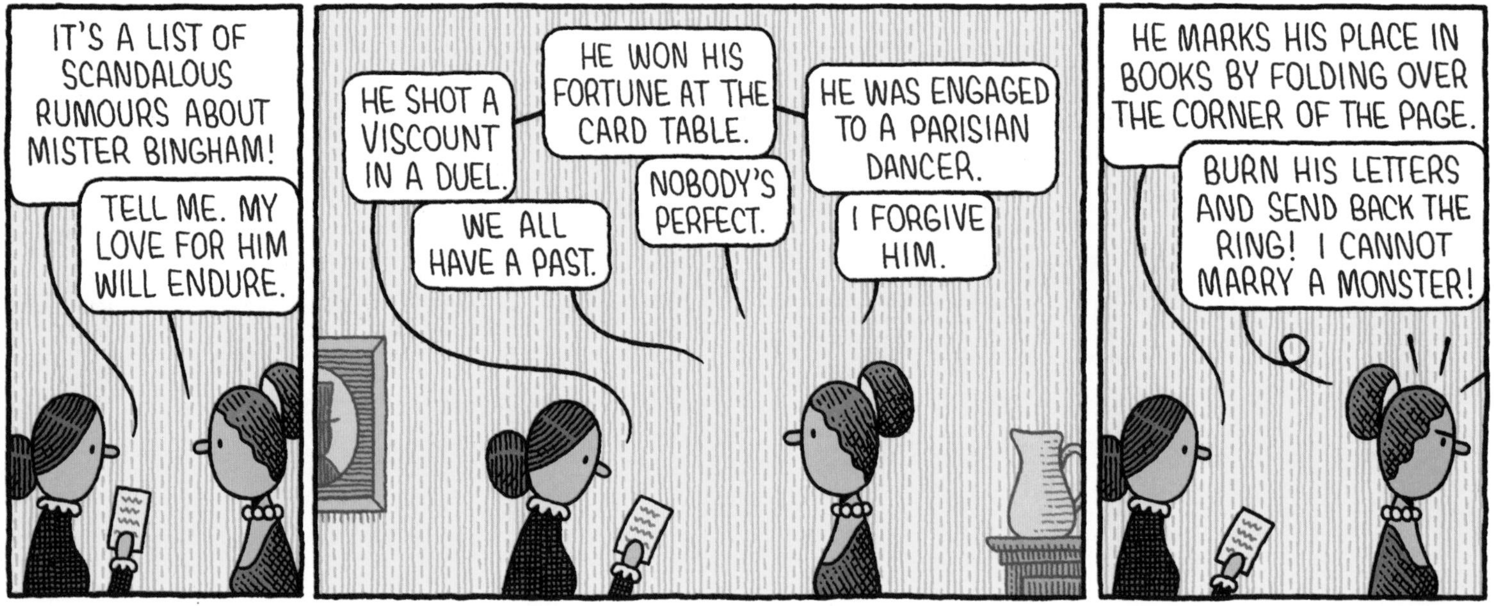
IT'S A LIST OF SCANDALOUS RUMOURS ABOUT MISTER BINGHAM!
TELL ME. MY LOVE FOR HIM WILL ENDURE.
HE SHOT A VISCOUNT IN A DUEL.
WE ALL HAVE A PAST.
HE WON HIS FORTUNE AT THE CARD TABLE.
NOBODY'S PERFECT.
HE WAS ENGAGED TO A PARISIAN DANCER.
I FORGIVE HIM.
HE MARKS HIS PLACE IN BOOKS BY FOLDING OVER THE CORNER OF THE PAGE.
BURN HIS LETTERS AND SEND BACK THE RING! I CANNOT MARRY A MONSTER!

WITH THE LIBRARIES CLOSED, IT WAS ONLY A MATTER OF TIME...

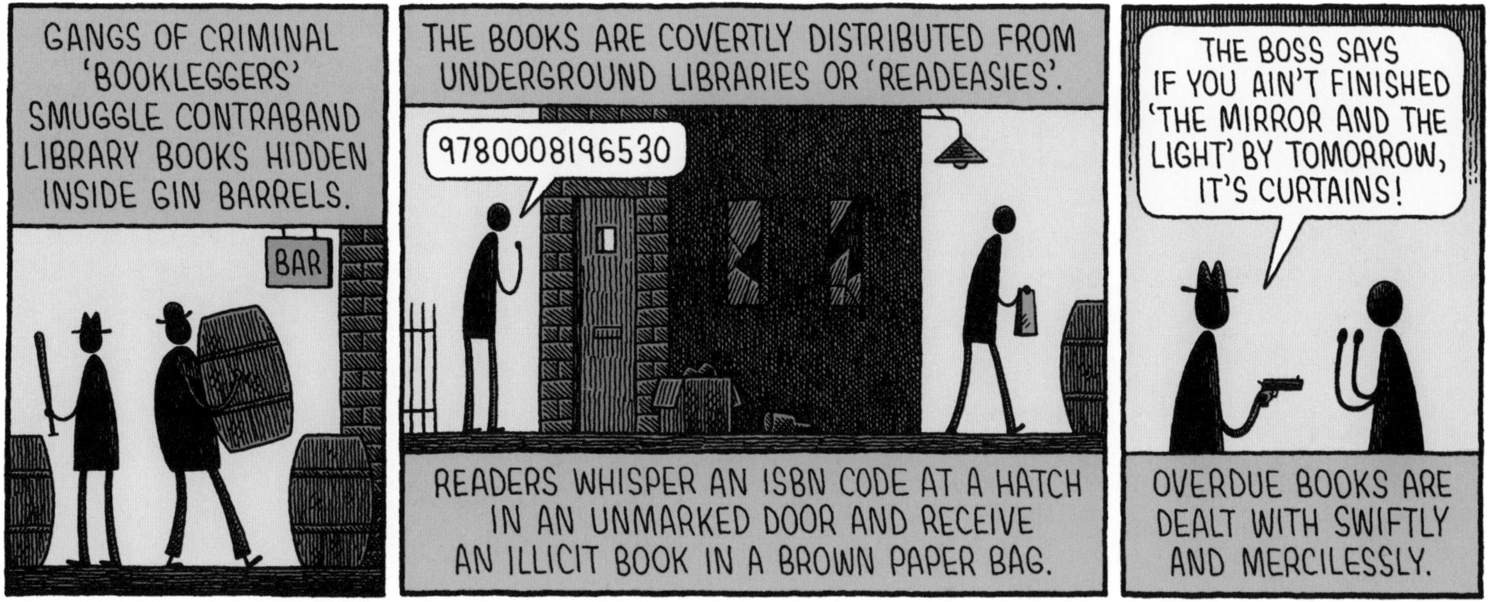
GANGS OF CRIMINAL 'BOOKLEGGERS' SMUGGLE CONTRABAND LIBRARY BOOKS HIDDEN INSIDE GIN BARRELS.
BAR
THE BOOKS ARE COVERTLY DISTRIBUTED FROM UNDERGROUND LIBRARIES OR 'READEASIES'.
9780008196530
READERS WHISPER AN ISBN CODE AT A HATCH IN AN UNMARKED DOOR AND RECEIVE AN ILLICIT BOOK IN A BROWN PAPER BAG.
THE BOSS SAYS IF YOU AIN'T FINISHED 'THE MIRROR AND THE LIGHT' BY TOMORROW, IT'S CURTAINS!
OVERDUE BOOKS ARE DEALT WITH SWIFTLY AND MERCILESSLY.

TOM GAULD WAS BORN IN 1976 AND GREW UP IN ABERDEENSHIRE,
SCOTLAND. HE IS A CARTOONIST AND ILLUSTRATOR.
HIS WORK IS PUBLISHED IN THE GUARDIAN, THE NEW YORKER,
AND NEW SCIENTIST. HE LIVES IN LONDON WITH HIS FAMILY.

THANK YOU: CHARLOTTE NORTHEDGE, LIESE SPENCER,
DAPHNE GAULD, IRIS GAULD, JO TAYLOR
AND EVERYONE AT D+Q.

OTHER BOOKS BY TOM GAULD:

GOLIATH
YOU'RE ALL JUST JEALOUS OF MY JETPACK
MOONCOP
BAKING WITH KAFKA
DEPARTMENT OF MIND-BLOWING THEORIES
THE LITTLE WOODEN ROBOT AND THE LOG PRINCESS

TOMGAULD.COM

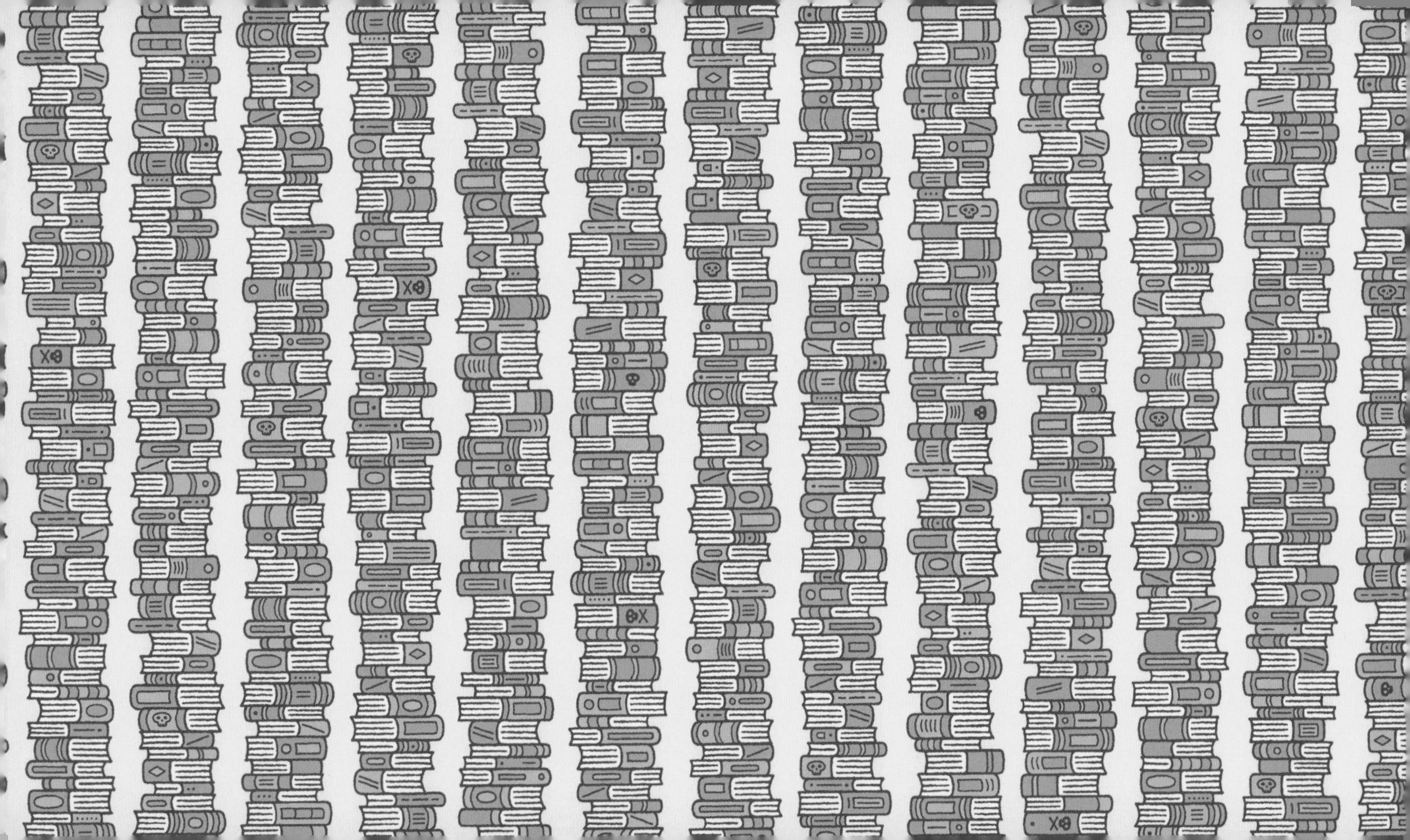

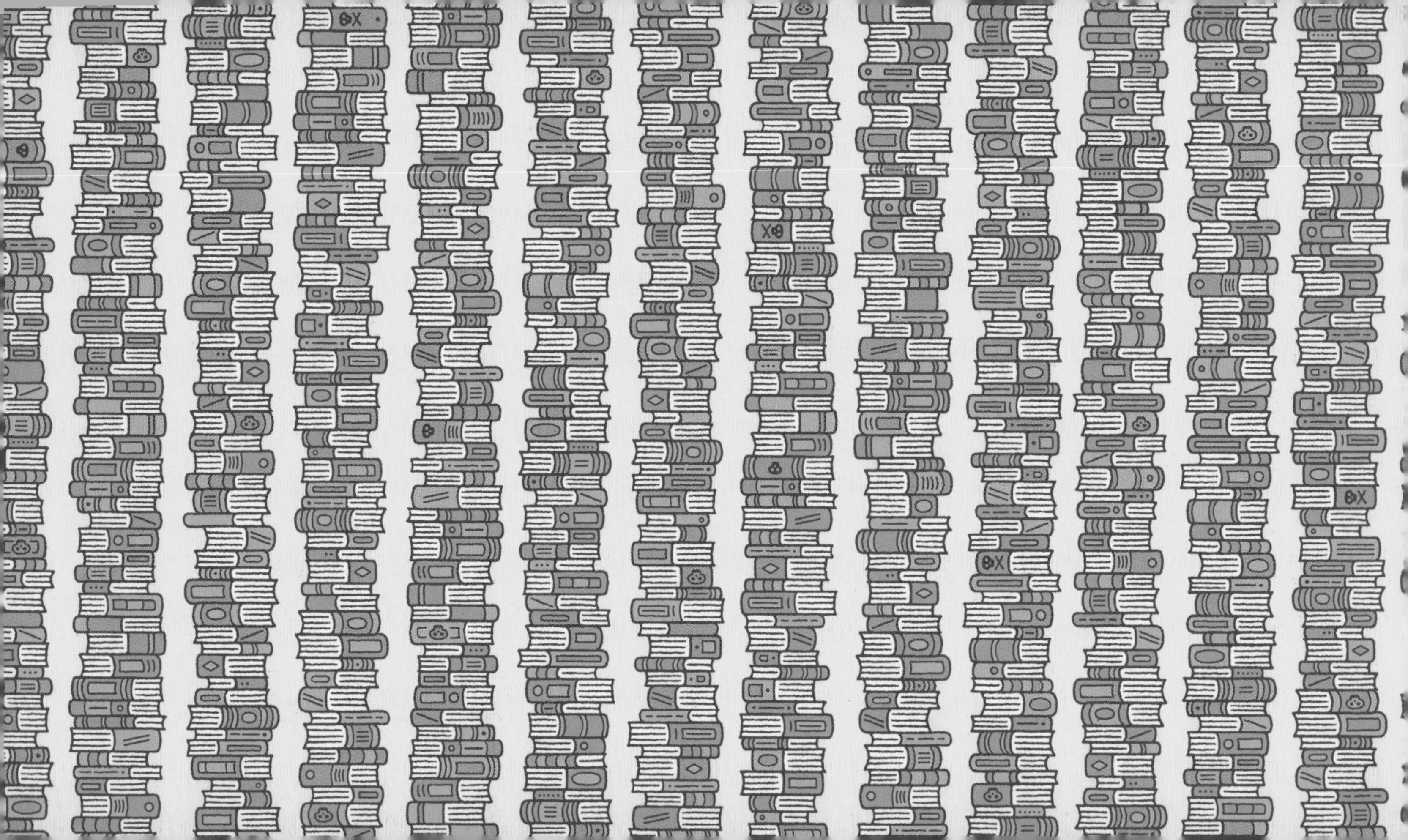